ELEVEN DOWN

The Frankie Funnybone
Memoirs
Volume II

John Gradwell

Published in 2023 by FeedARead.com Publishing

Copyright © 2023 John Gradwell

First Edition

The author has asserted their moral right under the Copyright, Designs and Patents Act, 1988, to be identified as the author of this work.

All Rights reserved. No part of this publication may be reproduced, copied, stored in a retrieval system, or transmitted, in any form or by any means, without the prior written consent of the copyright holder, nor be otherwise circulated in any form of binding or cover other than that in which it is published and without a similar condition being imposed on the subsequent purchaser.

This novel is entirely a work of fiction. Although certain characters may be loosely based on historical figures, events portrayed in the book are the work of the author's imagination.

A CIP catalogue record for this title is available from the British Library.

@jgradwell

john.gradwell@hotmail.co.uk

For Carole, Philip and Helen

1
Having a Gran Time

ALTHOUGH IT'S PAINFUL, I'm just about prepared to give Barney's hook full credit for helping me stay alive and end The Crossword Killer's reign of terror. The annoying twerp - Barney that is, not the slayer - insisted I use the hook to remove from the stage volunteers found wanting during our double act's 'impromptu' talent show. So, while lucky old Barney milked huge laughs from his persecution of these hapless extras, I had to hang around like a spare prick, pretending I was in on the joke.

Yet, but for that hook - a gaily-painted cross between a giant shepherd's crook and a giraffe's walking stick - my guts would have been blasted all over the front four rows of the stalls, bringing that particular show to a strange and gruesome end. Ironically by then Barney's own luck had run out ... but as usual I'm getting ahead of myself.

That I found myself in such peril was, you'll be totally unsurprised to hear, down to my dear wife and showbiz agent Nancy. After pointing out, a bit unnecessarily in my view, that it was two decades on from the Funnybone glory days as unofficial stooge to The Crazy Gang, she revealed it was time for her to resuscitate my career. This would be effected by pairing me with one of the new crew of comics, noisily emerging ten years into the peace and pointedly owing allegiance to nobody, particularly the recent past and its already fusty representatives. The latter, of course, were all over the place; your Hancocks, Howerds and Hills, desperate to transfer their success in variety and radio to the flickering world of television and its inviting new commercial channel. But in showbiz nothing stands still and these comic thrusters were already being overtaken by another generation sick of hearing how the war had been won by ENSA's shock battalions facing down peril in a thousand NAAFIs. Barney McAskill was one of this coming mob, developing comedy routines which not only lacked structure but traditional jokes as well. Accordingly, Nancy was keen to 'hook' my (as she saw it) flagging career to Barney's (as I didn't see it at all) rising star.

"But, Nance," I protested over breakfast toast and coffee at our town house in Earls Court, "I don't work well with anyone else."

"You don't work at all at the moment," came the cruelly terse reply from behind the latest copy of The Stage. "Besides," she added putting down the paper to reveal a wide and patently insincere smile, "double acts are quite the coming thing again. Look at Morecambe and Wise, Hope and Keen, Mike and Bernie Winters."

I waited for her clinching argument - the punchline as it were - before realising that was it.

"Mike and Bernie ...? Jesus, Nance, you've got to be joking."

Sadly, just like the new comedians of 1956, she wasn't joking at all and in no time, I found myself condemned to a summer season at the end of the pier in Mellish, a faded seaside resort not far down the coast from Blackpool but in showbiz terms a hundred million miles away. It wouldn't have been so bad if I'd been playing the impressive Grand Palace on its famous central pier. But sadly this structure had taken its final bow very suddenly during an air raid in 1941 and Mellish's remaining pier was tucked away by waste land at the north end of town and host to a large wooden shed known as The Coliseum

Theatre. Accordingly, I'd prepared myself for five months of tedium amid the candy floss, cockles and kiss-me-quicks. Just shows how wrong you can be!

Incidentally, in case you're wondering, I've sacked the chump who blighted the otherwise highly entertaining first volume of these memoirs. My view is that the book would have been even more sparkling if it hadn't been for this so-called "editor" continually sticking his oar in and trying to make out it was *me* that was some kind of dimwit. Saying that, the first volume did go down a storm with the people of Britain; I even received a letter from The Palace. Well, The Palace Theatre in Dunstable. The current ASM reckoned I'd been a great favourite of his grandad after my barnstorming appearance there in '48. This lad also admitted he'd enjoyed my memoirs but didn't believe a word of them. So, although I'm now 108 - they tell me it's the new fifty-five - I've decided to do without an editor in this second lot of rememberings.

Now, where was I? Oh yes, the fact that my darling wife and children had declined to make the trip to not-so-sunny Lancashire left me free to do whatever I wanted in my spare time. Which in Mellish amounted to not that much. After all there were only so many hours you could profitably spend in The Museum of Cod and Coley. The social highlights of my week therefore consisted of sessions where I'd get half-cut in the company of Wilf Holt, the Coliseum's caretaker and odd-job man. In fact a month into my sentence this had begun to happen so often it was already something of a tradition. After our double act had done its duties as number two on the bill to a nowhere near full second house Barney, without a word to me, would change and swiftly exit the building as if the hounds of hell were on his tail. He was usually followed in short order by our little repertory company of crooners, jugglers, knife throwers and roller-skating tap dancers. At least they were rolling down to the pub; Barney to god knew where! Meanwhile, I'd be left alone to scrape the five and nine off my face by the fading glow of a Hollywood dressing room mirror which had four of its ten lightbulbs out - an appropriate metaphor for the direction in which my "comeback" was going. Make-up removed, I would toddle along to the large broom cupboard next to the wings which Wilf grandly called his office.

This particular Tuesday night I'd stepped in to find the old rascal taking a break from cleaning-up duties and reclining deep in an armchair which, much like Wilf himself, had seen better days. In his right hand he slowly twirled a large glinting glass full of single malt while watching me, eyes full of mischief.

"You've still not replaced those bulbs," I grumbled. "It's so dark in there I could easily be scraping the make-up off someone else's face."

Wilf put down the Scotch and set fire to his pipe.

"The fact that you can't see yourself properly," he offered as the top half of his own head disappeared into a ballooning cloud of burning Gallaher's Condor Sliced, "could be a blessing in disguise."

I decided against returning serve with my wittiest riposte, mainly because it didn't yet exist. As a consolation I grabbed the whisky bottle and poured myself a generous measure.

"I see young Barney's pissed off quickly again," Wilf remarked as I balanced my backside on the only other berth in the room, a Charles Rennie Mackintosh dining chair with two wonky legs. "Never sticks around for a stiffener, that one."

"Miserable git," I replied, draining the glass in one. "Anyway, never mind him. Nice bit of stuff is that, Wilf. I reckon it's your shout to get the next bottle?"

"No it's yours and this is it, so that's fifteen and six you owe me."

"I didn't realise they had a branch of Fortnums in Mellish," I grumbled, handing over the cash while savouring the prospect of a second glass being poured by Wilf. He was still looking mischievous, almost daring me to ask what he was keeping up his sleeve. I knew this because when he was either nervous or excited, he automatically began twisting his thin sandy strands of hair.

"Get it off your chest then, you old rapscallion. What've you done?"

He breathed in deeply and shook his silvery locks.

"It's perhaps best you don't know."

For once I was tempted not to follow our already tried and tested ritual of me chasing Wilf round the houses before he revealed something I already knew or couldn't care less about anyway. But as there was no other show in town, I indulged an old man's whims. And, to be fair, what he told me was a step up in quality from the normal gossip. As you'll see.

"Right ho, what've you been up to?"

Wilf paused his top-knot twisting and replied with a satisfied grin, "I've shagged your grandma."

Wasn't kidding was I?

"You've done what!" I shouted, almost tumbling from my rickety perch.

He smiled again in dreamy contentment.

"I gave your granny one. And then I gave her another one!"

In a list of scenarios I could plausibly have imagined Wilf setting before me, this bombshell would not have made the top five hundred.

"My gran's been dead these past twenty-five years," I spluttered, "tell me you've not gone and dug her up!"

Wilf looked mortally offended.

"I certainly have not," he snapped, tugging even more furiously at his barnet. "Our romantic rendezvous took place on a pile of sacks backstage at the Bolton Grand when I was but an impressionable young gofer. It was only yesterday I discovered that The Blackburn Barn Owl was your grandma."

Well, he'd got her stage name right at any rate. But surely he was bluffing.

"If you … knew her as well as you say then you'll be able to tell me her real name."

Wilf took another long pull of Scotch before puffing reflectively on his briar.

"I think I do know that. Now let's see …"

He was definitely bluffing as well as puffing.

"Well, her surname was Thirkettle obviously - like thee."

A significant pause and another long draw on his pipe. Yes, I thought, definitely bluffing. Then a wry smile …

"And her first name was Molly."

Damn! He wasn't bluffing.

"OK, you're right but that doesn't prove you … knew her that well."

Wilf smiled triumphantly.

"Maybe it doesn't but I'm going to tell you all about it anyway."

"On reflection I'd rather you didn't. Have you seen the weather forecast?"

"I helped your gran rehearse the words of a song."

Oh, well that sounded fairly innocent.

"It was called 'She'd Never Had Her Ticket Punched Before'."

That didn't.

"Mind you," chuckled Wilf, "the words can't have been about your gran."

"I see Fleetwood's in for a proper soaking."

"Because by the time I knew her she'd got herself a first class go-anywhere season ticket - day or night!"

In the face of this exceedingly immature stab at humour, I opted for steely detachment and took a prim pull on the Scotch.

"Don't fret, kidder, it were only the twice," he explained, dabbing away mirthful tears.

"Thank goodness for small mercies."

"Yeah," he spluttered, a new punchline already minted, "you see there was always a massive queue. Ha, ha ha!"

Even though there had been the odd rumour down the years, it was unsettling to be told directly that your daft old granny, the one who would put linseed oil on her porridge (and, for all I know, condensed milk on her cricket bat), was a turn-of-the-century slapper!

Whatever, this slur could not go unavenged. Accordingly, I skilfully moved the subject onto ground guaranteed to stifle Wilf's jollity.

"So I take it this sordid business occurred before you became a 'hero' for four years spent whimpering in a ditch praying your very active dick wasn't about to be shot off?"

That appeared to do the trick.

"I'd like to see how you bunch of fairies from the last lot would have coped," Wilf growled, half rising from his seat. "Our lads couldn't run away in tanks and jeeps, you flamin' young perisher. We had to stay put and fight."

Thankfully back on more comfortable terrain, our banter now followed its established course; Wilf spelling out in grim detail what had befallen many of his comrades at Ypres; and me alluding to but managing to disguise the true nature of what I'd been up to in France, Italy and Yugoslavia. I wasn't ashamed of most things our unusual gang had been forced to do but it was still as much a secret as that circus at Bletchley, about which - amazingly - nobody had breathed a word either.

As usual we eventually agreed to disagree about who'd had the roughest war, which allowed Wilf to move on to other classic turn-of-the-century acts he'd known but hadn't quite managed to shag. Marie Lloyd, Vesta Tilley, Little Tich and even Charlie Chaplin were mentioned with awe if, in the case of the latter, without too much fondness. Wilf even had a good word to say about a more recent celebrity, my old sparring partner Frank Randle, one who definitely didn't spill more than he drank. In turn I reminded Wilf of my own stellar career which began at thirteen when I took on the mantle of Bendiest Boy in my home town of Butterthwaite, some thirty miles inland from Mellish.

"Do you know," I told Wilf proudly, "I could touch the back of my neck with both ankles."

"Aye, you got that off your gran an' all."

Enough was enough! I was about to warn Wilf off further discussion of my aged relative's sexual shenanigans but was silenced when he suddenly sat up, his lascivious smile replaced by a look of concern.

"Did you hear that?" he asked, half rising from the armchair.

"What?"

"Footsteps - in the auditorium."

"It'll be Alice just finished cashing up."

Wilf shook his head.

"No, Alice had left before you got here. There was hardly anything to cash up anyway."

That was true enough. Hours of battering rain had ensured that only a few brave souls had made the trudge north for our Tuesday second house. It had been like playing to a bus stop.

"Maybe it's Henry Shelvey then." He and his younger brother Marcus owned the pier and theatre.

Again, Wilf begged to differ. "Mr Henry wouldn't bother with such measly takings on a night like this. He'd leave 'em in the safe. Besides he's down in Liverpool sizing up some new turns."

"Then it must have been the wind."

Still Wilf looked unconvinced.

"You may be right but I think we should just check anyway."

"Tell you what," I piped up, eager to press home my advantage, "you stay here behind the lines while I go and face the enemy."

Bang! Wilf shot out of his seat like a jack-in-the-box, snatched up his broom and was through the door, all before I could move. Grinning, I picked up my coat and followed him down the corridor and into the cold, dimly-lit auditorium. For ten minutes we prowled up and down the rows of red plush seats looking for intruders, or maybe fans of mine who couldn't tear themselves away from the place. But of course, we found nothing. Figuring that Wilf's previous mischief needed a reply in kind, I stiffened and shouted to him in apparent terror.

"Quick there's someone here under the seat."

Wilf was next to me in an instant, broom in hand, and poised to despatch the trespasser.

"Oh, sorry, my mistake," I told him as he breathed heavily, "it's just Frank Randle sleeping it off."

For a second I feared Wilf might brain me with his brush but he stepped back into the aisle with a sour smile.

"I knew it couldn't be Randle," he said. "He's up the coast playing to a full house - unlike your extremely talented self."

It was cruel but true and we glowered at each other, neither sure of his next move. Then very carefully and solemnly Wilf stooped to lay his broom on the floor and raised his hands.

"This is the first time I've ever said this but ... I surrender. And I accept yours too."

I stared at him for a moment before we both burst out laughing.

"What on earth are we doing," I said, "rummaging around among fag ends and orange peel when it was probably the theatre cat you heard?"

"Or waves battering the pier," agreed Wilf. "It's a filthy night out there. You should get off."

"Sure you'll be OK?"

"I've survived these sixty-six years past, I think I can manage another night."

"OK but get off home as soon as you can."

"I will that."

I turned to go but then stopped. "Seriously, Wilf, I could stay until you've finished cleaning up," I told him. "Then I could walk you to the end of the pier."

"Seriously, Frankie, I could shove this broom up your backside. Now bugger off."

"Oh and, Wilf," I added with a grin, "don't forget to sweep up properly. This place is turning into a tip."

Dodging his swinging besom, I did a confident quickstep up the aisle, across the box office area and down another short, dusty corridor before exiting through the stage door and into the driving rain. The wind was really howling now and I hurried down the pier, through the turnstile at the entrance and away along the glistening, empty streets. It was more like Silesia in deepest winter than mid-summer in an English seaside resort.

Before arriving in the town I'd anticipated that Nancy would book me into one of Mellish's five-star hotels. However, as no-one had yet shown the gumption to build any of them, I found myself lodging at the home of my cousin Rose about half a mile from the theatre. During my childhood Rose's parents ran a boarding house at the other end of Mellish to which our lot, the Thirkettles, made a pilgrimage one week every summer for sea, sand and … well that was about it. Yet, despite this connection, Rose and I had never been particularly close, mainly due to the ten-year difference in our ages. In fact the last time I'd seen her was on her wedding day eight years ago. But she'd readily agreed to Nancy's request/demand to become a seaside landlady like her late mum Ivy. To be fair she'd taken to the role enthusiastically and seemed delighted to have someone else about the place. I couldn't really blame the woman either given that her husband Joe, a taciturn copper, was the type who wouldn't say one word when silence would do just as well. In the unlikely event of Joe Trueman attending a showbiz party, you wouldn't catch him looking round the room for someone more interesting or important to impress. He'd be scanning it for the exit because he didn't want to talk to *anyone*. However, no such hang-ups encumbered Cousin Rose. Before our first evening meal together four weeks previously she had been so happy and animated, even as she waved her table knife under my nose. When I was reassured that murder was not on the menu, Rose had a question about the knife.

"Don't you recognise it, Francis?"

"Er, no."

"But you must!"

While my answer remained resolutely the same, I felt, as an honoured guest, the need to make some kind of effort.

"Is it one of Solomon the Sword Swallower's hors d'-oeuvres? I do know he likes a light bite before …"

"Of course not, silly," Rose trilled, "it's part of your beautiful wedding present to us."

So I *was* right, I hadn't seen it before. Given Rose's outpouring of gratitude, however, I resolved to compliment my wife on her good taste.

"Solid silver too."

And her profligacy. What was wrong with Woolworths?

On this night, however, I would find my cousin in nowhere near as sunny a mood. I reached the small semi-detached in Woodcock Street cold and soaking but buoyed by the prospect of a generous portion of Rose's shepherd's pie. She'd promised to leave it on a low light in the oven before turning in and I fully intended to do it justice, with or without a solid silver knife and fork.

It took me by surprise therefore that, as I stepped into the darkened hallway, the lounge door swung open and Rose almost literally flew out like an agitated sparrow. On seeing it was me her mouth fell open in disappointment before she managed to compose herself. Obviously poor Rose had been expecting someone dearer to her than me; it was equally evident she'd been crying.

"Francis, you're soaked," she said, masking the hint of a sniff with a hanky from her pinny. Take those clothes off while I see to your supper."

"I'll sort it out myself, Rose. You go to bed."

"Nonsense, get up those stairs at once. And bring your wet things down."

By the time I'd changed into fresh slacks and shirt and returned to the lounge, Rose had laid out supper on a coffee table in front of a healthy-looking fire. She'd also poured me a welcoming glass of India Pale Ale.

"I thought it would be warmer in here than the dining room."

"Thanks, everything looks splendid."

As I ate, Rose arranged my damp togs over a clothes maiden which she placed to one side of the fire so as not to take away too much of the heat from me. Settling down in her armchair, she began to read what looked like a novel. Only I could see from her worried look that she wasn't reading at all, but thinking.

"What's that you've got on the go?"

Rose stared at the book as if she'd only just realised it was in her hands.

"Oh, just a silly romance. Boy meets girl. Boy leaves girl. Girl gets ... unhappy"

She thrust the book towards me. The picture on the cover showed an early nineteenth century dandy dragging a dark-haired beauty around a candlelit ballroom.

"Looks pretty potent," I said, taking extra care not to spray mashed potato all over my cousin.

Rose dropped her head and tried to look as if she was concentrating on her Regency romance. A decade younger than me, she was good looking enough for idle speculation that I might have fancied my chances. Had she not been my first cousin and married to a detective sergeant.

"Joe turned in, has he?"

Rose glanced up disconsolately.

"No he hasn't."

"On duty then?"

"No, he's ... out for a walk."

"On a night like this! He must be crackers!"

She immediately looked daggers at me.

"What do you mean, crackers? Joe's not mad."

The ferocity of her reaction threw me for a second.

"Er, I just meant he must be crazy, that is, er, misguided, to go out when the weather's so filthy."

I was prepared for another onslaught but at that point Rose simply crumpled. She dropped the book to the floor, bent forward and put her head in her hands. Now she was making little pretence of not crying. I leaned forward to comfort her ... and spilled what remained of my supper all over the fireside rug.

"Oh heck, Rose, I'm sorry."

Surprised, she looked up and noticing the mess, appeared to welcome an excuse for action.

"Don't worry," she fussed, her tears momentarily forgotten. "At least you've eaten most of it. I'll get the dishcloth."

She rushed to the kitchen, returning moments later suitably armed. I'd decided against mentioning Joe again but as she scrubbed it was Rose herself who brought up the subject, revealing much more than I'd anticipated. Apparently over the past couple of years they had been trying for a baby without success. And although she didn't say as much, I could tell that this had put a strain on the marriage.

"I wouldn't worry too much, cuz," I consoled her. "Plenty of time for kiddies."

She stopped scrubbing and looked up at me.

"Francis, I'm thirty in two months' time. And Joe turned forty in February."

"Come on, Rose, thirty's hardly ancient. I mean there's a woman in the paper today who had triplets when she was ..."

"Remind me how many children you'd had by the time you were thirty," she snapped. "Three wasn't it?"

"Three too many I sometimes think," I said, falling suddenly silent under the force of her glare. "Er, I love them all to little bits of course but well ... sometimes."

The memory of our eldest Julia as a three-year-old grassing me up to Nancy for eating butter beans out of the tin was still raw sixteen years on.

"Julia's at Cambridge isn't she."

"Yes she's doing - sorry *reading* - law. At Girton College. Nice old spot just out of the town."

"I'd love to have gone to university," said Rose. "By now I could have been established in a profession. Maybe accountancy."

She stopped scrubbing and hung her head. There was no attempt to hide her despair but I tried, without much hope, to lighten matters.

"You could always get yourself a job though."

"No I couldn't because Joe won't have it. He insisted I give up work when we got married."

She stood up and went into the kitchen without another word. Crikey, there appeared to be no consoling this unfortunate woman and I realised that, although she was my close relative, I knew next to nothing about Rose Trueman.

On her return a more composed Rose began to talk as if the previous conversation had not happened. She asked how the act was going and was good enough to listen sympathetically while I outlined in some detail the way Barney was hijacking the entire routine.

"I mean, do you know what the horrible little sod - pardon my French - did tonight. Just as I got to the top of the stepladder, he kicked ..."

We were interrupted by the telephone ringing and before I could finish my painful tale, she'd flown past me and into the hall. I heard her almost cry out Joe's name before falling silent. It was clear we'd both be better off if I was away to my bed but as I went into the hall, Rose looked up perplexed. She then offered me the receiver.

"He wants to speak to you," she said, still looking mystified.

"Joe wants to talk to me?"

"It's not Joe. It's ... well I'm not sure who it is. Here."

When she handed over the receiver, I immediately understood her problem. The voice at the other end of the line was cracked and indistinct; so unclear that it took me a few moments to realise that it was Wilf, the theatre's caretaker.

"What's to do, Wilf? You sound in a right state."

"Oh, Frankie, I am," he spluttered. "I think there ... there's someone in the theatre and, well, I'm right scared, I don't mind admitting it. Frankie, you couldn't ..."

"I'll be there in a jiffy. In the meantime you ring the police. And stay calm."

2

The Crossword Killer

RUSHING BACK through the glistening streets, I cursed myself for not remaining with Wilf. The poor fellow sounded in an absolute panic and it would have cost me nothing to stick around another hour or so before escorting him to his little terraced cottage two streets from the pier. Hurrying along, I half expected to come across Joe whistling a merry tune, which, to be fair, he wasn't generally prone to do. But the streets remained resolutely empty and echoing as I approached the pier at a breathless trot, hoping that by now the wanderer had returned to Rose.

The problem of how I'd breach the barrier at the pier's entrance was immediately solved but hardly in a reassuring way. Someone had kicked a large hole in a section of the wooden slats on which had been plastered a poster advertising Five Boys chocolate bars. Only two of the creepy quintet's images remained undamaged, leaving a space all too easy for an adult to squeeze through. Had this vandalism already happened when I left Wilf less than two hours before? The turnstile exit was a good ten yards away and I wouldn't have noticed it on my way out.

The worn and splintered boards of the pier amplified the sound of my anxious footsteps above that of the wind, which had mercifully dropped to an irritable sigh. I tried to be light on my feet as anyone approaching (or indeed fleeing as had happened during one particularly disastrous show) could sound to those in the theatre like a buffalo stampede. As the Coliseum loomed before me like a beached ocean liner in the faint moonlight, I switched on the torch I had borrowed from Rose. And what I saw nearly made me throw up in terror! Outside Wilf's room were a couple of small window boxes containing the kind of hardy plants that managed to thrive under his careful husbandry, even in these extreme conditions. The blooms gave the theatre's exterior a homely look and were often commented upon by admiring holidaymakers. But now Wilf's mini-garden lay broken into pieces across the boards. Cornflowers, sea pinks and geraniums were scattered among lumps of soil and the large wooden splinters of what were once gaily-painted window boxes. I don't mind admitting that this vandalism terrified me.

I paused by the window but it had been fully shuttered against the storm and there was no sound from inside. Hurrying past the barley sugar Doric columns at the theatre's entrance, I reached the stage door on the far side of the building. On discovering it was still locked, my hopes flared briefly as I fumbled for my key. Maybe it was just a bunch of nasty kids who'd desecrated Wilf's little garden and no-one had entered the theatre after all. Yet that thought didn't stop me nipping into my dressing room and grabbing a signed cricket bat that had been presented to me by my old drinking buddy and sporting legend Denis Compton. If there was an intruder lurking I would brutally - but stylishly a la Compo - cover drive him into the Irish Sea. Switching off the torch, I tiptoed past the box office and towards the end of a narrow corridor to Wilf's room, where the light was on and his door half-open. Stopping outside, I breathed in deeply before tentatively prodding the door wide open with the cricket bat.

Even the most fevered imaginings had hardly prepared my brain for the sickening sight that greeted me. Wilf lay slumped against the far wall next to his battered armchair, a rifle bayonet buried up to the hilt in his bloodied stomach. My newish old friend gazed at me in absolute desperation - and then his eyes flickered momentarily to the left. An insignificant movement for sure, yet enough to warn me that his attacker was still there, behind the door.

"Wilf, what on earth has happened? Let me help you ..." I shouted before giving the door an almighty kick and darting into the room with the bat swinging.

What appeared to be a large club cut through the air but my surprise attack had put the assailant slightly off balance and his downward whistling stroke, vicious though it was, just missed my right shoulder. As it did, I blindly swung my own makeshift weapon again and connected, sending the attacker staggering back against the wall. I quickly turned, stepping protectively in front of Wilf to face the intruder. Dressed all in black apart from a chequered cloth mask through which unusually deep blue eyes glittered, he was gloved and clutching a baseball bat which he immediately began to wield in quick jabbing movements, forcing me backwards. I tried to return the compliment with wide-arced batting strokes but the tactic was of little use against his evident skill and he was easily able to push me on to the retreat.

"Tek t'bastard's head off his showders, Frankie" wheezed Wilf, now just behind me.

"No, Wilf, we'll need his head and neck - for the hangman's noose," I replied hoarsely, the message's stilted bravado more than nullified by the fear and panic in my voice. The attacker, sensing my terror, rushed forward and connected with a swing to my left elbow. Howling with pain, I only just managed to hold on to the bat and parry a thrust towards my throat. Glimpsing a hunting knife in his belt, I realised with horror that the game would soon be up if I didn't manage to make significant contact. But, as he reached for his blade, the attacker froze and a second later I realised why. The room had begun to gently vibrate, a sure sign of running footsteps approaching along the pier. With what sounded like a sardonic laugh, the masked attacker turned and sprinted towards the door.

I was about to give chase when Wilf gasped, "Watch out, Frankie," as the man raised his right hand. Instinctively I jerked the bat in front of my face a moment before an object hit it with surprising force, sending me tottering backwards against the wall. When I managed to look up, the attacker was gone but he'd left a present - his hunting knife straight through the middle of Compo's scrawling signature. The vicious looking weapon, with its serrated edges, had nearly split the bat in two.

As Wilf gave a weak moan and tried to move, I laid my hand softly on his shoulder.

"Stay where you are, Wilf. Help's on its way."

But the old man's breathing was getting shallower and faster.

"The swine jumped me, Frankie," he wheezed and gazed disbelievingly at the bayonet embedded in his stomach. "I put one of these into a German, just a kid really, at Wipers in 1917. Not a day goes by when I don't wonder who he was and how his ma felt when she heard."

"Don't talk, Wilf. We'll soon get you to hospital."

A tear rolled down his grey-stubbled cheek but then he made a real effort and managed to grab my arm.

"He was in the bar, Frankie," Wilf gasped urgently.

"This guy attacked you in the theatre bar?"

Wilf sighed and shook his head.

"Look after my flowers," he muttered before rolling over gently to one side. I felt for a pulse but there was nothing there. Amid all this horror I couldn't help notice that Wilf's hair, which he was forever twisting into a top-knot had unravelled, showing him to be completely bald on top. At that point I hated the killer all the more for not even allowing Wilf a moment of dignity in death. I bent down and, gently as I could, closed his eyes.

There were heavy footsteps in the corridor and seconds later Ray Parr exploded into the room. Ray, a tall and beefy detective constable who worked with Rose's husband Joe, stared in disbelief at Wilf's body, his jaw dropping even further when he saw the bayonet.

"God save us, what's gone on here?" he exclaimed.

"What the heck does it look like?"

"You tell me."

"It looks like my pal's just been murdered by a maniac who only just missed killing me as well."

I had a sudden thought.

"Where's Joe?"

"I'm on my own," Ray replied, "but Joe knows there's an emergency and he should be here any minute."

I snatched up the cricket bat, the knife still embedded in its blade and before Ray could say or do anything, I'd flung open the window and almost knocked the shutters off their hinges with the bat. A rush of sea spray blasted me as I leaned through the window.

"Joe," I yelled, fighting against the sound of wind and waves, "he's coming down the pier. Stop him."

"I didn't see anyone, Frankie," said Ray, surprised.

"Then for all we know he's still in the building. Come on."

For the next few minutes we combed the theatre just as Wilf and I had done a couple of hours earlier - and with the same results.

We'd just got back to Wilf's room when Detective Sergeant Joe Trueman arrived with a police doctor and a couple of uniformed officers. Joe's outwardly purposeful walk could not disguise the heavy limp he'd had since a bullet shattered his right knee not long after D-Day. How the heck he'd passed a police medical exam, god only knew.

The doctor bent over Wilf, felt for a pulse at the side of his neck and with a shake of his head confirmed what I already knew. Joe gazed impassively at Wilf's body for a few seconds and turned to me.

"Who did this?" he demanded.

"How the hell can I say? The only thing I do know is that if you lot were doing your job Wilf would still be alive."

It was an unfair comment, prompted by my own feelings of culpability at leaving Wilf alone at the theatre, but to his credit Joe did not react. With a quizzical expression he merely glanced at Ray who almost imperceptibly shook his head. Taking a deep breath, Joe turned to me.

"Please, Frankie, could you tell us what happened?"

I carefully took them through the events of the evening from hearing footsteps in the auditorium two hours before Wilf faced his horrible end. As I finished speaking, Joe picked up the cricket bat and stared at the knife embedded in it as if he couldn't quite believe what he was seeing. His face was a mixture of such puzzlement and extreme worry that I wasn't surprised to see him actually reach for the knife.

"Don't touch it, skip," Ray said, gently putting a hand on his boss's shoulder and removing the bat from his grasp. "We'll get the bayonet checked for prints as well."

"Good luck but I don't think you'll have much joy," I told Ray. "I reckon this fellow left nothing to chance. He was wearing gloves."

"What else?" said Joe who'd returned to the land of the living.

"Black boiler suit, army boots, belt and a black and white mask."

"What stripes, like?" Ray asked.

"No. Checks. Like a chess board or a crossword puzzle or something."

Joe and Ray exchanged another brief worried glance.

"Oh, and he had piercing blue eyes. A bit like yours Joe."

Ignoring my final comment, Joe bent down to examine the bayonet in poor Wilf's guts. I hadn't noticed before but there was a small envelope taped around the locking ring and with a jolt I saw that the name written on it was 'Joe'.

Ray eased me away from the body of my old pal.

"We'll get a car to take you back to your digs and you can give us a full statement in the morning," he said, gently steering me towards the door. "Just call in at the station."

"Are you not coming, Joe?" I asked without thinking.

He gazed at me as though I was some kind of imbecile.

"There's a couple of matters that might just delay me a while."

These awful events had taken such a heavy toll on my nerves I feared I'd be tossing and turning all night. However, I immediately fell into an exhausted sleep and didn't hear Joe come in at all. When I awoke around nine o'clock and went downstairs, Rose told me he'd left for work a full hour before. You certainly couldn't fault the man's commitment.

I toyed listlessly with breakfast, unable to shake off the image of poor Wilf, despatched in such a ghastly way. When I finally pushed the plate to one side, the bacon, beans and egg hardly disturbed, I expected a telling-off from Rose but she just got on with her dusting, barely registering that I was there at all.

Something was worrying her and it wasn't the size of my appetite.

I got out of the house as soon as possible into weather that could not have been more different than last night's storms. Driving wind and rain had been replaced by a warm westerly breeze and the sun was playing a constant game of peek-a-boo from behind wispy clouds. One thing that had not changed, however, was my feeling of emptiness, almost impotence, over the fate of the friend I'd been gently ribbing a few hours ago. What we'd imagined was the theatre cat must have been the killer waiting to strike. But why leave it all that time? I'd been back at the digs well over an hour before Wilf's final frantic phone call at around one in the morning. What was the murderer's motive for even letting him make that cry for help? I could only conclude that he wanted me back there. Had he intended to kill me too? Or for me to bear witness; to demonstrate to the police just what they were up against. But then I remembered the knife, only parried by my last-second backward defensive stroke. If the killer wanted me alive then he'd displayed an amazing bit of knifemanship. And what of the note addressed to Joe?

I breathed in hard and my nostrils and throat were immediately assailed by the same salty tang that had hit me when I smashed open the shutters in Wilf's room. Deciding that a few more minutes to myself were advisable, I passed the police station and turned left on to the sea front. However, if solitude was my goal I was out of luck. Although it was only half past nine, the promenade was already heaving with folk taking advantage of the better weather after being turned out of their digs for the day by dictatorial landladies.

The sea air made me realise I was hungry after all and, on a whim, I bought a saucer-full of cockles from a small kiosk which backed on to the sea wall. As I drowned the slippery seafood in vinegar and pepper the kiosk owner, a skinny fellow of about fifty, began to nod his bald head sagely as if possessed of a great secret he was desperate to share. Knowing the type, I was less than keen to take him on but he piped up anyway.

"I see they're out in force. You know, trying to track him down."

"Can you blame them?" I snapped, angered that the news about Wilf was already fodder for gossips.

"No I can't. And if I weren't stuck here I'd join 'em. I could do with a fiver."

"There's a reward already?"

He looked at me oddly.

"You could call it that I suppose."

"You'd think it'd be more than five lousy pounds."

Was that all Wilf's life was worth?

The cockle man shrugged.

"It must mount up though, a fiver every time. I mean he was in Blackpool yesterday, Morecambe the day before. And I know for a fact he's off to New Brighton tomorrow."

The killer had embarked on some sort of macabre seaside tour? Hold on …

"What the blazes are you talking about?"

"That bloke from The Daily Sketch. What's his name, Tommy something or other? He's here today and they're all out searching for him."

He glanced up and down the prom and then spoke out of the side of his mouth.

"Apparently today's clue is 'the old queen's mad as anything,' whatever that means."

While I'd imagined a citizenry chasing down Wilf's killer, the town's attentions were actually consumed by The

Sketch's mystery man and the crisp white fiver burning a hole in his pocket. With a profound and despairing sigh, I turned away from the kiosk and found myself nose-to-nose with a pimply youth in a check sports coat and fawn slacks, a fag perched perilously on his bottom lip.

"What can I do for you, son?"

"I know who you are," he replied, nodding at me and grinning expectantly.

Never let any blasé showbiz types fool you that they don't like being pestered by their fans. Take it from me it's what every performer lives for. Even though I wasn't on top form, I smiled back graciously at the young fellow and inquired if he could use my autograph. The youth looked puzzled for a moment before winking and tapping me lightly on each shoulder with the rolled-up newspaper he held in his right hand.

"You are Timmy Trotter," he trumpeted, "and I claim my five pounds!"

Ah well, although he'd turned out not to be a fan at least he wasn't throwing stuff at me.

"Looks like it's your lucky day, young man."

The lad squealed with delight and spat his fag end on to the ground.

"I knew it, I knew it, I knew it," he burbled, "and ..." his voice dropped to a whisper, "I won't even mention anything about an old queen." He winked again.

"Here's your prize, son," I said, handing him the half-eaten plate of cockles. "Maybe you can sell those for a fiver."

I left the boy gawping at the saucer as if his five pound note might yet materialise among the vinegary bivalves.

Strolling back in the direction of the nick, I noticed a small, shabby-looking man squatting on the sea wall apparently engrossed in his newspaper. He was obviously a veteran because as I passed, he casually drew back the lapel of his threadbare demob suit jacket to reveal what looked very much like the VC pinned to his waistcoat. I was about to warmly shake his hand but then realised that the clue, 'old queen mad as anything' referred cryptically to 'Victoria Cross', the medal he was wearing. The man, who must have been in his fifties and could have fought in either or indeed both world wars, looked at me pleadingly as if he wanted the whole charade to end so he could get the train home. For a moment I did consider claiming my five pound prize from Timmy Trotter. But then I figured that it wouldn't look too clever if one of the town's so-called highly paid variety acts waltzed off with holidaymakers' cash. Besides, I didn't have a copy of The Daily Sketch to batter him with.

If one half of the town had been on the prom chasing Timmy Trotter's fiver, it was gratifying to find that the other fifty per cent appeared to be inside the police station. A crowd of men, mainly in their fifties and sixties, milled around in front of the inquiry desk while harassed uniformed and plain clothes officers tried to determine who they were and what they knew. One senior officer with three silver pips on each shoulder strode from group to group glaring at anyone who had the misfortune to catch his eye. Before I could join the scrum around the desk, Detective Constable Ray Parr appeared from a side room and beckoned to me.

"This way, Frankie," he said as we weaved through the crowd and down a short corridor to where two chairs stood outside a closed door. He insisted I sit on one and loomed over me.

"It seems old Wilf was a popular lad," he said. "Most of that lot back there are his mates and mad keen to catch the swine who did him in. And then string him up by his knackers."

"You can include me among the stringers."

The very important looking character with the three pips appeared at the end of the corridor, pausing for a moment to glower my way before he turned and marched off.

"Who's Colonel Blimp?"

Ray smiled to himself.

"That's Chief Inspector Hallows. Or Daddy as I like to think of him."

"I thought it was usually 'skip' or 'gaffer'?"

"It was - before I started going out with his daughter."

"And how does the very important Chief Inspector feel about that?"

"He doesn't know yet. You see she's still at school."

"For goodness sake, Ray!"

"Don't worry she's seventeen. Jenny's in the sixth form at Mellish Grammar. Maths, further maths and physics."

I glanced over at Hallows who glared back and signalled for Ray to join him.

"Your father-in-law needs to bond with you."

"Ssshh," he muttered nervously, "mum's the word."

"You be careful," I whispered back, "or the word *will* be 'mum' and soon after that it'll be 'shotgun'."

Ray's face assumed a mask of formality.

"Detective Sergeant Trueman will call you in very soon, sir," he said loudly before marching briskly towards the desk.

I sat there another five minutes before the door opened and my showbiz partner Barney McAskill stepped out of Joe's office. He was nearly as tall as Ray but lacked the copper's beefy build. Barney looked as if a breath of seaside breeze would knock him over. He glared at me as he closed the door and I caught a familiar strong draught of bad breath and body odour.

"You do realise that the Shelveys have closed the theatre for the rest of the week," he spat, as if the whole rotten business was my fault.

Pinching my nose, I put my other arm round his shoulder.

"Poor old Barney! Theatre owners are heartless swine aren't they! It takes just one insignificant caretaker to be horribly murdered and they immediately put your stellar career on ice. I'd write to The Daily Sketch if I were you. Better still, nip on to the prom and have a word with Timmy Trotter. Make a quick fiver to tide you over as well."

Barney angrily pushed my arm away.

"You're a funny man, Frankie," he said with a sour smile. "When you're not on stage."

"Whereas you are a miserable git all the time."

"The thing is though, I get the laughs."

Damn the man but it was true. Off stage Barney, with his wispy beard, bad teeth and teetotal ways, was about as much fun as diphtheria but when that curtain went up he became a Lord of Misrule, improvising wildly and getting huge laughs, mostly at my expense. I, on the other hand, found my carefully scripted routines - *our* carefully scripted routines for goodness sake - increasingly redundant as Barney dragged the act into unexpected places to which I was usually incapable of following.

"What did Joe, er Detective Sergeant Trueman want with you anyway?" I asked.

Barney shrugged.

"He seemed keen to find out if I knew Walt ..."

"Wilf!"

"Yeah him. But why would I know anything about the caretaker for god's sake? He might as well have asked me about the theatre cat."

Luckily for Barney, Joe opened the door just as I was about to snap the uppity swine in two.

"Could you come in please, Francis," Joe said before quickly disappearing back into his office.

I turned to face Barney.

"Why don't you take a holiday? Get as far away from this place - and me - as you can."

"Funny you should say that," he said, picking at his teeth. "I've been invited up to Blackpool. To stay with a real comedy star ... Frankie Driscoll no less." He looked at me smugly as if this was the punchline to yet another of his wonderful routines, which of course distinguished themselves by a lack of punchlines.

"Now, Barney, that is funny," I replied with a delighted grin, mainly because I'd worked with Driscoll and knew exactly what he was like. "After a couple of hours with him you might even discover that I'm not your least favourite Frankie in the world."

And before he could reply I stepped into Joe's office and closed the door.

"What are you grinning at?" Joe snapped testily as he bade me sit down. "Does murder amuse you?"

That wiped the smile off my face.

"No, it's just that my stage partner out there is such an amusing fellow."

"I know. I've seen your show. Now sit down."

I sat and Joe studied me unsmilingly, fingers steepled under his boxer's nose. It was a good few seconds before he spoke.

"We've found no trace of this supposed attacker."

"Supposed attacker! What are you saying? Wilf ran himself through?"

"I'm saying no such thing," replied Joe irately. "The question is who did stab him?"

And he gave me another hard stare.

"Oh, now you're insinuating that I had something to do with Wilf's death?"

"You said that not me."

"Look, Joe," I replied, struggling to keep calm, "your darling wife will confirm that a terrified Wilf phoned me at your house - at a time incidentally when you were nowhere to be found."

"Now you appear to be accusing me of something."

"No, Joe. I'm just pointing out that fingering me for killing the only good friend I had in Mellish is as daft as me thinking you're a wrong 'un - even if ..."

I paused and stared at him.

"Even if what?"

"Nothing."

"Spit it out, funny man."

"Well, it's just that your eyes are exactly the same colour as the killer's."

Now we glared at each other. Joe's eyes really were a deep and lustrous shade of blue. Luckily, before our ill-tempered conversation could go any further, Ray came in, slamming the door behind him.

"Phew, your mate *was* popular," he said, collapsing onto the chair next to mine and stretching out his long legs. "Something up, guv?" he added, glancing at Joe whose face could hardly conceal his anger.

"The comedian here reckons it was me who skewered his pal."

"Nah, Frankie," Ray said shaking his head, "Detective Sergeant Trueman would have been nowhere near quick enough to catch old Wilf."

I thought Joe might actually blow his top at that quip and a couple of seconds later he did explode ... with laughter, which got Ray and me going as well.

"You're a daft so-and-so, Ray," said Joe, wiping his eyes, "but I don't know what we'd do without you. Right, can we get serious?"

Joe began again to carefully take me through what had happened the night before while Ray wrote down what I said on a green evidence sheet. And at one point I remembered something significant I hadn't mentioned the previous night.

"Just before he died, Wilf said the killer was in the bar."

"The theatre bar?"

"I assume so. Maybe he attacked Wilf there."

Joe looked doubtful.

"Wilf was definitely stabbed in his own room. There were no signs of a struggle - or blood - anywhere else, including the bar."

"Just thought I'd mention it."

We continued on through the horrible events. Oddly, Joe became uneasy when as an afterthought I mentioned our regular military banter and that Wilf had been a proud soldier in the First World War.

Ray, who was still scribbling away, addressed his chief almost automatically.

"Looks like he's killing ex-servicemen."

Joe gave him an exasperated glare and Ray reddened.

"Er sorry, guv," he mumbled. "Forget what I just said, Frankie."

"What did you mean 'he's killing ex-servicemen'? Has he done this before?"

Ray, whose face had now turned from red to very pale, didn't respond. Instead he handed me the statement he'd taken down and asked me in a formal voice to read through it and sign it if I was satisfied it summed up what I'd said. The statement seemed fine and I put my name to it with a flourish. Then I pushed my chair back and looked over at the two detectives in urgent discussion at the other side of the room.

"Are you going to tell me what's going on or do I need to take a trip down to the newsroom for a chat with my friend Phil?"

Ray stared at me in alarm.

"Are you talking about Phil Halliday at the Mellish Express?"

I shrugged and said nothing.

Ray strode purposefully towards me and for a moment I feared he was going to smash his bear's paw of a fist into my face. But instead he dropped his massive forearm onto my shoulder.

"Frankie, it's like this. Phil or any of the other reporters won't be able to tell you anything because none of them know what's going on. And we'd like to keep it that way for now at least."

"So tell me."

Ray looked quizzically at Joe who nodded in exasperation.

"OK," said Ray. "Are you sitting comfortably? Then I'll begin."

His story went like this. The previous week, at about two o'clock on Monday morning, a beat bobby had been walking near the Cenotaph gardens when he noticed a fire.

"At first he thought some louts had set a pile of rubbish alight," Ray explained. "But when he got nearer, he saw it was altogether worse than that."

"What was it?" I couldn't help but show interest.

Ray glanced once again at Joe before continuing.

"What was blazing at the foot of the war memorial was the body of a man."

"A body? Who was he, Ray? And what the heck had happened to him?"

Once more Ray looked at Joe who was staring keenly at the inscription on his fountain pen.

"We thought he was a tramp at first and in a way we were right. He turned out to be a former serviceman who'd fallen on hard times. Let's face it there's enough of 'em around. And, er, the other thing was he'd been murdered."

"Let me get this straight," I said, struggling to control my anger. "You've known for over a week that there's a madman around who's already butchered one old soldier. And you said nothing to anyone."

"It wasn't as simple as that," replied Ray, reddening again. "You see for three days we didn't even realise the man had been murdered."

"Eh?"

"At first it was assumed he'd set himself on fire, drinking meths or whatever his favourite tipple was."

"God's sake, Ray," Joe grumbled, "show some respect."

"Sorry, skip, but it ain't exactly unusual among tramps is it? And there was an empty bottle next to the body. Anyhow, Frankie, it was Joe who uncovered the truth."

I gazed expectantly at Joe who sighed and reluctantly took up the tale.

"Something about it all didn't seem right to me."

"Like what?"

"I don't know, call it a hunch. So three days later I took myself back to the memorial gardens and, after a bit of a dig around, I discovered an envelope with a message inside it."

"Under the ground?"

"No, taped to the base of the cenotaph."

"And nobody had spotted it before?"

"Nobody had any cause to look," Ray interrupted. "It was well-concealed and anyway at that stage we didn't suspect murder."

"So, what did the message say?"

"We can't reveal its contents but it did lead us to believe that far from it being a tragic accident, this fellow had been murdered."

I felt myself becoming angry again.

"That three days' delay doesn't alter the fact that you then knew a killer was on the loose, free to strike again, this time at my poor old pal. But for you two clowns, Wilf would still be here. What sort of coppers are you?"

The last part of my tirade had risen to such a crescendo that Joe shot across the room and dragged me by my lapels from the chair, which went spinning across the room, and pinned me to the floor.

"Shut your bleedin' din, will you," he hissed, spittle flying from the corners of his mouth. "And I'll tell you why we said nothing."

He took a deep breath and released his grip. I took an even deeper breath after realising that Joe had been slowly choking me.

The door opened and Chief Inspector Hallows leaned in. Seeing Joe bent over my prostrate figure, he raised an eyebrow.

"Keep it down," he muttered. "We don't want a khaki panic out there. And Joe …"

"Yes, sir?"

"If you must torture him, do it quietly."

Shamefacedly, Joe stood up and stepped away from me. Rubbing my throat, I got to my feet and faced Hallows.

"Very well, funny man," he said with the trace of a smile, "these two 'clowns' as you put it will tell you why it's in everyone's interests, including yours, that you keep your trap shut for now."

I wasn't going to be fobbed off that easily.

"You might say that but …"

"Yes, I might say that," answered Hallows evenly, his smile having disappeared. "And I might say I enjoyed your double act too."

"And did you?"

But Hallows had already left, closing the door behind him. I looked at Joe who turned away and walked over to the window. Ray glanced at his boss and then at me.

"You OK?"

"I'm fine. Unlike my poor old pal Wilf."

Ray retrieved the upturned chair and set it down in front of me. He motioned me to sit which, after a moment's hesitation, I did. Ray perched on the desk.

"Look, we do understand why you're upset," he began slowly, "but the thing you have to remember is that this town relies on its well-deserved reputation for fun and frolics. People need to know they can come here and have a smashing time and go home happy."

"Without the inconvenience of having a rifle bayonet sticking in their guts."

"Exactly. You're really quick on the uptake."

Ray grinned at me encouragingly.

"Unfortunately," I reminded him, "while your happy holidaymakers are making sand pies and chasing Timmy Trotter up and down the prom, they don't realise that they stand a fair chance of ending up stretched out on the slab next to Wilf and the burning man."

Joe, who hadn't spoken for a couple of minutes, turned from the window to face me. He nodded very deliberately before speaking.

"What you say, Frankie, is absolutely correct. On the one hand we are striking a balance between security - and believe me police night-time patrols have been doubled and all leave cancelled - and on the other hand a wish to protect the public and avoid panic. My own view is that people do indeed have a right to know what is happening in their town but the powers-that-be have decided otherwise. That may of course change but until then we have to go along with it."

"And what if the press finds out?"

Joe took half a step towards me and stopped.

"We did tell them about the tramp on fire," he said. "But that was before we knew he'd been murdered."

"A fact you've failed to mention since?"

Ray nodded.

"Sort of. But be a good lad and say nothing for the time being."

"It's going to come out eventually and then I reckon you'll all be in deeper doings than if you'd been honest in the first place." I paused. "However, I'm not the one who'll be in the firing line so I'll say nothing and let you get on with the job for now."

"Good man," said Joe, smiling for the first time. "And don't go anywhere. We might need to talk to you again about Wilf."

"You still think I had something to do with it?"

Ray shook his head and once again put a big paw on my shoulder.

"We know he was a big mate of yours, Frankie," he smiled. "It's just that we have to cover every angle."

"Wilf was the only pal I had in this godforsaken town. We were close. Very close. In fact, he told me he'd …"

"He told you he'd what?" said Ray, suddenly intrigued.

"Er, nothing."

"It might be important."

"No, I assure you it isn't."

"We'll decide that. Out with it."

"Well, not long before he died Wilf said … he told me he'd … shagged my gran. Not recently of course," I added hastily.

Ray guided me gently towards the door.

"If he'd shagged *my* gran," he said with a huge grin, "*I'd* definitely have done him in."

3
Four-and-Twenty Bloodhounds …

"SEE O'ER YON," Ted the cab driver told me with conspiratorial glee, "what dost reckon them are?" He slowed down to point out two large sculptures, one atop each gatepost guarding the mayor's palatial residence. They appeared to owe their architectural origins to a mish-mash of Blackpool Pleasure Beach and the Third Reich.

"Dunno," I offered, "they look like enormous crowns to me."

"Aye they might look like crowns to thee but what they're supposed to be," said Ted, barely able to choke back a giggle, "is pies. Giant flamin' meat 'n' tater pies. Think on that."

My pathway to musing on the outer limits of what the Mayor of Mellish, Alderman Kenneth Boardman, considered good taste had begun an hour earlier.

On leaving the police interview I'd wandered up and down the prom trying to make some sense of what Joe and Ray told me. Why was the murderer targeting old soldiers? What would his next move be? And at what inevitable point would the police's subterfuge about the cenotaph victim be discovered?

The earlier crowds had thinned out. Evidently someone had cornered Timmy Trotter and relieved him of his white fiver. Or perhaps the old fellow had simply given up and caught the train home. I couldn't have blamed him as the promising weather of a few hours before had disappeared and it was starting to spit with rain. By the time I'd done another length of the prom it was teeming down and I had to hurry back to the digs. Although Rose chided me about wet clothes for the second time in around twelve hours she seemed somewhat detached, as if away in quite another place. Sitting in front of the fire next to a clothes maiden draped once again with my steaming gear, I resumed torturing myself over what had happened to Wilf and how I could perhaps have saved him. After a while, Rose came into the lounge and sat in the chair opposite with her sewing box.

"You OK?" I asked after twenty minutes silence.

Rose paused in her needlework and gave me a tired smile.

"I'm fine, Francis," she said. "How about you? You're not coming down with a cold or anything?"

"No don't worry, I'm fine as well."

But not really fine and a lot more tired than I'd realised. The next thing I knew I was being gently shaken awake by Rose, who told me I had a phone call.

"It's the mayor," she said in less than reverential tones.

I struggled into the hall and grabbed the receiver.

"Funnybone."

"How do, Frankie" boomed a voice at the other end of the line. "Ken Boardman here. I'm the mayor round these parts. Have you had your tea?"

"I should say not," I replied in surprise. "It's only just gone lunchtime."

"If you call four in the afternoon lunchtime then I suppose you've got a point."

Blimey! I must have been kipping for two hours or more. Takes it out of you does murder.

"So have you eaten yet?" the mayor repeated.

I told him that I hadn't whereupon he ordered me to get my backside up to his place sharpish.

"It seems I'm dining out, Rose," I told her while checking if my shirt was dry. She nodded wearily as if it mattered not a jot to her where I took sustenance.

An hour later I was in the back of Ted's cab listening to his tales as we bowled along the Preston Road. Apparently, he'd known Wilf well.

"Oh aye," he said, "the coward what did him in wouldn't have stood a chance in the old days. Wilf would have walloped him. And when he got up Wilf would have walloped the bugger again. Him and his brother spent most of their days fighting - when they weren't at it, if you know what I mean."

He turned round and gave me a gap-toothed grin.

"Yes, I believe he did hint at one or two bedroom exploits," I replied non-committally, desperately keen to reveal no family connections, "but I never heard him talk about a brother."

"Alf was killed at the Somme," Ted said with a sigh. "First wave on July 1st. South Lancashires copped it good and proper that day and not even tough guy Alfie could battle his way out."

"But Wilf did."

"No, he only got called up in autumn of 1916. Alf were a volunteer, see. What's your business with the mayor?"

I told him truthfully that I had no idea beyond that I'd been offered an evening meal. He guffawed at that idea and filled me in about the sculptures atop the gates. As the taxi stopped in front of Boardman's mansion, Ted leaned back and spoke out of the side of his mouth.

"His grandad started t'business and talk was that during the war - the Great War that is - he came by most of his meat via the doggy pound. Course it were only a rumour. But don't eat anythin' that might have gone woof, woof."

As Ted's cab trundled out of the gates, I turned to look at the house. With the Greek columns and porticos, it resembled your typical factory owner's idea of a grand home in the classical mode. I recognised the style because my dear father-in-law Joshua, a cotton magnate, lived in a similar heap which towered menacingly over our home town of Butterthwaite. In fact, the barley sugar Doric columns of the pier's Coliseum Theatre looked ten times more authentic than either of these mansions.

It was still tippling down so I abandoned my architectural survey and sprinted up the steps to the forbidding black double front doors. Before I could ring the bell, however, they flew apart and a large red-faced character with a mane of greying hair swept out, his arms extended.

"Frankie, nice to meet you. Come on in out o' t'wet."

After crushing my hand in his huge paw, the mayor led me into the large hallway.

"Bloody summer rain'll be the ruin of this town," Boardman grumbled. "Course, sun'll be cracking t'flags up in Blackpool."

"I doubt that," I told him. "They reckon the whole county's getting a soaking."

"No, no, you're not following me, lad. Thing is, every day in summer local evening newspapers all over Lancashire phone the resorts to check on the weather. And guess what? Why, it never rains in Blackpool! It can be peeing down all along the coast up to Barrow and down to Liverpool but somehow it's always sunny in Blackpool. You wouldn't credit it would you?"

"Not really."

"Me neither. That's why I've told the lads in the tourist office to make sure it never rains in Mellish either. I think Southport's caught on too. So has Fleetwood. That leaves poor old Morecambe as the only resort on this coast where you can still officially get a soaking. Ha ha ha."

"Does nobody round here tell the truth about what's going on in their town?"

Boardman's laughter stopped as suddenly as it had begun and for a moment I thought my grim face was about to take a beating, such was the glare he gave me. Then, just as quickly, his features relaxed.

"Come on, lad," he boomed, "time to tuck in."

I resisted the compulsion to inquire if we were having meat 'n' tater pies and I'm glad I did. Although Boardman appeared to be the usual tiresome civic bumpkin, his taste in food was anything but provincial. We sat down at one end of a massive polished maple dining table and were served pate de foie gras followed by boeuf bourguignon and fresh cherries with double cream, all dished up by Boardman's housekeeper Muriel, a grey-haired unsmiling woman of about fifty.

During the meal Boardman listed the variety acts he'd enjoyed, including my own apparently. Then he really floored me by mentioning that he knew Joshua.

"Oh aye, your father-in-law's a right character," he said with a grin. "Nobody in't'Lancashire Chamber of Commerce gets one over on old Joshua."

"Apart from me," I muttered just a little too loudly and was forced into the umpteenth re-telling of the story concerning my 1936 elopement with Nancy, which resulted in a hot and heavy pursuit northwards by Joshua and his armed bullies, ended only by the intervention of King Edward VIII on the moors above Balmoral. Oh, and that the randy royal stood for us at our quickly thrown together wedding the next day.

"Crikey," Boardman whistled, "the king was your best man! Who was chief bridesmaid, Princess Margaret?"

"Almost, but in the event the honour went to Wallis Simpson. It wasn't that long before she and the king staged their own elopement."

"Yeah, I remember that. Keep in touch, do you?"

"No."

"Even so, you're better connected and more influential than I thought, Frankie," said Boardman, refilling my glass with Chateau Lafitte 1938. "Which is all to the good."

He gave me a long and what he must have imagined meaningful stare. Aye, aye, I thought. We've arrived at why I'm here.

"Thing is, Frankie, these murders are doing nobody in the town any good at all."

"Least of all those who've been murdered," I answered cautiously. How did *he* know there was more than one victim?

"Oh yes, very good. I like your style," Boardman replied without the trace of a smile. "But people like you can do something about it."

"How am I supposed to stop a murderer?"

"You're not. That's down to those clowns at the nick. I'm meaning you can help the town out. Spread the word round your fellow professionals and tell the audiences that Mellish is still a safe place to come. Point out that the numbers are insignificant and you're no more likely to be butchered than be …" He waved his hands inconclusively so I supplied the punchline.

"… than be poleaxed by a flying meat pie?"

"Yes. No. You know what I mean. Spread the word around the business. Reassure the people you meet so they'll go home and tell everyone this is a safe place."

This conversation wasn't making much sense. I didn't generally dispense nuggets of advice to our audience members, unless I was pleading with them not to leave early.

"Oh, and perhaps," Boardman added airily, "try to persuade that old fool Shelvey to reopen the theatre pronto."

So that was why I'd been summoned! I took a long drink of wine.

"Look, Ken, I can't honestly pretend that I've much influence with Henry Shelvey. He's a nice fellow but he seems like a man who knows his own mind."

"Aye, that he does," said Boardman ruefully. "Let's say me an' him don't agree on much. But a bloke like you might have more influence with him."

"Very well, I will ask Mr Shelvey when he plans to reopen the theatre."

Boardman leaned back with a smug smile and noisily drained his half-full wine glass. His self-satisfaction was screaming to be punctured.

"But I won't make light of the fact," I added sternly, "that one of my pals was a victim of this madman and I only just escaped joining him in the morgue."

Boardman appeared chastened.

"Of course not, Frankie," he muttered. "I wasn't suggesting you do that. Forgive me."

"Already done."

"Good," said the mayor jumping to his feet and slapping me on the back. "You'll be needing the grand tour then."

He led me into the circular entrance hall, the walls of which I now noticed were infested with large framed posters advertising all manner of Boardman pastries. The pictures showed happy holidaymakers capering around on impossibly sunny beaches while jolly red-faced pie men - not unlike

Boardman himself, I mused - beamed out from behind stalls groaning with savoury delights. At the top of each poster was a suitable homily such as, 'Our Crust is a Must,' 'They're Thrilling, They're Filling,' and my favourite, in light of what Ted the cabby had revealed about the firm's dubious origins, 'It's Real Meat for a Real Treat.'

Boardman smiled proudly. "Made up all them slogans meself," he boasted.

"You're a poet, Ken. Instead of Boardman we should call you Bard Man."

My flimsy piece of whimsy tickled the mayor to such an extent that he slapped me on the back again roaring with a great deal more laughter than I'd earned at the theatre in recent times. He then led me up the wide winding staircase to the next floor to admire a couple of bedrooms, each with its own lavish bathroom, before taking me back downstairs and through a kitchen big enough to service a medium-sized hotel. At the far end, beyond the massive cooking range he opened double doors which led onto another staircase.

"My pride and joy!"

He smiled and beckoned me towards the stairs, which swept down in a wide graceful arc. At the bottom was a wall entirely of glass, behind which shimmered an indoor swimming pool at least forty feet long. Lights glittered beneath the surface bathing the room in an atmospheric bluish glow, the effect of which was somewhat ruined by Boardman switching on garish up-lights in the shape of medieval torches on the walls around the pool.

"I do fifty lengths every morning without fail," he told me proudly. "Can't take any risks with your health, I allus say."

"Amen to that," I muttered distractedly, because in truth I was only half-listening to Boardman's prattling. What had caught my eye was another glass wall at the far end of the pool which framed an extremely strange tableau. Beyond the glass was a kind of gymnasium containing what to me looked like instruments of torture. To one side of the room, hanging from the ceiling was a heavy leather punch bag which at that very moment - and there's no other way to put this - was under assault. A younger, larger and more muscular version of Ken Boardman, dressed in just a pair of grubby grey tracksuit pants and boxing gloves, was belting hell out of the bag. But he wasn't just punching it; he was actually kicking the thing as if it had just flashed at his maiden aunt. The young man was also clearly shouting angrily at the bag but I couldn't make out the words coming from behind the glass. I noticed Boardman glance once or twice at this bizarre scene while trying to preserve a pretence of normality.

"And I have a little fellow come in once a week to clean the pool and check the chlorination levels," he told me.

"Coronation," I replied, still distracted because to my astonishment the young boxer had now started head-butting the bag and I swear at one point actually tried to sink his teeth into it.

"God's sake," Boardman muttered angrily under his breath before marching down the side of the pool towards the gym. I was unsure whether to follow but curiosity got the better of me. I trailed behind as Boardman flung open the glass door and barrelled into the gym.

"Bleedin' 'ell, our John," he exploded. "It's supposed t'be Marquess of flamin' Queensberry not a brawl outside a chippy."

For a second the young man looked nonplussed, as if unaware of what he'd been up to. Without a word he immediately ended his assault and, breathing heavily, moved to another corner of the room where he began to hit a hanging speed ball with a great deal more control than he'd hitherto shown. He was good too, as the ball flew from side to side like a gossip's tongue on washday.

Boardman looked at me with more than a trace of embarrassment in his eyes.

"Francis, meet my son John. As you can see, he's in training for an important boxing bout. John, this is Francis Thirkettle, alias the comedian Frankie Funnybone."

"I know who he is," John replied without pausing in his rat-a-tat exertions. "I've seen his show."

And, after a pretty effective pause, he provided the sting.

"Comedian's putting it a bit strong, don't you think?"

Having heard stuff like this many times before, I tried to let the comment go with a practised sardonic grin which implied, "You get up on stage, psycho boy, and try your luck."

My host, however, was having none of it. With a roar which startled not only myself but John as well, Ken Boardman leapt at his son, grabbed him by the throat and pinned him against the wall.

"Apologise now, you little toe rag," he hissed.

I confess I was prepared for a bout of blood-spattered mayhem. John Boardman didn't look the type to take this sort of assault lying down, even from papa. However, to my surprise, I noticed the briefest moment of pure fear and shock sweep across John's face before he was able to compose his features. In the same moment the wild look in his father's eyes disappeared to be replaced by one of embarrassment as he relaxed his grip. Boardman wiped his hands down the front of his shirt and nodded at John who turned to me.

"Very sorry, Mr Funnybone," he said with a straight face. "I've suddenly remembered that your show was a hoot from start to finish."

"There, we're all pals again," Boardman grinned, patting his son lightly on the shoulder. "And from what we've just seen - especially with that speed ball - I wouldn't like to be in the other feller's boots next week."

John smiled sourly.

"Yes, Mr Funnybone, my prospective opponent will doubtless be quaking in those very boots as we speak. After all he only boxed for Britain in the Berlin Olympics."

"That was twenty years ago," I replied in an off-hand bid to reassure John that his big head had the ghost of a chance of remaining on those broad shoulders.

"Comedian and historian," muttered John but did not comment further after his father flashed him a dangerous look.

"I'd better be getting going, Ken," I said, keen to defuse the situation. "Thanks for the lovely meal. Could you ring for a taxi?"

"No need for that, Frankie," Boardman replied. "Our John will run you into town. You are going to that club tonight I take it?"

John nodded, picked up a towel and walked briskly towards the door. Opening it, he said without turning, "Fifteen minutes. In the hall."

Boardman and I followed John up the stairs, along the kitchen and into the circular hall. I could see the mayor was debating whether he should apologise again for John's boorishness but he was saved from further abasement by the appearance of a strikingly beautiful woman with light brown wavy hair, who came in through the front door holding hands with a pretty little girl. They were followed by a very small, middle-aged man in a chauffeur's uniform and cap who carried a tiny sleeping boy over his shoulders like a sack of spuds. The woman, who was surely no more than late thirties, smiled at Boardman who rushed over to embrace her.

"Frankie, meet my wife Marjorie," he gushed with pride. "And the kiddies Alan and Wendy. Everyone, this is the distinguished comedian Frankie Funnybone."

Marjorie had the good grace to hold out her hand and confess she was delighted to meet an actual star, although it was clear she'd never heard of me.

"We don't get enough real personalities in this house, Mr Funnybone," she said with a dazzling smile. "The people my husband mixes with are very pleasant of course but a touch …" she dropped her voice to a whisper, "uninteresting."

I threw an anxious glance towards Boardman but he was grinning inanely, obviously entranced by his wife's allure. He spent the next few minutes proudly informing me how she and the children had been for a motor ride around the Lake District, while I speculated how long the tiny chauffeur could continue to support the child without collapsing and how many cushions he needed to sit on while driving. Luckily, Muriel the housekeeper, who was a heavy-set woman, appeared on the scene to relieve the driver of his burden. Without a word she lugged young Alan upstairs, ushering little Wendy in front of her.

"I'll be up to say goodnight in a sec, Mu," said Marjorie.

"And then you can have a bite and tell me all about your day," Boardman said excitedly.

Marjorie's face fell.

"Oh, Ken, I'm so sorry. I promised I'd go to visit Polly and stay the night. She's still suffering with her trouble. That's on top of Arthur being his usual beastly self to her."

"Polly! Again? Ah well, if things are that serious then it can't be helped," said Boardman, trying without much success to hide his disappointment and irritation.

"I'll be back tomorrow as early as I can," cooed Marjorie, giving her husband the ghost of a peck on the cheek. "Delighted to meet you, Mr Funnybone."

I nodded as she turned to meet John coming down the stairs.

"Off out on the razzle again, mummy dearest," he said with an unpleasant grin.

Marjorie patted him lightly on the shoulder.

"You really are the most terrible little shit, John," I heard her whisper before she continued on upstairs.

It was obvious Boardman too had witnessed the exchange because he looked as if he was considering thumping his son. John, however, had the sense to continue walking briskly towards the front door.

"Come on then, jester," he shouted without turning round, "your carriage awaits."

I made to follow him but Boardman grabbed my arm urgently. All the bonhomie had disappeared from his countenance.

"Remind that landlord of yours - the copper," he muttered, "that people come to this town to have a belting time and a good feed. Not to get ritually bleedin' slain. Tell him he'd better catch this sick so-and-so pronto."

With that he let go of my arm and patted me gently on the back, the baleful glare replaced by a not altogether convincing benevolent smile.

"And the next most important thing is get that theatre reopened. Like I said, Frankie, spread the good word. Especially to old Shelvey."

With that he nearly pushed me down the front steps.

I had barely settled into the plush leather front seat of John's sporty Jaguar before it was already halfway down the long drive. John propelled his car with the same disturbing intensity he showed in tackling the heavy bag and it was a minute or so before I was confident enough to fully open my eyes and speak.

"I must say, John, your mother looks very er ... well. A most handsome lady."

John let out a huge guffaw, swinging the vehicle dangerously towards the grass verge.

"As my mother's been dead these past ten years, I doubt that very much, Mr Comedian. However, if you're talking about my step-mother Marjorie then I must reluctantly agree, although what she sees in my Dad god only knows. Apart from his millions. Ha ha ha."

Well, it was nice to see him with a smile, albeit a crooked one. We drove on in silence for a minute before John made a surprise announcement.

"You know she used to go with that copper you're staying with."

For some reason this piece of news astounded me and I had to check what he'd actually said.

"You're saying that *Joe Trueman* went out with Marjorie?"

"Yep, before my old man snatched her off him. I can tell you that led to fun and games when Mr Plod finally plodded home from the war. Your cousin, is he?"

"He's married to my cousin."

"Ah yes, the little mouse."

Seeing me bridle at this off-hand dismissal of Rose, John moved quickly to clarify his comment.

"No offence, my friend. Joe's ten times better off with your cousin than my evil step-mother. Merely a turn of phrase, I assure you."

I quickly steered the subject away from romance and towards boxing which darkened John's mood as I knew it would, and serve him right. Apparently, Ken Boardman was sponsoring next week's amateur tournament and had persuaded John, against his better judgment, to take part.

"It's true that the bloke I'm up against, Brian Pike, was fighting twenty years ago but he's still only thirty-eight. Jesus wept, Joe Louis was still boxing when he was thirty-seven."

"Until he was taken apart by Rocky Marciano."

"The difference is, friend, I'm no Marciano. Pike will do to me what I was doing to that punch bag. Here's the terminus."

He brought the vehicle to a screaming halt and I tumbled out, relieved to be in one piece. Before I could even thank him, John had slammed the car into gear and roared away, his tail lights receding quickly into the distance. In fact, he'd dropped me about three streets away from Joe and Rose's house but I wasn't bothered. The evening was warm with all trace of rain gone and I enjoyed the stroll back, listening to mothers calling their older kids in from the streets.

As I walked, I reflected that Boardman had just wasted a good meal on me. I couldn't influence public opinion one way or the other - not that I had any intention of trying to - and had little sway with Mr Shelvey, who would doubtless reopen the theatre when he was good and ready. Besides I'd earned one or two days off, having worked harder these last few weeks than at any time since before the war.

On reaching the house there was barely enough time to put my key in the front door before it flew open and there stood Rose. At first I thought she was expecting Joe and my arrival, like last night's, would be greeted with dismay. But instead she flung her arms round me in relief.

"Thank god you're here," she sighed.

"What's up, cuz, toilet blocked again? Is it a job for my trusty plunger?"

Rose gazed up at me in fear and agitation.

"Oh, Francis," she cried, "there's been another murder."

4
Don't Quote Me

IT WASN'T THE SCREAMS coming from Rose and Joe's bedroom that filled me with dread, although heaven knows, the racket was disturbing enough. No, what really got to me was the persistent low guttural sobbing. And the fact that the tortured soul making this hullabaloo was Joe. Creeping along the landing to the door of their bedroom, I'd paused, weighing up whether to go in. After all, surely the secrets of their marriage bed should stay under the covers. But as the alternating screeches and sobs grew in intensity, I decided there was nothing else for it. So I threw open the door - to be greeted by an alarming sight. It wasn't so much that Joe was in the middle of a nightmare, clawing the air above him and moaning the same name over and over that shocked me; it was more the fact that throughout it all Rose lay peacefully asleep next to him.

This unnerving scene was the climax of a fraught twenty-four hours for our household and its three occupants. Rose's delight at seeing me the previous night had been swiftly overtaken by confessions of acute anxiety about her husband. She wouldn't elaborate on the causes but did reveal the little she knew about the latest murder, which boiled down to the fact that the body had been found in the cellar of a pub. Eventually, a little after midnight, I managed to coax her upstairs to bed before staggering to my own room and going out like a light.

When I'd awoken at eight and gone downstairs, Rose was still in her bedroom but the evidence of an eiderdown neatly draped over the back of the sofa showed that Joe had slept there so as not to disturb her and was already out of the house. As I'd thought more than once, if sheer bloody hard graft from the lead investigator counted for anything then this villain should soon be doing the Strangeways Shuffle on the end of Albert Pierrepoint's rope.

Rose still hadn't appeared by gone nine so I left the house on a mission to discover more about the latest crime. And it became immediately clear that the streets were alive with fear and wild speculation. Passing the ironmonger's, I observed two elderly women chatting.

"Nailed to a cross he was, just like our good lord," one whispered to the other. "Whatever next!" her pal replied.

I'd decided to avoid the nick and clear my head with another brisk stroll down the prom, when I literally ran into Ray. He appeared without warning from a back alley whereupon we collided. And it was easy to see why he might be somewhat distracted; on his arm was a teenage stunner in a school uniform, light enough on her feet to dodge the collision.

"Watch where you're ... oh it's you, Ray."

"Sorry, Frankie, didn't see you there. Er, Jenny, this is the comedian Frankie Funnybone, you know the one I mentioned. He's staying with Detective Sergeant Trueman."

Jenny nodded and politely shook my hand but didn't seem remotely interested in who I was. She whispered something to Ray and then excused herself before dashing off down the road.

"Shouldn't she be at school?"

"Free period. They're trusted to manage their own time when they get to A-levels."

"Let's hope she gets good grades then."

"She will. Fancy gate-crashing the press conference?"

"You organised that quickly."

"Not exactly. It was originally just about Wilf. But I'm sure he won't mind sharing."

As we walked, Ray told me what he knew about the previous night's grim discovery. A cellar man at The Fusilier on Butterthwaite Road had gone to change a barrel and discovered the body of a former coal unloader at Liverpool docks. This poor fellow, an ex-infantryman, had been blindfolded and tied to a post with a paper target pinned over his heart. He was dead of course from three shots, all straight through the bullseye.

"A firing squad!"

"Grim ain't it?"

"This guy's got to be strong to overpower a coal heaver."

"He'd been sleeping rough for years apparently," said Ray. "That doesn't half take it out of you."

"Was there a note?" I asked.

"Yes, but mum's the word. We won't be mentioning any of those this morning."

Approaching the cop-shop, he slowed down and put a hand on my arm.

"But we will be telling them most of what we know about Wilf's death. So, if you'd rather …"

"No, no. I'll be interested to hear what you have. What about the first victim?"

Ray looked uncomfortable.

"Powers-that-be decided not to link him in … yet."

"That's ridiculous."

"Ours not to reason why," he said with a shrug. "Come on in here. Tradesman's entrance."

Ray led me down an alley that was barely wider than a man and through a side door into the station. In the corridor we stopped at the doorway of a large room. At one end there was a raised platform with a table and two chairs. The rest of the room, already filling up with a pea-souper of pipe and cigarette smoke, contained about twenty chairs. To my surprise most of them were already occupied by bored-looking press men. A couple of photographers lounged by the platform.

"Sit at the back there," Ray whispered. "And tell anyone who asks that you're from The Beano. I'll be up on the stage."

"With your father-in-law?"

Ray's swagger evaporated in an instant.

"Ssssh," he hissed with a worried glance at Chief Inspector Hallows, who had just entered the room and was striding towards his place on the podium.

Hallows, however, had much more important things to do than take note of idle chit-chat from underlings. Brushing imaginary specks of dust from his immaculate cuffs he gazed haughtily at the journalists before introducing himself and Ray. And, as the press conference proceeded, I had to admit he was handling it well. Without revealing too many vital details - he'd withheld the bit about the paper target for example - Hallows gave just enough away to keep the reporters interested and dealt easily with their excited but somewhat routine questions. He also presented them with a short rundown of what had happened to Wilf two nights ago without, I noted, mentioning my role in the tragedy. Ray chipped in with prosaic details about the second victim, the coal heaver and ex-soldier whose name was a rather unlikely Terence Poynter-Mann, before Hallows finished off with a strong plea for calm and a pledge that the case would soon be solved. The killer, after all, had left a ton of clues which meant it was just a matter of time before he'd be facing the hanging judge.

It was at this moment of apparent triumph that Chief Inspector Hallows made his big mistake. Imagining the conference to be over, he stood up and came out with what he must have considered was a jocular aside.

"We should all really get back to work now," Hallows smiled graciously. "After all, this fellow won't catch himself."

As he turned to go, a voice cut through the smoky air.

"From what we've seen so far, neither will you."

The speaker, who was sitting on the back row a couple of chairs away from me, was a slim young man. But for the beginnings of a wispy beard, he could have been mistaken for a schoolboy. Unlike the other journalists he was not smoking and didn't even appear to have a notebook. Hallows regarded the young man with a mixture of condescension and exasperation.

"What paper are you from?" he asked in a tone which invited the other press representatives to pity the presumption of this poor deluded interloper.

"The Express."

Hallows shook his head more in sadness than anger.

"I must warn you, sonny, that I am on extremely good terms with the editor of the Mellish Express."

"The Daily Express."

Take it from one who knows, as punchlines go it was a killer. Hallows staggered back against his chair, open-mouthed. He couldn't have looked more astonished if he'd just been booted in the ribs by Lord Beaverbrook himself. Before the chief inspector could reply, the Express man moved in for the kill.

"Perhaps you could explain a little more about the fact that this poor man wasn't just murdered."

There was a theatrical pause which convinced me that this kid could give Barney a run for his money; he even looked like him.

As Hallows squirmed, the reporter continued in a calm but icy voice.

"The poor fellow was executed, wasn't he? Tied to a post and shot through the heart, over which was fastened a paper target. That's what I'd heard at any rate. Your comments."

Crikey, this guy's police contacts were good. Either that or Marvolio the Magical Mind Reader had a serious rival. Furthermore, I knew enough about the press to realise that if this reporter was willing to make such a potential scoop public then he thought that his rivals in the room knew, or suspected they knew, as much as he did. Maybe he was their spokesman. Whatever the situation, it was now vital for Hallows to throw these sharks some tastier morsels. Unfortunately, he failed to grasp this. When the chief inspector's mouth finally stopped opening and closing like a gormless guppy's his next comment was hardly inspiring.

"We won't rest until this person is caught," Hallows declared, lifting his papers from the table in a way that clearly indicated the show was now over. But as he swiftly began to take a few steps towards the exit, he was stopped in his tracks.

"What about the notes?"

This came from a plump fellow two rows in front of the Express man. At least Hallows had enough sense not to question which newspaper this chap represented.

"Notes?"

"He's been taunting you with crossword clues, hasn't he? About the war."

"Er, well, as we are into operational territory here, we must maintain the confidentiality of the investigation," Hallows blathered as the younger journalist prepared to administer the coup de grace. Express delivery, so to speak.

"So do tell us," said the wispy-bearded boy, with an insincere smile, "when were you going to mention Michael Donaghy?"

"Michael ... Donaghy?" Hallows croaked.

"Yes, you might just recall him. Another former serviceman. Murdered a week-and-a-half ago at the cenotaph. Barbecued to a crisp."

There was a gasp of surprise from more than half the journalists in the room. Evidently not every press man and woman were in on that little secret.

"I assume it was the same killer. Cryptic note, 'a ton' of clues and loads of gormless provincial coppers chasing their own tails."

All eyes were now on the chief inspector, including those of the seated Ray who gazed up expectantly at his boss. Hallows had become a rabbit in the headlights. With what he hoped was a final, "I can't comment on that," he turned and marched towards the exit door behind the platform. Even then he couldn't dodge the Express reporter's final barb.

"Incidentally, as we're talking about ex-servicemen, remind us all what you did in the war."

Hallows was already clutching the door handle.

"I did my bit for our great country," he muttered before disappearing towards what he mistakenly imagined would be sanctuary.

Meanwhile, Ray stood up with a smile.

"That's all, folks," he announced before giving a faultlessly executed military salute, which raised a huge laugh from the press crew. As Hallows fled through the doorway, I glimpsed Ken Boardman furiously grabbing his arm and dragging him to one side.

While the press pack drained out of the room jabbering excitedly and comparing notes, I carefully approached the door behind the platform, which was still ajar. Peering round I saw no sign of the chief inspector or of the mayor. No sign, but considerable sound! Every step I quietly took up the corridor brought a withering tirade by Boardman into sharper relief. By the time I was outside the chief inspector's office, it was clear that Hallows was receiving a furious dressing-down.

"I really don't think that's appropriate, Mr Mayor," he was protesting.

"And I don't think it's appropriate," countered Boardman, "that my town is being threatened by a murdering madman who seems to do what he damn well pleases. Now get a grip, or get on your bike!"

"Really, Mr Mayor, this is too …"

"Out of my way, you pen-pushing prick."

The conversation was evidently over and I moved quickly away from the door in case Boardman spotted me and suggested that I walk up and down the prom on my hands with a target on my backside. As I hurried round a corner, I bumped into Ray for the second time in an hour.

"Hello, Frankie, you really shouldn't be back here, you know."

"And you really shouldn't be giving your boss's daughter …"

"OK! Fifteen all," shouted Ray quickly, his muscular right arm steering me gently but firmly towards the main entrance. His grip relaxed only when we got to the bottom of the steps whereupon he puffed out his cheeks and smiled.

"Press conference went well don't you reckon," he said with a wink.

"If the point of it was for your chief to make a complete arse of himself, then yes it was an enormous success."

"Hmmm."

"Especially as it was followed by a steamrollering from Boardman."

"Ah, never worry. I'm sure Daddy'll get over it."

"You'd better bloomin' well hope so. Where's Joe today?"

I could see he was debating whether or not to tell me.

"Come on, Ray, we're all on the same side."

"Joe's gone to Altonford University," he said finally. "To talk to a code-breaking expert."

"Armed with the crossword clues?"

"I can't really say …"

"… which the whole country will know about tomorrow morning."

"If you put it like that then yes."

"Can I see the clues?"

"You can ask Joe. Ta ra for now."

I watched Ray ascend the steps very nimbly for such a big chap. For some reason I imagined him gliding across the dance floor with Jenny in her ballgown. It was an oddly comforting thought.

On the spur of the moment I decided to visit someone I'd intended to see for a day or two. Accordingly, I stopped at the florist's round the corner from the nick. While waiting for my small gift of roses and lilies to be put together I glanced through the shop window and smiled with delight. Assuring the florist I would be back in a minute, I rushed across the road to a bus shelter in which sat my stage partner Barney McAskill. He seemed not at all pleased to see me.

"Howdy, pardner," I cried with extravagant bonhomie. "I could have sworn you were rubbing shoulders with the comedy elite in Blackpool."

"I don't know what you're talking about," he muttered, turning away from me.

"But surely you were invited to stay with my good friend Frankie Driscoll. Ah, dear old Frankie, I remember being on the same bill as him at Great Yarmouth in, what would it be, oo-er 1947."

Barney jumped up furiously and I could swear there was murder in his eyes.

"You knew, didn't you? You damn well knew."

"Knew what, dear boy? Oh, did I forget to mention that Frankie's prone to get, let's say a bit fruity? Especially when there's a good-looking young chap around. Or even in your case."

"Shut up, you has-been nobody," yelled Barney, drawing anxious glances from one or two passers-by. I smiled indulgently as if to reassure them that I had everything under control. But by now Barney's eyes were on stalks.

"I heard today that we reopen on Monday," he spat.

"Oh goody. We'll be able to resume our fruitful partnership."

Barney smiled, showing off his rotten teeth.

"Yes, we'll be back performing together and you, you dinosaur, won't know whether you're coming or going. I'll have you jumping all over that stage and you won't even have the wit to respond because you're slow and stupid and rubbish."

"Something to look forward to then. By the way, you haven't got a much better-looking brother who works on the Daily Express have you?"

He stalked off, evidently forgetting that he'd been waiting for a bus. Well, at least a few lucky passengers had been spared the joy of Barney's presence. When I went back into the shop the florist appeared extremely excited.

"Was that young Barney from the pier show you were talking to?" she said, handing me a stylishly assembled bunch of blooms.

"Yes, it was. I'm his psychiatrist. The poor chap's delusional, you know."

She looked genuinely pained.

"That's such a shame, I was at the show last Wednesday afternoon."

"Ah yes, the shopkeepers' matinee. Did you enjoy it?"

"Oh, I did," she gushed. "I thought young Barney was brilliant."

She paused and sighed.

"Delusions, you say? I suppose that is the price of fame."

"Indeed so, madam. It is a sad fact that many of our comic geniuses are tortured souls. Er, what did you think of his partner?"

"Partner?" she replied with a puzzled frown. "I don't remember him having a partner. That'll be three and sevenpence please."

I hailed a taxi, as the twenty-minute walk would have allowed me to dwell excessively on what was undoubtedly in store for me on Monday. Matinee and evening performance, Barney would tie me up in knots more completely than the Crazy Gang ever did. But maybe, just maybe, the killer would get to him first. It would be truly tragic but understandable. After all, murderers have standards too. Perhaps Barney himself was the killer. Oh, wouldn't that be even more fantastic! I could pause the act, announce I was making a dramatic citizen's arrest on stage and stove Barney's head in while I was at it. I'd be the hero of the hour, everyone's shining knight and nobody, but nobody, would be laughing at me! Er, what I mean of course is …

"Wakey wakey, captain. We're here."

I paid the driver and walked up the short path through a small, neat front garden. The bungalow's front door was opened by Wilf's sister Ethel and I felt so relieved when it became immediately clear that I didn't have to explain who I was.

"Come in, please, Frankie." Ethel said with a sad smile. "Wilfred told me so much about you."

And not one single mention of Barney bleedin' McAskill. Yes!

Over tea and ginger nuts, Ethel accepted the flowers with my condolences and tenderly told me all kinds of stories about Wilf, her rapscallion big brother. Why he never married - was a bit too fond of too many ladies. Why he loved his job - got to meet all sorts including Charlie Chaplin. Imagine that! Her Wilfy hobnobbing with someone who would become the most famous man in the world.

"Something to tell the grandkids about," I said, before remembering Wilf didn't have any grandchildren, none that he knew about at any rate. He'd had my grandmother of course but his sister definitely didn't need to know about that.

After we'd traded reminiscences over a pleasant hour I was about to leave when Ethel mentioned she was the final survivor of five brothers and sisters. Sensing she was about to stray into emotional territory, I put my exit on hold while Ethel reeled off a grim litany.

"Little Dorothy went of the flu of 1919, just five she was. Then poor Neville was killed in the pit. 1933 that was. Who does that leave?"

"Alf."

"Ah poor Alfie, dead on the first day of The Somme. Like so many others. Now Wilf's gone and there's just me. My hubby Jim was killed at Tobruk." She tried to suppress a sniff but she couldn't hide the tears welling up in her eyes.

Ethel had had it rough and no mistake.

For the next few moments we sat in silence as she collected her thoughts. Then I tentatively prepared to leave.

"I'm so sorry about your husband," I told her. "But at least Wilf missed the start of the Somme. That was a very lucky break."

I stood up to go but Ethel remained in her armchair, staring into the fireplace's empty grate. I thought at first that she'd dropped off, but a few seconds later she looked up at me.

"Those are exactly the words that young fellow used to Wilf. 'A very lucky break.'"

"Young fellow?"

I sat back down, curious to hear rather more about this chap.

Apparently, a fortnight or so before he died Wilf was having his regular Sunday lunchtime pint when he was joined by a man who claimed to be a local historian. As per usual Wilf mentioned his war record - hence the lucky break comment - and reminisced about the variety acts he had known. The man had received all the information gratefully and duly noted it all down. But his greatest interest was reserved for the Coliseum Theatre itself. How long it had been built, what materials were used and particularly how it was laid out. This was meat and drink to Wilf, his own domain as it were. He'd even supplied a little diagram with details, including the fact he kept window boxes which were his pride and joy.

While Ethel was talking it became progressively harder for me to retain a façade of calm, but inside I could feel my excitement rising. Could this be the encounter in the bar Wilf had mentioned just before he died? I needed to hear more about this 'lucky break' fellow.

"Did Wilf mention what he, er, looked like?"

"Bearded. Wore glasses. Just a youngish man, he said. Mind you they were all young compared to Wilf. Nice bloke though. Bought Wilf a few pints."

"A very nice bloke then. Did your brother say anything else about this chap?"

"He said there was one thing about him that really stood out."

I took a deep breath.

"Would it be that he had the most brilliant piercing blue eyes?"

"That's right. Did Wilf mention the man to you as well?"

"Listen, Ethel, please try to remember. Did Wilf give any details to this chap about his war service?"

Ethel looked down at the carpet in embarrassment.

"Frankie, one thing you should know about our Wilf," she said, "is that after a couple of drinks he'd get maudlin', very maudlin'. And this fellow was very free with his cash. He wouldn't once let Wilf pay his turn."

"So Wilf would have told him about the German that he'd bayonetted at Ypres?"

"I'm sure he would have. Mind you, he wasn't proud of it, you must understand that."

"I know he wasn't."

"He just had to get it off his chest. It was like a sore that never healed."

I didn't mention that the incident was virtually the last thing her brother had described to me ... to anyone. I was too busy wondering how I could keep Ethel from panicking when she realised that Wilf had met his killer not once but twice. In the end I said nothing about it, merely adding that the cops might want to speak to her, just routine you understand, and maybe it would be best if she locked and bolted her doors at night. You couldn't be too careful these days, especially with a killer on the prowl. I hope I didn't frighten her unduly.

Ten minutes later I was sitting in the vault of Wilf's local, a street corner pub called the Prince George, far enough from the prom to contain no pesky holidaymakers with their flippin' odd ways. It wasn't too long before a few regulars recognised me and started to chinwag about Wilf. They'd heard about my encounter with the murderer and were happy to buy me a pint and take one or two more in return off the man who had battled to save their old pal's life and nearly lost his own in the process. Toasts were drunk and the conversation, lubricated by my largesse, ranged across many topics - both world wars, showbiz and Wilf's legendary prowess with the ladies (although my Granny Thirkettle remained thankfully unmentioned).

The talk grew ribald without becoming riotous and, as Wilf's mates and I became confidantes, I mentioned in passing a mutual friend who often turned up in these parts. Youngish chap, glasses, beard and bright blue eyes, maybe here a fortnight or so ago? Worked behind the scenes at the Theatre Royal in Preston. However, none of them remembered Wilf talking to someone of that description. Although outwardly calm I was screaming inside, "One of you must have seen him!"

I'd decided I was out of luck and was about to cut my losses when one of the drinkers, an ancient who could have been Wilf's great grandad, held up his gnarled, knobbly forefinger.

"What day did you say your young mate was here?"

"I'm pretty sure it was a Sunday."

They all began to nod at each other. Evidently the conundrum had been cracked.

"Ah well," the old chap said, "Wilf liked to take his Sunday pint in the saloon."

"There's a lounge bar in this place?" I exclaimed in surprise and was directed through a side door into an almost identical room to the one I'd just vacated. The only differences were that the seats were padded, there was no dartboard and a gold-framed image of our newish Queen gazed uncertainly down from the back wall. There were fewer drinkers too but one of them, prompted by my offer of pints all round in memory of a good old pal, recalled that Wilf had been sitting in that very corner with another man a couple of weeks before. A young fellow with bright blue eyes.

"Ah," I replied. "That could well have been our mutual mate, er, Benjamin."

"It couldn't have been Benjamin though could it," said the drinker, whose name was Jack and looked a bit younger and sharper than the average Prince George regular. "It couldn't have been him because he didn't know Wilf."

"I thought they were talking together?"

"Yes but they hadn't met before. When this chap came in he asked at the bar which of us was Wilf Holt."

"He mentioned Wilf by name?"

"I just said, didn't I?"

"And you'd recognise him again, would you, Jack?"

"I reckon so. Oh, and there was another thing about him."

"What would that be, Jack?"

"This fellow had quite a bad limp. I noticed it when he went off for a pee. The right leg from memory."

I spent a few more minutes chatting but my mind was racing in quite another direction. Lots of people limped, but still … After a few minutes more I bade my farewell to both bars. The episode had set me back a few quid but I considered it money very well spent.

Making my way home I tried to rationalise and put out of my mind the fact that the young man limped. After all, Joe was hardly unknown in these parts and surely someone would have realised if it was him talking to Wilf. No, my immediate worry was how to tell Joe that I might have made a significant breakthrough in the case - without treading on his size tens and upsetting him any more than he already was.

But although it was only just after eight when I let myself in Joe was already away to his bed exhausted. I'd intended to pump Rose for background information Joe might have let slip but, noticing my slurring speech, she administered a gentle lecture about the evils of excessive drinking so I buttoned my lip. I wasn't actually all that drunk and when she went up a short time later, I made a pot of coffee and mulled over what I'd learned.

The murderer had stalked Wilf and the other two victims as well. That was now clear. They had been targeted not so much for who they were as for what they had been and had become; military men who ironically could no longer put up much of a fight. The killer was methodical about finding out more about them and didn't seem too worried about being recognised, although paradoxically this seemed to make him harder to recall. It occurred to me that at some stage he'd probably checked the regimental records of each veteran, maybe a useful line of further inquiry? But a couple of fundamental questions remained. Why was he targeting old soldiers in the first place and, more worryingly, what was Joe's role in all of it? I felt he hadn't told me the full story of his involvement but what was he hiding? Maybe something about the note at the cenotaph he'd so conveniently found. And what about the crossword clues? No amount of black coffee could tease any answers out of my brain and I went to bed at about half past nine, being careful to set my alarm for seven o'clock.

Then at about 2am came the incident with Joe thrashing around in his bedroom, yelling out a strange name while next to him his wife slept like a baby throughout the whole thing. Seaside folk! A proper rum bunch!

5
Olly Old Pal

I COULDN'T QUIZ Rose about those bizarre bedroom goings-on as I had to leave the house early for a hastily arranged rail trip to see Nancy's eldest sister Alexandra. She and her husband Ralph were completing the renovation of a small country hotel up in the hills near Lancaster and, with no shows until Monday, I'd invited myself up to have a look at the place before it opened.

I'd always had a lot of time for Alex. She was the only one of Nancy's siblings who'd stuck up for us during her mad Dad's reign of terror, and had suffered for it by becoming the second of Joshua's daughters to be struck out of his will. So I was pleased to see that the nearly-finished hotel was a handsome place with twelve rooms and a large garden which would hopefully bring in enough cash to ward off any financial worries in later life. It was also a relief to talk to normal people who weren't chasing murderers or their own demons. After a hillside walk, we settled down to an early evening tea at a pretty ivy-covered pub by the banks of the River Lune and swapped tales.

Eventually, without giving away too many details I briefly mentioned the murder spree going on down the coast. Alex was appalled and admitted that she feared for my safety - before going on to seek my valuable opinion on fixtures and fittings; curtains versus blinds, that kind of nonsense. Ralph, a thoughtful chap, was silent on the matter of murder until he was driving me to Lancaster station after we'd dropped Alex off at home. Thankfully Ralph wasn't a big drinker. He couldn't have had more than four pints.

"This fellow," he said, not taking his eyes off the road, "he's unlikely to be a veteran."

"How do you work that one out?"

Ralph, who had been in a tank battalion at El Alamein, gave his opinion that anyone who'd survived wartime action would respect the second chance given to someone in the same position. Although I argued back that many veterans hadn't faced life-threatening action, I had to concede that Ralph's point was a valid one. By the time we pulled into the station car park our discussion had become philosophical and so engrossing that I only just managed to tear myself away and catch the last train with a connection to Mellish.

I had hoped to sneak in and go straight to bed because it was after eleven and I felt certain Joe and Rose would be asleep. But the best-laid plans and all that! Propped up against the front door, I fished into my coat pocket and found I'd forgotten my key. Silently damning myself for a fool, I speculated whether I could shin up the drainpipe to my room, which overlooked the front garden. I knew I'd left the window slightly ajar that morning but in the gloom I couldn't see if anyone had since closed it. And, although I'd only had a few drinks, it wouldn't be the safest move to start jumping around fifteen feet up the side of a house. It might also prove unwise to play cat burglar at the home of a copper.

Then I remembered that the back door was occasionally left unlocked so, eager not to disturb anyone, I tiptoed down the side of the house - and froze. Someone was prowling around in the small back garden. I could just about hear careful footsteps on the flagged area near the French windows. Catching my breath, I peeped round the corner of the house. At first I could see nothing but as my eyes grew accustomed to the gloom I made out a figure trying to peer through a gap in the dining room curtains. The intruder moved closer to me and scanned the kitchen through the window. Then, slowly and quietly, he pulled down the handle on the back door. Sure enough, it was unlocked and he stepped quickly inside.

It was a good job I hadn't had time to speculate whether this was the murderer.

"Right, you sneaky swine," I yelled and rugby tackled the figure, who flew into the kitchen and hit his head against a cupboard. But as I jumped up, the intruder neatly hooked his legs round mine and sent me flying. Immediately he was up on the balls of his feet and before I could react, he'd kicked me hard in the ribs. As he swung his foot a second time, however, I grabbed it and pulled him to the floor again where he hit his head with another satisfying crack. This time I was up a split second before him and succeeded in smashing a quick left and right into his face, whereupon he subsided with a groan. At that point the kitchen light came on, revealing Joe standing in the doorway in his dressing gown. I grabbed the intruder by the throat intending to give him another smack for good luck when he gave a yell.

"Call off your attack dog, Joe."

I paused, my fist raised in mid-punch, and stared in confusion at Joe who, after a few seconds, nodded reluctantly. I cautiously relaxed my grip on the burglar. He was small and wiry with a rat-like appearance, and could have been mistaken for a tramp but for the fact he was wearing a new and expensive-looking light-brown overcoat.

The man stood up, exaggeratedly smoothing the coat as if to emphasise his right to be there. Then he smiled. It was not a pleasant smile.

"Hello, Joe," he wheezed, "are we not drinking to an old mates' reunion?"

I glanced uncertainly from one to the other. The rat man still wore a superior smile whereas Joe looked as if he'd seen a ghost.

"I caught this character sneaking around the garden," I told him.

The man laughed.

"As if I'd be sneaking around outside an old pal's house, eh Joey? Now what about that drop I mentioned?"

Still silent, Joe closed the kitchen door behind him and took out a quarter full bottle of whisky from the sink cupboard. He poured some into a small glass and handed it to the man who immediately downed three-quarters of it. The guest smacked his lips and smiled again, revealing two rows of uneven tobacco-stained teeth.

"Not drinking, Joe? We could have a toast to the old times."

"Or I could arrest you."

It was the first thing Joe had said and the words, while outwardly combative, came out in a dull monotone.

Again, the man laughed as if Joe had cracked the best gag he'd heard in a long time.

"But you won't will you, Joey? I mean why should we bother ourselves about courts - or a military tribunal for that matter? Got nothing right last time did it?"

Joe stared almost hopelessly at him, inadvertently rubbing his bad right knee. Our unwelcome visitor noted the movement and nodded.

"Still gives you gyp, eh? You were luckier than some though."

This pantomime had gone on long enough for me.

"Look, chum, I don't know who you are but say your piece and then clear off, there's a good chap."

The man grinned again and took out a packet of Craven A, offering one to me but pointedly ignoring Joe. When I refused, he took his time lighting up before theatrically blowing smoke at the ceiling. He then faced me.

"You might not know who I am, Mr Comedian, but I know you. I watched Jimmy Nervo and Teddy Knox boot you all around the London Palladium in '36, just like that kid's doing these days."

Blimey, he'd seen me both with The Crazy Gang twenty years ago and obviously on Mellish Pier in the last month. Satisfied with the chastening effect he'd had, the man pointed at me.

"I'd appreciate it," he declared, "if you didn't spoil the reunion of two old comrades. I mean me an' Joe here go back a long way. We could chunter on till the cows come home, couldn't we, Joey?"

I ignored his pointed look at me and stood my ground. No way was I leaving Joe alone with this menace. After pausing for a lengthy pull on his cigarette, he decided to ignore me and carried on.

"You won't have forgotten about poor old Mack McKenzie and Pete Maybury, will you, Joe? Oh, and your good pal Corporal Gibbo."

Mention of the final name set Joe's eyes flashing dangerously.

"What exactly is it you want?" he hissed.

Our visitor appeared to be growing in confidence with every second. He took another long drag on his cigarette and swigged the last of the Scotch theatrically before grabbing the bottle from the draining board and pouring a much larger shot. He tilted his chin and began to stroke it as if in an on-stage reverie. Throughout, however, his eyes remained hard and focused. Then he went too far.

"What was it poor old Lieutenant Iris said? That's it, Corporal Gibbo was mummy to all of us! But as I recall, he was a bit more than that to you."

With a roar Joe flew at the man, knocking the nearly-full glass out of his hand, and wrestled him to the floor before kneeling up and smashing his fist twice into the face of the intruder much harder than I had done. Blood burst from his damaged nose and he began to howl like a child, all self-confidence gone. I was about to reluctantly drag Joe off him when the kitchen door flew open and there stood Rose in her nightgown.

"Joe, what on earth is going on here?"

Joe froze in mid-punch, as if someone had doused him in icy water. Looking suddenly confused, he released his prey and stood up swiftly. The man also got up slowly, took a yellowing handkerchief out of his coat pocket and dabbed at his bleeding nose. Then he picked up the still burning cigarette and extended his other hand to Rose.

"Delighted to meet you, Mrs Trueman. Bernard Ollerton. I was in your husband's platoon."

Rose glanced at Joe, who was breathing heavily, before she shook the hand offered to her.

"Coffee, Mr Ollerton?"

"No thank you. And please call me Olly."

"*Olly* is just leaving," said Joe.

"Yes," said Olly, still dabbing his bloody nose, "must dash. Lovely to meet you, Mrs Trueman and you Mr Comedian. Don't get pushed around more than you have to."

He held out his hand and reluctantly I shook it. Joe, however, ignored his proffered paw. Olly merely smiled and walked past him towards the front door. Joe followed, with me a few steps behind them. I could hear Rose take the dustpan out of the cupboard under the sink and begin to clear away the broken glass.

Olly opened the front door and turned back.

"I'll be in touch then, Joe," he grinned.

"If I catch you round here again," Joe hissed, "I'll break your bleedin' neck."

Olly laughed and took a pull on his fag.

"Bye, Mrs Trueman," he said loudly and added a whisper that I could only just hear, "It won't be *my* neck that's broken when the law finds out what you did, Joey. You're in more bleedin' bother than you could ever dream."

And, almost casually, he flicked the cigarette into Joe's face. Startled, Joe brushed his right hand quickly across his hair a couple of times and looked back up in fury. But Olly had already disappeared into the night. Joe took a deep breath and quietly closed the front door then went back into the kitchen where Rose was emptying glass into the bin. But before he could say anything, she walked past him.

"Don't be too long," she muttered and climbed the stairs without looking back.

Joe raised his eyebrows with an effort and signalled for me to follow him into the lounge. He closed the door behind us and poured two generous glassfuls of single-malt whisky he had taken out of the sideboard.

"I wasn't giving that little creep any of the proper stuff," he said, smiling weakly. "Cheers."

"Here's how."

We clinked glasses and I resolved to pursue the matter of Olly no further that night. However, unprompted, Joe proceeded to explain how he and our recent visitor were part of a unit that had landed in Normandy on D-Day.

"You'll not be surprised," he began, "to hear that Olly was as useless a soldier as he is a human being. If it hadn't been for our corporal, the one he was having a go at …"

"Gibbo?"

"Yeah. If it hadn't been for Gibbo's organisation and skill none of us would have got off the sand alive that morning. As it was, we lost only two out of fifteen in our section. One killed, the other wounded."

"What about your officer?"

"That useless shit," spat Joe with real venom before glancing anxiously at the door in case Rose was lurking behind it. "He'd have been staining Sword Beach red with the rest of us if it hadn't been for Gibbo. As for Olly …" Joe shook his head. "He was a liability. If he hadn't been such a good scrounger - or thief as we call them on the force - I swear someone would have …"

"Shot him?"

Joe's eyes flashed briefly. Then he grinned.

"Not even Olly was that bad."

He went on to describe the platoon's terrible progress towards Caen after the landings. If the beach action had been bad enough, what followed was even more harrowing.

"We lost more men in those terrible lanes than on the beach."

"Between the high hedges? Les bocages?"

Joe stared at me in surprise. "You were there?"

"No but my brother Tommy was. Remember him from your wedding?"

"Of course."

84

"It took him a good few years to get over what he saw in Normandy. In fact I can't be sure he's ever got over it."

"I'm not surprised. Do me a favour, Frankie."

"What?"

"Don't press Tommy about what went on in those terrible lanes."

"I never have."

"Good." He paused. "Having said that, we'd have lost a lot more but for Gibbo."

When he picked up my empty glass, I thought he'd drawn a line under the evening and it was time for bed. Instead he refilled both glasses and flopped back into the armchair.

"Now," he said, "you can tell me all about the press conference yesterday."

It turned out he knew most of what had gone on, particularly the way Hallows had made a fool of himself. He guffawed over Ray smartly saluting the press corps, and shook his head in despair when I described how Boardman had been laying down the law to Hallows. In the circumstances, I opted not to quiz him about his relationship with Marjorie Boardman, although I was itching to find out.

Because Joe had actually begun to relax, I realised I wasn't really looking forward to spoiling the moment by telling him about Wilf's encounter with the limping blue-eyed man in the bar. And when I finally did, he duly hit the roof.

"You've been sitting on this information for nearly two days!" he barked.

"Well, I had to go to my sister-in-law's. Near Lancaster, you remember?"

Come to think of it, my mitigation did sound a trifle lame.

"Well-appointed place, your sister-in-law's is it?" Joe replied, which threw me a bit.

"Er, yes. Very nice."

"But obviously not well-appointed enough to have any connection to the telephone network. What are you, some sort of comedian?"

"A couple of people reckon so."

Joe glared at me, blue eyes blazing - before his scowl dissolved into a smile and he actually began to laugh.

"That's quite good," he chuckled. "In fact, very sharp."

"Thanks. And it might be nice to recognise how sharp I'd been in uncovering the pub lead in the first place. And in giving you more witnesses to talk to."

My own annoyance served to placate Joe, who agreed and said he'd follow up the information. He further revealed that the expert he'd seen at the university was a literature professor who had been as baffled as anyone by the messages on the three notes. But he had suggested that a colleague who lived in a village a few miles from Mellish might be able to help.

Joe took a long pull of his Scotch.

"Apparently this fellow was at Bletchley Park," he said with a hard look at me. "You won't have heard of it."

"Code breaking centre north of London," I replied promptly. "Did more than anything to win the war. Top secret and must never, ever, be mentioned. No, I've never heard of it."

Joe smiled.

"I suppose I deserved that. But if anyone can help it's surely got to be one of those bods."

"True enough. Can I see the messages?"

Credit to Joe, he didn't hesitate. Pulling a file from the top drawer of the sideboard, he took out a large black and white photograph.

"Not a great copy," he said, handing it to me, "but you'll get the idea."

The message shown in the photo was a couple of sentences of what appeared to be gobbledegook. On cheap lined notepaper, someone had typed, 'Wit Oskar messed up and the world went Wild. Jive Free.'

"That's the first one I eventually found near the war memorial where poor Michael Donaghy was …"

"Done to a turn?"

"I suppose so," Joe replied gloomily. "Make any sense to you?"

I stared at the message in the photograph.

"The wit he mentions has got to be Oscar Wilde hasn't it? But he's spelled both his first name and surname wrong."

"I noticed that too," said Joe, handing me a second photo. On the same sort of paper was typed, 'Time Joe and his buddies delivered. Won Free.'

Joe winced visibly as I said it out loud.

"This was the one found on Wilf?"

"Yes."

"It appears to mention you."

"Yes."

I waited for further explanations but none came. After looking at the photograph again, I turned to Joe in puzzlement.

"What do you imagine you're supposed to be delivering?"

"I have absolutely no clue."

He passed me a picture of the third message. It said simply, 'Action Station. Sex Too late.'

Something very basic struck me.

"If these are crossword clues, then where does it say how many letters and words there are in the answer?"

Joe picked up each photograph and studied it.

"I mentioned that to the university chap and he was stumped too."

"Hold on," I exclaimed, "pass them to me again."

He handed the photographs over and, after a quick glance at each one, I started to laugh.

"This maniac, whoever he is, has a sense of humour. Look at the last sentence of each message - and think! Maybe they should be in brackets."

Joe picked up the photos and screwed up his eyes. "'Jive Free, Won Free, Sex Too Late' Oh my goodness, you're right. Five three, one three and ... six, two eight. That was brilliantly, worked out, Frankie."

I smiled modestly. Nobody had described my work as brilliant for a good while; 1938 from memory and he'd turned out to be on drugs. I studied the photographs again.

"Now we need to unravel these clues and, with your permission, I'll give Nancy a crack at them. She's coming up here in the next couple of days."

Joe looked doubtful.

"I know she's your missus but …"

"But nothing, Joe. Nancy does Ximenes every Sunday and more often than not completes it."

"Ximenes?"

"A torturer from the Spanish Inquisition. And a noted crossword compiler in the Observer newspaper. Hardest in the world some reckon. And like I say, Nancy's got his measure."

"Very well then," Joe replied, looking mightily impressed, "I'll be interested to see what she makes of the messages."

He poured us each a third generous portion of Scotch and, prompted by his more general questions about Nancy, I spent the next half-hour going over our dramatic elopement twenty years before which had ended with those regal blessings at Balmoral I'd mentioned to Ken Boardman. When I finally paused, he stared at me admiringly.

"To think all I did was just get down on one knee," he whistled.

"I would have done that too but her Dad might have put a bullet in me while I was down there."

Joe commiserated and, unprompted, went on to tell me how he had been going to marry Marjorie a few years before he met Rose.

"I suppose that tub of lard Boardman claimed that he'd stolen her off me?"

"Er, no. But his lad did."

"Well it's not true anyway. Marjorie and I had already parted when I went into the army, a good while before that suet pudding scooped her up."

I couldn't resist a quick smile in the face of such vehemence.

"So no hard feelings then?"

"None whatsoever!"

As if to emphasise the point Joe drained his glass and slammed it down on the table.

"That's me done for the night."

"Me too."

Joe took the glasses into the kitchen while I switched the two standard lamps off. I stood in the kitchen doorway and watched as he rinsed the glasses and carefully put them on the draining board. Maybe it was the drink but I couldn't help returning to the subject of Joe's erstwhile love rival.

"Did Boardman see any action during the war?"

Joe wiped his hands on a tea towel and turned to me. To my great surprise he was grinning broadly.

"Oh, indeed he did. In fact at one point things turned extremely hot for him."

"What, he served in North Africa?"

"No, one of his dodgy meat pies exploded all over him."

For a second, I thought I'd misheard. And then we both started laughing fit to burst. Joe was guffawing so much he had to use my shoulders as support.

"Ssssh," he sniggered. "We'll wake Rose."

"It's not me doing the cackling. Well it is, but …"

"Come on," said Joe wiping his eyes on the tea towel and tossing it to one side, "up those wooden hills."

As we got to the top of the stairs, Joe indicated the bathroom. He was giving me first run at it, a heartily appreciated gesture as I was bursting. I moved to go in, whereupon Joe placed a hand on my arm.

"I'd be grateful if you didn't mention to anyone about that little shit who was round here earlier," he whispered.

"Olly?" I replied, reprising an earlier wisecrack, "never heard of him."

When I came out of the bathroom a couple of minutes later Joe was still on the landing, apparently deep in worried thought. I remembered his anguished dream the night before and patted his arm gently as he went past me into the bathroom.

"Sleep well, mate," I told him.

Joe nodded back at me.

"And, Joe, keep out the way of exploding pies!"

6

Teddy Boys' Picnic

"TELL YOU THE TRUTH," I informed Rose, "I'm not much of a dancer."

"Tell you the truth," came Joe's reply from behind his copy of the Daily Express, "you can't be any worse than me."

Rose nodded eagerly in agreement.

Tell you the truth, I was feeling better than I'd imagined I would when I'd flopped into bed the previous night. Turning over Olly's dark hints about Joe's wartime exploits, I fully expected to be kept awake half the night. But whether it was the long trip to Lancaster and back, the satisfaction of smacking an intruder who'd turned out to have richly deserved it, or merely the effects of what felt like a gallon of Joe's best single malt, I fell asleep after a couple of minutes and did not even hear Joe flushing the toilet. In fact, I didn't wake until I heard Rose and Joe arguing downstairs and it was after half nine when I joined them in the dining room.

Joe was looking most uncomfortable while his wife was clearly on the warpath. I hesitated in the doorway, wondering whether I could avoid getting embroiled in a row about the goings-on with Olly the night before.

"Tell him, Francis," she commanded as I reluctantly entered the room.

"Rose, I'm the comic not the mind-reader. Tell Joe what?"

"Tell him what a good idea getting a television would be."

I breathed a silent sigh of relief, but I also knew better than to become involved in a domestic spat - bitter experience had taught me that - so I mumbled that perhaps, on the one hand, they should sort things out between themselves and on the other, I'd be better employed making everyone toast and tea. Slinking off into the kitchen and cremating a few slices of Mother's Pride, I fervently hoped a line had been drawn under the matter. However, on returning with my burnt offerings ten minutes later, I found Rose was still at it.

"Marion reckons it's great. The telly's never off in their house."

"Why does that not surprise me about your sister?"

Joe's irritable remark had come from behind his newspaper.

"And now they've got ITV," Rose pressed on. "Take Your Pick. Double Your Money. Popeye."

"You've just proved my point!"

"Which is?" said Rose, angrily pushing the newspaper aside and glaring down at her husband.

"That we don't need a television at all when we have the gramophone."

"Aaaaargh, if I hear another song by Guy flamin' Mitchell, I swear I'll have a seizure," she yelled and stomped off into the kitchen, still chuntering to herself.

Joe looked at me and shrugged.

"She has a point about Mitchell," I said. "Me and him were on the same bill in Margate three or four years ago. We didn't get on."

"That doesn't make him a bad singer."

"Just thought I'd mention it."

Joe didn't labour the point but indicated with a tilt of his head that he would prefer Rose not to hear his next observation. I drew close, thinking he might be about to comment on the events of the previous evening, but what he actually said took me completely by surprise.

"Could you take Rose to the dance tonight?"

"What dance?"

"This thing at the rugby club. Ray got us tickets but I'm doing an extra late shift." He drew even closer and murmured, "Rose has been really looking forward to it."

"Well, if you put it like that then how can I refuse?" I replied in my finest stage whisper.

"Good man."

"Yes, thank you, Frankie."

I spun round to see Rose smiling at me.

"At least someone in this house appreciates a bit of fun on a Saturday night," she said, with a glare at Joe.

"Tell you the truth," I informed her, "I'm not much of a dancer."

Joe's reply, after his retreat to the safe haven behind his newspaper, confirmed that I would probably be the more adequate partner for Rose after all. A couple of minutes later he jumped up and left for work, giving Rose a peck on the cheek and shaking my hand warmly. Of the previous day's happenings, he made no mention. While Rose went upstairs to get changed for a weekly cinema outing with her sister I chewed listlessly on the few edible bits of my toast, trying unsuccessfully to work out the last time I'd been on a dancefloor. When I'd eaten and washed up Rose hadn't reappeared so I slipped on my sports coat and left the house.

I thought I might catch him at his cheap showbiz digs but the landlady there said she hadn't seen the fellow even for breakfast and her look suggested she wasn't too bothered if she didn't clap eyes on him for dinner, tea or supper either. She did, however, recommend I visit a café round the corner which I duly did. Sure enough my quarry was sitting immobile at a corner table, all but invisible and keenly observing the holidaymakers as they tackled their Saturday elevenses. He saw me immediately and I noticed his body stiffen in anticipation of a scene. But I waved as cheerily as I could and indicated by waggling my right hand in front of my mouth that I was offering to buy him a cup of tea. Barney nodded, still wary.

The truth was that, while I felt no less antipathy than usual towards my stage partner, it was in my considerable self-interest to mend fences. With Henry Shelvey having decided to reopen the theatre in two days' time, I needed my career quickly back on track, a livelihood that had been almost fatally undermined in the past month by this weasel. And I was well aware that he could do it terminal damage if I didn't get back on his right side. Accordingly, after stumping up for a pot of finest Hornimans and the establishment's one Eccles cake that didn't look like its best days were long behind it, I expressed my sincere regret for not having warned him about Frankie Driscoll's proclivities. That earnestness and maybe my generosity, because he was a notorious tightwad, must have impressed Barney as he began to relax, although he didn't touch the Eccles cake. In truth the fellow was just too busy, continually scribbling on to his paper napkin whenever he heard particularly fatuous phrases from the other customers. One of these, a plumpish man in his mid-thirties, sat at the next table reading the Sketch, oblivious to the problem his harassed wife was having with their son who looked about fourteen. The kid was continually fidgeting and whining on about how - unlike Barney - he'd prefer to be in Blackpool.

"It's rubbish 'ere," he kept on complaining. "There's nowt to do."

His sister, aged around ten, was also at the table equally oblivious, crayoning like fury into a colouring book. Finally, the mother reached breaking point and exploded all over the cafe.

"Just stop your bleedin' moanin', our Neville," she bellowed, "or I'll flamin' well batter the spunk right out of you!"

While other startled customers wrestled with the anatomical conundrum contained in this bizarre threat, Barney's face betrayed the ghost of a smile and he quickly resumed his scribbling on the napkin without even looking what he was writing. As the embarrassed woman quickly chivvied her family from the cafe, the husband still with half a marshmallow sticking out of his gob, I turned to Barney.

"How long before that wee gem finds its way into the act?"

"You'll just have to wait and see," he replied with an inscrutable smile.

"And therein, Barney, lies the problem!"

Over the next twenty minutes it all poured out of me. How I was at my wits' end trying to anticipate the latest method he'd find to humiliate me on stage. The fact that I actually feared for my professional future. Why I was hardly sleeping and had resorted to prescription drugs. The whole performance was carefully designed to have an effect and, as I threw the odd sly glance at Barney, I knew it had. Sensing he was about to speak, I silenced him with a raised hand and added that while audiences didn't mind us bashing each other with wooden mallets, they were less keen on one of us humiliating the other.

"So it's to both our professional advantages if I look less of a chump," I concluded.

There was half a minute's silence while Barney digested what I'd said. I knew that even if my supposed health worries (I couldn't even name a prescription drug) caused him little concern, then the prospect of committing professional suicide just might.

"I can see your point, Frankie," he said warily, jotting down something else on his napkin. "So, what do you suggest?"

This was more like it and for the next hour or so, fortified by more tea, we hammered out our new manifesto.

I pledged that I wouldn't object to him steering the act down bizarre pathways as long as he first let me in on the secret and I knew broadly what to expect. There would be no more humiliating me either, and I was to take a greater part in the hook game he played with the audience. We could, however, go after each other with mallets at any time.

That final comment was the first thing I'd said that had ever made him laugh and, newly energised, he went on to outline a number of ideas we could explore. These were without exception inventive and funny. Despite being an annoying twerp, this chap really thought about his craft. Even better, he seemed to accept the few ideas I offered up with a show of enthusiasm I'd never witnessed before. All things considered, it was a productive couple of hours and, if we didn't exactly part as bosom buddies, then I felt that at least a corner had been turned. I left him with yet another pot of tea, crouching like a spider sizing up its prey and continually scribbling on his napkin, which by now looked more like the Rosetta Stone.

A fair few of Barney's suggestions had set me thinking about how we could combine our ideas on stage and I promised myself that, like him, I'd write more things down in the comedy bible, ie a primary school exercise book I kept in our theatre dressing room.

Reaching the pier, I couldn't help but notice that the hole in the fence at the entrance had been patched up and all sad traces of Wilf's shattered window boxes cleared away from outside the theatre. Recently-arrived families milled happily around the pier or eagerly dropped worm-baited lines into the gentle waves below, oblivious to the horror of what had happened here just four days before.

Sighing, I prepared to let myself in at the stage door when I felt a tug on my arm and looked down to see a boy of no more than ten waving a small leather-bound book. With his left hand he brushed a hank of blond hair away from his face.

"Autograph please, sir," the boy piped up. I smiled and took the book from him.

"Who shall I sign it to, son?"

"Er … you'd better put Walter."

"You sure that's your name?"

"Oh no, I'm Terence."

I scrawled my best wishes to "Walter and/or Terence" and watched as the lad excitedly ran to show the message to his tall, muscular dad who was smoking his pipe ten yards away. The man glanced at the book in delight and held up a huge hand in appreciation, a gesture I reciprocated before closing the stage door behind me. Then the thought that he might well have watched me on the boards when he was his son's age brought me back down to earth with another sigh.

Turning away from the door deep in melancholic contemplation, I almost collided with the theatre owner Henry Shelvey on his way out. We apologised at the same time and then simultaneously began to speak before both pausing and bursting into laughter. Mr Shelvey was a good twenty years older than me yet at that moment, he looked like a mischievous schoolboy even though he was dressed like an Edwardian gentleman of leisure.

"Sorry, Frankie," he said, nervously fingering his yellow spotted cravat, "I was just on my way out. Are you all right? You seem rather contemplative."

"Just pondering the inexorable march of the years, Mr Shelvey."

"Ah yes," he replied wistfully, "time like an ever-rolling stream that bears all its sons away."

"Couldn't have put it better myself, Mr S. Don't let me keep you."

He nodded but paused before opening the door.

"You know we reopen on Monday," he said.

"Yes indeed. In fact, Barney and I have just been putting the finishing touches to a new part of our act."

"Oh, I'll definitely look forward to that," he replied and I didn't doubt it. He'd be there at most of the shows and was famous for rolling up those expensive sleeves if scenery needed shifting or something was stuck up in the fly loft.

"Er, Frankie, can I ask you a question?"

Hand still on the doorknob, he turned to face me. His look was one of embarrassment.

"Ask away."

"I know I was talking about time's ever-rolling stream and all that, but do you think just short of a week is long enough? To pay our respects to Wilf?"

"More than enough," I smiled. "In fact, I'm sure Wilf would say the same if he could. Before ordering you to bloomin' well get the show back on the road."

"I do think you're right," laughed Mr Shelvey, looking relieved. "Did you know Wilf had been with us since 1922 when my father was in charge? He was always a good worker but he'd also been a bit of a lad, if you understand what I mean."

"I know exactly what you mean," I replied, trying once again to suppress the eternally disturbing image of Wilf and my gran.

"A lot of fellows who'd been in the war were like that," he mused. "Some were understandably withdrawn, particularly the ones who had been badly wounded and disfigured. But Wilf and his chums wanted to live life to the full after what they'd been through."

He paused and banged his fist angrily against the door.

"It should never have happened," he said with considerable vehemence. "What is the world coming to? Your cousin's husband must ensure he brings the man responsible to justice."

"He will, sir. Have no fear of that."

Mr Shelvey prepared to open the door but once again turned back.

"There was something else I wanted to speak to you about but it's gone clean out of my head."

"Nothing to do with the mayor is it? He is rather keen to see us back open."

"No, it's definitely not about *him*," Mr Shelvey replied and I swear his lip curled slightly at the mention of Boardman. "Good day, Frankie, I shall look forward to the new routine."

I unlocked our room and took the exercise book out of my dressing table drawer. With sadness I read the most recent entry which was from the night before Wilf's murder, and chronicled my concerns over Barney flying around the stage like a demented bluebottle while I had remained more or less static. These worries now seemed absurdly irrelevant in light of what happened the following night, but I used the idea as a starting point to develop what I thought could be a profitable new direction for the act. This, unsurprisingly, involved me claiming centre stage while Barney was off on his manic manoeuvres. So completely absorbed was I in making the notes and imagining my triumph, that I didn't hear the menacing footsteps until they were almost outside the door.

Startled, I quickly grabbed Compo's cricket bat, the one that had saved me when I faced Wilf's killer. I'd employed the same plank of willow to teach the great run scorer how to do the reverse sweep, a stroke Dennis had used sparingly but usually to great effect before being warned by the bluff Lancashire off-spinner Roy Tattersall that he'd get thumped if it happened again off his bowling. I prayed that, should anyone be handing out a beating in the immediate future, it would be me.

The footsteps outside had stopped. I stood up as quietly as possible and held the bat firmly, poised to reverse sweep the intruder into a week next Thursday. But then came a knock at the door, followed by a low but firm voice.

"Caretaker here. Who's there?"

Sighing with relief, I swiftly put down the bat and opened the door to be confronted by an enormous thirty-something fellow with wild dark hair. He was holding Wilf's brush in a threatening manner, similar to the way I'd been brandishing the cricket bat. So that was the info that had slipped Henry Shelvey's mind! I quickly apologised to the new caretaker for not telling him I'd arrived and in a low Scouse accent he accepted my regrets with good grace, inviting me to his room for a glass of something when it suited me. Half an hour later, after estimating that the act was now in better shape than ever, I closed my exercise book with a satisfying snap and strolled across the foyer. It still felt strange and sad to approach what was Wilf's old lair.

The new man, whose name turned out to be William Pitt, poured me a small Scotch and himself a rather larger helping from the remains of the bottle that Wilf had bought and I'd paid for. It was now less than a quarter full, but I decided not to get the relationship off on a wrong footing by mentioning the fact.

"So, Bill … do you mind me calling you Bill?"

"I'd sooner you used 'William', if that's all the same."

I thought he might be joking as it's rumoured Merseysiders are occasionally wont to do, but not a flicker troubled his deadpan features.

"Right. It's just that, well, you know with the name and all that."

"Most folk haven't a clue who William Pitt was, them as do know I'm not him and the rest couldn't give a flying you-know-what."

Well, this bloke was going to be a barrel of laughs and no mistake. However, I persisted with the charm and managed to drag out of him that, after a short career welding plates at Cammell Laird's ship yard in Birkenhead, he'd entered showbiz, latterly as caretaker at the Palace, New Brighton. Oh, and that he'd never seen my act.

"You've got a treat on Monday then," I replied with a lightness I wasn't particularly feeling.

"What would that be?"

"You'll have to wait for the act."

"I'll be much too busy for those sorts of goings-on."

Nobody could accuse me of not trying. I gulped my meagre portion of whisky and slammed down the glass.

"Thanks for the drink, Bill, er William. We really must do this again."

I turned but before I reached the door Pitt spoke up in his soft insistent tone.

"Where was it they found him?"

"Eh?"

"The old guy who was here before me. Where did he die?"

"Well, it was just in that corner over there. But look I wouldn't worry, William. The killer's hardly likely to strike again in this building." (If I'd only known.) "You'll be perfectly safe."

It appeared that I'd seriously misjudged Pitt's concern because, throwing me an odd look, he spluttered into mirthless laughter.

"It'd take more than some seaside joker to bother me, pal," he spat. "I was a Royal Marine."

"Wilf fought at Passchendaele and that didn't save him."

"Yeah, because he was old and weak. Like I said, I've no worries about this character."

"Then why did you ask where Wilf had been killed?"

Pitt took a long pull of Scotch and smacked his lips.

"Because I'm going to photograph the spot."

"The police have already done that."

"This is for my own records."

"Records! Are many people slaughtered at your places of work?"

"Not all that many."

That return drink was not about to be any time soon if I could help it. Pitt's bloodless and detached manner continued to disturb me long after I'd taken my leave of him. Indeed, I was still discomfited enough to mention it to Rose a few hours later as we strolled to the rugby club dance.

"He's probably shy or something," was her verdict.

"He didn't seem at all shy. The reverse in fact. I mean why would you want to photograph a murder scene?"

"I wouldn't."

"But why do you think Pitt does?"

"Maybe he's putting together his own crime display. Joe told me that some people do."

"Yeah, they're usually the ones who end up being photographed themselves - from the front and the side."

"You old cynic," she laughed.

"I'll mention it to Joe though. Seems odd behaviour to me."

It had turned into a beautifully sultry summer's evening, the sort of which I'd rarely experienced in Mellish and it made me calmer than I had felt for a while. Rose must have been feeling much the same because she gently took hold of my arm with her left hand and linked me with her right. I caught a whiff of her scent and for a moment it went straight to my head before I remembered who we both were.

"Steady, cuz, people will talk."

Smiling, she went up on tiptoes and kissed me on the cheek.

"That's for agreeing to take me to the dance. And if 'people' want to make something of it then they jolly well can."

"Give it to 'em, girl! That's the spirit of Dunkirk and The Battle of Britain. Did I ever tell you that I know Winston Churchill?"

"Yes."

I smiled and gave her arm a gentle squeeze. It was good to see Rose in what, for her, constituted high spirits. No wonder too as she and Joe hardly ever went out together. I was more than likely doing them both a favour.

Mellish Rugby Union Club's recently-built HQ turned out to be a surprisingly spacious, boxy two-storey structure with a large function room on the first floor. Climbing the stairs, I concluded that there was more than a bit of money sloshing about the club, an impression confirmed by the fact that its social committee had hired a twelve-piece dance band and crooner, who were already in action on the large stage at the far end of the room. I recognised them too; it was Eddie Edison and his Treetones, resident band at the Coliseum. Well, I couldn't blame them for moonlighting when the theatre was shut, even though I knew that Henry Shelvey was paying them a retainer.

Ray, who was sitting at a table halfway down the room, called out for us to join him. As we walked across the largely empty dance floor, I nodded at Eddie who was busy murdering The Yellow Rose of Texas. He gave me a quick thumbs-up just as Rose whispered into my ear.

"Guy bloomin' Mitchell again. Can't get away from him. How can anyone dance to this crap?"

"Not too many are," I replied, trying to ignore Rose's uncharacteristic profanity. She was right on the button though as, apart from a trio of middle-aged couples shuffling aimlessly back and forth, no-one seemed too bothered about cutting a rug.

Ray jumped up from his seat, grabbed Rose's hand, and kissed it extravagantly.

"Madame," he purred in a cod French accent, "you grow lovelier by ze second. Whereas the monsieur ici …" And he turned slowly to me. There was a pause before everyone burst out laughing.

"It's great you could both be here," Ray said guiding us into the chairs opposite him and his girlfriend. "You already know Jenny."

Rose quite obviously did because they hugged each other enthusiastically. Jenny then sprung a surprise by apologising for not taking enough notice of me when we first met that time in the street. I graciously waved away her apology and resisted the temptation to suggest that she'd probably had geography homework on her mind.

While at the bar, I mentioned to Ray what Rose had said about the turgid music, omitting the profanity of course. After all, I didn't want to get her into trouble with Joe. Ray nodded sympathetically.

"She's right," he said and added with a wink, "but watch this space."

It was unclear to me what he was on about until the band finished their first set. As Eddie and the musicians trooped out on to the clubhouse balcony for a smoke, another gang immediately sprang into action. Two burly chaps carried a box each on to the stage while a similarly built third man quickly ran a wire from one of the boxes to the band's speaker. After a minute or so he gave a thumbs-up and a fourth man, smaller and less muscular, jumped on to the stage. He drew a black disc from one of the boxes and carefully placed it on the other. With no warning, a driving high-pitched American voice began to yell unintelligible lyrics, reinforced by an urgent saxophone backing. The dance floor immediately filled up with young couples intent on hurling each other around. Ray showed he could move unexpectedly smoothly for a big man while Jenny looked as if she'd been born to dance. Rose and I watched the scene entranced.

The first record with its odd words, which I later discovered was Tutti Frutti by a lively young chap called Little Richard, gave way to one I did recognise. Over recent months it had been the background music to newsreels showing scenes of mayhem in dance halls and cinemas up and down Britain. Now I realised that rock 'n' roll was making inroads into this part of the country too. As Bill Haley and His Comets belted out Rock

Around The Clock, the sense of excitement, anticipation and almost danger around the room became palpable.

However, nobody looked as if they were about to slash curtains or smash seats, apart from one likely lad who leapt away from his family group brandishing a chair above his head. He sat down on it quickly enough though when his mum jumped up and gave him a thick ear.

But it was on the dance floor where the real confrontation was bubbling up. Most of the couples had already fanned out to the edge, ceding centre stage to two pairs who were giving it all they'd got. One of the duos flinging each other up and around was Ray and Jenny and it became clear they were in a kind of unofficial jiving competition with the other couple, a very small stick-thin woman and a bear of a man with slicked back hair. This giant wore a long blue drape jacket with a black velvet collar and shoes with thick soles that made him look even more gigantic - and no less ridiculous. Yet even in those diver's boots he moved with such surprising swirling grace that his lithe female partner could hardly keep up.

As the sweat flew from both pairs, the dancers round the outside halted their steps completely and began to clap rhythmically. This seemed to drive on the two competing couples to even greater excess. The contest, a keen one, was heading for a draw as far as I could see when calamity struck. The Comets' final few chords were being belted out when the dizzy duos converged and the men collided heavily with each other. Only at this point did I realise with a jolt that the Teddy Boy was Ken Boardman's son John.

"Why, if it isn't the flat-footed flatfoot," he sneered, roughly pushing Ray away.

"You want outside, Daddy's boy?" was Ray's immediate response as he squared up to Boardman.

"No, let's do the show right here," John growled before shooting out a quick left jab, which Ray only just managed to block. Ray replied with a right over the top of Boardman's guard which he in turn managed to parry. So far so Marquess of Queensberry. Sadly however, within seconds both had tumbled to the floor, wrestling and kicking seven bells out of each other. Women screamed and scattered while a dozen burly men, closely, but not too closely, followed by myself, rushed in to split up the gouging gladiators. Yet none of us was as swift as the chap who had been playing the records. In a single bound he was off the stage and … that proved to be his downfall. For, as he moved to intercede in the row, John Boardman ever so casually straightened his right arm and, without even looking, smashed him across the face. The record man flew across the dance floor, apparently out for the count. But impressively, he was on his feet again and back at the combatants before his rugby mates could get started on making mincemeat of Boardman.

"Grow up for god's sake," he snapped, stepping, arms extended, between the pair both of whom looked fully intent on continuing the mayhem. However, by now they were surrounded by a phalanx of rugger buggers keen on demonstrating their expertise in the gentle art of scrummaging.

Our peacemaker dabbed at his nose, which was beginning to bleed. Then he relaxed and gave both combatants a grin.

"Look, boys, we're not licensed for fighting. Just fun. So let's start having some eh?"

Ray, by now beginning to look a touch sheepish, nodded but Boardman barged angrily through the rugby players and stalked off, dragging his tiny girlfriend behind him.

"You should watch him," the peacemaker told Ray, "he's a well-known rich prick. 'Scuse the lingo, ladies."

"I know who he is," said Ray, "and I look forward to seeing that amateur champ beat the crap out of him next week," he added with a raised voice.

But, if he heard, John Boardman did not react and disappeared through the main entrance.

"Apologies too, girls, for the language," said Ray as everyone began to drift off the dance floor, the music having come to a sudden stop.

Over at the bar a small, middle-aged bald man in thick spectacles was speaking urgently to Eddie, who nodded in agreement and led his band down the room towards the steps at the side of the stage. Their progress however was interrupted, by what appeared to be forwards from the entire First, Second and Third Fifteens, an evil-looking bunch of hulking villains. Thing was, I knew that the musicians' ranks contained more than a few who'd battled all the way to Berlin and weren't the types to be cowed by a bunch of overgrown schoolboys. The scene was set for another violent showdown before our peacemaker stepped forward once again. Clutching his bloody handkerchief, he inserted himself between the two groups and addressed the band.

"Listen, boys, treat yourselves to a longer break. Give the new music a chance to breathe, eh."

A rumble of discontent rippled among the musicians; it was obvious they suspected their fee was about to be trimmed. But, as if mind-reading, the peacemaker clapped Eddie on the shoulder.

"And of course we'll still pay you in full."

That did the trick and the band, their cash assured, immediately marched off to the bar in celebration. All except Eddie.

"See that little fellow over there," he told the mediator, "he insists we go on again."

"Yeah, that's the club secretary. Not an ounce of fun in him. Just give us another half an hour …"

"Well, I don't know."

"… and there's an extra fiver in it for you."

"I didn't realise you spoke fluent musician," Eddie replied with a smile before strolling after his men, no doubt weighing up whether to tell them about the offer.

"Right, girls," cried the diplomat to his hulking mates. "Let's shake it up!"

In the half hour of rock 'n' roll that followed even I was persuaded by an enthusiastic Rose to lumber on to the dance floor, and try vainly to look as though I knew what I was doing. In truth I didn't need to do that much as Ray and Jenny, now with the floor to themselves, dominated proceedings. Nevertheless, by the time an extremely refreshed Eddie and the Treetones reappeared, everyone else also seemed ready for a drink.

I was joined at the bar by the conciliator, who by now had stopped bleeding and didn't look to have suffered too much damage from Boardman junior's casual act of thuggery. He introduced himself as Conrad Ross, a computer scientist, whatever that might be, and was gracious enough to claim that he'd heard of me. Indeed, he promised to catch my act at the first opportunity.

"In that case I'll arrange complimentaries for you and your girl."

"Thanks but I'm unattached at the moment," Conrad grinned. "So you'd better keep your eye on that little stunner you're with or I might steal her off you."

It took me a couple of seconds to realise he was talking about Rose. However, Conrad must have mistaken my puzzlement for annoyance and swiftly apologised for any offence caused. I was equally quick to assure him that there was none taken.

"She's my cousin," I told him.

"Oh," Conrad replied wryly. "Well, never mind, I'm sure the geneticists don't get it right every time."

"No, no, we aren't going out together. I'm lodging with Rose and her husband."

Conrad balled his fists in mock rage.

"Husbands! What earthly good are they? Here let me help you with those drinks."

Conrad's first action when he joined our little group was to grab a startled Ray's right wrist and wave his arm in the air with a cry of, "and the winner is ..." This neatly broke the ice and his particular brand of self-deprecation quickly helped him integrate with the rest of us. For instance, it wasn't long before he was explaining how he was by far the worst rugby player in the club.

"As you might have just witnessed," Conrad informed us with a straight face, "I'm no Dickie Jeeps. So, when the Thirds are short of a player, they call the Women's Institute, then the Brownies and if they have nobody available then they give *me* a ring ... and ask if I know anybody."

Amid the laughter, Rose insisted that surely he couldn't be that bad but Conrad confirmed that, regretfully, he was actually even worse that than that, before turning to Ray.

"Unlike this splendid giant I'll be bound. What's your position, Ray? I'd guess prop."

Ray lowered his head a fraction as if supressing a painful memory.

"No, Conrad, I was never front of the scrum. But I did play number eight for the firsts here before I bust my ankle a couple of years ago. Must have been before your time."

"I've been here eighteen months."

"And he's transformed our funds in that time."

The speaker was one of the heavies who'd blocked Eddie's path to the stage. Up close I could see that the top of his right ear looked as if it had burst and bubbled out over the side of his head.

"Watch it, Teddy," said Conrad, "you'll ruin my reputation as an amiable blunderer."

The big guy gave a winning smile and placed a huge paw around Conrad's shoulder. "Best flippin' treasurer we've ever had, this one. How's it going, Ray? Comeback on the cards?"

"Not bloomin' likely, Ted. The missus here would kill me," he added, dodging a good-natured blow from Jenny.

In the couple of hours that followed, something rather pleasing happened. Conrad, now recovered from his ordeal, confirmed his comedic credentials by gently encouraging me to perform an unofficial double act with him. And boy did it go down a storm! We bounced jokes, quips and comments off each other as if we'd been playing together for years. Indeed, at one point Rose whispered that the act had miles more going for it than the one I had with Barney. Conrad, who had been paying particular attention to Rose all evening, overheard and when informed what a rotter Barney was, promised to let the First Fifteen's front row loose on him.

"They'll take him to an away match, use him as the ball and then lose him in the long grass," he said, assuring an anxious Rose that he was joking while winking broadly at the rest of the table.

As the evening's jollity continued there was just one slightly jarring note. At one point, Rose left the group and did not reappear for about ten minutes, long enough even for Conrad to quietly comment on the fact. On her return she didn't look quite right somehow and I was about to quiz her about it when, without warning, Conrad took our double act up another notch. He launched into the popular monologue Albert and The Lion but turned it into a two-hander by inviting me to supply alternate lines. It proved a scream too and when it fell to me to voice the feelings of the (apparently) recently bereaved Mrs Ramsbottom, my declaration that, "Eee, I am vexed," brought the house down, with Rose laughing as much if not more than anyone.

The fun carried on in this vein but all too soon Eddie and his boys were racing through the National Anthem (I still couldn't get used to not singing God Save The King) and it was time to go. However, Rose hung back after Ray and Jenny had left, explaining she wanted to talk to Conrad. Approaching the stage where he was coiling up a length of wire, she whispered something in his ear. For a second Conrad looked nonplussed but then nodded and Rose scribbled something on a piece of paper and gave it to him. She smiled, skipped back over to me and we left the room. However, we hadn't reached the bottom of the stairs before Conrad came clattering breathlessly down behind us.

"Rose are you quite sure?" he shouted.

She turned to him.

"I'm positive. Come for tea tomorrow."

Conrad looked perplexed.

"What do you think, Frankie?"

"It appears Rose has invited you to tea tomorrow."

"But it's such short notice!"

"Then come another time when you can fit us in to your busy schedule."

"Not short notice for me, for Rose! Plus, you hardly know me."

Rose put her hands on her hips and shook her head.

"Honestly. Men!" she said. "You call *us* indecisive. I've invited you for tea - you're coming. Is that clear?"

Conrad held up his hands in mock surrender.

"I don't fancy another beating so it looks like I'm joining you for tea. But, Rose, please allow me to make the main course, a kind of special stew, and you provide the vegetables."

"Very well," Rose agreed, "I'll do the spuds and greens, a dessert too and you bring your stew."

"It's a deal - which might include the odd bottle too."

"I'll drink to that," I said.

As Rose and I walked across the car park Conrad yelled after us.

"Tea is the evening meal in these heathen parts, right?"

Rose turned back, wearing a smile that illuminated the whole of her face.

"Yes, don't be arriving at ten to three," she shouted back, "or I'll have you peeling the spuds. See you at six."

My cousin was now in such a good mood that I suggested we stretch our legs on a longer route home, to which she readily agreed. The night was mild and frankly Mellish did not give the impression of a town cringing in fear from a maniac.

We strolled on the prom, among the late-night revellers whose kids were up long past their bedtimes, while Rose admitted she hadn't had such fun in months. She also stumbled, revealing that perhaps she hadn't had as much alcohol in months either. But what the heck! I too was merrier than I had been for a long time and mentioned this in a spirit of fellow feeling. At which point Rose giggled and I made an awful blunder by thoughtlessly asking where she'd disappeared to during those ten minutes at the club. I regretted it immediately as the comment squeezed all the joy out of Rose like air from a punctured bicycle tyre.

"Why do you imagine a woman would suddenly disappear to the toilet for ten minutes?" she snapped back at me.

"Oh the toilet was it? Er, dunno, maybe a dodgy vol-au …." And at that moment even my daft head got itself round what had happened.

"Oh, Rose. Sorry, I'm such an idiot."

"No need to apologise, Frankie," she replied flatly. "After all, it's just a monthly cross Joe and I have to bear." She sighed deeply. "I really thought this could be … I mean, you tell yourself not to build up hopes but you can't help making little plans in your head, the bedroom, the cot, the …"

She sighed again and I put my arms around her and gave her a hug for which she seemed grateful - right up to the point where I made my second blunder.

In my anxiety to change the subject more than anything else, I tackled her about something that had been on my mind for forty-eight hours; the bizarre episode during which Joe thrashed around in his sleep howling a strange name, while she slept like a baby angel.

Rose detached herself firmly from my embrace, walked over to the sea wall and lit a cigarette. The tide was right in and she gazed down at the waves gently lapping against the concrete. For half a minute she didn't speak. Then she turned to me.

"Was the name he shouted Freddy?"

"Yes. Who is he?"

"I have absolutely no idea, Francis. The only thing I know is that he's part of something that happened to Joe in the war."

"A friend who was killed perhaps?"

"Who knows? Joe refuses to talk about it. Despite the fact that he screams the name in his sleep and has done so at regular intervals ever since we were married."

With that, Rose angrily tossed her half-smoked cigarette into the waves and stalked off towards the road. By now she was so upset I swear she would have walked straight into the path of a speeding taxi if I hadn't dashed across and caught her arm. She looked up as though she'd forgotten I was there.

"I'm going home," she snapped and strode off without another word.

While regretting causing my cousin pain, especially after such a splendid evening, I was intrigued to have been allowed a further small insight into the odd bod she had married. I was still wrestling with the conundrum known as Joe as we turned into Woodcock Street. Whereupon, Rose urgently grabbed my arm.

"Look," she said, pointing with trepidation at her house, "there's a light in the parlour."

"You probably left it on."

"No, never. Joe hates to waste electricity."

"He's come home early then."

"I'm afraid not, Francis. He's on duty until midnight and it's still only half eleven."

"Yeah but maybe …"

"You don't know Joe. He's such a flipping stickler for routine. Oh my goodness, look."

Behind the net curtains both of us could clearly make out the shape of a figure moving around.

"Don't worry, cuz," I muttered unconvincingly. "If it's a burglar I'll deal with him."

"What if it's that horrible little man who was here last night?"

"Then I'll enjoy dealing with him all the more. You stay here."

"Not likely, I'm going in with you."

I must admit that, for all her usual outward timidity, our Rose did not lack guts. As we crept up the path, I signalled for her to hand me the front door key. Without a sound I let us in and we carefully approached the lounge door, which was half ajar. I was about to kick it fully open when Rose pressed something into my hand. It was a stout, curved-handled walking stick. Shoving her gently back a pace, I stepped up to the door and pushed it slowly.

The blue table lamp by the gramophone was switched on but there was no immediate sign of an intruder. Mindful of what happened when I discovered poor Wilf, I kicked the door fully open and quickly stepped round it with the stick raised. There was no-one behind the door. But then I felt a tug on my arm and turned to see Rose gazing in fear at Joe's large high-backed armchair, which had been turned to face the fireplace. From the chair there curled a slim column of cigarette smoke.

"All right," I said, carefully approaching the chair with walking stick raised, "get up slowly and don't try anything or I'll scatter your brains over the hearth."

There was an exhalation and the thin plume of smoke became a fog. Then a figure rose slowly from the chair and turned to face me.

"I must say, that's a lovely way to greet the wife you've not seen for a month."

7

Poets Cornered

IT'S NOT OFTEN I get annoyed with my missus - matters of that nature generally happen the other way round and it's Muggins here who finishes up on the business end of a fine old shellacking. But a combination of drink, the memory of Rose's previous vile mood and the sudden unravelling of a huge knot of fear made me abandon all restraint. I gave it to Nancy both barrels blazing.

"Don't you know there's a killer around who nearly nailed me? I could have dashed your brains out, you silly woman! What on earth were you thinking sneaking around like that?"

These admonishments were perhaps a touch more severe than I'd intended because something happened that I had very rarely witnessed; Nancy burst into tears. While I stood there paralysed with shock, Rose showed the good sense to rush to my wife and put a comforting arm around her.

"I'm so, so sorry," Nancy sobbed. "I thought it would be such a wonderful surprise for you but all I appear to have done is ruin things. Waaaaaaah!"

"You've not ruined anything," Rose soothed, while glaring at me.

Well, at least I was back on more familiar terrain; having to grovel to the women in my life. Time for boot-licking to begin.

"Look, Nancy," I began cautiously, "I wasn't angry with you as such - well I was - but only because I didn't want to see anyone get hurt, especially you. No offence, Rose."

Nancy dabbed at her eyes with Rose's clean white handkerchief and blinked hard a few times.

"I accept your apology, Franco," she sniffed.

"It wasn't an ap … well, yes of course that's exactly what it was. I'm very, very sorry," I said.

"That's OK then. Is there anything to drink in this place? I'm spitting feathers here."

Rose gazed at the rejuvenated Nancy like a rabbit in the headlights before scuttling off to find sustenance for my wife, who pulled me towards her.

"What's up with the mouse?" she whispered.

"I'd guess she's relieved about not having to do battle with a killer. Or indeed you. How did you get in here anyway?"

"Key was under the big plant pot by the front door. Not, in my opinion, the best example for a copper to set, or indeed the safest of hiding places when an assassin is on the rampage. Now where *is* that drink?"

The last bit was blasted out at least ten decibels louder than her previous words and had the immediate effect of bringing Rose scuttling back into the lounge with a quarter full bottle of brandy.

"Will this do?" she said nervously.

"*This* will do splendidly."

A relieved Rose poured out two glassfuls but Nancy refused to drink until our hostess had included herself in the round. We then toasted absent friends.

"I'd have come earlier," explained Nancy kicking her shoes off and stretching out in Joe's armchair. "But I took a detour to visit Daddy at Fresh Fields."

"I was so sorry to hear that Sir Joshua is in a nursing home," said Rose.

So are the nursing home staff, I thought, judiciously keeping the opinion to myself.

"How is he bearing up?" Rose added solicitously.

Nancy studied her brandy for a moment.

"Do you know, Rose, I have no idea. He wouldn't see me. The man is still bearing a grudge after two decades."

"Pig-headed old goat."

This zoological flight of fancy was meant to be another of my silent ruminations but unfortunately it turned out I'd said it out loud.

Rose stared at me in shock and surprise but Nancy merely nodded in agreement.

"Franco's right, Rose. The old fool hasn't spoken to me for twenty years and now it looks as if he never will again."

"How awful." Rose bit her lip.

"Don't distress yourself," said Nancy. "I'm certainly not, in fact …"

Nancy put her hand across her mouth but not before she'd started to splutter with laughter.

"Sorry, people, I'm just remembering my wedding day that never was."

In all likelihood Rose had heard the story before but we told it again anyway because, let's face it, the tale was a crackerjack. We recalled how, at the church gate, I'd snatched Nancy from the arms of her intended, Sir Charlie Chinless-Wonder or whatever his name was and we'd galloped off together into the sunset.

By now Nancy was nearly wetting herself with laughter.

"Oh, Rose, you should have seen it. Frankie was in a perfectly ridiculous disguise …"

"I thought I looked quite distinguished."

"… in this ludicrous get-up, then he pulls me up on to the carriage and we charge off, tipping my Dad over the church wall."

"Goodness gracious," said Rose. "I hope he wasn't hurt."

"Oh, he was livid."

"I meant physically."

"Don't worry," Nancy replied with a shrug, "the Protheroes are made of hardy stuff. My brother used to kick me down the stairs for fun. It's a good job I learned to walk. Anyway, we made our escape with me in just my wedding dress and a pair of riding boots."

"The boots were integral to the plan," I hurriedly explained to Rose, who was staring at Nancy as if she were a creature from another dimension.

Without pausing for breath, my wife galloped on to another subject completely, letting me know among other things that it was her intervention with Mr Shelvey that ensured the theatre would reopen on Monday - which by this time was tomorrow.

"I know the old caretaker chap was a pal of yours, Franco, but face it, the show must go on."

"Nobody's said that all the time I've been here."

"Well they have now and, getting back to the show, I must say that I'm really excited about seeing you and Barney on the stage together."

Rose threw me an anxious glance and I nodded ever so slightly to signal that I wasn't about to launch into a nuclear tirade against my stage partner. After all, we had just signed a non-aggression pact.

The three of us were again toasting absent friends when another one appeared on the scene. The front door banged shut and Joe limped into the lounge looking puzzled.

"Whose is the sports car? Oh hallo, Nancy."

Nancy leapt up to greet him. "Nice to see you again, Joe. It's been such a long time."

As they embraced, I peeked through the curtain and saw the soft top of Nancy's air force blue Morgan Plus 4 peeping over the low privet hedge.

"Crikey, Rose," I said, indicating the car, "we could have saved ourselves a lot of grief if we'd noticed that, eh?"

"It's called being a detective," Joe sighed, his voice heavy with irony, as he took a bottle of Scotch and a glass from the sideboard and slowly subsided into the armchair.

Following a slight hesitation in which I felt sure Rose was wondering whether to tell him that his guest had been sitting there, she quickly insisted that Nancy take her own chair. After apologies all round, we settled ourselves and Joe began to fill us in on the day's events. It wasn't good news. The hunt for the murderer was not proceeding at all well and Hallows was going barmy. Nothing in the background of the three victims, apart from the military connection, suggested that they had anything in common and the killer's many clues - notes and knives to name but a few - had yielded nothing substantive.

I was about to suggest that he show the notes to Nancy but before I could do so, Joe finally remembered he was among friends and actually forced a smile. He then asked how the evening had gone. Relieved, Rose enthusiastically told him about the rock 'n' roll, which he seemed delighted to have missed, and the bust-up involving Ray and young Boardman, which, it turned out, he wouldn't have minded catching.

"I thought they were going to kill each other," Rose exclaimed breathlessly, "and they might well have done but for Conrad."

"Who?" said Joe, his frown returning.

"Conrad, the club treasurer. John Boardman biffed him on the nose but he got right up and separated them. And then told them both off for good measure."

Again, Joe looked puzzled before laughing harshly.

"I'll bet that went down well with Ray."

"Ray wasn't the problem," I told him. "Boardman was. He stormed off like a big baby."

"A nasty piece of work, that one," said Joe. "He should have been in court countless times for bad driving, drunkenness and … more. But Daddy was always there to pull the right strings. Grease important palms."

There was a silence while we digested this. It was broken by Rose piping up hesitantly, "Anyway, I've invited him for tea tomorrow. Later today actually."

Joe's mouth fell open in amazement.

"You've invited John Boardman for tea? Have you lost your wits, woman?"

Rose burst out laughing.

"Not John Boardman, you silly sausage. I've invited our peacemaker Conrad Ross."

For a moment Joe was lost in puzzled contemplation. Then he reached into his inside coat pocket, pulled out a black notebook and flicked through it.

"Conrad Ross!" he exclaimed after a few seconds of scanning. "That's cleared matters up."

"Clear as a cracked bell," whispered Nancy who was next to me on the sofa.

"What are you talking about, darling?" said Rose.

"This Ross fellow is the computer expert I've been trying to contact. You've done me a favour, Rose. I'll show him the clues when we've eaten dinner."

Mention of the killer's odd messages grabbed Nancy's keen attention and I half expected a set-to with Joe invoking the sanctity of a police investigation. But whether it was the whisky or that he had run out of ideas and was willing to try anything, he immediately produced the three photographs he'd shown me the night before. After a couple of minutes carefully examining them, Nancy bestowed her opinion upon us.

"All three are cryptic crossword clues with the number of letters also given cryptically at the end of each. I've never seen that done before."

Joe glanced at me but didn't speak.

Nancy carefully placed the photographs on the small coffee table in front of her.

"The first is extremely odd so I might need a bit of time to work on it but the second! Come on, Joe, I can't believe nobody at your nick has got it."

"I'm sorry, Nancy, but you'll have to believe it. Surprise us."

"Time Joe and his buddies began to deliver," Nancy read from the photo. "The note isn't saying it's about time Joe and his pals did something. It refers back to the time when you actually did it."

Joe still looked perplexed.

"Oh, for goodness sake," snapped Nancy and I could tell that she was a whisker away from slapping him, which would have made the evening considerably more interesting.

"You were there or thereabouts on June 6th 1944, weren't you? That's the answer, won free, one three, D-Day. The time you - Joe - and your pals began to deliver Europe from the Nazi menace. Good work by the way."

If her throwaway compliment was meant to make Joe feel better it didn't work too well. At the first mention of D-Day he seemed to collapse in on himself. Indeed, Joe looked so sick he could have been back in that troop carrier, a terrified kid waiting for the ramp to open and expose him and his comrades to a blizzard of German fire. Making a real effort, he addressed my wife.

"Thank you for that, Nancy. I'll have a think about it. Now excuse me but I need to go to bed. It's been a long and tiring day."

"Don't you want to hear the answer to the third puzzle? That's easy peasy too."

Joe forced himself to listen as an ebullient Nancy explained that 'Action Station' simply referred to another of the most celebrated events in British history.

"Just change 'Action' to 'Battle' and 'Station' to 'Waterloo' and you get Battle of Waterloo, sex too late. Sorry, six, two, eight. Another military reference."

"That's amazing, Nancy," Joe replied, but without much enthusiasm. "Now if you'll all excuse me."

For a moment after he had left the room nobody spoke. Then all at once Rose began to apologise for Joe's rudeness and I babbled on that it mattered not a jot as we were going to turn in ourselves. Ten minutes later Nancy and I were lying side by side - thank god their spare bed was a double - trying to puzzle out what had just happened. After all, my brilliant wife had just cracked his clues for him and all he could do was give a grudging acknowledgement and slope off to bed.

"Don't worry about it, darling," said Nancy. "He's obviously had a hard day."

Then she bashed the pillows and made herself comfortable.

"I've really been looking forward to this moment," she whispered, "But having Darby and Joan on the other side of this wall doesn't exactly put you in the mood for you know what."

"I know what you mean."

"Something feels wrong as well." My wife was warming to her theme. "I mean by the look of him - and Rose - they haven't been making the bed rattle for years."

"Well, that's where *you're* wrong. Apparently they've been trying ages for a baby - but with no luck."

Nancy whistled softly.

"No wonder he limps."

We both collapsed into a fit of tipsy giggling.

When I awoke Nancy was already up and busy filling a suitcase with a selection of my clothes.

"My stars, I didn't realise you still wore this abomination," she said, dangling my favourite cardigan, a rather fetching mustard-coloured number, far out in front of her as if it were a decaying rodent. "I'll have a little man burn it immediately."

"You most certainly will not! How come you're messing with my stuff anyway?"

She leaned forward and whispered.

"We're leaving. I've booked us in to a hotel a couple of miles out of town. I can't sleep here another night, Franco. Come on, rise and shine."

She broke the news to Joe and Rose in such a way that you'd think we were doing them a massive favour. How Nancy really did not want to run up a huge bill on their telephone while she busily went about her business; how she didn't care to see a greedy pig like me eating and drinking them out of house and home; how every couple like them needed - nay deserved - a bit of space in their lives, especially at this *delicate* juncture. After all that, *I'd* have booted us out onto the street, hurling our belongings, including beloved cardigans, after us. But Joe merely shrugged; I wasn't even sure if he was listening. Rose, however, seemed doubtful about the idea that the house might somehow function more smoothly without my presence. Nancy confidently assured my cousin that years of experience had taught her that, yes, it really would. So, with a promise to return for the evening's meal featuring Conrad, we were speeding off in the Morgan less than an hour after I'd opened my sleepy eyes.

It had to be admitted that the hotel was surprisingly plush - god only knew how much we were paying for it. The room was smart and modern and instead of a cracked jug and bowl on the side table there was a bathroom actually attached, a bit like in one of the main bedrooms at Ken Boardman's mansion. Meanwhile the double divan was the size of the Kon-Tiki, although thankfully minus cabin and Norwegian sailors, so it seemed a shame to waste the opportunity. Accordingly, Nancy and I spent the rest of the morning reconnecting with each other under its covers. Indeed, apart from a break for lunch in the downstairs dining place, we spent the whole day in the bedroom, catching up on each other's news when we weren't otherwise reacquainting.

Nancy's exclamations of horror at hearing the details of just how close the murderer had come to spearing me with his evil serrated-edged hunting knife were, however, quickly eclipsed by her excited declaration that she'd solved the first clue. This threw me somewhat as I couldn't help wondering at what point she'd actually been working on the solution.

"What is it then?" I asked but Nancy just shook her head.

"I'll wait to see what this Conrad fellow says first," was her reply. "There's also the problem of the … but we'll leave that one too."

"So the long and short of it is you're telling me nothing."

"Aw, don't be like that, Franco. Why don't you ask me what made me choose this place?"

"What on earth made you choose this place?" I dutifully parroted while flicking though the handy Gideon Bible, so thoughtfully left on the bedside table for the edification and salvation of the hotel's wealthy clients.

"Daddy used to go on about it," Nancy replied with a grimace as she attacked her matted blonde thatch with a wicked looking long-handled silver comb. "They used to hold their County Chamber of Commerce frolics here."

"Well," I pronounced, seconds after satisfyingly launching the good book into the furthest corner of the room, "I bet the staff are relieved they'll never again be subjected to the pleasure of Joshua's company."

Nancy turned to me and I was surprised to see tears in her eyes.

"Don't say that, Franco," she sighed. "Daddy isn't in a position to hurt us or anyone else ever again."

I'll believe that when everyone who knows him is jitterbugging on his freshly-filled grave, I thought to myself while gently and solicitously trying to extract the evil comb from Nancy's tangled coils. To my surprise she began to giggle.

"Is it something I said? Only I haven't managed to make anyone laugh for a good while so I could do with making a note of it."

"No, it's not you," she grinned, oblivious to my stab at irony. "When I was with Daddy at the home yesterday, he became desperate for a wee."

Bloomin' heck, I really could do without chapter and verse on Joshua's plumbing problems.

"Well it does happen. But hang on, I thought he didn't talk to you."

"You're right, he didn't even look at me. He just shouted for the nurse to bring him a pan."

She began to giggle again which irritated me slightly, even though it was Joshua she was laughing at.

"Like I said, Nance, we all get caught short. Even the very worst of us."

"Yes, but I was thinking about that time near Balmoral where he … you know …"

"When he almost peed all over us!" I exclaimed, suddenly remembering how as eloping fugitives we hid behind a dry-stone wall as her Dad approached with the intention of making the wall - and therefore us - much less dry. Now we were both laughing like drains.

"He would have done too," Nancy said, "if it hadn't been for that bodyguard of his saying there was a pub just up the road. What was the chap's name? Dreadful fellow!"

"Lake. Maurice Lake."

I closed my eyes in an unsuccessful bid to block out memories of the duffing Lake had given me minutes after Nancy and I first had sex. At least the man hadn't interrupted us in the act. That *would* have made him a truly dreadful fellow. Yet, although Lake was the toughest of nuts, my father-in-law's deranged antics eventually became too extreme even for him. Two years later he went out of his way to warn me that Joshua had put hired killers on my tail. Which was why in October 1938 I fled for sanctuary to Nazi Germany - yes, it was that serious - and had my mad Munich adventure. In case you were somehow unlucky enough to miss the first volume of my memoirs, allow me to briefly explain that this particular escapade involved the Prime Minister Neville Chamberlain, four bodies, two of them in a roll of carpet, and a dead-eyed assassin from the British Secret Intelligence Service. It had been my unwitting introduction to the world of international espionage. (And if that doesn't boost my royalties for Volume I, nothing will!)

    Nancy turned and smiled at me.

    "They were such fun times, weren't they?"

    "Yes, I always look back fondly on those merry moments when your Dad was pursuing us up and down the kingdom accompanied by a pack of shotgun-toting desperadoes."

    "Don't be too hard on him, Franco. After all it was directly because of Daddy that the King stepped in to be your best man."

    "Suppose so."

    "I saw him the other day you know, the King, well the Duke of Windsor as we know him these days."

    "Did he wave?"

    "He was on the newsreel, you silly ass. President Eisenhower was entertaining him at the White House."

    "I'll wager he still looked as perplexed as the day he stood next to us during our little ceremony."

    "And tried to steal a quick kiss off me."

    "Before Wallis landed him one." I put on my best Brooklyn accent. 'Dave, get your goddam mitts off de Limey broad!'"

    Nancy laughed in delight and jumped to her feet. I had half an idea she was about to plant a not-so-chaste kiss on my cheek but she swept past me and took from her handbag an envelope which she handed over. It contained photographs of our daughter Julia. Cambridge was easily recognisable from the usual backgrounds - ornate bridges, shimmering water meadows and plummy-voiced traitors peeping around every corner. In each picture Julia was with the odd female friend plus a succession of boys.

"What our daughter got up to in her first year at Girton," said Nancy, lighting a cigarette. "You must admit she takes a good picture."

"How many boyfriends has she got?" I said flicking through the photos in amazement. "There's enough here for a rugby fifteen, plus reserves."

"She assures me they're just friends who are boys," said Nancy, expelling a plume of blue smoke across the room. "But don't worry. Anticipating all that, I gave her a jolly good talking to before she went up. And a box of condoms. So at least she's been protected the whole time."

"A box of … good god, woman, were you expecting a queue?"

"Of course not. And don't be vulgar."

"I mean, what on earth …?"

Nancy glared at me.

"And what were you up to at her age, Franco?"

I considered this for a moment.

"Well, there was the rather messy incident involving Jean Tomlinson and my pushbike … but as we know it's different for girls."

"It certainly is and ten times more serious. Anyway, when we get home you can have that same conversation with Baz."

The very idea that I should broach the subject of sex with our sixteen-year-old son Balthazar (don't ask) filled me with eye-swivelling horror. And as for producing a box of noddies! Finally noticing my obvious discomfort, Nancy stubbed out her ciggie, sashayed over and gave me a smoky kiss.

"After all, darling, you are somewhat of an expert," she purred, wrestling me on to the bed.

With one thing and the other, we were half an hour late arriving for the meal at Joe and Rose's. We hadn't even noticed it had been raining for most of the day. As Nancy pulled up, I jumped out of the Morgan, sprinted up the path and hammered on the door (I'm still not sure where that burst of energy came from). There was no answer and after a couple more knocks, I reached under the flowerpot and found the spare front door key still there.

"Talk about 'mind how you go'," Nancy muttered, using a compact mirror to check the sheen on her new coat of lipstick.

Once we were inside it became clear why nobody had heard us. Huge hoots of laughter billowed from the dining room accompanied by the tinkling of glass on glass. I couldn't help noticing that the merriment while loud also held something of an intimate quality. Nancy noticed it too.

"Sounds like Darby and Joan have recently renewed their campaign to increase the population," she whispered, pushing me forward down the corridor. "You first. After all, you are family."

With some trepidation, I tentatively opened the dining room door and was surprised to be confronted with Rose and ... not Joe but Conrad, both of them grinning guiltily like a couple of rubbish gunpowder plotters. They were seated opposite each other at the table and by the looks of it they had already put away three quarters of a bottle of red wine. Rose, who was wearing a rather fetching blue-flowered frock I hadn't seen before, smiled radiantly at us.

"You're here," she said.

"Yes," I replied, "sorry, we're late."

"But I'm so relieved it didn't cramp your style," Nancy added pointedly. "Any dregs left for us?"

"Never worry," bellowed Conrad, "leaping theatrically to his feet. "I brought at least four bottles. You must be Nancy. I'm Conrad."

Introductions completed, we ascertained that Joe would be along shortly and that, while the meal was cooking, Rose and Conrad had embarked on a wine-tasting session. The kind where you can't be bothered to spit the stuff out.

"What's that delightful smell from the kitchen, Rose?" Nancy inquired, sniffing the air like a starving bloodhound.

"You'll have to ask Conrad about that," she simpered tipsily.

"Ah yes," said Conrad, putting down his glass. "I'm warming up a pan of my magical concoction - or goulash as the rest of the world calls it. Picked up the recipe when we lived in Eastern Europe. My dear old Dad was in the diplomatic corps out there before the war."

"Well I hope it tastes as delicious as it smells," said Nancy. "Now I could have sworn someone mentioned wine!"

There were three extra glasses on the table. Conrad quickly half-filled one and handed it to Nancy before dashing to the kitchen and returning with another open bottle from which he poured out the same amount for me. Nancy sniffed her drink approvingly before picking up the empty bottle.

"Hungarian," she said, scanning the label. "Daddy used to buy this stuff occasionally. It was definitely a cut above our usual French vinegar. Well done, Conrad."

Conrad smiled and bowed exaggeratedly.

"That's down to my old man as well. He was something of an oenophile."

"They can't touch you for it these days," I quipped, eliciting the sort of restrained amusement to which I'd grown accustomed during my summer of fun in Mellish. "Here's to absent friends!"

Joe's continuing absence did not inhibit further toasts being proposed and, fuelled by too much wine and a lack of food, the gathering began to behave in an increasingly eccentric fashion. At one point, Rose went into the kitchen to check on her boiled spuds and returned still holding the steaming pan in front of her like a baffled entrant in the giants' egg and spoon event. Then Nancy fell off her chair and began shrieking with laughter in the manner of a well-brought up fishwife.

Another hour - along with two-and-three-quarter bottles - had disappeared when we heard the front door slam. Seconds later Joe slouched into the dining room trying to disguise both his limp and his worried expression. He succeeded in neither enterprise.

"Darling, you're back," said Rose, stumbling slightly as she got up to embrace him.

"Yes, sorry I'm late, everyone," he sighed. "But I see you've managed OK without me."

"Joe," said Rose now rocking back and forth ever so slightly, "this is Conrad the code baker ... breaker."

Conrad leapt to his feet and extended his hand.

"Joe, so pleased we could finally meet. I've heard a lot about you."

"Any of it good?" replied Joe, shaking Conrad's hand and slumping on to the remaining dining chair.

"You'd be amazed," smiled Conrad. "Wine?"

"I'll have a Scotch if you don't mind," Joe replied, loosening his tie.

The meal, served minutes later, had the effect of calming everyone down. The hysterical tone of the previous hour gave way to an earnest silence as we all marvelled at just how tasty Conrad's goulash was and that Rose's spuds and carrots had survived at all, given the circumstances. When we'd all finished eating, it was Conrad himself who gave a definitive verdict on the meal.

With a polite burp, he put down his knife and fork and announced, "I'm done. My compliments to … me."

Everyone laughed, even Joe.

"Yes, very tasty indeed," he agreed. "Now I believe you might have some information based on what I told you over the phone?"

"Joe!" scolded Rose, "have the decency to let Conrad digest his food before you begin interrogating him."

"Oh, sorry, Conrad," Joe said with a puzzled stare at his wife, "as you were."

"No problem, old fellow," smiled Conrad. "I'd be delighted to discuss the messages. Unfortunately, I'm not sure how much I can tell you. Can I see the originals?"

Joe glanced over at Nancy who took the photographs from her handbag and laid them on the table where Rose had quickly cleared a space. Conrad studied each picture for a few seconds and then nodded.

"The second clue has a simple solution but the first is giving me problems and I'm still working on it."

Nancy threw me what she must have imagined was a knowing glance. Sadly, she just looked cross-eyed. But I realised where she was coming from.

"The misshus has sholved it," I slurred, pointing at Nancy. "It's about the Battle of Trafalgar and Nelson's Column. No, wait a minute, it's …"

Conrad politely allowed me a few moments of confused rumination before he continued.

"I'm sure you've all realised the second message refers to D-Day and your part in it, Joe. Am I right?"

Joe nodded, never once taking his eyes off Conrad.

"And the third one isn't about Trafalgar, Frankie, but Waterloo."

Joe nodded again.

"It's this first one that's bothering me," Conrad added, betraying a hint of exasperation.

"Then let me enlighten you, Mr Codebreaker."

This was from Nancy who leaned across the table and snatched up the first photo, almost tipping Conrad's wine all over him. However, as the glass wobbled, Conrad stretched out a languid but firm hand to keep it upright.

"We almost had a dreadful disaster there," he laughed. "Now what about the clue, Nancy?"

"What we have here," my wife revealed, "is another battle, or rather a complete set of them."

I glanced round. She had everyone's complete attention.

"'Wit Oskar messed up and the world went Wild. Jive, Free.' The first bit's simply an anagram."

"I thought so," said Conrad. "'Messed up' is standard crossword setter's code for jumbling the letters. But I still couldn't make anything of it."

"You obviously didn't go to the sort of school I did," Nancy said smugly.

"I should hope he didn't," I interrupted. "It was a posh girls' academy in Switzerland."

"I have to admit that my schooling wasn't half bad either," muttered Conrad, "But still I'm stumped."

"Kito's War," Nancy announced triumphantly. "Rose, look it up in those beautifully bound encyclopaedias on the shelf there. The ones I'd guess haven't been opened since that well-scrubbed young salesman persuaded you to pay far too much for them."

Like most folk eager to do Nancy's bidding - and that did seem to be most folk - Rose jumped to attention. And a minute after opening Volume 4, JA-LO, she informed us that Kito's War was an insurrection against Roman rule in Egypt and across a wide area of the Middle East; a particularly bloody set of campaigns by all accounts.

"Hence 'the world went wild'," explained Nancy, her eyes still looking slightly foxed. "The bit of it that was known about at the time anyway. Tell us the date, Rose."

"Rose squinted at the large volume balanced on her knee. "Er, AD 115-117."

Conrad slapped the table. "That confirms it then."

Joe looked hard at him. "Confirms what?"

"Great work, Nancy," Conrad said excitedly. "Now I reckon I can unlock the second part of the puzzle. What the dates actually mean."

He got up and began pacing the room, which was in silence as all eyes followed him back and forth. Even Nancy, who'd looked a bit miffed when he spoke, was intrigued.

"Wow," said Conrad, noticing for the first time that he had a captive audience, "this must be what it's like on stage eh, Frankie?"

"Even *our* audiences aren't usually this quiet," I said. "Go on."

Conrad laid it out remarkably simply. After establishing that we all knew how a 24-hour clock was configured, he pointed to the dates of each battle 115-117, 1944 and 1815.

"I think," he went on, "these dates refer to times that are significant to each murder."

Joe jumped out of his seat and began to quickly scrabble at the inside pocket of his jacket. He drew out a small leather-bound notebook and flicked through it.

"What time do you reckon Wilf died?" he said slowly, directing the question at me.

"It must have been around one o'clock in the morning. Maybe just after."

Joe glanced at the notebook then held it up as if swearing in the assembled group. "According to your statement you discovered Wilf at one-seventeen. And the third victim, Terry Poynter-Mann was found by the pub's cellar man at around eight in the morning."

Conrad rubbed his chin. "But that doesn't correspond with 1944 at all," he murmured.

"It does," said Joe triumphantly, "since the pathologist estimated that he'd been dead for twelve hours."

Nobody spoke for a few moments until Rose added quietly, "Waterloo, 1815. That means the next murder will take place at a quarter past six in the evening. But when?"

"That's the bit I can't fathom," Conrad admitted with a baffled expression. "The dates of the killings must be hidden in the messages but I'm damned if I can see where."

"What are the dates of the murders?" I asked.

Joe scanned his notebook, flicking quickly through the pages. "May 31st, June 8th and June 10th. I can't spot any pattern there."

"Me neither," I admitted.

Although we were only a bit further forward, I realised that the mental effort getting there had gone a long way to sobering me up. My wife must have had the same experience because I noticed her eyes had uncrossed and she wore a familiar expression. The one which announced, 'I'm back in the driving seat so watch out, buster'.

Nancy lit a cigarette and surveyed the surrounding company. "Let me give you all something else to think about," she said blowing out a plume thick enough to announce the arrival of The Spanish Armada. "The messages also give clues to where the murders will take place."

There was a silence before Joe said, "Go on, Nancy."

She smiled and theatrically stubbed out her cigarette. "First message, Kito's War, Romans, ie the Coliseum Theatre. Second one, D-Day, Fusilier pub although that's a bit tenuous if you ask me."

Joe was immediately on the edge of his seat staring at her. "They hold annual D-Day reunions there."

Nancy nodded. "There you go then. So the third message indicates that the next murder scene will have a connection with the Battle of Waterloo."

I butted in, mainly because I hadn't contributed much to the last few minutes' discussion and I didn't want everyone running away with the idea that Nancy was the only clever clogs on the Thirkettle team.

"So we're looking for a pub called The Duke of Wellington." I sat back, more than pleased with myself - before my wife once again brought me down to earth.

"Maybe, Franco," she muttered, "but I reckon that this fellow considers himself something of an artist and wouldn't want a near repeat of the previous venue."

"Then where?" said Rose.

"We're going to have to give a bit more thought to that one," Nancy replied. "In the meantime, we must address the final problem."

Blimey, it was like being married to Sherlock Holmes.

"And that is?" Joe asked tentatively.

"Our final problem is, paradoxically," she said holding up the three photographs, "where's the first message?"

It took a few seconds for everyone to digest the implication of her question. Oddly enough it was me who got there first.

"She's right," I said. "The message that predicts the first murder. Where is it?"

Everyone turned to Joe who kept a poker face for around five seconds before quietly sighing and opening the file. He took out another photograph and placed it carefully on the table. It showed a rectangular envelope with his name and address typed on it. In the top corner was a threepenny stamp.

"It arrived here on May 28th. Three days before the badly burned body of the first victim, Michael Donaghy, was found on the war memorial. I didn't think much of it at the time but don't worry, I declared it immediately the second note was found near where Donaghy's body lay. It's now part of the evidence file. Like the others, it's a blue envelope."

I was about to pick up the photograph but paused. After all, wasn't *it* part of the evidence file too? Nancy, however, showed no such reservations, scooping up the picture and staring at it for fifteen seconds before pronouncing her verdict.

"Typed like all the others and on the same machine I'll wager. You can see that the tail of the 'e' in 'Trueman' is ever so slightly chipped."

"Well spotted, Nancy," said Conrad.

"Thanks," replied Nancy. "So where's the note that was inside it?"

Joe handed her another photograph from his file which Nancy stared at for a full minute.

"Perhaps you could share your valuable insights," I said, a trifle impatiently.

Nancy gave me one of her looks.

"If you wouldn't mind awfully," I added hurriedly.

"It reads, 'Remember me when I am gone away'."

"That would explain why the body was found at the war memorial," said Conrad. "And there's nothing else?"

"He didn't sign it, if that's what you mean," Nancy shot back. "What made you hold on to the letter, Joe?"

"Good question. It just looked odd that's all."

I laughed.

"And I suppose it's not every day you get sent love poetry."

Joe looked sharply at me.

"What do you mean?"

"Well it's a line from a poem. 'Remember me when I am gone away. Gone far away into the silent land.' Robert Browning, if memory serves me right. Don't tell me you didn't know."

"I … I …"

For the first time since I'd been in Mellish Joe did not appear to be fully in charge of his reactions. He could be unsure or even fearful but he usually looked as if he had a firm hand on the tiller. Now he seemed caught out - and I'd guess my drunken triumphalism wasn't exactly helping matters along.

"Do they not teach poetry at schools in this one-donkey town?"

Joe's eyes narrowed.

"We learned all sorts of things," he replied grimly.

"I'm not talking about knitting candy floss or nobbling the coconut shy."

"Browning, you say," replied Joe ignoring my insult and writing something down in his notebook. "Doesn't get us anywhere with the dates though, does it."

"Let me give it a try," Rose said unexpectedly.

"Are you handy with figures, Rose?" said Conrad with the ghost of a smirk.

"Well, I am a computer," she replied to general mystification.

"Wow!" Conrad's eyes widened. "I can vouch for the fact that they've never built a computer like you."

"Don't be silly. I operate machines for calculating wages."

"That's what she did before we were married," Joe interrupted grumpily.

"Er, well actually not only then, Joe," Rose replied hesitantly. I've just got myself a job at Tatlocks."

Nobody saw that one coming - least of all Joe. And immediately it sent the room temperature through the floor.

"When were you going to tell me that?" Joe hissed.

Everyone went very quiet. I was about to congratulate Rose on her upcoming brand new life adventure when a warning look from Nancy told me to hold my stupid tongue. Conrad must have sensed similar vibrations because he jumped up from his seat and announced, "It's been a lovely evening but I'm afraid I must go."

Rose looked absolutely crestfallen.

"Don't leave," she pleaded. "We're not going to start arguing, are we, Joe?"

"Are we not?"

As merrily as he could, Conrad continued, "I really must get to the rugby club. They simply won't start drinking if I'm not there. Seriously though, it's been a super evening."

He patted Joe's shoulder and pecked Rose on the cheek.

"But your saucepan," Rose pleaded in desperation.

"I'll pick it up some time. Thanks again. Bye."

Conrad hurried out and moments later the front door slammed. Rose turned angrily on Joe.

"Did you have to be so beastly?"

"It's not me who's been keeping secrets."

"Oh, for god's sake grow up," shouted Rose and ran from the room. We could all hear her footsteps pounding quickly up the stairs.

Meanwhile Joe carefully put the photographs back in the file and returned it to the sideboard drawer.

"I need a breath of air," he announced and was out of the door before either Nancy or I could reply. The front door slammed for the second time in a minute, leaving us on our own. I stared across the table at my wife.

"Are *you* thinking of leaving very suddenly?" I asked.

"No but you are."

"Eh?"

"Follow Joe and see he's OK."

"He'll be all right."

"He's under more pressure than we realised. Make sure he doesn't do anything stupid, or come to any harm. Go on, it's stopped raining."

I groaned inwardly. In my view experienced coppers who'd battled their way across northern France didn't need their hands holding. However, I was under orders.

Thus ejected from the property, I managed just a glimpse of Joe before he turned the corner at the far end of Woodcock Street. Blimey, he'd been moving much quicker than normal - gammy leg or not - and I set off at a trot to overhaul him.

However, it wasn't until we were nearly at the recreation ground - about a quarter of a mile further on - that I felt near enough to shout for him to stop. Either he didn't hear, or more likely ignored me, because he continued down a rough path and disappeared into the trees. Although darkness had not fallen completely, the dripping leafy canopy made it gloomy - and slippery - enough to force me to watch every step. I'd thus given up on the prospect of catching up with Joe when all at once I collided with him. He whirled round and shone a torch straight into my face. I also noticed that his right fist was raised in a most threatening manner.

"Joe, it's me - Frankie," I yelped hurriedly.

"Frankie," he mumbled, sounding for all the world as though it was the first time in his life he'd heard the name.

"What are you doing here, Joe?"

Without a word he slowly turned round and shone the light up into the trees, which continued to shed raindrops into our eyes. Through the liquid haze I saw, gently swinging like a grotesque pendulum, the body of a man. He appeared to be in a parachute harness connected to a number of thin ropes, the other ends of which were looped around a large branch. His head was slumped on to his chest and strands of lank hair hung down over his forehead like a greasy curtain, revealing a large bald spot. I was immediately reminded of Wilf just after he had died. But it was the dead man's clothes which fascinated me. While his trousers and shoes looked worn and shabby, the overcoat was brand new. Where had I seen it before? It took another few seconds before I realised with a jolt that the body lazily swaying under the damp canopy of leaves was that of Joe's former comrade in arms.

"That's, that's ..." I stammered, wiping water from my eyes.

"Olly," Joe said quietly. "And I'd always imagined the little swine was indestructible."

"How did you know he'd be up there?"

"I didn't. I usually come this way on my … evening strolls."

"Evening strolls … blimey, Joe, what does all this mean? What the hell is going on?"

I don't mind admitting that I was scared out of my wits. And, as Joe turned to me in the near darkness, I could see that those bright blue eyes were also wide open with fear.

"It means we have a fourth victim," he said, struggling to control his emotions. "Now listen, Frankie, I'm going to use the police call box at the end of this path. Please stay here and don't let anybody near that tree."

Joe handed me the torch and disappeared into the gloom. I half expected him not to return, leaving me stuck all night with only the gently swaying Olly for company, no more fun in death than he had been alive. But five minutes later Joe was back, limping heavily and breathless with exertion.

While he'd been gone, I'd managed a perfunctory check on the state of the body and the immediate area around the scene. An upwards sweep of the torch told me that Olly had not come crashing down through the tree canopy, and therefore someone with considerable strength had somehow hauled him up there. It was hardly a comforting thought and I nervously swept the flashlight beam around the path and over surrounding bushes to confirm that I was alone. I'd already tackled the killer once and barely escaped intact; I definitely didn't fancy my chances a second time. I also noticed that an envelope was stuck to the inside leg of Olly's trousers, either with thread or perhaps glue, but I could not make out who it was addressed to. However, it was undoubtedly light blue like the other four. As Joe came wheezing back up the path, I flashed the beam upwards again.

"Shall we try to get the letter down?"

Joe shook his head.

"Leave things exactly as they are. Ray and the forensics boys are on their way. I've asked for the pathologist as well. Poor sod'll be fed up of the sight of me."

He gazed up at what had once been Olly and grimaced.

"So someone finally nailed the rotten little twerp," he said with surprising vehemence.

I glanced back nervously down the path.

"Steady on, Joe."

"There's no getting away from it, Frankie," he said in a voice that was becoming rapidly more strident with every sentence. "In war and in peace this man was a bleedin' liability. Mind you he wasn't the only one …"

He stopped and exhaled loudly.

"But then there's no point in raking over old ground while he floats above us, dead as a … whatever."

"I think you're right, Joe." I paused to reflect then added, "If the last note is anything to go by then he'll have been killed at around 6.15 this evening. But … but that means it all happened in broad daylight so someone must have seen something odd - even if it was only the body spinning around up there."

I shone the torch and we both took in Olly's final sad pirouette.

"Don't worry, Frankie, we'll check every angle. It was raining hard at the time though, so there won't have been many potential witnesses and besides, people don't tend to look up when they're hurrying along."

"You did."

"I … I must have heard something to make me stop."

My silence could not help but have told him that I considered his explanation a bit threadbare. There was also another question.

"We established there would be some connection with Waterloo. But I can't see it."

Joe was breathing so heavily I pointed the torch at his pale white face to check he was OK.

"This patch of land we're on," he replied quietly, "has been known as Wellington Common for as long as I can remember."

I suddenly felt even more cold and vulnerable, as if the killer was watching our every move.

"Who is this guy?" I exclaimed. "He seems to pass through the town like The Invisible Man, taking lives on a whim. Except there's nothing whimsical about it. Like the military theme it's all planned down to the last detail."

I was now frightening myself and to his credit Joe spotted this.

"Go back home, Frankie, please," he urged. "There's nothing you can do here. Our lot will be along soon and we'll take a formal statement from you tomorrow. Go and get some rest."

I wasn't about to object. I handed him the torch and he flashed the beam back down the path.

"It comes out of the trees after twenty yards," he said, trying to sound comforting. "There's a decent moon tonight and you'll have no trouble finding your way back to the road."

He patted my shoulder and I moved off. At that point, however, I realised what had been nagging away at my subconscious since the end of the meal. In the circumstances it seemed inconsequential but nevertheless I turned back and shouted.

"Joe, I've remembered something."

"What?"

I could hardly see him and was barely able to hear his voice.

"The line from that poem we were talking about," I shouted back.

"The one by Robert Browning? What about it?"

"That's the thing; it wasn't written by Browning."

"Who then?"

"I'm pretty sure it's by Christina Rossetti."

There was such a long silence that I turned to go. Perhaps he hadn't heard me. But then Joe's voice filled the air with terrified bewilderment.

"What name did you say again?"

"Rossetti. Christina Rossetti."

Although he tried to stifle it, the groan was audible, and I could just make out a dark figure sinking to his knees in the middle of the path. I wasn't entirely sure but it looked as if Joe's head had fallen onto his chest in despair, reflecting exactly the terrible pose of his former comrade in arms whose body swayed languidly but ominously in the light seaside breeze ten feet above him.

8
Desert Rat

"MY BOYS, MY brilliant, brilliant boys," Nancy enthused, her arms draped around both myself and Barney as we scrummed down in the middle of our tiny dressing room. Normally I'd balk at having to share my wife's affections with any man, let alone the egregious Barney, but even I was forced to concede that these were special circumstances. So I basked in Nancy's adulation as she whispered sweet somethings in both our ears. I couldn't help it. Just as characteristically Barney completely ignored her show of admiration, even contriving to continue scribbling in a tatty little notebook as if reporting on Nancy's ravings for The Knott End Trumpet. Had it been me jotting down the observations I might have mentioned how it was the first time I'd been so close to Barney; and that he smelled like a pigsty. However, I have to admit that would have been churlish, as Nancy's comments and the celebration were entirely warranted. The combination of myself and Barney had left two packed houses clamouring for more. And they had been great shows, albeit with just the one small piece of unpleasantness. An extremely eventful day had ended a lot more propitiously than it began.

After I'd left Joe kneeling on the woodland path, apparently praying for salvation, there had been a short but fraught walk across the common and a sudden violent sprint through glistening echoing streets until I was back in the safety of Rose's spare bedroom. If this mad slayer was going to finish me off second time round, he'd at least have to clock a world record for the hundred yards dash. Exhausted, I tumbled into bed next to Nancy, who I'd already deduced had not gone back to the hotel because her car was still sitting outside. There, I *was* a detective after all! Not that my wife would know or care. She was gurgling away merrily, her snoring undoubtedly fuelled by the heroic intake of Conrad's plonk; but it wasn't this cacophony which kept me awake until nearly 3am. My fevered imagination did that. A maniac was loose in the town, stalking Joe and by extension the people around him. He was hugely strong, worked in a silence that bordered on invisibility and had proved totally ruthless. Oh yes, and he was clever. He'd taunted everyone with cryptic clues that even Nancy had found challenging to decipher. Any of us could be his next victim, although I drew a tiny bit of comfort, as I watched Nancy's snores flutter the curtains, that so far his victims had all been male. Yet sleep when it finally overtook me provided little comfort. I was soon transfixed by demons swirling and swooping around the room and above the bed, while in the background the voice of my old teacher Mr Finch intoned the same lines from Paradise Lost over and over again.

"'Better to reign in Hell than serve in Heaven,' would you not agree, Thirkettle?"

"Not so sure about that, sir, especially as it appears to be coming from a teacher. Er, Mr Finch, are those fallen angels on top of the wardrobe here for the duration?"

"Be silent, Butterthwaite's Bendiest Boy. And bend over!"

To put the tin lid on everything, I awoke with a start to discover a ghastly demon with snakes for hair glowering at me full in the face while pummelling my ribs. It came as only partial relief to discover the terrible apparition was Nancy demanding to be appraised of what had gone on after I'd pursued Joe. I wearily told her I would talk about it in the morning but she became so insistent that I ended up describing everything down to the last grisly detail. Whereupon she fled to the bathroom and was violently sick. Staggering back to bed, Nancy then had the nerve to blame Conrad's goulash for her infirmity.

"Conrad's gallon of vintage vino more like," I observed, taking another demonic dig to the ribs for my troubles. Eventually I managed another couple of hours' shut-eye before wakefulness and worry drove me from bed at around seven o'clock. Even after a cold rinse I still felt tired and dirty as all my clean clothes were at the hotel.

Rose was busying herself in the kitchen while predictably Joe had already left for the station. Despite the strained circumstances, however, there seemed to be a new zest about my cousin. She even warbled a couple of verses of Some Enchanted Evening, the type of musical stuff she usually disdained. It was a couple of minutes before I remembered she was beginning her job the day after tomorrow.

"Wednesday's a funny day to start," I observed as she brought me a cup of tea.

"Not really. I was due in next Monday but they've a big new order going out on Friday and they needed some extra help with the invoices. And then there's the overtime to calculate."

"What exactly do Taylors do?"

"They make clothes, Frankie."

"What sort of ...?"

"*Tatlocks*, however, manufacture soft furnishings. Settees, chairs, that kind of thing."

"Sounds good. *And* you'll be able to rest your weary legs."

"I don't anticipate much free time. Don't want it either."

Rose's enthusiasm for hard work heartened me, holding as it did the prospect of some new purpose in her life, despite Joe's misgivings.

"Joe didn't seem too pleased when you told him you'd got a job."

"He's got enough on his plate without worrying what I get up to," she said with some vehemence, adding with a literary flourish, "and I'm damned if I'll continue to wander this place like a latter-day Miss Havisham."

"Is she your old Sunday School teacher?"

"No, Francis, she's a character in Great Expectations. Charles Dickens, remember?"

"I know, Rose. It was a joke. I am a comedian."

"So you are. I'd clean forgotten."

There was a pause then we both burst out laughing, stopping only when Nancy could be heard clomping down the stairs in her seven league boots.

"I wouldn't even entertain working if I thought a baby was anywhere on the horizon," Rose whispered quickly. "But as it is …"

She scurried back into the kitchen just before Nancy entered the room. My wife looked even ghastlier than anything John Milton could have dreamed up and was in a correspondingly diabolical mood. Before she'd even sat down there had been a dig about not making myself useful to Rose when she was starting work in a couple of days' time. While finishing off my drink I pondered whether there were any circumstances in which I could stop *her* from doing what she damn well pleased. There were not, I concluded, as I swallowed a mouthful of tea leaves.

"Stop slurping! It's like feeding time at Chester Zoo," snapped my darling better half.

Not particularly keen to start World War III, I made my excuses and left for the police station with a threat of death hanging over me if I wasn't at the theatre by one o'clock. Dying wasn't too far from my mind either as I approached the police station. At the very least, I expected the building to be heaving with potential witnesses just as it was the day after Wilf had been killed. I'd counted at least five lurid contents bills outside newsagents on my way there. The Daily Express's seemed to capture the mood succinctly as one billboard screamed, 'Seaside Slayer's Latest Victim'. How they'd latched on to that so quickly, god alone knew, or maybe on reflection it simply referred to the previous victim. Whoever it was, surely the town would be queuing up to help catch the killer.

But no, the nick was largely empty and quiet - at least until I walked in whereupon the outsized desk sergeant, Ernie, loudly proclaimed, "Hey up, Raymondo, the turn's arrived."

Ray wearily poked his head around the door of the squad room just up the corridor from Joe's office. Although he had every reason to look worried, it was still unusual to see this normally sunny man in such a gloomy state. Nor did Ray try to hide it. Before I sat down, he'd curtly established that I wanted a cup of tea and then barked an order to the other side of the room, where another giant was making himself comfortable by draping his long legs across the desk.

"Hey, Clarkson," Ray shouted, "if you can't even pretend to be working then you might as well make me and this gentleman a pot of tea."

The reply from behind The Daily Sketch was curt and uncompromising.

"Do it yourself, I'm not your bleedin' slave."

Ray considered this for a moment before he got up and strolled across the room.

"Ned, my very good friend," he said, towering over his colleague, "I find myself struggling to apprehend a fiend fully intent on slaughtering as many inhabitants of our beautiful little town as he can. Whereas you appear to be debating whether to put a shilling each way on the favourite at Lingfield. So kindly shift your arse and get us some tea."

The final sentence, laced with false bonhomie, was followed by Ray sweeping Clarkson's feet off the desk. Clarkson jumped up immediately, savage intent across his bruiser's face, but something held him back from further action - possibly the prospect of a good hiding from an even fiercer character. With a forced smile, he turned to me and said, "One sugar or two, sir?"

"Milk and two lumps please," I mumbled, feeling a bit uncomfortable about Ray's bullying performance which was not quite over. As Clarkson was leaving the room, Ray shouted, "Three sugars and just a splash for me."

Sitting down, Ray relaxed and grinned sheepishly.

"He'll probably take me literally and pee in it," he said.

"You can't really blame him. Is everything OK with you, Ray?"

"Yeah, no problems at all," he replied without much conviction. "Now let's get your statement down. This is becoming a habit isn't it?"

I went through what had happened the previous night, leaving out only the top and tail of the narrative; Joe's anger at his wife's announcement of her employment and his obvious anguish when I revealed who had actually written the poem. A couple of minutes into my story, Ned Clarkson came back in and placed two mugs on the desk. Ray cast a critical eye over the teas.

"You've not pissed in them, have you?"

"Not in his."

There was a moment of absolute stillness before Ray burst into laughter.

"Thanks, Ned, he spluttered. "Sorry I was a bit off with you before. Still all right for that drink after work?"

"Only if it's your shout," replied Clarkson, while pointedly putting both feet back up on his desk.

"We love each other really," grinned Ray and, while unsure if his warm words had totally healed the wound, I was relieved to hear them as his previous behaviour had been worryingly out of character.

A minute later the side door opened and Joe's head popped out. Seeing Ray was taking my statement, he turned to Clarkson.

"Ned, be a good chap and make a pot of coffee for three. A few biccies too if you can pinch any. We have an 'important' guest."

With a glare at me, he closed the door. Ray looked at Clarkson, who stared angrily back. Then both started howling with laughter.

"It's like one of them Brian Rix farces, is this," said Clarkson shaking his head.

"Watch the door doesn't smash into you on the way out," chortled Ray.

"And don't let the vicar come in through the French windows demanding a stiff one," I joined in, whereupon both gazed at me uncomprehendingly - before erupting into laughter again.

After Clarkson had slouched out again still shaking his head, the comedy was put to one side as Ray returned to the matter of my statement. Worryingly, he began to circle round a point which was troubling him but could not easily be stated out loud; Joe's role in all of this. Had I seen anyone else? No, but then I was rather drunk and concentrating hard on following Joe. Was Joe in my sight the whole time? Most of the time but not quite all. However, not long enough for him to have done anything 'significant'. Certainly not hauling a full-grown man up a tree.

Ray seemed relieved at my answers but by now I was becoming seriously troubled. Surely the cops - his own buddies - weren't actually speculating that Joe could have had anything to do with these atrocities?

I was about to tackle Ray on this point when an almighty shouting match erupted in the office next door. Much of what was being yelled was unintelligible but the argument was clearly between Joe and Hallows. Joe was evidently seething too as one of his few phrases clear enough to make out was labelling his chief 'a stay-at-home yellow belly.'

Ray glanced at me and rolled his eyes.

"We're back to war service - or the lack of it," he whispered.

Unsurprisingly, the slur propelled Hallows into a furious rant, which included a threat to have Joe's badge. Next, I was even more astonished to hear Ken Boardman's trademark growl urging both men to hold their din. It was remarkable enough that two senior police officers were having a semi-public row; the fact that it was being conducted in front of the town's mayor was almost unbelievable.

My version of events from the night before was put on hold as Ray crept over to the side door and placed his ear against it. He put a finger to his lips when Clarkson came bustling back in carrying a wooden tray on which stood a large white coffee pot, three cups and a plate of chocolate biscuits. As Ray knocked loudly on the door and pushed it open, the shouting stopped immediately. Ray whispered something to Clarkson as he went in. Seconds later he came back out, leaving the door slightly ajar.

For a moment I thought the performance had ended but it merely turned out to be the prologue. A dainty tinkle of spoons on the sides of cups was immediately followed by more ugly hostilities and it was now Boardman making the running. After weighing in with yet another barbed demand for the killer to be caught, he gave his considered opinion that both officers "were sitting on their backsides letting this swine rampage at will." At which Joe exploded again and things turned deliciously vicious.

"Don't tell us we're doing nothing, you fat prick," he yelled, at which even Ray and Ned Clarkson looked shocked.

"Don't call me fat," Boardman bellowed back, "I could still take you."

"You mean like the last time I kicked your big *fat* backside."

"That was before someone gave you that gammy leg. You useless cripple."

Snorting in disgust, Joe shot back with, "Yeah, the gammy leg I got while you sat on that same fat backside making money while real men died."

A cup shattered, two chairs skittered across the room and there followed the unmistakable sounds of two grown men grappling.

"For god's sake," shouted Hallows, obviously struggling to separate them. "This is a police station not an ale house. I'll have you both in the cells!"

There was more grunting and groaning before the fracas calmed down. I could hear Joe breathing heavily and Boardman wheezing.

"Detective Sergeant Trueman," Hallows barked. "You will apologise to Alderman Boardman."

"What, for defending myself?"

"For calling him a ... a rude word."

Joe took a deep breath.

"Sorry I called you a fat prick, Alderman," he replied with a sniff.

Boardman gave a harsh laugh.

"We all know what this is about," he announced, his voice frostily calm. "It's not my fault that the sergeant here is unlucky in love."

"This is not personal," said Joe, also making an unsuccessful effort to sound even-tempered.

"Have it your own way," Boardman fired back. "But I'll tell you what is personal."

"Must you?"

"Yes, I bleedin' well must," Boardman spat back. "Whether you like it or not this murder business is all about Joe Trueman. The notes, your dead mate, the attack in the theatre; this madman's doing it all because of you. Don't ask me why - that's your department - but I'm damned sure he is."

"I assure you the last victim was no 'mate' of mine," snapped Joe, missing a chance to refute Boardman's accusation.

"The mayor is right, Joe," Hallows weighed in. "This fellow has something against you and we must discover what it is."

"Preferably before all the visitors decide to go home and never come back!" Boardman declared angrily.

"Excuse me, gentlemen, but I have actual work to do," Joe said calmly. Ray took a quick, guilty step back from the door as it opened but Joe ignored him and limped slowly across the squad room without a glance at anyone. I decided the wise course would be to refrain from pointing out that his tie was wrapped Just William-style round the back of his neck. And his shirt was missing two buttons.

"Detective Sergeant, come back in here at once," yelled Hallows, appearing in the doorway just as Joe left the squad room through the far exit.

Hallows glared at the three of us and slammed the door shut. The two remaining voices were now indistinct but still it was apparent that Boardman was not letting up. One of the few exchanges we could clearly make out ended with the mayor growling, "People come to Mellish for a great holiday and to scoff my pies - not get ritually bleedin' slain."

"He must like that one, he used it on me," I whispered to Ray who signalled it was time to go.

"Me an' Frankie here are just nipping out, Ned," he told his colleague. "Try to make sure they don't kill each other."

"I'll give it my utmost attention," Clarkson replied without looking up from the racing pages.

Closing the door behind us, Ray whispered, "Goodness knows what he did to *their* drinks!"

I assumed we were all set to chase down our arthritic fugitive but Ray didn't even pause at the desk to ask Ernie which way his skipper had gone. Nor were we about to visit last night's murder scene. Instead, Ray steered me in silence towards the sea front and into a café just off it. It was a few moments before I recognised it as the same greasy spoon in which Barney and I had signed our non-aggression pact a few days before. Like then, the place was about three quarters full even though it was not yet ten o'clock.

Thinking of the number of lurid newspaper billboards we'd seen on our way, I whispered to Ray as we stood at the counter, "Seems a nice murder or two draws the tourists in rather than scaring them off."

"Just wait until he kills one of them," came the lugubrious reply. "You'll not see 'em for dust. Then watch the mayor's fat head really fly off."

We settled down with our mugs of tea at a corner table.

"We can talk in here," Ray said. "That place is a madhouse sometimes."

"Especially when cops start punching politicians. I wouldn't mind knowing what all that was about."

So Ray told me. In a nutshell, all three men were young coppers together before the war. Joe and Hallows were serious about the job but Boardman, who was a few years older than the other two, had allegedly joined the force as a protest against his old man not giving him enough responsibility in the family business - but really to escape service in the approaching conflict. While Joe heeded the call to battle, Hallows stayed behind to begin his rise through the ranks. Boardman too remained in Mellish until the fighting ended and then quickly quit the force to rejoin the family firm. And when his wife died suddenly, he started to court Marjorie who, as far as anyone knew, was still officially going out with Joe.

"And that's why the skip's got an outsize chip on his shoulder about the other two," said Ray draining his mug, "although if you ask me, he got a much better deal when he married Rose. She's ten times the person Marjorie is."

I was tempted to quiz Ray on how he had reached this intriguing conclusion regarding the second Mrs Boardman, who'd seemed to me a perfectly respectable woman. But before that, I needed an urgent answer to the biggest question of all. I stared hard at Ray.

"In your opinion," I asked, "would Joe have taken Boardman just then?"

Ray grinned and surprised me with his answer.

"I wouldn't like to bet on it, Frankie. Boardman may look like a barrel of lard but he's a really hard and vicious so-and-so, as many in the town can testify, and don't forget Joe's got his gammy leg. Whatever the outcome though it would have been one hell of a scrap."

The image of the mayor angrily seizing his terrified bruiser son by the throat suddenly came back to me.

"So not only does Joe have a terrible time in France and comes home half-crippled, he gets shafted by those who stayed behind?"

"Spot-on," said Ray. "It took him years to get over all that and become the little sunbeam we know and love today."

If he ever did get over it, I thought, recalling Joe's night-time rantings as Rose slept on serenely beside him.

"Has Joe ever mentioned someone called Freddy?" I asked as casually as I could.

Ray shook his head. "I've never heard him talk about anyone called Freddy. Who is he?"

"I don't know. Someone from the war perhaps."

"In the four years I've worked with him Joe's hardly mentioned what happened to him in France. But …"

"But what?"

"Well I've pieced together the few things he told me with what other people have said."

"And?"

Ray hesitated and then sighed.

"I shouldn't be doing this and it's probably not relevant to what's going on now."

"It might be. Who knows, it could actually hold the key to the murders."

There was a pause, filled with the screaming of a five-year-old as his exasperated mum boxed his ears for an unknown crime.

"It was something about Joe's unit taking down a German sniper and everything going to … you know what. And that's all there is."

I stared at him.

"You must have more than that."

"Not really. As I said, Joe's hardly opened his gob about it."

"Was it the sniper who got Joe in the leg?"

"Yeah but Joe was lucky. Before that the Jerry had managed to wound another lad and kill Joe's best buddy."

"Gibbo," I said, recalling Olly's mocking words which had so enraged Joe the other night in his kitchen.

"That's right, the sainted Corporal Gibson. You seem to know more than me. Oh, and I forgot to mention that Joe's CO then shot the sniper who managed to fire back and kill him."

"Phew, that turned into a jolly day out."

"Too right," Ray muttered, "and the most ironic thing …."

"Is?"

"…that Joe was a sniper himself."

"I never knew that."

"Best shot in the regiment apparently. He won cups for it. But you'll never see any on display in his house, if he even still has them."

I tried to weigh up this unsettling nugget of information but could make little of it. The events in northern France had become a bit clearer though. Three dead including the German, plus our sniper Joe and another soldier wounded. Yet the only thing I could be absolutely sure of was that the one person who'd emerged unscathed was Olly. And look how he'd ended up.

"Nothing else?" I asked. "Joe wasn't Monty's double as well, was he?"

Ray stroked his chin.

"Not that I'm aware of. But I do know that when he was up and walking again, he got himself seconded to the British Field Security Police. Ended up as an investigating officer on Airey Neave's staff at the Nuremberg Trials. You've probably never heard of Neave. I hadn't."

As a matter of fact, not only had I heard of Major Neave but had actually encountered the slippery so-and-so as the war drew to a close. However, as it related to a classified matter, I decided I wouldn't mention the meeting to Ray. I shook my head noncommittally.

"So maybe Joe was affected by what he saw and heard at Nuremberg."

"I doubt that," Ray replied with a shake of his head. "Joe told me that the Nazi High Command reminded him of a gang of retired ironmongers who'd been caught pants down in a brothel. He was definitely not impressed! Where were you in the war, Frankie?"

"Here and there. You?"

"Too young. I even missed Korea. Did my National Service in Catterick."

"Probably a bit safer than Korea."

"You've obviously never been to Yorkshire," Ray said with a grin.

"You should be a comedian."

"Somebody should."

"Hmmm. Now what about the latest message from our madman?"

I noticed Ray hesitate for a fraction of a second.

"It's best you show me if you want my wife to work it out."

Ray sighed and took a folded photo from his pocket, showing the murderer's most recent communication. There it was; the same type of envelope with Joe's name on it. The message read, "Saints Alive! Sam, Alan, you've gone mad. Sex to heaven."

"No idea who Sam and Alan are," said Ray. "Or what drove 'em bonkers."

"I'll wager they're not really relevant, or if they even exist," I told him, copying the message on to a paper napkin. "But we'll see what Nancy comes up with. Thanks for the drink."

I handed the photograph back to Ray and was about to get up when he put his huge hand on my arm.

"Would you stay a bit longer?" he asked with a frown, "I really could do with your advice. I'll get some more teas."

"My shout," I insisted and, while the bored looking girl behind the glass counter was pouring the drinks, I wondered what Ray was about to reveal and whether it concerned Joe. When I returned with the teas, he was biting his lip and fiddling with the frayed end of his tie. Like his boss after the dust-up with Boardman, he looked for all the world like a naughty schoolboy. Just Raymond!

"The thing is," Ray blurted out before I'd even sat down, "Jenny's in the family way."

Holy Virgin Mary so he *had* been a naughty boy!

"She told me the happy news last night," he groaned, "what should I do Frankie?"

How the bloody hell would I know? My three kids had all been (more or less) wanted and above board.

"I take it 'Daddy' isn't aware of the situation?"

"Christ almighty, no. He doesn't even suspect …"

"… that you're 'stepping out' with the apple of his eye. If you don't mind me asking, does she want the child?"

Ray slumped down into his seat.

"Jenny does want kids," he said with a sigh, "but not yet. She wants to go to uni and qualify as a doctor."

"This needs sorting out quickly then."

"Problem is, as I'm sure you know, abortion is illegal."

"So is homosexuality," I replied as witheringly as I could while whispering, "and I'll bet there was none of that at Catterick."

"Good point," he agreed, "but that doesn't make our problem any easier. I mean, where would we go?"

"I know where you shouldn't go. To any of those back-street butchers."

"You're right. I've arrested more than one."

"Scrape a couple of hundred together any way you can and get her to a decent clinic in London. But do it as quickly as possible. Things'll only become more risky as time goes on."

He groaned. "It's a real mess, isn't it?"

"Yeah and it's your mess so it's down to you to clean it up."

Despite my uncompromising tone, I felt desperately sorry for both of them. It also angered me that they would be forced to sneak around like criminals when their only offence was falling in love.

"Look," I said, tentatively putting my hand on Ray's arm, "If you like I'll get Nancy to have a word with you both. See what she can come up with. And no, I won't tell Joe - or Chief Inspector Hallows."

He gave me a weak smile.

"Thanks, Frankie. You're a sport."

"You're welcome," I replied, "and for the record, if you'd done that to my daughter, I'd shoot you."

"If I'd done it to your daughter, I'd load the gun for you," he groaned, "but thanks anyway."

The café was nearly full by now. Crikey, these people had only just finished breakfast at their digs but were already tucking in again. For some reason it made me feel hot and irritable but I managed to bid Ray a civil goodbye and headed straight for the theatre, a full two hours before the time Nancy had decreed I should be there.

As I walked, I reflected that even if Hallows did find out that one of his officers had impregnated the apple of his eye, he'd be hard put to react as murderously as Nancy's Dad did when she eloped with a comedian. That fellow had absolutely no sense of humour.

It wasn't yet eleven when I arrived at the theatre to find that the only person there was William Pitt, who greeted me with a surly nod as he swept the stalls. Having put the matter of Ray and Jenny to bed for the time being - so to speak - I was free to spend the next half hour in my dressing room turning over the deepening mystery of Joe's connections to the killer.

Reluctantly, I prepared to face up to a thought that my brain had been trying and failing to bat away. Could it actually be him? Apparently, he hadn't been at home or at work when the first victim was murdered. Ray had confirmed as much. And when Wilf and I were attacked, Joe had turned up after Ray arrived and reckoned he hadn't seen the killer in flight. Well, he wouldn't have would he if he were the madman himself? But then there was the way the attacker moved - with a lot more speed than Joe dragging his shattered knee surely possessed. He did have the same deep blue eyes though and was about the right height. He would have had chances to commit the third murder too and actually had a motive for the fourth, although exactly what hold Olly exerted over him was still unclear. Obviously, Joe could not have killed the little rat and strung him up in the short time he was out of my sight. Yet he might have done it earlier and then deliberately led me there. But again, why? All at once I felt angry and guilty that I was even having these thoughts. Joe was an upright citizen, model husband and good copper. He could no more be a deranged killer than I. And yet! He had been through the mill during wartime like many others who were reduced to gibbering wrecks. Conflict leaves its scars on the mind as well as the body. As my battle-hardened younger brother always said, it never really leaves you.

The whole business was tying me in such knots that I was actually relieved when Pitt bobbed his fat head round the door without as much as a knock.

"That mad bat on wheels wants a word with you," he said, and would have left it at that if I hadn't intervened

"Hold on a second, William," I said jumping to my feet. "Any clues about where I can locate this deranged mobile rodent?"

He gave me his usual look; a mixture of annoyance and contempt.

"She's on stage, making more work for me as usual."

Evidently that's all I was going to get as Pitt closed the door without another word.

I had half a mind to ignore our creepy caretaker's exasperatingly cryptic comments but curiosity got the better of me and I wandered down the corridor. At first I thought that Pitt, in an uncharacteristic moment of whimsy, had tricked me as none of the stage lights were on and the only illumination came from a couple of dim bulbs in the wings. But then I saw her at the front of the stage, idly dangling her roller-booted legs over the edge of the orchestra pit. As I stepped on to the stage, she turned to me and smiled.

"Frankie! I thought Bigfoot hadn't given you my message."

I grinned at this (very apt) characterisation of the caretaker from one of my best pals in our little troupe. Dorothy Burgess had been a showbiz friend for years.

"How do, Dot. Would Pitt the Welder not let you put the lights on?"

Dot grinned back at me.

"Even he's not that tight - or stupid."

She explained that she was practising in the near dark so the moves would be even more automatic when she was on a brightly-lit stage.

"You've not done too bad over the past six weeks from what I've seen."

"Yes, but you won't have missed that the other two, Roz and Betty, are just kids and a lot fitter than me. I'm not getting any younger, Frankie."

"You and me both, Dot."

I'd first met Dot just before the war during a short season in Redcar. At the time she was a little saucepot, the youngest member of The Rolling Hills, a three-woman skating troupe led by the redoubtable Freda Hill. Freda and her sister Kath were long retired but Dot had kept the group's name going.

"People always have a bit of a laugh about it," she'd told me over a reunion beer or two when I'd first arrived in Mellish.

"So what can I do for you, Dot? Apart from switch the lights on."

"It's maybe what I can do for you, Frankie. Listen to this."

Apparently, after a quarter of an hour going round in circles, Dot had stopped for a smoke in much the same position, legs dangling over the pit, when she noticed someone was up in the circle.

"So this bloke, and it was a bloke but don't ask me to describe him, hasn't noticed me. He goes to the front, crouches down and …"

"And?"

"And he's hidden by the balcony so I can't see what he's up to. But about a minute later he's up again so I shout 'are you having trouble, mate?' Well, Frankie, he bloody well froze!"

"He obviously hadn't spotted you."

"Too right. But when he realised someone else was there, he got out pretty sharpish."

"Say anything?"

"Not a word the whole time. I thought it was right odd, especially with what happened to poor old Wilf."

"Yeah, you were right to mention it. I'll get one of the detectives to have a word with you. Did you notice anything odd about this guy? Maybe his eyes."

"Yes I did. *And* I saw he had three gold fillings, two at the front and one at the back … for goodness sake it was nearly dark in here."

I shrugged and Dot smiled.

"Sorry, Frankie, I shouldn't be making fun of it. I know what happened when you tried to help Wilf. You're a brave, brave lad."

Luckily, the semi-darkness meant she couldn't see me blushing.

"Well, I should get me skates on, so to speak," Dot said as she wobbled to her feet. "Maybe we'll see you at the pub some time."

"Yeah, if the missus lets me off the leash."

Dot rolled gently to the middle of the stage and turned in a sharp pirouette.

"When you tell the police about this, make sure it's that nice big young lad who interviews me and not the miserable old bugger."

Back in the dressing room I barely had time to raise a smile over Dot's description of Joe before an even more miserable face blighted my day. Barney shambled in and pulled up in amazement at seeing me there a full two hours before we were due on stage for the matinee. But he quickly recovered and seized the opportunity to go over the new routines one last time. In truth, I was glad of the extra rehearsal time because I knew from experience that, half an hour before we were due on, he'd withdraw into himself and clam up until he burst onto the stage as The Lord of Misrule.

The first stage of this faintly disturbing transformation having duly taken place, I quickly applied my make-up and phoned Ray about what Dot had told me. Then I hurried off to watch the opening acts, including the very impressive Rolling Hills, from the wings, both to give them my support and to gauge audience reactions. And what a crowd - a full house no less! It was clear that the killing spree had not put people off coming to the show. On the contrary, our absence had truly made their hearts grow fonder. Of course, as Ray had speculated, that could change if the killer turned his twisted attentions away from vagrants and hustlers to guests in the hotels and boarding houses. But for now, like the good northerners they were, they wanted value for their money and were determined to enjoy themselves come what may.

We were due to wind up the first half and as Tommy Sacks the Prince of Wails had almost completed the mangling of his final song - this town was overflowing with foul murder - my partner appeared next to me.

"It's packed out," I told him under my breath. "Nancy's on the front row as well."

I didn't expect an answer because Barney had fully entered his trance, but I did want him to be aware that if he entertained ideas about going rogue, the presence of my wife - his agent - should at least give him pause for thought.

Watching Nancy enthusiastically applauding Tommy Sacks took me back twenty years to the first time she'd seen me on stage, with The Crazy Gang at the London Palladium. It was the same night we'd ended up in my hotel room, the first time we'd …

"Those terrible twins, Frankie and Barney!"

"Come on, slowcoach," shouted Barney, slapping my bum as he rushed past me on to the stage, totally ignoring The Prince of Wails who'd been good enough to give us the big build-up.

"Cheers, Tom," I muttered as I sprinted past him and promptly shunted straight into the back of Barney, who'd stopped dead.

"Whoa, Frankie, I reckon we're in the wrong place here," he exclaimed, gazing beyond the footlights with wide-eyed, exaggerated amazement.

"How come, Barney?" I replied rubbing my nose and following his gaze, desperately hoping this unscripted intro was not going to end with me scraping yet more chucky egg off my face.

"Didn't that yellow-bellied swine who killed our great pal and war hero Wilf boast that he'd have everybody in the town cowering in their digs?"

Quite apart from the fact that the killer uttered not a word while I fought with him for my life, Barney was taking a bit of a liberty calling Wilf his mate. However, having seen how expertly he could manipulate an audience, I was willing to go along with it.

"I do believe he did, Barney."

Barney stared back at the expectant faces and slowly shook his head.

"Well, somebody forgot to tell this cussed lot."

There was silence for a couple of seconds then a great roar of approval went up, mixed with a gale of cathartic laughter which only increased as a straight-faced Barney began to yell back at them.

"No, no, you're in deadly danger. Hurry up back to your digs at once. Do you hear, all of you get yourselves under those sagging bed frames right now!"

Barney was just following the old showbiz maxim that the best way to get an audience onside is to stroke their egos while making them laugh, but all the same it was gratifying to discover the tactic still worked. After that, they were putty in our hands.

And despite this unscripted start, Barney stuck faithfully to the routine we'd agreed with the laughs generously divvied up between us. And what laughs! They hardly stopped during the full thirty-minute act, even when one of our victims, called up from the audience, got mighty stroppy with me, a ding-dong which almost came to blows.

It is with some humiliation that I must admit to the lion's share of the blame for what happened. The hook had been

Barney's idea and in the month we'd been performing together, my skill at wielding it had vastly improved, and a good job too. I recalled with shame that in the first week I whipped the false teeth from a woman's mouth - top and bottom set together - which would have counted as a magical feat had I not merely been trying to tap her on the shoulder. Although the fiasco had raised easily the biggest laugh we'd had in our four weeks of performing, I was aware that the situation was far from satisfactory and had therefore been practising furiously. At first glance the hook, all twelve feet of it, looked lightweight and easy to handle as it was coated in plastic; in fact it was fashioned from ash, one of the hardest woods, which made it quite heavy and difficult to manoeuvre. However, I'd developed one or two decent techniques by now and it was nothing for me to hook someone off the stage without even looking when I got the signal from Barney. Sadly, my burgeoning over-confidence and the fabulous response we were getting led to a degree of slackness on my part. So, instead of justifiably hooking off the latest offender - he *was* murdering The Old Rugged Cross after all - I tapped him on the shoulder and, when he turned in surprise, poked him in the eye. That wasn't the finish either. As the victim doubled over in pain, I somehow got the hook stuck in his shirt collar and half strangled him as he came lurching offstage, to the noisy delight of the audience. This fellow, a bar-room bruiser by the look of it, was unfortunately seriously unamused by my ham-fistedness and less-than-fulsome apology. Well, it had been funny and I couldn't conceal a smirk.

"You clumsy idiot, you half strangled me," was his mildest comment as he threateningly clenched his huge fists. By now we were in the wings, which was lucky in one way because the audience couldn't see what was going on, but less fortunate for yours truly as there would be no witnesses when *he* throttled me. The issue was resolved, however, in a sudden and surprising manner. Our creepy caretaker William Pitt materialised as if from thin air and squared up to the fellow. Who checked out his prospective opponent and took a step back. While the guy was big, Pitt was a full head taller.

"Now then, wack," Pitt bent down to whisper in the bloke's ear, "I've gorra sweeping brush here that'll fit most anywhere."

He waved the broom menacingly at the man, who took another backward step.

"So stop spoiling everyone's enjoyment or I'll shove it where the sun don't shine. Now get back to your seat, start laughing and don't stop 'cos I'll be watching you."

Whether out of shock, fear or both, my erstwhile aggressor quickly did exactly as he was told. With a nod of gratitude to Pitt, I bounded back on to the stage just as the next sap was entering from the opposite wing. In an inspired move I hooked this chap off by his waistband before Barney had even introduced him - he wasn't the only one with the ad-libs. Even better, as the guy flew across the stage towards me, he had the good grace to hold his throat in mock terror and roll his eyes as if being strangled, which raised a mighty laugh. His reward was to be escorted by me back to centre stage where I laid the hook down in front of him and bowed in mock supplication. We then let him sing his song, I Parted My Hair in the Middle, all the way through, to the delight of everyone as he was surprisingly good and could easily have given that prize boob Formby a run for his money.

It was a triumph, evident not only from the gales of laughter and applause sweeping over us but also from the gentlest of taps on my back that Barney gave me as we exited. It was the first time he had shown even the most basic appreciation of my skills. Much as I didn't care for the guy, at that moment I felt as if I'd been crowned the most popular boy in school. This euphoria lasted precisely up to the point where Barney closed the dressing room door and turned on me in fury.

"You've not been practising, you stupid dolt," he yelled with such force it made me jump. "How many times do I have to say it, that hook needs careful handling. You just about got away with it today but it won't be long before you actually take someone's eye out. And that, I assure you, will not be funny."

Well, I hadn't exactly been expecting a gold watch and the freedom of the municipality, but this was too bloody much. So I let him know it.

"You little shit," I growled, grabbing my truculent partner by the lapels and swinging him into the wall. Now it was my turn to lay down the law.

Yet, where I'd expected fear in his eyes the expression reflecting back at me was one of sardonic amusement. It was only the second time I'd seen Barney smile and it shocked me so much I released my grip.

"Good," he said with a nod of satisfaction, "at least it shows you're half-serious about the act."

I half-seriously considered battering the priggishness out of him, but the moment had passed and he was already rabbiting on about a change he wanted to make to the second part of our routine, which would provide the show's penultimate section. It was as if the previous exchange hadn't happened and I had no choice but to go along with both his sudden switch in mood and the amended routine, which was more wordplay than slapstick. I suppose it was meant to show off our versatility. Which it did forty-five minutes later. As Barney had confidently predicted the audience lapped it up and we were given a rousing send-off, aided and abetted by bill topper, BBC radio crooner Ronnie

Hallworth, who unexpectedly wandered on to the stage and called us back for a couple of encores.

Some top-line acts don't appreciate the lower orders getting too much applause but old Ronnie wasn't like that. After all, it suited him if the audience were in a good mood when he made his appearance.

As we came off after the second encore, I remarked to my stage partner that Ronnie's action had been generous. Barney just stared steely-eyed at me and replied, "*I'll* ... we'll be top of the bill by the summer's end."

With that gracious assessment he stomped off towards the dressing rooms. And, in a way, he was right. Before summer reached its conclusion, his routine would indeed prove to be an amazing solo spectacle - although perhaps not quite in the manner he'd envisaged.

I stayed in the wings to watch Ronnie's act, partly because he'd been decent to us but mainly to see if Mr Shelvey was going to say something at the end of the show.

Sure enough when the general applause had died down, the theatre owner joined the acts on stage and made a proud and passionate speech praising our skills and the audience's fortitude in the face of our recent terrible hardship.

He didn't elaborate but everyone knew what he meant and gave him - and by extension themselves - another rich round of applause.

It seemed to bring the company together too, apart from one of its number. After I'd finished shaking hands and patting backs, I returned to the dressing room to find that Barney had already departed; to where, god only knew - or cared.

Accordingly, when my wife bobbed her head round the door, I was more than ready for a chat about how things had gone. But even Nancy didn't hang around, promising we'd talk after the second house. Then she scarpered as well.

Show business can be a solitary life even on stage in front of an audience of hundreds. When the lights dim and there's just you and a surly caretaker, ever ready to brandish his broom in an unsettling manner, it becomes even lonelier. So I used the odd and indeterminate period between matinee and second house to do what I often did; go for a walk in the desert, where I had one of the more surreal encounters of my life.

A short tram ride did more than take me to the sand dunes at the southern tip of the resort; it immediately transported me back to my childhood and our family's annual holiday. Thinking back, it amazed me that our lord and master Joshua even allowed us the luxury of a week's break - after all his estate contained so many important chimneys up which young 'uns needed to be stuffed. But allow us a yearly holiday the old skinflint did, and it was here that our Dad Les would encourage me, my brothers and sisters to fly his home-made kites while he was digging elaborate bunkers and planning mammoth games of hide and seek. These memories came tumbling back as I tramped through the strength-sapping sand and sharp-edged marram grass which, as I no longer wore shorts, could not whip my legs to bits - one memory I was content not to relive.

The purpose of this jaunt, clearing my head of its clutter, was accomplished as I took in deep lungfuls of clean air. It was a lovely day, the clearest of the summer so far and I had little difficulty picking out the major peaks of Snowdonia looming up well beyond the Mersey Estuary.

The clear late afternoon skies and uninterrupted views briefly allowed me the illusion of complete solitude and it therefore came as something of a shock to discover I was not alone after all.

As I walked, I noticed a figure had appeared behind me in the middle distance; a man for certain but I could be no more positive than that about him or his intentions. What I did know was, as I tramped on increasing speed all the time, that he was nevertheless gaining on me. I'd now gone at least half a mile from the tram terminus and was a fair distance from the coast road. If this chap meant me harm, I was a sitting duck.

But of course, I told myself that was all perfectly ludicrous. The murders had spooked everyone and had us all jumping at our own shadows. Like me, this fellow was merely taking advantage of the fine weather to clear his lungs and noggin. Nonetheless, I quickened my pace even more and struck out right to get nearer to the road and safety.

Cresting the summit of a particularly huge dune, I glanced back and saw to my alarm that the pursuer, dressed in a smart overcoat and homburg hat, was now a mere one hundred and fifty yards away.

Matters then took an even more sinister turn as I watched the man reach into his overcoat, draw out what looked like a weapon and point it at me. Wise old soldiers - and I include myself in their ranks - don't generally wait for the bullets to start flying before hitting the dirt and half a second later I was rolling over and over until I reached the bottom of the giant sand hill. Breathless and afraid, I quickly sat up and looked around. In front of me, maybe a quarter of a mile away on the crest of another particularly high dune was a concrete pill box, one of a string built to guard the area during the war. Maybe I wasn't thinking straight, but I reasoned that somehow this bit of coastal defence might provide the cover needed to give me a chance of disarming my pursuer.

Sweating mightily, I discarded my light jacket and hurried on, panting across the heavy sand. It brought to mind basic training at the start of the war and by the time I staggered up to the bunker I realised how out of condition I'd become. Dodging round the far side, I cautiously peeped back round the way I'd come. No sign of my pursuer. Maybe he'd parked his murderous thoughts and gone home for tea and stickies. Or perhaps, I reflected, my imagination had gone haywire and he hadn't been chasing me after all.

I sat back wheezing for another minute and was about to peep round again when I heard the muffled sound of footsteps and of sand being displaced. Someone was labouring up the dune towards the pill box and if I didn't move I'd be a sitting duck.

Taking a deep and anxious breath, I began to creep quietly round the structure in a clockwise direction. When I'd reached a quarter to, I heard him pass on the other side. Without hesitation, I hauled myself on top of the half-buried bunker, flew across it and launched myself at my stalker. He didn't even have time to look up as a flying Funnybone smashed into the small of his back, knocking him flat and pushing his face into the sand. And before the man could even think about reacting, I'd twisted his right arm up his back and quickly reached for the weapon inside his coat. However, to my bewilderment, what I pulled out was not a gun but a telescope. Furthermore, the mystery stalker seemed to know me.

"Heaven's sake, Francis," he spluttered testily into the sand. "Are you trying to suffocate me?"

I quickly jumped up off his back and flipped him over. Even though the sandy mask that smeared his features should logically have added to the mystery of his identity, there was no mistaking who this fellow was; the very last person in the world I'd expect to find flat out on a Lancashire sand dune.

"Philby!" I cried. "What in the devil's name are you doing here?"

Kim Philby sat up and began to fastidiously brush the sand from his eyes and nostrils. It was obvious he was seething but making a considerable effort to control himself.

"Well, Francis, this is a f...f... fine greeting for an old chum who just wants to say hello again," he stuttered.

"Well then, you shouldn't have chased me. For goodness sake you must know there's a murderer on the loose."

"A murderer?" Philby looked shocked. "Good lord, no, I hadn't heard. And I wasn't *chasing* you, old fellow. I just wanted to talk. I saw you get on the tram and by the time I'd followed in my car and parked up, you'd hared off like you were pace-making for Roger Bannister."

Philby stood up and brushed the remaining sand from his overcoat and trousers. He was much as I remembered him from our last meeting five years before, but I couldn't help noticing there were fresh networks of burst blood vessels around his nose and eyes. He picked up the homburg and popped it on after smoothing back his hair. Now he looked much more like the debonair Kim of old. He even smiled for the first time ... and handed me the coat I'd discarded.

"You appear to have dropped this in the confusion," he grinned. "Doesn't quite look ready for the jumble sale."

"Oh, er, thanks," I replied, accepting the garment.

"How are you, old friend," he said, extending his right hand which I grasped firmly if unenthusiastically.

"I'm fine now. But what on earth are you doing here? I thought your lot broke out in a rash if you ventured northwards of Potters Bar."

"Let's get to the road and stroll back, eh, chatting as we go," he said, putting an arm round my shoulder.

As we made our careful way down the sand bank, Philby explained he'd just sailed in from Ireland where he had been visiting a friend. Disembarking at Liverpool docks, he'd noticed a playbill for the Coliseum and, on a whim decided to motor up the coast to Mellish and catch my act.

"After all, you did once promise me complimentaries, old fellow," he reminded me as we reached the road and shook the remaining grains of sand from our clothes.

Yes, I thought, that was before you set that mad Russian goon on me, recalling with an inward shudder my fight to the death with an armed intruder at home in London just after the war.

Although I'd said nothing, Philby read the look on my face.

"I say, old fellow, you're not still blaming me for the Bilyatov nonsense, are you?" A decade on and he even remembered the evil thug's name! "I can assure you that his presence in your home was just terribly bad luck."

"It was for him," I answered noncommittally, recalling how by sheer good fortune, the Russian had finished up dangling like a puppet, fatally skewered on a particularly sharp coat hook.

The reply seemed to amuse Philby because he gave a sharp laugh and clapped me on the back.

"It certainly was. The burglary rate in Earls Court went down to zero after you'd dealt with him. I think that was the last time we met wasn't it?"

I studied him closely to see if he was joking or just being the usual slippery Kim. But, judging from the jaunty air of his walk, he must have believed what he'd just said. I therefore took great pleasure in puncturing his self-satisfaction.

"But, Kim, you surely can't have forgotten New York in 1951."

He paused for just a fraction of a second before reassuming his nonchalant air.

"Of course not, old fellow, how could I forget you poking a gun into my back in ... Central Park wasn't it?"

"Times Square, actually. And it was just a toy pistol. Hopalong Cassidy, if memory serves."

I'd been ordered to bring it home as a present for Julia, who was going through a tomboy phase.

"It was a joke," I reminded him.

"Yes, most amusing."

So funny in fact that he'd actually pissed himself.

I became aware that the weather had suddenly turned as cool as the atmosphere between the unsmiling Philby and me. The sun was now obscured by angry looking grey clouds. I looked back and saw that the view of Snowdon and its surroundings had been completely obliterated. Moreover, it was clearly raining across Merseyside.

Philby turned up his collar, which made him look even more like the double agent he undoubtedly was. I'd long ago worked out that he'd been in Manhattan to consult his Russian handler over the imminent unmasking of Donald Maclean as a Soviet agent. At the time he'd told me, in apparent despair, about their mutual friend and dissolute diplomat Guy Burgess's unbalanced antics in Washington which included driving around madly while drunk and assaulting a traffic cop. These were all ruses to get Burgess, a former lodger of mine, sent straight back to Britain where he could organise Maclean's flight to Moscow.

I expected Philby to quickstep around the subject or talk about something else - Surrey's chances of retaining the County Championship perhaps - but what he actually said astounded me. With a smile, he nodded and replied, "Ah yes, that was such a strange time. Lots of talk about a Third Man."

"Indeed, I wonder who that could have been." My voice dripped with irony but Philby affected not to notice.

"Oh, I know full well the identity of the Third Man," Philby continued, with a supercilious glance at me.

Crikey, was I about to elicit a confession that the combined efforts of MI5, MI6 and the mother of parliaments had failed to extract? I struggled to remain calm.

"The Third Man, Kim? Who would that have been?" I replied as coolly as I could.

He stopped suddenly.

"Why," he said with a smile, "it was you, old fellow."

I too came to a dead stop. Surely the man could not be serious! This was akin to being accused of child abduction and rodent abuse by The Pied Piper of Hamelin.

"What on earth are you talking about?"

"Well, old b...b...boy, correct me if I'm wrong but was it not you who drove Donald and Guy down to Southampton for the start of their ... great adventure?"

"Blimey how did you know about that?"

I paused while he smiled to himself, no doubt under the impression he'd trapped me into a confession. In fact, I was just thinking things through. And then it came to me. Of course, Anthony Blunt was leaving Maclean's house in Kent that evening, as I arrived with a limping Burgess (the reason he couldn't drive the car himself).

"It was Dandini who told you, wasn't it?"

"Dandini?" Philby appeared puzzled for a moment and then gave another wicked smile. "Ah your little nickname for Tony. Very good!"

"Yeah, when he saw me he nearly soiled his silk drawers."

"Oh dear," Philby intoned, "he must have swallowed something disagreeable."

"Yes," I replied, "there's definitely something very disagreeable about all this. In fact, I'd be perfectly happy to take the whole thing further."

Philby's smile disappeared. "W…w…what do you mean, my dear fellow?"

"That we should test your Third Man hypothesis … in court perhaps."

Now Philby looked positively alarmed.

"I mean you were ever so keen for that MP, what was his name …"

"Lipton," he spat almost without thinking. "Marcus bloody Lipton."

"… to repeat his allegations about you outside the protection of parliament. Come to think about it, I wouldn't mind putting the whole business in front of a learned judge myself. Then we could determine which of us is more likely to be Harry Lime; me or you!"

Philby took off the homburg and wiped his forehead with a clean white handkerchief, which the increasingly strong wind nearly snatched out of his hand.

"You forget," he said, replacing the hat and regarding me with cold eyes, "that the Foreign Secretary gave me a clean bill of health."

"Kim, you may have been able to pull the wool over the eyes of that dodderer Macmillan. And you seem to have convinced the world's press - no doubt after plying them with gallons of your mother's best sherry - that you're a fellow to be trusted. But let me tell you, *old boy,* I saw the newsreel of that performance and I thought you looked thoroughly shifty - guilty as hell in fact. So go on, sue me as well."

He took a step forward and I actually thought he might go for me. But Philby was a desk jockey not a field agent, and if he had turned nasty, I would have taken great delight in stuffing his head back into the sand. Philby obviously sensed this and gave what he must have imagined was his most relaxing smile. It made him look constipated.

"I was making a joke, old fellow. I never had any notions about you being the Third Man. I realise that it was Guy who asked you to drive them both to Southampton. Why, you probably didn't even guess what they were up to, did you?"

I didn't reply. I wasn't going to let him know that I'd worked out exactly what Maclean had been doing. Philby waited an age for my response but, when he realised this was fruitless, he took off his hat once again and smoothed his hair. He must have had some notion that this bestowed upon him a devil-may-care air. What on earth did they teach them in the KGB?

"I mean," he added, once more carefully putting the hat back on his head, "Guy won't have told you anything, I know that." There was a short pause. "He didn't, did he, old man? Maybe a final message to good old Blighty?"

I stared hard at him for about five seconds before exploding into laughter.

"So that's it," I hooted as Philby tried hard not to look like a prim schoolmistress confronted by the naughtiest boy in the class - a role he'd have had years to perfect with Guy Burgess as a close pal. "Yes, I see it all now."

In truth I saw merely what was peeping out above the surface but it would do for the time being.

"I'm not sure I understand you, old man," Philby mumbled.

"Let me enlighten you then, Kim. Your chums in the Kremlin are desperate to know why Burgess tagged along for the ride."

I watched his face carefully and there it was; the merest flicker of an eyelid proving I'd hit home.

"I mean the jig was up for Maclean. It was the Tower and quite possibly the rope for him if he'd not scarpered."

"We don't generally hang traitors in this country anymore," protested Kim.

"No, you're right, we give 'em the run of Buckingham Palace instead. Maybe Maclean should have hung around for tea with the Queen, although I'd guess he was expected for a nice cuppa from the KGB samovar. But blundering old Burgess! What possible joys could miserable Moscow hold for him? And that …" I grabbed Philby by the throat, "… is what your Soviet paymasters have tasked you to find out isn't it? Why someone who had no need to defect took that final irrevocable step. Was it just silly drunken Guy acting on a whim? Or was he going to some lengths to disguise that he was in fact a very clever triple agent."

Philby began shaking his head vehemently.

"You don't know how wrong you are, Francis."

His voice was thick, whether with anger or the pain of being half-throttled I didn't know and couldn't have cared less. Instead I released my grip and gave him a history lesson.

"Let me tell you what actually happened on that evening in May 1951."

"If you really must, old boy," Philby replied, affecting a nonchalance immediately betrayed as false by another flickering of those ferrety eyes.

So I explained how I'd driven the pair to Southampton and Burgess had gone onto the ship, the Le Havre-bound SS

Falaise, to see his mate off. And how I'd quickly bribed a steward to lock them both in Maclean's cabin until the boat was in the middle of the Solent.

There was a gasp.

"I ...d...d...don't understand."

And from Philby's anguished expression I could see that he genuinely did not comprehend. Ignoring him, I went on to explain that even though I'd signalled from the dockside that the departing Burgess faced the gallows if he ever set foot back on Blighty, I actually had nothing on him. In fact, if he'd taken the return crossing, he could quite easily have brazened things out.

Philby was silent for a good half minute before he looked at me in extreme puzzlement.

"Why on earth would you do such a thing, Frankie?" he said. It was the first - and last - time he ever called me Frankie.

"Because, Kim, at the time I was under the impression that Guy had set that murderous Russian goon on me."

Philby looked exasperated.

"Guy had absolutely nothing to do with ..." He stopped but it was too late.

"No, *he* didn't have anything to do with it. You more than anyone know that."

"I'm sure I have no idea what you're talking about."

"Of course you don't, old man. Anyway, all a long time ago now isn't it? But let me spell one thing out in the here and now. Your Soviet chums don't know what they've got with Burgess and they're nervous. So it's your task to put them straight."

"I still don't understand."

"OK understand this. If anything other than advanced alcohol poisoning should strike down Guy, then *I'll* name you as the Third Man and furnish proof. And if by then you've buggered off to Russia - as I know you inevitably will - I'll unmask Blunt as the Fourth Man. And if he's already minced off to cooler climes then I won't hesitate to name Cairncross as the Fifth Man."

Again Philby's eyes flickered momentarily with surprise and I knew that my hunch about the civil servant John Cairncross - and it was based on nothing more than a couple of things Guy had said while he was off his head with the booze - had hit the target. For the second time in a few minutes I dissolved into laughter.

"You really should brush up on that tradecraft, Kim. Then you'll be better placed to 'persuade' me to have a go at naming the Sixth and Seventh Man. A pair who've done their utmost to make this country a complete laughing stock."

This time Philby made no pretence at obfuscation.

"Laughing stock? The Sixth and Seventh Man?" he spluttered, bewilderment mixed with astonishment. "Who on earth are you talking about?"

"Isn't it obvious? When I've finished with your gang, I'm finally going to deal with Mike and Bernie Winters!"

The punchline duly delivered in a manner even Barney would have been proud of, I strode off leaving Philby with his mouth opening and closing like a fairground goldfish, a job well done. Although I was relieved that I would never again share oxygen with Guy Burgess, I couldn't help but retain some affection for the old scoundrel. He'd brightened up many a dull post-war evening during his brief stay chez-Funnybone, usually by falling down stairs or tumbling out of a window. And you could always rely on him for an entertaining string of near-the-knuckle anecdotes before that day's alcohol intake finally poleaxed him. Furthermore, as I'd always suspected and Philby had just inadvertently confirmed, Burgess had nothing to do with the murderous attack on me by the Russian goon I'd left dangling from the back of our study door.

However, when I tried to feel rotten about my part in Guy's flight to Joe Stalin's palace of varieties, I couldn't quite manage it. I just hoped that my response to Philby, when it reached the Kremlin sooner rather than later, would be enough to deflect any triple agent suspicions away from Guy and give the old fellow a bit of peace in his final few Moscow years. On the other hand Philby, like his exiled pal the traitor Maclean, could go hang; I would have willingly pulled the lever on both of them.

I glanced back to check if Philby was still gawping like a guppy but to my surprise he was nowhere to be seen. His sudden disappearance unnerved me, and the ten-minute stroll back to the tram terminus became a series of jittery ducks and feints while I scanned the dunes in anxious anticipation of a sudden assault - as Philby no doubt anticipated I would. However, no toxic blow dart or poisoned umbrella attack rendered my return ticket superfluous and I was soon back on the Mellish-bound tram breathing a lot easier. I did note, however, that the small car park next to the tram terminus contained no vehicles at all. So, unless Philby had run the mile or so back across the dunes at Roger Bannister's pace, it was clear he was lying. Someone else had given him a lift there - someone who had probably been tracking us as we walked.

That unsettling thought cast a cloud over my journey but thankfully by the time I was back in the theatre dressing room all thought of tossers and traitors had disappeared from my mind as I prepared for the evening show. Which went even better than the matinee, in that I didn't cripple anyone with the hook and raised a fair number of laughs off my own bat. It was just like old times and, to make things all the more peachy, Nancy gave

Barney and me her full attention after the show and made the effusive remarks with which I opened this long and eventful chapter. Even better was the news that she had been on the phone all afternoon to bookers from Blackpool who'd promised to be in the audience some time very soon.

"This could be a whole new start for my boys," she said excitedly, which even prompted the merest ghost of a smile from Barney.

9
Magic Numbers

I SHOULD HAVE SLEPT well that night. I had put one over on that utter rotter Philby and drunk in the sincere, if unaccustomed, praise of my dear wife who now lay snoring like a porker beside me in our hotel room. But it wasn't Nancy rattling the windows and drawers that was murdering my prospects of sleep. I had, after all, been married to the woman for twenty years and was well used to the racket, even though Nancy stoutly denied she ever made a sound. No, what was keeping me awake was straightforward worry; about Joe and more particularly my cousin Rose.

I'd swept over every angle of the four murder cases and finally decided that, even though circumstantial evidence might finger Joe as the killer, logic and common sense said this was rubbish. Why on earth would an experienced detective intent on a murder spree leave so many clues pointing to himself as the culprit, including cryptic notes with his name on them? Unless previous traumas had rendered him deranged enough not to care. Blimey that was a definite poss … no, come on, Frankie! Let's rule out that sort of rot once and for all. But even if the notion of Joe as a murderer was obvious nonsense, it was equally clear that something in his military past held the key to what had been happening. And while I wished Joe no harm, I definitely didn't want the affair to give my poor cousin any more grief. I therefore needed to accompany her hubby on a journey into his past to see what light it threw on the present. And that possibly dangerous mission needed to be undertaken very soon.

If thoughts of murder and madness weren't disturbing enough, the matter of Barney reared up suddenly to further compound my anxieties. For sure, the whiffy weasel had been good as gold and willing to be generous about my part in the double act while headmistress Nancy was on patrol. But the flames of Barney's ambitions burned fierce and bright and it was only a matter of time, I reasoned, before I'd be the one on top of the bonfire.

Then there was Philby, a master of cunning and deception. What if Guy Burgess's motives for fleeing eastwards weren't Kim's primary reason for his unsettling appearance in the sandhills of Mellish? Maybe there was an altogether more diabolical scheme afoot. What if the master spy was in league with the murderer and planning to do me a … Fortunately at that very point I must have drifted off into slumber and would no doubt have remained in that happy state until late morning but for a sharp, unwelcome dig in the ribs.

"Franco!"

"Uuuurgh."

"Wake up. I've got it."

"Well don't give it to me." And I turned over.

"You absolute ass!"

Nancy didn't sound at all pleased, even though by rights it should have been sleepy old me on the warpath.

"I'm talking about the answer to the fifth clue," she said.

Nancy switched on her bedside light, cruelly forcing me to abandon all ambitions of sleep. She sat up, eyes gleaming so brightly, I knew it would be unwise to suggest we leave the matter until a more suitable time - such as the middle of next week.

"Do you not want to hear it?"

"Go on then. After all, I am wide awake."

"You don't look it."

Best not to disagree.

"I'm all ears, darling."

"The answer is the Battle of Almansa."

"Never heard of it. Can I go back to sleep now?"

"No! Didn't they teach you anything at that school of yours?"

"Not much. Apart from what would happen if you didn't wash down there."

"Well, at my slightly more prestigious school ..."

Slightly! It was a young ladies' academy in Switzerland, for goodness sake.

"... our history tutor Madame Fourais taught us that one of the skirmishes in the War of the Spanish Succession was the Battle of Almansa. Seventeen oh something."

Mention of that particular campaign reignited a memory from twenty years before. It was my first visit to Chartwell, Winston Churchill's impressive pile down in Kent, where I'd unwisely gone toe to toe with the old rascal in a drinking session. Finding myself somewhat befuddled, I'd staggered off in search of the bogs and ended up in Winston's study gazing stupidly at proofs for his latest book about the most distinguished Churchill up to that point.

"Ah yes," I told Nancy with some authority, "the War of the Spanish ... whatever you said. I believe that was the finest hour of John Churchill, First Duke of Marlborough. An ancestor of my old mate Winston, who coincidentally had his own finest ..."

"Stop name-dropping, Franco," snapped Nancy. "It's unbecoming."

Her mention of such one-upmanship triggered another memory of that Chartwell visit. Winston had been swanking on to me about the best man at his wedding being some Lord Snooty character so far up the social ladder you could barely see his posh backside.

Fortunately, I was able to trump his Duke of Wherever with the name of the best man at my own wedding - King Edward VIII. OK, it's not something you'd shout about these days, what with one thing and another, but in 1936 when Nancy and I got hitched, he was the monarch and that was as good as it got.

Of course old Winston didn't believe a damn word of all this bragging. And my absolute insistence that it was the truth - plus the half gallon of Johnny Walker Red Label he'd shifted - helped drive the man so far off his trolley that he actually ended up phoning the King. At two o'clock in the morning! Whereupon Winston was given a well-deserved earful of flea before being informed that yes, His Britannic Majesty had acted as best man for an up and coming star of the music hall and what damn business of his was it anyway? Thang yow and goodnight!

All of which went unremarked as I reckoned Nancy probably wouldn't care for any more blather about my drunken one-upmanship with the previous Prime Minister, or indeed of our own unconventional wedding. It was much safer to stroke her ego.

"So enlighten me, oh wise one, as to how you unravelled this fiendish puzzle."

"The whole thing was dead easy really," Nancy replied with her customary modesty. "It's simply an anagram of the names Sam and Alan as denoted by the word 'crazy'."

"And the bit about Saints Alive?"

"God, Franco, I can't be expected to know everything! Get your best buddy Conrad on the job next time you see him."

Which turned out to be sooner rather than later.

Next morning Nancy ordered a bleary-eyed me down to breakfast while she stayed in the room making more phone calls to the bookers who were interested in our act. When she finally appeared downstairs, I was already mopping my plate with the last of the fried bread, whereupon she ordered me to brush my teeth and get my coat so she could drop me off in Mellish before driving on to Blackpool.

Protests about being denied my life-sustaining daily intake of toast and marmalade were brushed aside with the observation that my career would look like burnt toast if she was late for the meeting she'd just organised. Besides, she'd make sure the rest of my breakfast didn't go to waste. Twenty minutes later she'd dropped me outside Mellish police station and was roaring away Tower-wards to flatter a bunch of showbiz impresarios. On reflection, perhaps I should have mentioned that she had a large smear of my marmalade across her chin.

Having grown accustomed to the idea of playing the wise elder statesman, I dropped in to the nick, keen to give Ray more fatherly advice about the delicate situation regarding his boss's daughter. But Ernie the desk sergeant informed me that Detective Constable Parr was busy down at the coroner's office and that Joe was nowhere to be seen either. So I nipped into the library next door for a constructive half hour, followed by a stroll to Joe's on the off-chance I'd find him skiving.

I still had a key and was about to slam the door behind me when I caught Rose's unmistakable giggles coming from the lounge. Crikey, I thought, Joe *is* bunking off. And he's finally learned how to tell a joke! I closed the front door quietly and was about to burst in on them when a male voice, not Joe's, completed the punchline of a gag, definitely not one of Joe's because Rose exploded with laughter. As the door was slightly open, I looked through the narrow gap and observed my cousin sitting on the sofa smiling adoringly at Conrad Ross, who was sitting next to her. Oh bugger, not again! On top of everything else, I really did not need this.

I backed away slowly, hoping neither had spotted me, opened the front door quietly, then slammed it shut and stomped back down the hall.

"Hullo, it's only your friendly neighbourhood merchant of mirth," I boomed in my best impersonation of Charlie Laughton as Henry VIII.

Throwing open the lounge door, I observed that Conrad was still on the sofa but Rose had somehow re-materialised in Joe's chair by the fire.

"Oh, sorry, am I interrupting something?"

"No, no, Francis" Rose said, quickly jumping up and wiping her hands on her faded blue and white gingham apron. "Conrad's only starting work late today so he thought he'd call round and pick up his saucepan. You remember from the other night."

"I remember we were all well sloshed but, despite all that, the divine taste of Conrad's goulash is engraved into my memory. Thanks again, matey."

Conrad acknowledged my compliment with a modest nod.

"My sincere pleasure, old fellow. But I didn't only come round for the saucepan."

This threw me and it obviously troubled Rose too, judging from the way she pulled at her pinny.

"No," Conrad continued, "I called in to drop this off."

He stood up, reached into his jacket pocket and took out an envelope which he handed to Rose with a gallant little bow. Surprised, she tore it open and pulled out a greetings card.

"It's just a small message of good luck for when you start your new job. It is tomorrow?"

Rose smiled and nodded.

"Thank you, Conrad. How kind and thoughtful of you."

Bugger again! This fellow was a good sort, I'll grant you, but he was making the rest of us look like unfeeling northern clodhoppers.

"Er, yes, Rose," I quickly interrupted, "I was going to get you a card too but I …"

"Didn't?" volunteered Rose helpfully after my agonisingly long pause.

"I suppose that's about the size of it."

"Well thank you for the thought, Francis - however belated it was."

I suppose I deserved that but it was delivered with such a beautiful smile that I didn't feel too embarrassed. Instead I reflected that I'd never seen Rose look happier. Even on her wedding day.

"I'd better get going," said Conrad. "Computers won't programme themselves. Well, they will one day but probably not before this afternoon."

"Actually, Conrad," I interrupted, "before you go can I pick your brains about the most recent clue?"

"Of course, old fellow. Fire away."

I told him about Nancy's brainwave concerning a little-known battle and the mystery that remained about the phrase. 'Saints Alive'.

"So there *is* a Battle of Almansa?" mused Conrad. "I'd played and played with that word but couldn't get anywhere."

"Oh yes," I said authoritatively. "It was an action during the War of the Spanish Succession between Philip V of Spain and his Habsburg rival Archduke Charles of Austria. If memory serves, Almansa took place on April 25th 1707. Charles finished runner-up."

That half hour in the library had definitely not been wasted.

Conrad nodded, evidently impressed, and Rose had the decency not to look too shocked at my uncharacteristic feat of scholarship.

"The only thing that's missing," I added, "is this 'Saints Alive' thingy."

"What if …" said Rose, suddenly snatching a small book from a shelf in the sideboard. "What if," she added flicking through the slim volume, "it refers to the Saint's Day corresponding to that date? Ah yes here we are. April 25th, St Mark."

"I'm not sure …" I began.

"St Mark the Evangelist's Church! You know, the one on Antcliffe Road."

I didn't but it made as much sense as anything else.

"That's brilliant, Rose," said Conrad with a smile which slowly turned into a frown. "But I really don't see any modern military connection in the clue."

Rose considered this for a moment.

"What if," she said for a third time, "it refers more to the function than the name?"

"How do you mean?" I asked.

"Well, you won't know this but St Mark's is the largest church in Mellish."

"And?"

"And it's the venue for the town's Remembrance Day service before everyone marches to the Cenotaph."

Conrad shook his head angrily.

"So this animal is about to defile a place of worship. Shame on him."

I nodded vigorously. "I'll echo that, Conrad, but although we know where he's going to strike and what time - 1707 or seven minutes past five - we don't know the exact date."

"I just might be able to help there," Conrad mused. "We could run all the numbers in the clue through our computer down at the university."

"Will they let you do that?" Rose asked nervously. "The people in charge."

"As 'the people in charge' are myself and my colleague Miles Paddon, I would have thought so - as long as we ask ourselves nicely. In fact, you could both come down and see the magic in action."

"What, now?" I said.

"No time like the present. I'll drive."

Rose shook her head sadly.

"I have to get the house straight before tomorrow. My new job, remember?"

"Of course. Silly me! How about you, Frankie?"

"Sorry I've got a matinee at two-thirty."

Conrad glanced at his watch.

"It's half-nine now. We'd be there well before eleven. A quick shoot round then straight back. And the Mellish public will still get their daily Funnybone fun ration."

"I don't want to put you to any trouble or get you the sack."

"As I said before, although I'm prone to doing silly things, giving myself the push is not one. And I assure you it's no trouble at all."

So, to quote Stanley Holloway, that was decided upon. Conrad gave Rose a quick peck on the cheek - for good luck he claimed - and grabbed his saucepan. Five minutes later we were already on the outskirts of Mellish, speeding south towards Altonford in Conrad's nippy Triumph TR3 Roadster, air force blue like Nancy's Morgan. Conrad appeared as revved up as the car, emitting a constant stream of chatter about his life so far. How he'd tried to enlist in the RAF straight from King's College, Cambridge in 1939 but they wouldn't have him - under orders from the boffins who were setting up Bletchley and had already earmarked him for greatness. How he had played a (very small) part in breaking vital German naval codes under Gordon Welchman in Hut Six. How one day he would build a computer no bigger than a garden shed. It all sounded mad scientist bollocks to me but I had the good grace to smile encouragingly and the gumption to ask "Gordon who?" despite having met the chap briefly in 1942. Luckily Conrad didn't inquire about my war, which suited me fine.

His spiel and - thankfully - the car's speed slowed considerably as we hit traffic in the northern suburbs of Altonford. Yet we still managed to pull up outside the university's red brick main building at a quarter to eleven, and were in the corridor outside his department five minutes later.

"Here we are, the holy of holies," Conrad smiled, taking hold of the door handle. Then he paused.

"Listen, Frankie," he said, his smile turning into a frown. "If I'm going to get you back to Mellish on time, I'll have to see one or two colleagues pretty sharpish. Could you manage by speaking to Miles Paddon on your own?"

"Yes of course. He doesn't bite, does he?"

"Only if you touch something you shouldn't." Conrad grinned and gave a wink. "In you go."

He opened the door and gave me a gentle shove - into what appeared like another dimension. So immediately fascinating was this arcane new world that I didn't even notice the door close behind me. I was in a high-ceilinged windowless room about thirty feet square, the walls of which were lined with what looked to me like sophisticated equipment from a telephone exchange. Instead of wires, however, there were hundreds of glass tubes sticking out at right angles. In the centre of the room obscuring the far wall was a large light green metal box about eight feet high and fifteen feet wide into which was built a desk with a large keyboard. And sitting at the keyboard with its back to me was a figure in a faded grey lab coat, looking for all the world as if he was about to play the opening bars of All Things Bright and Beautiful. The figure did not turn when I entered the room but continued to tap the keys on what looked on closer inspection like a large typewriter, all the time gazing up at a board of flashing lights. There was a low continuous hum which got louder as I approached the figure.

"Hello," I said, "I'm a good friend of Conrad … er."

Damn it, I'd forgotten his surname!

"Not that good a friend apparently," the figure drawled while continuing to type. "It's Ross by the way. Conrad Ross on the off-chance you wish to become even better acquainted."

"That's it. Conrad Ross. He said you might be able to help me."

"Are you the funny man?"

"Yes, I suppose I am. Frankie Funny … er Francis Thirkettle."

The man spun round in his swivel chair and faced me. He had longish dark hair, with a grey streak swept back from his forehead, and piercing blue eyes that scanned me keenly. He was unsmiling.

"Looks like you're not too sure about your own name either! On the other hand, I'm pretty certain that I was christened Miles Paddon."

"Pleased to meet you, Miles," I said, holding out a hand. Paddon didn't take it, instead indicating a chair about ten feet away.

"Drag that up and sit on it so you don't do any harm. We don't want any vacuum tubes blowing, do we?"

"I should say not," I agreed, quickly grabbing the chair and squatting down next to Paddon. "Nice place you have here."

Although I was mildly irritated by the man's attitude, it probably wasn't advisable to grab him and give him a shake. Who knew what damage even a stray vacuum tube could cause when it blew?

"Huh, not nice enough," replied Paddon. "Manchester's set-up is ten times the size of this. Mind you they have ten times the resources."

"Sounds like you'd rather be there than here."

"You don't know how right you are. And all things being equal, I would have been there instead of festering in this backwater. Alan promised me as much in 1939. But … well things happen don't they." Suddenly Paddon sat up straight. "So let's see it."

"What? Oh right, the message."

I passed him the piece of paper which contained the Almansa conundrum.

"We think we've got a time and a place but what day? That's the problem so Conrad thought you could, er, feed it into your computer."

"I could do that," Paddon agreed. "But I could, er, also do this."

For a moment I thought he was going to screw up the piece of paper and toss it aside; or maybe eat it. This oddball had wrong-footed me from the moment I'd stepped into his den so nothing he did or said would have been particularly surprising. Instead, he picked up a pencil from the desk and quickly began to scribble on the paper.

"Sixteenth of June," he said, tossing the pencil aside after just a few seconds.

I was astounded.

"How do you work that out?"

"It's basic binary. Look, you simply swap the first two numbers …"

"I'll assume you're not lying," I said quickly, gratified to see disappointment flash across Paddon's features. "So, the sixteenth of June, eh? That's only four days from now."

"Is it?" said Paddon turning back to his desk. "I wouldn't know. But I do know that Ross must be losing whatever touch he had if he couldn't work that one out. Mind you, maths was never our 'free thinker's' long suit. Bloody crossword puzzler!"

Blimey, there was something going on here and no mistake. Time to shake things up a wee bit.

"So you were both at Bletchley?"

Paddon swung back to face me. "How the devil does someone like you know about Bletchley?"

Again I was gratified to see him thoroughly rattled.

"Oh you'd be surprised what 'someone like me' picked up during the war, Mr Paddon."

Including a dose of cupid's measles, I might have added, although definitely not in Nancy's hearing.

Paddon shook his head as if remembering something disagreeable.

"I was at Bletchley very briefly and that's where I renewed my acquaintance with Conrad Ross. You see we'd …"

"… been at King's together, I know."

Paddon stared at me.

"Indeed. And I suppose I should be grateful he remembered me ten years later when he was setting up this place."

This last comment was so heavily laden with sarcasm that it was clear gratitude was not the first emotion Paddon felt when considering his work at Altonford.

"So you'd both have worked on …" but I didn't get any further as at that moment Conrad breezed into the room.

"I told you they'd be short meetings," he said to me. "I hope Paddon's been keeping you entertained with his bumper fund of hilarious anecdotes, Frankie. Perhaps you'd consider teaming up on the stage with him. You could call yourselves Funnybone and Funny Cove."

Paddon shook his head again.

"It's not me who's the comedian. Call yourself a code breaker and yet you couldn't work out a primary school problem."

"Ah, you got it as well, eh? The sixteenth of June. A gold star for you, prof."

Paddon and I stared at Conrad.

"Sorry, Frankie," he said sheepishly. "I wasn't a hundred per cent sure but I'm relieved Charlie Chuckles here has confirmed it."

Regarding Conrad with utter disdain, Paddon said, "Your killer, whoever he is, reckons he's being really clever and wants you and the police to think it too," he said. "But anyone with a quarter decent education could have put this clue together."

That left a disturbingly high number of suspects, including the angriest people in all of Mellish and probably beyond, Ken and John Boardman. Plus Joe. Who would have to hear about this right away.

"Thanks very much for your help, Mr Paddon. I think it might be time to get back, Conrad."

Without a word, Paddon turned away from us and once more began to tap on his keyboard. It would be some time before I spoke to him again but when I did a lot of things had become much clearer - and many lives changed.

Forty-five minutes later, and true to his word, Conrad dropped me back at Mellish police station, by which time I was seeing Miles Paddon in a considerably different light.

On the journey back, Conrad had explained that after university, where they'd moved in totally different circles, they met up again at Bletchley briefly in 1941 before Paddon had decided code breaking wasn't close enough to the action for him and joined up. That was the first surprise. I told Conrad I hadn't exactly envisaged his lugubrious colleague as a man of action. That was when he unveiled his second shocker. Paddon, he revealed, was on the last troop ship into Singapore in February 1942 as the Japanese invasion began, and spent the rest of the conflict as a prisoner of war.

"Paddon doesn't give much away as you might just have noticed," Conrad told me as he drove. "But you don't have to read too far between the lines to know the Japs did more harm to him than any of us will ever know. Then when he got home there was, as he saw it, the great betrayal."

Apparently, it had taken Paddon two years to recover from malnutrition, shake off his more persistent demons from having been a PoW and return to a state where he could just about function properly. Unfortunately, by then things had moved on, including the world of magic numbers. Computer genius Alan Turing had assembled his own team at the Victoria University in Manchester and that mob did not include Paddon.

"You see," Conrad had explained, "when we were both at King's just before the war Alan Turing was the brightest star at the university. Paddon idolised him and was ecstatic when Turing apparently told him that he'd be part of his big plans for computer science when the war - which everyone knew was inevitable - was over. But it never happened."

I remembered our conversation a few minutes before.

"He told me he'd planned to work in Manchester with someone called Alan. Do you think that maybe Turing harboured a grudge about Paddon leaving Bletchley and joining up?"

"Maybe," said Conrad deep in thought. "I never got to the bottom of why he did that. But it was more likely that during the post war launch work Paddon was in no fit state for anything. And when he'd recovered, the ship had already sailed and there was no place on board for him."

"Did Paddon hold that against Turing?"

"He wasn't happy, I know that. But I do remember him shedding a discreet tear when we heard that Turing had killed himself a couple of years ago, so I'd reckon he still held him in high esteem. By then of course he was firmly established here. And even though he's an awkward cuss, we're all jolly glad to have him around."

I could have told Conrad that the feeling wasn't exactly mutual but I held my peace about Paddon's dissatisfaction with where he'd washed up. I also kept quiet about another matter - a blue-eyed recent addition to my mental list of suspects.

For the second time that day I watched a blue sports car roar away after it had deposited me in front of the police station.

This time, however, I found Joe was in his office and, surprise, surprise, he didn't bite my head off or snap that I should have told him all I knew the day before yesterday. He listened more or less respectfully as I outlined Nancy's and Rose's theories about the clue, and finally the contribution from Paddon and Conrad. I did mention that Conrad had called round obviously without adding that I'd caught him on the sofa with Rose.

"So, Saturday at St Mark the Evangelist. That's good work, Francis."

"Nowt much to do with me, old lad."

"But you helped pull all the strands together. And in police work that's often half the battle."

"Well, if you say so."

"I do indeed." There was a slight pause. "By the way, what was Conrad Ross doing at our house?"

Always the bleedin' copper! Good job I was ready.

"He'd come for his saucepan. You know from the other night when he made that tremendous, what's-it-called, goulash."

"I wouldn't know. You'd guzzled it all by the time I got home. Remember?"

"There *were* others involved, Joe," I told him, unhappy at his suggestion that I was some sort of selfish glutton. However, I couldn't resist turning the knife.

"And take it from me, while goulash might sound like something you'd find on the bottom of your shoe, it tasted like heaven. Goodness knows where Conrad got all that lovely meat."

For a moment Joe stiffened with a look that suggested he might set off on this line of inquiry like a dog after a rabbit. Or a copper chasing a spiv. It might also have occurred to him, however, that meat rationing had ended two years before. There was one more thing.

"Did Ray tell you about what Dot, our skater, saw in the theatre?"

"He did, yes, and we've had a poke round upstairs in the circle. Nothing conclusive I'm afraid but I'll mention it to Hallows along with everything else you've just told me. And then we'll draw up a plan to give this character the reception he deserves on Saturday."

"What, a kind of church social?"

"It won't be very sociable, I can assure you."

I mused on this not so vague statement as I left the station. Under normal circumstances even the suggestion of police brutality appalled me but in this case I would happily take one arm or leg if Joe and his boys decided to give our bright-eyed killer an early Christmas bump - and then sling him from the top of the church tower. It was the same in wartime. You'd never consider murdering a defenceless man - until you'd seen the horrors he'd inflicted on your good pals.

These dark matters were dominating my thoughts to such an extent that I failed a) to notice the portly fellow entering the station as I was about to leave and b) to moderate my response as we collided.

"Hey, watch yourself, Porky," I muttered, "… oh sorry, Alderman, I didn't realise it was you."

"Frankie! How you diddlin'?"

Ken Boardman held out his hand, which I clasped with as firm a grip as I could muster. He wasn't going to crush my pinkies this time. But no doubt because I was now a pal, Boardman didn't seem in the mood for any more displays of one-upmanship. Au contraire, as he never would have said, the mayor was bonhomie personified which made me rather relieved I'd met him on his way in - and that apparently he hadn't caught my 'porky' comment. However, I reckoned that after another half an hour discussing the latest murder and mayhem with Joe and Hallows, that expansive smile would be turned on its head.

All of a sudden Boardman slapped me hard on the back and for a moment I feared he *had* heard my insinuation that he was a barrel of dripping. But it was merely his clumsy way of showing appreciation

"Well done, buddy, for getting the theatre reopened. It's just what the town needed."

"Mr Shelvey's idea, Ken, not mine," I wheezed, struggling to get my breath back.

"Ah but you put in a word didn't you."

"Maybe the odd adverb."

The mayor nodded before reaching into his inside jacket pocket. He pulled out an embossed card and handed it to me.

"As promised," he said, smiling as he handed it over. It was a ticket to a boxing tournament due to take place that evening.

"Remember, the sportsman's dinner I mentioned? Our John's fighting that bloke who boxed for Olympic bronze in 1936."

Under normal circumstances I could have dreamed of nothing more agreeable than watching the boorish John Boardman cut down to size by an expert. Unfortunately, it wasn't to be.

"That's really thoughtful of you, Ken, but don't forget I'm working tonight. We do two shows a day, you know."

"And damn fine efforts they are," said Boardman, nodding emphatically, "but we don't get to the meat and potatoes of *our* fine show until late on. So, when you're done with the mirth-making get yourself over to Collins Hall sharpish and prepare to be amazed by a feast of fisticuffs."

I'd estimate that ranked somewhere alongside "Our Crust is a Must" down in the slogan relegation zone. But I was prudent enough not to say so.

"OK, Ken. I'll try my very best. And thanks."

"No problem. Your mates'll be there too. Joe and his buddy."

This came as no surprise to me as both, particularly Ray, would relish seeing Boardman junior getting his clock cleaned with neither of them having to lift a finger.

Taking leave of the mayor, I strolled across to the pier and realised that I hadn't thought once about my troublesome stage partner all day. This unnerved me somewhat. I was all too aware that when I took my eye off the ball, every manner of indignity tended to come barrelling my way, courtesy of Barney.

However, the smelly twerp was on his best behaviour and the show passed without incident. Furthermore, Nancy greeted us in the wings with the news that a veritable posse of Blackpool bookers - well a couple at any rate - would be running the rule over Monday's show. While welcoming the news and praising my talented missus to the rafters, I judged it wasn't quite the time to mention that I was determined to snare a killer at church on Saturday evening. And if that interfered with our last performance before the talent scouts saw us then that was how it would have to be.

"That's tremendous work, Nance. Eh, Barney?"

"Yeah great."

"You're very generous, boys," said Nancy, overlooking my stooge's lack of effusiveness. "Just polish the act till it gleams."

The evening show did shine brightly too and left me admitting - albeit reluctantly - that Barney was indeed a talented so-and-so. He made no attempt to freeze me out either and our routines hummed along, delighting the packed galleries. Those bookers were in for a treat on Monday evening.

For once I was quicker away from the theatre than Barney - which really disconcerted the troublesome tick - and within ten minutes of taking our final bow I was barrelling through the front doors of Collins Hall. Rushing down the corridor, I almost collided with Ray coming out of the toilets. He hadn't seen me as he was still fiddling with his fly buttons.

"What's up?" I asked. "Forgotten where you put it?"

He looked up in surprise and I saw that his eyes were barely half-focused. One, two or maybe even more drinks had evidently been taken.

"Oh hullo, Frankie," he grunted. "No, I can remember exactly where I put it. That's the problem."

I let the comment pass as I hadn't the stomach for a discussion on the rights and wrongs of his and Jenny's situation. Instead I decided to raise the tone.

"Has Boardman junior had his face turned inside out yet?"

"No," said Ray giving me a lop-sided grin, "you're just in time. In fact, here he is - everyone's favourite spoilt brat."

John Boardman, clad in an expensive looking silk dressing gown and shiny brown boxing gloves, had appeared from behind a door further down the corridor, accompanied by a small wiry fellow in his late fifties who I took to be his corner man. They strode through the entrance to the main hall, where I could hear the MC introducing John to raucous applause and cheers. When that lot had died down, another door opened and out stepped his opponent who looked a full head shorter than John. This guy had nobody with him and wore only frayed shorts and a faded blue vest. Yet, despite his threadbare appearance, it was obvious that he was still in superb condition for a 38-year-old.

"Brian Pike," Ray whispered almost reverently, although why he was keeping his voice down god only knew as the place was a bear pit. I noticed that Boardman's opponent, now in the main hall, was getting even louder cheers than him.

"Fought for Olympic middleweight bronze in Berlin," added Ray. "Unlucky to lose on a split decision by all accounts."

Following the boxers into the hall, we were immediately assailed by a tidal wave of barely suppressed male violence, very little of which was coming from the ring, where Boardman showily practised a few routine shadow moves. Pike, in contrast, stood still and impassive, while being urgently lectured by a muscular chap who looked as though he could be the fighter's brother.

Ray led me to a table where Joe was sitting alone. The whole place was laid out café style as if to lend an aura of class to the proceedings; but that hadn't really worked. Men with wild hair, flushed faces and unknotted bow ties were on their feet shouting and gesticulating at the fighters - and all this before a punch had been thrown. Even the occupants of Ken Boardman's table next to the ring, all local worthies, looked as if they'd been on a three-day bender. There were no women to be seen apart from the young waitress who took my order for three pale ales with commendable efficiency. I sat down and nodded at Joe, who leaned over.

"This guy Pike, he's a steel worker from Sheffield."

"I know. He looks like he forged himself."

Joe smiled, something you didn't often see.

"He'll have the skin off young Boardman's face," he told me before leaning back smugly, ready for the action. Which didn't look as if it was far away.

The referee, a smallish fellow with the dishevelled look of my old chum Robb Wilton, was going through the rules with the boxers, both of whom appeared totally disinterested in him and his message. Pike presumably because, after a couple of hundred amateur fights, he was well acquainted with the Marquess of Queensberry's do's and don'ts; and Boardman, judging from the deranged performance I'd witnessed in his home gym, because he had no intention of abiding by them. He looked as if he couldn't wait to get on with causing mayhem, staring threateningly down at Pike, whose face remained blank as a sheet of glass. When the ref had finished his talk, the boxers turned and went to their corners.

"Ding, ding," Ray muttered excitedly, "all aboard for a rough ride."

To be fair to Boardman, the first two minutes of the opening round appeared to go his way. Pike seemed initially unwilling to get mixed up in any close-up brawling and was continually forced on to the back foot by John's windmilling haymakers which, while looking the part, didn't connect with anything much at all. However, it soon became evident that the more experienced fighter had merely been weighing up what his opponent had to offer as, in the final minute of the round, he clicked into gear. Two crisp jabs and an uppercut suddenly had Boardman puffing and blowing as he staggered backwards. With fifteen seconds to the bell, and expending little discernible extra effort, Pike doubled his opponent up with one in the guts before dropping him to the canvas courtesy of a vicious right cross to Boardman's chin.

The place erupted. Some, mainly younger, spectators were screaming that the stomach punch was low which it clearly wasn't. The rest were simply excited that the bout had caught fire.

Boardman was on his feet at eight, but still groggy, and the ref took the remaining few seconds of the round to establish that he was able to carry on. Boardman then tottered back to his corner, flopped on to the stool and began drinking desperately from a taped water bottle.

"John Floored-man," said Ray with a sparkle in his eyes and I wondered how long he'd been saving that one up. Whatever, it couldn't hold a candle to my Ken 'Bard Man' line.

"The demolition has begun," said Joe without much relish. "Whose bright idea was it to put a boob like Boardman in with a proper fighter?"

Of course, he knew full well that the brains behind this mismatch was sitting at the VIP table, smoking a big fat cigar and cracking dirty jokes with his posh pals. Meanwhile, in between struggling to take deep breaths, the son glared down at his Dad. In the other corner Pike sat almost still; his only discernible movements were slight nods of the head as his brother, or whoever he was, pointed out what Pike had been doing wrong. Which, to be fair, wasn't very much.

Boardman was lucky to kiss the canvas only twice in the second round and by the bell for the start of the third he was a sitting duck. Pike seemed a decent fellow and not one to draw out his opponent's agony. So, in that spirit of cordiality, he nearly lifted Boardman out of the ring with a savage left hook to the chin and that was that. Then the violence really started.

A table of five or six young bloods a few feet away from us began throwing out challenges to all and sundry and, when there were no takers, they turned on each other. One stocky young welterweight flattened a couple of his pals before leaping on to the table, scattering bottles, glasses and ashtrays. As he berated us all for cowards who hadn't the guts to take him on, I realised with a jolt that this caterwauling bruiser was actually the nice young chap from our local butchers who politely handed me Rose's weekend meat order after the matinee every Friday. I made a mental note never again to have a go at his black puddings.

Meanwhile, in the ring, the referee waited nervously to formally announce the winner while John Boardman stayed slumped on his stool, looking as if he didn't care if the whole crowd beat each other unconscious. In the opposite corner, a relaxed and amused Brian Pike chatted with his trainer/brother as if assessing the fighting merits of each brawler. It was significant that none of the crowd - even the butcher's attack dog - had jumped into the ring.

In the best tradition of coppers through the ages, the two at our table kept a keen eye on the mayhem while opting to let the participants punch one another senseless. Joe sat there impassively while Ray twitched, evidently more eager to sort things out. Finally, on Joe's nod, he leapt out of his seat towards the table of trouble where our butcher's boy was still gobbing on about how he'd dismantle anyone in the place, unwisely as it turned out. Reaching the table in three large steps, Ray simply lifted the meaty mauler into the air with one hand, dropped him to the floor and skimmed the unfortunate lad across the room into the far wall where he lay without moving.

"Right, you bunch of wankers," he told the rest of the battlers, "the two guys up there have put their bodies on the line tonight ..."

Ray curtly nodded towards John Boardman who gave back the ghost of a sour smile.

"... so sit down, shut up and let the ref get on with things. Or I'll turn really nasty."

Like good little boys the erstwhile bruisers sat down meekly as their leader limped back across the room, to be guided by Ray firmly into his chair. The referee was then free to announce the hardly shattering news that Brian Pike in the blue corner had won the fight by a knockout. Pike shook John's hand and modestly acknowledged the cheers.

As our peacemaker sat down, Joe leaned over to him.

"I think you're losing your touch," he told Ray, without the trace of a grin.

If John Boardman was grateful for Ray's intervention, he didn't show it, disappearing from the ring in double quick time. His Dad, however, was full of bonhomie, congratulating Ray with hearty slaps to his back. Brian Pike also came over and shook all our hands before being led away towards the dressing room in earnest conversation with the mayor.

"They'll be discussing his fee," Joe told me.

"Aren't they both amateurs?"

"You're dead right, Frankie" said Ray, "so I give you official permission to pop into the dressing room and confiscate Pike's purse."

"He might put up a bit more of a fight than young Gordon here," Joe observed, indicating the shamefaced butcher's boy, who was hovering by our table.

"Sorry Mr Trueman, Mr Parr … oh and Mr Thirkettle too," he muttered, "I think I got a bit carried away there."

"I think you got a bit thrown away, Gordon," said Joe, producing one of his extremely rare zingers, "but as long as our Friday meat order's packed full of nice lean cuts we'll say no more about it."

"You've no worries on that score, Mr Trueman."

The main bout of the evening was something of an anti-climax. The two light-heavyweights Gardner and Evelyn, who'd both boxed for England, were well-matched with Gardner getting the nod from two of three judges. This time everyone at the tables, particularly those around the ring, behaved themselves which I must admit I regretted slightly, as I wouldn't have minded seeing Ray wade in again. The technique he'd used to skim young Gordon across the floor like a paper plate was a thing of beauty.

However, as the boxers left the hall, I found myself becoming nervous and restless. The thing was, I knew that a packed event like this - there must have been around two hundred blokes in the place - would be a magnet for the killer. With Joe and other coppers plus the cream, if you could call it that, of Mellish society present, this grim showman would surely be unable to resist being there, laughing behind his hand at these worthies. Equally, of course, the killer could easily be one of them. I glanced at Joe chatting amiably to Ray and Ned Clarkson, who had been sitting at another table. Surely not, but ... Then over there was Ken Boardman, holding forth to the few members of his party who hadn't managed to beat it to the sanctuary of the bar to protect their eardrums. A blustering buffoon certainly, but still ... And, of course, I couldn't forget Boardman's son, comprehensively humiliated tonight, but obviously physically and maybe psychologically capable of murder.

It was while I gazed idly around the hall, half-hoping that the solution might suddenly land in my lap, that I thought I saw someone I knew, but couldn't immediately place. He was leaving the hall on his own and, as he disappeared through a far door I realised where I'd seen his unsmiling face before. I was fairly sure that it was Miles Paddon, Conrad's sidekick down in Altonford University's computer department. For some reason his presence unnerved me, and I dashed across the hall, keen to find out why he hadn't mentioned earlier that he would soon be in my neck of the woods. But at the entrance to the building there was no sign of Paddon so maybe it wasn't him after all. Probably as well because the last thing the town needed was yet another unstable character around the place.

10
Farewell to a Friend

FOR THE SECOND time in three days, again much to his annoyance, I was quicker off the stage than Barney. And before he could begin berating me for my awful timing, lax positioning and all-round crapulousness, I was already halfway out of the door. As I waved Barney a fond goodbye, I harboured a tiny sliver of hope that I wouldn't make the second house - because I would be far too busy frog-marching the newly-captured (by me) killer down to the … wherever they dealt with newly-captured killers. You may discern that my fantasy was still a work in progress.

Mind you, my smelly sidekick would have had a point. Since the day after the boxing brutality, I *had* barely been able to focus on such insignificant matters as punchlines and pratfalls. Even Nancy, never usually one to meddle in the nuts and bolts of her clients' routines, had shaken me awake early Saturday morning to give me the benefit of her expertise.

"It's the bare bones I'm worried about," she told me as I rubbed my newly-opened eyes in confusion. Bones? What on earth was she jabbering about? The only bones I'd seen were the ham ones handed to me with the rest of yesterday's weekly order by an unusually sheepish butcher's assistant.

I sat up straight.

"Look, Nance, if you have any complaints about the quality of Rose's meat order then take it up with the butcher himself. I for one am not risking life and limb by tackling a character who makes Rocky Marciano look like …"

"Franco, what in god's name are you burbling on about?"

"Well, I'm just saying …"

"Shut up and listen. I'm talking about the bones of the act. And lately, no matter how you look at it, Barney has been carrying you. You seemed hardly there yesterday evening."

"I have a lot on my mind."

"We all have things to worry about. But the majority of us realise that to function properly we must leave these concerns at the factory gate, in the office reception area or, when it comes to your case, in the dressing room."

Nancy had evidently rehearsed her spiel - something she clearly felt I'd been neglecting. And I couldn't deny she was dead right. All week I had been filled with equal amounts of trepidation and excitement over what would happen in St Mark's Church just twelve hours from now; so much so that my partnership with Barney seemed almost an irrelevance.

However, I was wise enough not to share that thought with Nancy - or Barney when we met up a couple of hours before the Saturday matinee. Good job too as he was still steaming about last night. Some rubbish about me having burst out of the cupboard on totally the wrong cue, thus cocking up his carefully choreographed mayhem. I say cupboard but it was more like a brightly painted upturned coffin if you can imagine such a thing. (Incidentally that simile, while perhaps not the best I've ever dreamed up, would prove all too sadly prophetic).

Anyhow, the cupboard had been part of the act for around a week ever since it arrived at the theatre, addressed to Barney. Apparently on his Blackpool jaunt, he'd been rescued from Frankie Driscoll's clutches by Mungo the Magician, a gloomy Scot - real name Graham Pettigrew - who was keen to recruit Barney as his new drinking companion. Whereupon, the bevvied-up pair had set about analysing each other's act or something because the upshot was that Mungo - Graham -

decided what Barney and I really couldn't do without was a brightly painted upturned magic coffin. Apparently, he'd grown tired of this part of his act and was keen to develop the bit where he sawed his partner's head off.

While thankful things weren't the other way round - the idea of Barney sharpening a saw on stage gave me the willies - we were still getting used to the new prop. I say 'we' but as you'll have divined it was actually me struggling to come to terms with what I was supposed to be doing. You see, Barney had had this bright idea that part of the act would consist of him becoming a magician with yours truly as his unlovely assistant. However (and here's the trick) Barney and I would turn out to be useless at the old magic and much enchanting hilarity would ensue. It sounded like a load of bollocks to me - the audience would actually be paying good money to watch two idiots cock things up - but the upshot was that it turned out to be rather funny. When I could be bothered to get things right! You see, everything depended on me emerging from the box at the most inappropriate moment. For instance, Barney would announce that he truly feared I had disappeared forever into the ether, whereupon I'd gormlessly stumble out onto the stage asking if anyone had seen my bike. However, I frequently tended to forget about all this and would emerge at totally the wrong - ie the right - time. In fairness I reckon these contortions would have taxed someone at the top of their game but for a fellow obsessing about catching a killer, well you get the picture.

I had hoped that the Saturday matinee would prove a turning point. And in a manner of speaking it did; I was worse than ever. Far from emerging at the wrong (right) time I didn't leave the box at all. Instead, in my eagerness, I managed to topple the whole thing over so the door was against the stage and I was firmly trapped. To be fair, Barney did turn what could have been a disaster into a comic triumph in which volunteers were invited onto the stage to give their opinion about how (or if) I should be rescued. But, even with laughter and applause ringing in our ears, I was keen to make another quick escape off stage. Accordingly, Barney was able to fire off only a couple of his savage barbs before I was racing away to keep my date with a killer.

In the event I needn't have bothered as my taxi was ten minutes late and it had gone 4.45pm when I arrived one street away from St Mark's Church. A quick glance round told me there was no-one about, but as I prepared to approach the church, the window of a dark Ford Pop parked across the road slid open.

"God's sake, funny man," a voice hissed, "why not parade up and down with a sandwich board and a megaphone. Get in. Quick!"

I hurried across and climbed into the back seat. Behind the wheel was Ned Clarkson sitting next to his boss Chief Inspector Michael Hallows, who turned to me in exasperation.

"What are you doing here? You could compromise the whole operation."

"Sorry, sir, but I thought I could be useful."

Hallows shook his head in annoyance.

"You'd be more use at home ironing. Just sit there and keep quiet."

Clarkson turned and began nodding severely at me like his chief. Yet I could make out the faintest trace of a smile on his lips. Just then a walkie-talkie radio that must have been on Hallows' knee burst into action. The voice was indistinct but Hallows definitely understood what was being said because he switched off the device and swore.

"You know how Brabourne was supposed to be watching the south door?" he barked at Clarkson.

"Al Brabourne, sir, yes that's the plan."

"Well he isn't there."

"Where is he, sir?"

"He's just arrested a pair of drunks for fighting on the prom."

Ned stroked his chin. "Couldn't he have left it to the uniforms?"

"Not really. These two hooligans were fighting him. The upshot is he won't be here in time."

"Sir," I butted in quickly. "I could monitor the south door."

Hallows turned to me and glared. "You're a bloody civilian. How will it look if this character kills you?"

"He didn't manage it the last time we met."

Hallows and Clarkson looked at each other.

"He'd be better than nobody, sir," said Ned. "I think."

"And don't forget," I reminded them, "that I did take part in undercover ops during the war … which, incidentally I'm not supposed to talk about."

Hallows looked as if he was wrestling with a particularly challenging philosophical premise. Or perhaps he was just constipated.

"Very well then, keep quiet and listen to me," he said finally, without smiling. "Get yourself round to the south door but for god's sake stay out of sight. There are officers on all the other doors and Joe and Ray are already inside waiting."

"I won't let you down, sir. Er, have you got a spare radio?"

With a grin, Clarkson handed me a whistle.

"If you see anything blow that like you're refereeing the cup final."

"And don't," Hallows ordered, "even think of tackling this character. You're a civilian and you're just there to keep a look-out."

"Righty ho, sir. You wouldn't happen to have a spare firearm about your person?"

Hallows' head nearly flew off his shoulders.

"What the hell have I just said? Just stay hidden near the door, and on no account follow him. Just blow the whistle when he's been inside a few seconds. We'll be the ones carrying weapons."

"I'd better get cracking then."

Clarkson pointed out of the car window.

"Go down that side street and turn left. The south door's about fifty yards further on. What you waiting for - an encore?"

Fat chance of one of those in the town showbiz forgot! I tumbled out of the car and sprinted off down the terraced street opposite, quickly arriving at another similar thoroughfare which appeared deserted. Around a hundred yards away to the left the red-brick tower of St Mark's loomed over the houses in its shadow. The south door turned out to be thirty yards closer to me than the tower and was guarded by gravestones. These were approachable through a lych gate and for just one moment the scene reminded me of my horse-drawn elopement with Nancy all those years ago. However, any smiles at the memory of her Dad going backside first over a wall quickly faded as I realised that the killer could actually be watching me.

Thankfully, as I cautiously approached the gate, there didn't seem to be anyone around. Then just for a second, I thought I heard something - maybe a door closing - in the far corner of the churchyard but when I spun round to look there was nobody there. I waited a full two minutes, taking deep breaths before opening the gate, sprinting across the lawn between the graves and dropping down behind one of the more imposing headstones. A few more seconds went by before I peered around the stone at the door, which was still firmly closed. A salty breeze rustled dried dead flowers in a metal vase by the grave next to me but apart from that there was hardly a sound.

    I glanced at my watch. Five minutes past, so just two to go before ... whatever was about to happen happened. I noticed the inscription on the neighbouring gravestone and drew a quick breath. It read 'Francis Thurston Taken unto God July 15th 1887 aged 56.'

    The similarity to my own name was unnerving. But at least if it were an actual augur, I reckoned that at forty-one I should be good for another fifteen years, like the Francis resting six feet below me. A sudden memory of the body of someone I'd briefly known floating gently away into the Med south of Salerno in 1943 made me catch my breath. That image faded and turned into one of Wilf wheezing his last breaths as a howling wind battered the pier outside. What the hell was this - all my bleedin' yesterdays? Next thing it'll be that mad Russian ...

    My reverie was shattered by two gunshots in quick succession from inside the church. Instinctively I glanced again at my watch. Seven bloody minutes past! Then came an unearthly wail - a human voice registering the deepest of pain. Sod sitting on my bum for a living! I sprinted towards the door while blowing three huge cup final-ending blasts on the whistle. For a couple of seconds the door refused to open but I managed to wrestle it ajar and dashed through the porch into the church. To be confronted by a terrible sight.

    Halfway down the aisle Joe was crouching by a prone figure which, as I approached, I recognised as Ray. A red stain was spreading slowly across the front of his shirt and he looked up desperately and fearfully at Joe, who seemed frozen to the spot. At that point there were what sounded like running footsteps up at the far end of the church near the door to the tower.

"I didn't see him, Frankie," Ray gasped before inclining his head towards Joe. "Go on, get him, skip," he added, his voice barely audible. "The others'll be here soon. Frankie, take my gun."

I picked up the weapon which lay by his side and, after a second's hesitation, followed Joe, who was already hurrying across the church towards where the footsteps had come from. As he pushed open a studded door, we were confronted with the stairs to the tower. Opposite them was a door to stairs down to the crypt. It was half open.

Joe looked at the flight to the tower and for a moment he seemed unsure of himself.

"I'll do the crypt," he said. "You watch nobody comes down from the tower."

"OK."

"And, Francis."

"I know. Don't approach him. Just blow my whistle."

"No. Shoot the bastard, first in the chest and then right between the eyes. Then do it again for good luck."

Well, there's nothing like good clear instructions, I always say. Joe took a surprisingly large torch from his coat pocket and set off slowly down the crypt steps while I moved away from the tower's spiral staircase back to the studded door and levelled my pistol at the bottom few steps.

Behind me in the church I could hear shouts and hurried footsteps, almost certainly Hallows and the rest discovering the grim truth of what had befallen Ray. Then I picked up another sound, this time from the tower. A footstep? A door slamming shut? It was too indistinct to tell. I hesitated; although I was armed, my orders were not to go looking for trouble. Just watch, wait and report. Oh, and pop one between his eyes if you get the chance.

My indecision lasted two seconds. With half a glance at the open crypt door, I began a slow ascent of the tower, fretting that every step could bring me face to face with the killer. An immediate consolation that I was left-handed and thus able to quickly aim around the curve of the staircase, lasted until I worked out that anyone up there would more than likely be right-handed and have the same advantage on their way down. In fact, the murderer was undoubtedly right-handed. I remembered the dexterity with which he'd flung the knife at me - only deflected by a celebrity's old cricket bat. If the killer's skill with a gun was equal to his knifemanship then I was in big trouble.

As I took each step slowly, leaning on the central column of the spiral for support and trying to stop my left hand shaking, I was once again forced to face the truth that I was out of condition. Sure, I'd been able to best Philby a few days before but this character was in a different league; if he got the drop on me, I was as good as dead. It was therefore with some considerable relief that I reached the top of the stairs without incident to find the door to the tower roof was indeed banging open and shut in the light sea breeze. I quickly checked the flat roof area but there was nobody lurking and I was congratulating myself on a job well done when sounds of an almighty racket came billowing up the spiral steps. Someone was yelling for help at the top of his lungs.

I took the stairs two or three at a time, bouncing off the wall but somehow staying upright. In no time I was outside the door to the crypt from where the pandemonium issued. As far as I could tell, it was Joe who was yelling for help. I hesitated a second, mindful that it could be a trap, but then pressed on down the steps. The crypt was in almost total darkness and my small hand torch hardly lit up a thing. However, I couldn't have missed where Joe was. Loud insistent cries led me to focus on a heap at the bottom of the stairs and my torch beam just illuminated the prone body of a man - Joe. He sounded out of his mind with fear but he still had the wit to yell a warning.

"Watch the bloody stairs!"

It was a good job he did too. As I cautiously made my way down, I nearly slipped on what must have been the middle step of the flight. It felt like sheet ice. Seconds later I was next to Joe but I realised, even though he'd just shouted out a warning to me, he had no idea who I was. He gazed at me with wide blank saucer eyes.

"Joe, it's me. Frankie."

"Frankie, thank goodness."

"Don't worry, old fellow, I'll get you out of here in no time."

"I fell down the steps. I think I've bust my ankle."

I picked up Joe's more substantial torch which was by his side and switched it on. Joe was lying across the bottom two steps with his left leg bent underneath the top of his right leg. I gingerly moved him and, though he grimaced, he didn't cry out which told me the ankle was most likely unbroken.

Then Joe grabbed my arm.

"He could still be down here, Frankie."

Jesus Christ, I could have done with that information a touch sooner! I pointed Ray's pistol out in front of me and swept the torch beam around but there was nothing to be seen apart from Joe's weapon on the floor a few paces away, next to what looked like an envelope. At the far end of the crypt was the entrance to a dark passageway.

"I heard him running off so I tried to take the stairs two at a time," Joe told me. "But I slipped and dropped the gun. When he realised that, he stopped and walked back, ever so deliberately and stood right over me."

By now Joe's breathing had become ragged.

"Joe, what did he look like? Did you shine your torch at him?"

"Yes, he was wearing that mask again. But I saw those eyes Frankie. Deep blue. Just how you described them. Then he …"

"Then he what?"

"He picked up my gun and pointed it at me. I thought that was it. But he … he just tossed it aside, reached into his pocket and took out an envelope, which he dropped as well. Can you see them?"

"Yeah, I won't touch them though. He might have left prints."

"Good thinking."

"So what happened then?"

"Nothing, thank god. He just disappeared into the gloom."

"Looks like there's a passage of some sort, I'll go …"

Before I could finish my sentence two more powerful torch beams lit up proceedings and a pair of size tens came clattering down the stone steps. They were attached to a couple of uniformed officers. Both carried pistols.

"Watch those steps," I yelled. "They're really slippy."

The pair halted just in time or else I'd have been underneath a whole heap of injured coppers.

"You lot took your time," I spat angrily. "The detective sergeant here could have been killed."

The older of the two officers, also a sergeant, looked as if he was seriously considering shooting me before he took a deep breath.

"There were reports of someone running from the east door," he said. "We had to check but it was a false alarm."

"Then here's some more reliable advice. The killer escaped down that passageway." I fixed the torch beam on it. "Perhaps you could … you know."

The coppers glanced at each other and I wondered if they were about to ignore what I'd said. But as they dithered, Joe piped up, "He's right. Our man's somewhere down there."

Duty prevailed over annoyance and the pair set off into the gloom. At that moment Ned Clarkson appeared at the top of the stairs and picked his way down carefully after another warning from me.

"Can you get up, guv?" he asked Joe.

"I think so with a bit of help."

Ned and I took an arm each and gently eased Joe to his feet. He was still shaking. Then because the stairs weren't wide enough for three, Ned, who was a head taller than me and as powerfully built as Ray, slowly guided Joe back up to the main body of the church. As I followed, I noticed, almost guiltily, that Joe had wet and possibly soiled his trousers. When we came to the slippery step I bent down and rubbed it lightly. My hand came up covered in grease.

We reached the top of the steps and Joe stared into the body of the church as if suddenly remembering a desperate trauma. He turned back to us.

"Ned, is Ray … OK?"

Clarkson paused just a fraction too long before answering.

"Don't worry, guv, they'll get him to hospital as soon as possible."

Joe's head dropped on to his chest in abject misery. In the aisle I could see two ambulance men gently easing Ray on to a stretcher. They had obviously been working furiously on our pal's chest wounds as his shirt was ripped open and bandages were wound tightly round his upper body. But Ray's grey pallor and shallow breathing told the story that all the medical attention may not have been enough. Joe obviously understood this because he lurched forward and fell to his knees by the stretcher.

"I'm sorry, Ray," he cried out. "I'm so sorry."

Hallows, who was standing to one side, glared at him.

"What the hell are you sorry for?" he snapped. "You didn't shoot him. Did you?"

So wild and savage was Joe's returning glare that for a brief moment I fancied that he would leap at his boss and try to throttle him. And if that happened I, for one, would not intervene. But as suddenly as it came, Joe's energy drained away to nothing, leaving him in a sobbing heap on the stone floor.

"Get him into the other ambulance," Hallows barked. "I will not tolerate one of my men breaking down like this in public. It smacks of cowardice."

Before I could angrily remind Hallows that *he* hadn't been the one risking his life on Sword Beach twelve years earlier, Ned had raised Joe gently to his feet and they followed the ambulance crew carrying Ray down the aisle. As this grim procession reached the door, they were met by the two uniformed coppers who had pursued the attacker into the darkness of the crypt. The pair stood respectfully aside to allow the retinue past and then joined us. Their disappointed faces revealed they hadn't come close to catching the murderer. That did not, however, prevent Hallows asking a damn fool question.

"Well, Adams," Hallows said to the older of the two uniforms. "Did you get him?"

"No, sir, he'd gone by the time we got there."

"Gone where for god's sake? How did he get out of that crypt?"

"There's a flight of stairs which leads up to a hatch in the far corner of the graveyard," Adams explained.

I was about to blurt out that I might have heard the killer using the hatchway to slip unseen into the church; but I held my tongue. After all, I couldn't be sure it had been him.

"You wouldn't know the hatch was there at all," Adams went on. "I reckon this guy must have reconnoitred the area. It might be worth speaking to the vicar, see if anyone's been hanging about or asking questions."

"You do *your* job, sergeant, and I'll do mine."

"Yes, sir."

I'd had just about enough of this pompous pillock throwing his weight around so I waded in.

"You might start doing *your* job by picking up the rest of the evidence."

"What are you rattling on about, funny man?" Hallows said as I stood nose-to-nose with him. "You do realise I could have you arrested for insubordination."

"Don't be bleedin' ridiculous," I snorted. "I'm not one of your underlings. Now listen carefully."

Hallows glared at me but took a pace backwards.

"Joe had a terrible experience in the crypt. He had to face down the killer who pointed his own gun at him. It's still down there along with another message. Maybe things would become a bit clearer if you went and got them."

"So why didn't you bring them up yourself?"

Again, I could not believe Hallows had asked such a stupid question.

"I didn't bring them up because the killer's fingerprints will be all over both. It might be an idea to handle them with care."

Hallows paused to take a breath and then reached into his pocket. He pulled out a medium-sized brown paper bag folded in half and handed it to the younger copper.

"Put the gun and letter in there, PC Jameson. And wear gloves when you pick them up. Carefully now."

"Yes, sir," said Jameson hurrying off.

"Adams, you get down to the vicarage. Ask the minister if anyone suspicious has been hanging around."

"Very good idea, sir."

Frankly the sergeant was not doing too splendid a job of disguising his smirk but Hallows must have decided not to draw attention to his blunder and ignored Adams's triumphant look.

"But first," Hallows added, "make sure nobody comes in here until the forensics boys arrive."

He turned to me. "You, come down to the station and give us your statement."

I looked at my watch. Crikey, even after all that had happened it was still only just gone half past five. I could easily make the second house - if I showed a touch of humility. Ah well, here goes.

"Er, Chief Inspector, please would you allow me to come in to the station after the show? Only I really need to be getting to the theatre. And, er, sorry I was so rude before. I was upset about Ray and Joe but still, it was an unforgivable way to speak to a man of your stature."

Hallows nodded and relaxed.

"It's been a stressful time for everyone," he replied. "Very well, you can go to the theatre but make sure you come in straight after the performance."

"I will, I promise."

And I did, but not before possibly the least convincing performance of my career. We were lucky that Barney was on effervescent form and able to carry the act on his own, because I was staggering around the stage like a drunken zombie, struggling to get the images of Ray's dreadful injuries out of my mind. Not that the audience appeared to notice or much care judging from their enthusiastic applause at the end. Still I was expecting - and prepared to take without a murmur - an after-show bollocking from my partner. Surprisingly, however, Barney was most understanding and solicitous, asking after Ray and Joe and commiserating with me over my ordeal. If I'd had my wits about me, I might have suspected something wasn't quite right, but tonight Barney and his feelings were totally incidental to me.

At the station, an uncomfortable looking Ned Clarkson told me he had heard nothing about Ray's condition and quickly began to take my statement. I tried to be precise and thorough - up to a point. While chronicling my nerve-shredding trek up the church tower steps, I once again failed to mention I had heard - or thought I'd heard - someone in the churchyard just before all hell broke loose. No point in looking like a complete dick is there? Ned read the statement through when I'd finished, nodding intermittently before asking me to sign it. He exhaled loudly and poured me a large whisky into a tumbler he produced from his drawer. I began to sip it unthinkingly before slamming the glass on to the table.

"What the hell is this for? What's happened?"

Shamefaced and wretched, Ned replied, "Ray died on the operating table at the General two hours ago."

I gazed at him, open-mouthed in horror. "But you told me he was OK when I arrived."

"I said there was no news."

"It was a damned lie however you look at it," I shouted, my eyes filling up.

"I'm really sorry for misleading you, Frankie" said Ned, close to tears as well. "We needed you to concentrate on your statement."

"You could have said."

"I know and I'm sorry. But think how the rest of the lads are feeling. How I'm feeling. I loved that guy. We did our training together, me and Ray. We've knocked the crap out of each other more times than I care to remember."

"I'll bet he knocked more out of you than vice-versa."

He gave me a grin through the tears.

"You're dead right there, Frankie. I tell you, nobody got the better of Ray during a dust-up - in a fair fight at least."

Still smiling weakly, Ned sat down, poured us each another double and told me the tale of Ray's recent encounter with a Teddy Boy he'd been at school with. Apparently, this guy was a real roughhouse who'd just been released from the cells after being arrested for brawling the night before. He was on his way out of the station as Ray arrived for the morning shift.

"Ray takes one look at this character with his funny haircut and daft drainpipes and says, 'Hello, Gilbert …'"

"Gilbert!"

"I know. I couldn't stop thinking about Gilbert Harding. Anyhow, Ray says, 'Hello, Gilbert' and the Ted comes back with, 'I'm known as Gil these days.' And Ray says, 'whatever you're known as, you've got to be wearing that lot for a bet?'

"By now we're all splitting our sides, which upsets the Ted who shouts at Ray, 'I could always tek you at school, you fat prick.' So Ray pats his stomach, looks at the desk sergeant and signals to Interview Two. The sarge nods and Ray and the Ted disappear inside. Two minutes later Ray reappears dusting himself down while we have to wait another ten minutes before the Ted crawls out, covered in blood. And, as he's staggering away, Ray shouts, 'remember me to your mother, Gilbert.'"

Ned burst into a gale of laughter at the memory but he was still close to tears. I got up from my seat and patted his shoulder.

"It's how we should remember him, mate. Kicking the whatsit out of clowns. Now what about Joe, is he still in hospital?"

Ned was unsure of the present whereabouts of his sergeant but revealed they had talked on the ward about what happened in the church. Joe told him that he and Ray were crouching at either end of a row of pews when there was the noise of something metallic rolling across the floor. Both jumped up, fearing a grenade whereupon there were two shots and Ray's shirt front turned red.

"You pretty much know the rest," he added. "After all, you literally blew the whistle on the whole business."

His brief rundown was indeed much as I remembered, and I felt a sudden stab of guilt for not even thinking of Ray as I made my uneasy way up the tower's spiral steps or when I descended fearfully into the crypt.

Ned mistook my wave of remorse for more basic wretchedness.

"Frankie, there's only one person we should be blaming for all this," he said, planting his grizzly bear arm around my shoulder. "And when we catch him - which we will - I'm going to give the swine nearly as good a beating as Ray would have handed out."

"Then that'll be one hell of a pasting, Ned. Please promise that you'll let me hold your coat."

Ned let me use his office phone to call the hotel and tell Nancy that I'd be staying at Joe's tonight. Even if Joe wasn't there, I reasoned that my cousin would need emotional support.

Turning the corner of Woodcock Street, I expected to find the place in darkness yet was surprised to see it was not only lit up but also playing host to a small army of visitors. Cops, plainclothes and uniformed, were ferrying all manner of items - boxes, papers and even a coal scuttle - down the garden path and depositing them in the back of a large unmarked van. Neither Joe nor Rose appeared to be around.

I recognised one of the plunderers as Al Brabourne, yet another of the station's beefy detectives, the one who was supposed to have been watching at the church's south door that afternoon but had ended up in a brawl on the prom. Those two drunks may well have saved his life.

"Now then, Al, what's all this?" I said approaching him. "Should I be calling the police?"

He deposited his package into the van and turned to me.

"It's all above board, Frankie. Hallows is keen to gather all the evidence and Joe gave him permission to do it without a warrant. It was lucky he let us have a key as his missus doesn't seem to be around."

"Where is Joe?"

"Still at the hospital I'm told. He's been making an almighty fuss though. Says there's nothing wrong with him. Not on the outside at least."

I looked sharply at Brabourne.

"Did he say that?"

Brabourne appeared uncomfortable. "No, that was just me sounding off. Sorry, forget I spoke."

He turned to his colleagues who seemed to have finished their plundering.

"Right that's us done. Give Joe this key back will you, Frankie."

When they'd all cleared off and I'd checked that Rose wasn't hiding under the sink, I went on a quest to find something to drink that was stronger than dandelion and burdock. To my relief I discovered a couple of bottles of Magee's light ale at the back of a corner cupboard and was well into the second when I heard the front door slam. Convinced it would be Rose - it was gone eleven o'clock after all - I jumped up as the parlour door opened. It was therefore a huge surprise to see a haggard looking Joe come limping in and flop down on the sofa.

"I hope there's some of my bloody whisky left," he said, staring accusingly at me as if the pale ale in my glass were his best Glenfiddich.

Fortunately, there *was* some of Joe's whisky left, even if it was the second rate stuff he kept below the sink for uninvited guests like Olly. I poured him a generous measure and watched him put it away in a few seconds. Not wanting to refill his glass right away I was about to put the bottle back under the sink but Joe jumped to his feet, grabbed it off me and did the pouring himself.

"So your ankle wasn't broken?"

"Nah, just sprained. They managed to patch me up so I can limp on both legs now. Maybe I'll learn to walk on my hands."

"If you did, we could find you a spot on the bill."

"I might need a showbiz job the way things are going," he said as his eyes swept the room. "Did they take much?"

"I'm not sure. I haven't been upstairs yet."

I was half-expecting an outpouring of anger at the intrusion but Joe just shrugged. Nor, unlike Ned, did he share any fond memories of Ray apart from saying, "Welcome to the second most wretched day of my life."

What he did do, however, was kick off his shoes and proceed to tell me all about the most wretched day.

"I mentioned about that stuff that went on around Caen, didn't I?" he said as if resuming a conversation from seconds rather than days ago.

At first, I thought I'd misheard him.

"Did you say Caen?"

"That's right. The bocages. Those high hedges the German ambushers hid behind."

"You mentioned it before. Do you remember I told you my brother went through the same thing?"

Joe nodded. "So he did - the poor sod."

He was silent for about a minute and then forced himself to carry on, presumably to take his mind off much more recent horrors.

"That fighting around that part of Normandy was rough. Luckily during our last leave before the big one, our corporal …"

"Gibbo?"

"Yeah Jimmy Gibson," Joe smiled, no doubt for the first time since seven minutes past five. "Before D-Day, Gibbo ordered us all to go out and buy knives; bloody large hunting things you keep in a sheath. Said they could save our lives and he was proved right more than once. For some units it was hand-to-hand."

"Look, Joe, there's really no need to do this."

I was expecting an explosion but Joe merely shook his head.

"No, Frankie," he muttered. "It has to be done. I'm more and more convinced that these murders relate back to what happened in Normandy."

I decided against interrupting him again and he continued.

"Anyway, after three weeks of that lot we were out on our feet but the unit was still largely intact. We camped in this wood miles from anywhere and for once it was quiet. We'd had a really restful twenty-four hours; a bit of kip, a few running repairs and one or two beers that we'd managed to stow away in the Sherman; Gibbo's idea of course."

The smile that had spread across Joe's face remained for a few more seconds before disappearing in an instant.

"Then the staff sent up a message. There was this sniper in a church tower."

I remembered Ray giving me a brief outline of this story a few days ago in the café. God, what wouldn't I give to be talking to him now!

"Joe, if all this is too painful …"

"No!" he snapped, slamming his fist onto the table. "As I said all this … bloody stuff now is somehow bound up with what happened there in 1944. I owe it to Ray."

"OK then. In your own time."

Joe took a deep breath.

"It went really badly from the start. Gibbo pleaded with the lieutenant - his nickname was Iris - to take our Sherman and blast the sniper to kingdom come. But he wouldn't do it."

"Why the hell not?"

"Because he was high church and the idea of a tank destroying the tower offended his religious sensibilities. A couple more months of fighting and he'd probably have burned down Cologne Cathedral if he'd … but for the moment it was all, 'I will not have a hand in destroying the house of Our Lord.'"

"Jesus wept."

"As well he might."

Joe took another long pull of whisky.

"So then Gibbo came up with the idea of him and our sniper - me - doing a quick recce of the scene and maybe getting off a decent shot. But this know-it-all, who knew nothing, couldn't accept that a mere corporal had had a better idea than an officer so he ordered a full assault. Half a dozen of us were to get up there supposedly to increase the odds of shooting the sniper."

Joe shook his head and took another belt of Scotch.

"Quite apart from the fact that most of the lads weren't great shots and a couple couldn't hit a cow's arse with a banjo, they'd all be putting themselves needlessly at risk."

"So, a dangerous enterprise."

"You haven't heard the half of it. As Gibbo argued with Iris, I swear his hand hovered over his hunting knife he was that angry and desperate. Gibbo knew what was at stake and the hell our lads had already been through. But the lieutenant was adamant so Gibbo takes a deep breath and picks up the map. And after a couple of minutes he's tracked the perfect spot two hundred yards from the church. He reckoned we could approach through trees without being seen and I'd have a clear line of vision. Then - and I still can't believe this happened - Iris snatches the map off Gibbo and says he'll navigate.

"So there we are, six of us all squashed into a jeep like we were off to Blackpool for the day. Iris, our master map reader, assures us that we're half a mile from the tower when the jeep screeches round a corner and there's the church, about two hundred yards distant. Gibbo yells for the driver to stop and all of us to scatter into the ditches either side of the road. We all made it too," and here Joe let out a huge regretful sigh, "apart from the driver, a big, daft lad from Glasgow who ended up with half his head shot away."

"Joe, we really don't need …"

"Yes, Frankie I'm afraid we do. Anyway, we've got poor old Mack Mckenzie lying there in the middle of the road, obviously beyond help and we're pinned down. Worse still, the sniper's managed to hit the jeep's fuel tank and it's on fire."

"Nobody left in it, surely?"

"No but although we'd all grabbed our rifles and the radio, Pete Maybury our grenadier has had to leave his launcher on board."

"Where it's burning to a cinder."

"Exactly. Anyway, we wait for Iris to issue orders but there's sweet Fanny Adams coming from that direction so Gibbo takes charge. Not for the first time, I might add. Gibbo uses hand signals to get everyone away from the burning jeep and manoeuvre us all into strategic positions around the church where we have a clear view of the tower.

"I've made it to the side wall of a medium-sized churchyard. The others are in a copse facing the tower. Trouble is, it's a country parish and there's a large area of open ground in front of the churchyard. Gibbo makes it clear he needs me to take on the sniper while Pete Maybury, who's still got a belt full of pineapples, makes a dash towards the churchyard wall. So I get set, take careful aim and go boom bang bang, for about five seconds as Maybury careers across open land ready to launch one of his grenades at the sniper's nest. Tower's only about forty feet high, that's nothing to a strong arm like Pete."

Joe stopped once more to take a drink. He was lost in the memory and his hand movements showed he was almost literally weighing up what had happened. This time I didn't try to interrupt him. All this stuff remained so real to him he was now speaking solely in the present tense.

"Pete's about to throw his first Mills bomb," he resumed, "when my bloody rifle jams. You see it a lot in the films but take it from me it doesn't happen very often. So Pete's without cover on open ground but he's still about to chuck the thing when the sniper nails him."

"So now there's two dead."

"Maybury's not dead and luckily his grenade landed behind the church wall so he wasn't blown to bits either. But his right shoulder's pretty badly shot up and I can't do anything but wait for the German to finish him off. Yet of course he doesn't."

"He left him there as a target … a trap."

"Dead right, Francis."

There was sweat forming on Joe's upper lip and he was beginning to tremble. He took another long drink and with an effort resumed his story.

"I'm out of the game until I can strip down the rifle and reassemble it but that's going to take some time seeing as my cover isn't great. From my position behind the side wall I can make out Olly at the far end of the copse talking furiously into the radio and doing his best to keep his head down. A few yards nearer to me, the corporal and the lieutenant are arguing. Gibbo's pointing my way and obviously saying something like, 'Give Joe a chance to mend his firearm.' But Iris is waving his own rifle around like it's a Zulu spear."

"He was offering to provide cover?"

"Yeah, which would have been great if he'd been an even half-decent shot."

Joe sighed again. "I'm desperate now because I know ... what could happen. So I start to strip the rifle, which is the easy bit. All the time I'm watching Gibbo arguing with Iris, trying to buy a bit of time.

"When I've got it stripped, I see the problem and it's something and nothing. An overload of grease and dirt around the firing pin. So I pull off this neckerchief I wear to keep the sun off me and get rubbing. The dirt and gunge are gone in seconds and I can start to put it back together. I notice Gibbo's stopped arguing and has started to crawl to the nearest point of cover to Maybury who's still lying there twitching. I have to get this bloody gun back together and normally I could do it in twenty seconds. But of course things aren't normal. I'm shaking and the bits won't fit into each other. Now I see Iris levelling his rifle and as he begins to fire, Gibbo's up like a shot and reaches Maybury in a few seconds. Iris is doing better than I'd hoped in pinning down the sniper and I've nearly got my rifle back together. Gibbo's starting to drag Pete back to cover in the trees. And then ..."

Joe stopped and stared at the wall. Because I knew what was coming, I hadn't got it in my heart to even think about prompting him. Again, his hands seemed to map out what was happening, more for his own benefit it seemed to me. Joe gulped and continued his narrative in the past tense as if to put more distance between him and those terrible events.

"... then the sniper fired off a couple of rounds at Iris, who dived back behind his tree. Fair enough. But if you're covering somebody you've got to start firing again quickly or else ... but there was nothing. At first I thought he'd dropped the rifle but I then I saw him there behind the tree shaking.

Meanwhile my piece was nearly reassembled when I saw Gibbo go down. I thought that was it for him but it turned out *he'd* been hit in the shoulder as well. That didn't stop him trying to drag Pete though and I was just about ready to fire when Gibbo got hit again … in the head. And this time he didn't get up."

Joe wiped away a tear. I didn't want to hear any more.

"Look, Joe, I get the picture. Gibbo was a brave man in the middle of a balls-up."

Joe continued as if I hadn't spoken. And now he's back in the present.

"For a moment it's all quiet and then there's a ferocious yell. It takes me a couple of seconds to realise it's me doing the yelling. Next thing I'm up on my feet firing like mad at the tower. Either I get lucky or I'm actually aiming properly, I just can't remember but anyway I must have hit him because I see him fly backwards. Dead or wounded? I dunno but I'm going to find out. I vault over the wall and get to the side door of the church …"

Someone began to unlock the front door whereupon Joe and I jumped out of our skins as if we were both cowering in front of that French church. The living room door opened and in walked Rose. She stared at us.

"What are you two up to? You both look as if you've seen a ghost."

Joe was first to recover.

"We're … er … we're remembering," he said.

"Oh please," Rose exclaimed in exasperation, "not *those* ghosts, Joe. The damn war ended a decade ago."

Rose took off her coat. She too had begun to shake.

"You're so right, darling. But we were also remembering Ray."

Joe sat his wife down and talked her through the terrible events of that afternoon. As he did so Rose's hostility evaporated and she broke down sobbing.

"Poor Jenny. What will she do?"

It was something that hadn't even crossed my mind in these last few desperate hours. But now, thinking about it, I hoped she'd get herself to that clinic as soon as possible.

11
Gunning for Joe

THIS CHRONICLE has now reached a point where the home straight is in sight and there is light at the end of a very dark tunnel. Chickens may well be coming home to roost too. But before the clichés drown us and the book is finally closed, we'll have to deal with the deaths of two more people and very nearly a third (me, in case you were at all worried).

And as it stood, someone other than Joe would now have the job of untangling the skein of threads - clues, messages and motives - that might lead to a rational conclusion. I didn't envy that someone, as the list of suspects grew larger by the day. Along with the barmy Boardmans and Barney (oh yes, I'd had my eye on him for a while) we now had to consider Paddon, Philby, the battling butcher's boy and probably Conrad, although why he'd want to risk his status as Mellish's new Mr Popular was a conundrum worthy of Professor Stanley Unwin who, incidentally, had also crept onto my suspect list. I even began to wonder if the killer was Nancy; after all, she never appeared to have much regard for the male sex and could very well harbour a hidden desire to drastically deplete its numbers. But then again if my wife had gone bonkers enough to embark on a murder spree, then it was odds-on that the first victim would have been me. A very dry run, so to speak. So I could (probably) rule her out.

However, looming larger than any of those names and casting a considerable shadow over the case, was the figure of Joe Trueman. Poor Ray in those final moments had trusted his skipper to watch his back. But what if, from the opposite end of a row of pews, Joe had distracted Ray with something that sounded like a rolling hand grenade and then, for whatever reason, gunned down his oppo? All three of us had heard what we thought were footsteps, but had we? The sound could just as easily have been that door at the top of the tower, clattering in the wind. And I had the sinking feeling that whoever had pulled the trigger, it would eventually be established that Joe's weapon was the one that had killed Ray.

It was a gloomy Sunday morning and I had the house to myself. Joe was away facing the music at the station and for some unspecified (to me at least) reason Rose was desperately needed at her new place of work. It was with some concern, therefore, that I was jolted out of my musings on murder by the sound of the front door slamming loudly. And, before I could even begin to worry about a mad intruder, one appeared in front of me.

"Hello, Joe, you're back soon. Have they decided to let bygones be bygones?"

He stood in the frame of the lounge door and regarded me with annoyance.

"Where's Rose?"

"At work."

"Good for her," he replied, flinging himself grumpily on to the sofa. The move was, I noted, becoming something of a habit. "They've suspended me."

"Oh, that's rotten luck."

"Hallows would argue that bad luck had little to do with it."

Then Joe told me what I'd already feared; that it looked very much like his was the gun that had killed Ray. I had to confess that, like him, I was baffled.

"Look, Joe, I know you didn't shoot your mate twice in the chest. I mean it's not possible."

He snorted. "Your vote of confidence is very valuable to me."

"But how the hell ...?"

Joe suddenly sat up straight as if commanded to do so by an invisible headmaster. Or Nancy. "It's so obvious," he replied with a peculiar smile. "He must have switched guns in the crypt."

"But he can't have known that you'd drop the weapon ... ah!"

"Exactly! The slippery stair. He figured I'd have to let go of the gun to stop me breaking my neck. The bastard was right too. Dear god, I have to admire him in one way."

But now something much more basic was troubling me.

"If he switched the gun, how could the one they found be yours?"

And come to that, I thought, how could he have used it to shoot Ray *before* he took it from Joe? Something wasn't adding up, but while I was wondering how to ask that question, Joe spoke again.

"They think the weapon they found, the one that had been fired twice, was my old wartime service revolver. It should be right at the back of the bottom drawer of the sideboard there."

For a moment Joe seemed unwilling to test his hypothesis so I opened the drawer, reached right to the back and groaned. Apart from a couple of faded tea towels and a tin of Uncle Joe's Mintballs, it was empty.

"Your mob must have found it last night."

Joe shook his head vehemently.

"Al Brabourne swore that what they'd found didn't include my revolver."

"What *did* they find then?"

"He didn't elaborate."

I paused a moment to think this through.

"So the killer must have got into here and took it?"

"Looks that way."

"Think, then, who's been in the house recently? Me, Nancy, Conrad. Conrad?"

He shook his head vigorously.

"You don't get it. The gun was probably taken weeks ago."

"How do you reckon that?"

"Something Hallows said. Just take it from me, he must have broken in then - or found the key outside - and I haven't missed the gun until now."

This was becoming stranger and stranger.

"But if he had your personal weapon, then what did you have? What the heck did you drop in the crypt when you slipped on his booby-trapped step?"

"I'd never use my service revolver for official duties. Ray checked out two pistols from the arms store. He had one, I had the other."

"There you are then. There'll be a record."

"I wouldn't bank on it. Ray was never exactly one for protocol - and we were rushing. But that's all part of what I want you to clear up. Go and see Ned. Find out what he knows. Please, Frankie."

If I was about to make myself even less popular at the station, I had to know all that Joe knew. And I was certain he was keeping some-thing back. At first he blustered and denied it but when I told him he was on his own and stood up to leave he raised both hands in surrender.

"Hallows said unofficially that the gun was mine and was about to tell me something else when he went all pompous and clammed up."

"Pompous? That doesn't sound like Chief Inspector Hallows at all."

Joe managed a weak grin.

"I think it's about what Al mentioned - something else that they found here. But I can't imagine what. Genuinely I can't, Frankie. That's why I'm hoping Ned will tell you. After all he's the one in charge now."

"They've made a constable the lead officer?"

"He's acting Detective Sergeant Clarkson now."

"Bloody hell, do I bow or curtsey?"

"Just use flattery. Despite the extra stripe he's still Blockhead Ned as Ray calls him."

Joe might have been willing to tell me more but for the inadvertent mention of his dead colleague. Breaking into a fit of coughing to hide his sobs, he blurted out that he was going upstairs for a rest and hurried from the room.

I'd been hoping that by now Rose would have arrived home to rustle up the delicious breakfast I hadn't quite got around to making myself. But half an hour's hopeful hanging about yielded no such luck.

So, as it became clear that my cousin had so selfishly decided to further her career instead of keeping me alive and I didn't fancy tackling Blockhead Ned Clarkson on an empty stomach, I made my way to a seafront greasy spoon I knew would be open on a Sunday. There I spent a relaxing hour stuffing my face with black pudding and fried bread while considering an intriguing philosophical question raised by my perusal of the Sunday papers. I mean why in the name of Socrates was the gorgeous film star Marilyn Monroe planning to tie the knot with a dusty old writer nobody had ever heard of? The only Arthur Miller I'd ever come across used to catch rats back in Butterthwaite when I was a kid and I felt pretty sure Marilyn wouldn't consider him too much of a prospect. These inconsequential silver screen musings did largely manage to keep my mind off murderers and victims (unless you counted the rats) but as the final piece of toast and marmalade, disappeared I was forced to concede that my confrontation with Ned could no longer be put off.

It was awkward, especially as I didn't feel like being anywhere near the station. Of course, I wanted to know what else they had on Joe nearly as much as the man himself. But at the same time, I was extremely unsure - not to say fearful - about the reception I would get. Like most front-line professionals, cops are an insular lot and react badly when one of their own is taken. Quite understandably I suppose, considering they rely on each other for their safety day after day. Anyway, as I gingerly entered the nick my fears seemed to be well-founded. Ernie immediately raised the lid of the counter and came hurtling out at me, his huge ham hands outstretched, looking ready to strangle any comic who strayed into his path. Then he hugged me.

"The lads reckon you did all you could and more in that church," he sniffed, clutching me so tightly to his sergeant's tunic that the buttons dug into my cheek.

"Anyone would have done the same, Ernie," I mumbled, gently easing myself from his grasp. "I didn't know Ray as well as the rest of you, but he'd already become a good mate."

"And you went after the bastard who did for him and that merits a medal in my book," he added, wiping away a tear.

An unlikely prospect if you asked me but I wasn't about to argue the point. Instead, I tentatively tested the water.

"Ernie, do you think Joe did it?"

The desk sarge stared at me as if I'd lost my marbles.

"That man's as awkward a cuss as there is and many's the ding-dong I've had with him," he spluttered. "But Detective Sergeant Joe Trueman a murderer? You may as well suspect Princess Margaret."

Having had a brief but lively run-in with our new monarch's younger sister *(see Volume One),* I wasn't entirely consoled by the comparison. After all she'd nearly set me on fire with her cigarette when she demanded to know who the devil I was and I reminded her that she definitely knew me because she'd once shown me her knickers. OK, I didn't mention she'd been doing handstands and she was only six. Whereupon the grown-up princess had replied with gusto, "I'm afraid that doesn't narrow it down all that much."

However, I understood exactly what Ernie was trying to say and felt grateful on Joe's behalf.

"So is the new detective sergeant in his office or is he having a lie-in.?"

"Probably both," Ernie replied. "Ned is in his office but he may well be kipping. He's been in all night, you see."

Sure enough, a tentative push at the door to what until yesterday had been Joe's domain, revealed Clarkson spark out across a heap of files littering the desk. A mug with a few dregs of tea still in it lay horizontal on the floor next to his chair, and I could just make out a shortbread biscuit stuck between the side of his head and the desk.

Feeling it would be uncharitable to rouse him, I was about to back out when Ned jerked upright and pointed at me.

"I wasn't asleep, I was thinking."

I was thinking too. I was thinking Ned looked terrible.

"I'll let you get on with your musings then," I told him and began to close the door. But he signalled me back.

"No, no, come in. We need to talk."

Sitting in the chair opposite, I waited while he straightened his collar and tie and removed the biscuit from the side of his head. To his great credit, I don't think for a second he'd considered eating it.

"I suppose," Ned began, dropping the shortbread in the bin by the desk, "that he's sent you to try to make me spill the beans?"

"Why what are you guilty of?"

"*My* conscience is clear," he said, staring unblinkingly at me. "But can we say the same thing about your mate?"

My mate? Up until now I'd thought Joe was Ned's pal as well. Surprising what an extra stripe can do to a man's loyalties! But I decided those thoughts were best kept to myself.

"Look, detective sergeant - and many congratulations on your promotion by the way - you surely can't believe that Joe would shoot his best buddy dead?"

Ned let out a huge tired sigh and seemed to physically deflate.

"No, I would never have said that until …"

"Until the real killer swapped his weapon for the one that killed Ray?"

"You have to admit, it's a strange tale. And Joe's are the only prints on the pistol."

"That's because it's his gun and the killer wore gloves."

"You saw him then, did you?"

"I heard …"

Again, I decided not to elaborate on the fact that I *might* just have heard the killer on his way in to the church and done nothing about it. Instead I tried to change the line of inquiry.

"Well, what about the fact that Ray checked out two weapons from the armoury? There has to be a record of that!"

"I'm afraid not." Ned said, reddening slightly. "We're only a small nick and there is no armoury as such; just a gun safe and the book we sign to say we've checked out the weapon and how much ammo. But it's been happening so much in recent weeks that some of us tend to forget. Looks as if Ray was one of 'em."

"Who holds the key to the gun safe then?"

Something in Ned's eyes suggested he was giving me a silent round of applause for a valiant effort on Joe's behalf, and I was relieved that my earlier fears that he had turned against Joe seemed to be unfounded.

"That's a good point, Frankie," he sighed, "but unfortunately Ernie keeps the key in his drawer, something everybody in the station knows. When we're in a hurry we tend to lift it if he's not around. Don't mention that to Hallows though, will you."

I told him I had no intention of even being in the same room as Hallows. He seemed relieved and as we now appeared to be on the same side, I hoped my next line of questioning would be more productive.

"I heard … that you'd found something else at Joe's you thought might be incriminating."

Apparently, we still weren't quite the best of buddies though. Ned glared at me and I feared he'd had enough of this already and was keen to pitch this unwanted intruder from his new office. But after staring silently at me and taking a deep breath, he selected one of the mountain of files, took a photograph from it and handed it to me.

"Ever seen that before?"

I studied the picture, which showed a medium-sized black Remington typewriter, the old-fashioned sort. I had to admit I'd never clapped eyes on it.

"The thing is," Ned went on, "we're waiting for official confirmation that this is the machine which our man used to write the notes."

He handed me the photograph of the killer's first message.

"Look closely at the word 'Remember'. You'll see that the 'e' key is worn down on the tail - exactly like the one on this typewriter."

He tapped the photograph and I remembered Nancy drawing attention to the same defective key stroke. I didn't know where he was going with this but a knot started to form in my stomach all the same.

"Surely the 'e' would be like that on any machine," I tried to argue with mounting trepidation. "It *is* the most used key."

"You'd think so but those in the know say every key impression is unique - a bit like your fingerprints. And I'm afraid this machine was found hidden at the back of a wardrobe. In Joe's bedroom."

I hadn't seen that one coming and it floored me for a second or two.

"But ... but why on earth would Joe keep the typewriter in his house? Surely if he was guilty, he'd have hidden it properly or got rid of the thing."

"Not if he wanted to write more notes. Before killing more people."

"I know!" I said, sharing my latest inspiration with Ned, "the typewriter must have been planted in Joe's wardrobe. By the killer."

"Then why are Joe's the only fingerprints on it?"

Damn the man, he had an answer for everything. But so did I.

"This is absurd," I replied gamely. "What if he was wearing gloves, same as in the church?"

Ned steepled his fingers under his nose as if in prayer. "OK then, Funnybone of the Yard. Tell me how the killer, if he isn't Joe, wrote the notes."

"It's completely obvious," I began, genuinely unsure of what my next words would be. "The killer broke in, stole the gun and … wrote the note at the same time."

"And then he broke in again, wrote the second note, then broke in again and wrote the third … do you see my problem?"

I did indeed. And I was running of plausible excuses. But still I was sure it couldn't be Joe.

"He might have written the notes all at once," I spluttered. "The one thing we do know about him is that he plans ahead."

Ned hung his head wearily.

"Have it your own way. But we've still only Joe's word there was actually another person there in the church. I mean, did you see anyone else?"

"I heard something … there were footsteps running away after Ray was shot. That's why we chased him."

"But did you *see* anyone?"

"No but …"

"We really have to consider the possibility that there might not have been anyone else. If Joe told you someone was running away you wouldn't have stopped to think, would you?

And you told me last night the door to the tower roof was blowing in the wind."

"That doesn't mean there weren't footsteps as well."

Ned put his head in his hands and breathed in heavily for five seconds or so. He then looked back up at me.

"Frankie, I really don't want to believe it was Joe. But we're duty bound to look at all the evidence. And when that evidence also includes instances of violence …"

"Violence?"

Flicking through another folder, Ned pulled out a single sheet of paper and stared at it.

"Bernard Ollerton," he said, as much to himself as me.

"The next to last victim, yeah. Joe's already told you he served with the guy. They were both at D-Day."

"But he didn't tell us he'd kicked seven bells out of this Ollerton bloke a few days before he was found strung up on Wellington Common."

"Joe hardly touched him."

"You were there, were you?"

Now he was really interested. Why couldn't I keep my big trap shut?

"Look, Ned, I found the little weasel sneaking round the back garden at midnight and tackled him. Then Joe came down to see what the commotion was about and ended up …"

"Kicking seven colours out of him?"

"The guy provoked Joe, right? Got under his skin. Something about an incident during the war."

"Yeah we know about that too. Military records etc, etc. But let's leave it for now. We're going around in circles."

Tell you the truth I was more than happy to park the matter there. Although I hadn't liked Olly from the kick-off, I felt Joe's response *had* been unduly violent - he'd really lost his rag - and I'd been mightily relieved when Rose appeared. That led on to another awkward thought.

"Who told you about Joe tackling Olly?"

Ned smiled wearily as he replaced the sheet of paper in the file.

"I'm under no obligation to keep you abreast of any aspect of my investigation."

"Yet you still want my assistance."

"And I thank you for giving it, Frankie."

"I don't mean about Joe. You'll still need help with the note. I take it there was a note?"

That wiped the smirk off his face and for an instant I thought he was about to issue me with marching orders. But he paused before handing over a photograph from the first file. It was written in the now familiar style and try as I might I could not stop myself focusing on the chipped 'e'. I noticed too that the message lacked the killer's odd cryptic way of revealing the number of letters in each word. It was almost as though he had grown tired of taunting us. However, if that was the case, he hadn't exactly decided to make himself crystal clear. I read out the note.

"'Demise of treacherous laughing nobleman, we hear. What a spectacle. Three, three, two, three, four, four.' What does Conrad Ross say?"

Ned shrugged. "I haven't been able to contact him yet. What do you make of it?"

I studied the note, more for form's sake than anything as I was sure we'd have to pass it on to Nancy or Conrad for enlightenment. But suddenly, I realised that rather incredibly, the solution was staring me in the face. I turned things over in my mind for a full minute before deciding I was on the right trail.

Then with the faintest of smirks, I prepared to mess with a copper's mind.

"Er, let's see. Demise equals death," I began haltingly, as if unsure of myself.

"Thanks for working that one out," said Ned, who was trying hard not to grin. It was clear he thought that I hadn't a clue what I was talking about.

"And nobleman could be a duke or earl - or maybe a peer. Which added to 'we hear' and spectacle might give us - the end of the pier show."

Ned wasn't grinning any more. In fact, he'd sat bolt upright and was staring at me.

"Go on," he said cautiously.

"But hold on a dashed minute, why 'treacherous'?" By now I'd decided to milk this for all it was worth. "Let's see, what I think we have here is a traitorous peer. Well, Ned, who else could that be but Lord Haw-Haw, which would also explain the reference to laughter. So the next murder will be at the end of the pier at around quarter to eight."

"How do you work out the time?" By now Ned wasn't even attempting to hide his amazement.

"I'd have to check but I'm pretty sure the execution - or demise - of William Joyce, Lord Haw-Haw, was in 1945 or 1946. Our twenty-four-hour clock, remember?"

He nodded slowly.

"And when is it going to happen?"

I bloody well knew he was going to ask that!

"I might have to make one or two complicated mathematical calculations - possibly involving sines and cosines - and get back to you on that."

The grin was back on Ned's face.

"Tell you what, let your pal Conrad do the maths, eh? Much safer."

Fair play to him, he'd got me back there.

"Ok, I'll contact Conrad but I'll have to hold on to the photo."

"Very well, but if you show this to anyone bar Mr Ross or your wife, I'll personally …"

I never found out what he was about to threaten me with as at that moment Hallows swept into the room without knocking. He pulled up sharply when he saw me sitting there and I readied myself for yet another bout of verbal fisticuffs. But surprisingly, and I have to say extremely unsettlingly, Chief Inspector Hallows gave me what he must have considered to be his warmest smile.

"Ah, the man of the moment," he intoned. It was a description which had me scrambling to wonder what I'd done right.

"You were absolutely right," he added, "to warn the officers about handling the gun in the crypt without gloves."

It was him I'd warned!

"And because of you, we were able to determine that the only prints on the weapon belonged to Detective Sergeant Trueman."

Not so clever then. My intervention had merely served to punch another gaping hole into the sinking ship that was Joe Trueman's life and career. I desperately tried to redress the balance.

"Thank you, Chief Inspector, but the killer could have set up Joe by cleverly switching weapons. And of course by wearing gloves."

"It's a theory," he replied in a manner which suggested that as theories went it wasn't much of one.

I then made matters a zillion times worse by unthinkingly asking, "And how's your daughter?"

In an instant Hallows' benevolence disappeared and he stared at me with thunder and lightning in his eyes.

"My Jenny? What damn business is it of yours?"

Oh crikey, what had I done? The fact that she'd been going out with Ray had never been officially acknowledged.

"Er, I'd heard, that is I was told that your daughter, Jenny, was, er, going to go to university."

"And where did you hear that?"

It was my distinct impression that I was no longer flavour of the month.

"Er, I think it was when she came to the show."

"She never mentioned she'd been to see your … show."

"Oh yes, I remember it quite distinctly. She came backstage afterwards and introduced herself. Told me she planned to study medicine at university. Oh, and how proud she was of her old Dad."

"Did she now? Well I'm proud of her too. So proud that I've arranged for her to spend a few months abroad to help boost her studies."

About nine months would be my guess.

"Ah good thinking, sir. Nothing like learning a new language. Especially when you're studying … medicine. Please mention that I was asking about her."

Hallows nodded curtly and turned to Clarkson.

"I want your preliminary report, drawing together all the different threads of the case on my desk by five today."

On that note he walked out of the office without so much as another glance at me.

Ned and I paused just in case Hallows decided to come flying back in and torment us further. But, after a few continuing moments of blissful silence, I ventured the whispered question, "Do you think he suspected anything?"

"Not at all," Ned replied with a straight face, "I'm sure he swallowed your feeble tale and doesn't suspect for one moment that you know his little angel's got a bun in the oven. Now clear off and find out when this maniac's going to strike again."

I left the nick worrying that I might encounter Hallows again and be forced to admit at glarepoint that I knew the apple of his eye was carrying a dead cop's baby. Mercifully he was nowhere to be seen - probably too busy jabbing underlings with sharp objects.

However, the possibility of Hallows materialising like Dracula discouraged me from asking Ernie if I could use the phone at the front desk to contact Conrad. Walking slowly towards the prom where I knew there was a phone box, which hopefully contained no senior police officers, yet another suspicion hit me. The person who'd benefited most from Ray's death and Joe's suspension was their colleague, the newly-promoted Detective Sergeant Clarkson. I couldn't help but recall that flash of intense anger in his eyes when Ray dismissively swept his feet off the desk. But then I also remembered last night when, with tears in his eyes, he told me how he and Ray had been the very fastest of friends. This bloomin' case was making me imagine all sorts of things, most of them frankly ridiculous.

Conrad wasn't in when I phoned the university and I rejected the chance of being put through to Paddon as I didn't fancy being made to feel I was back in the babies' class. Leaving the phone box, I toyed with the idea of a walk along the prom. It was a dull but dry Sunday morning and a jaunt to the dunes and back would have given me a fine appetite for my roast dinner with Nancy back at the hotel. However, with the image of Joe fidgeting at home uppermost in my mind, I abandoned the idea of a relaxing stroll and made my way slowly back to Woodcock Street.

Joe was out of his chair and into the hall before I had even closed the front door.

"Well?" he said, unable to stop himself from sounding as though he was about to question me under caution. So I mentioned the gun which he knew about already and the typewriter, which he didn't.

"I don't even have a typewriter."

"Well, they found it in your wardrobe and they reckon your prints are all over it."

All at once Joe gasped and grabbed my arm.

"Is it a big black antique thing?"

"Yeah, a Remington."

"That's right," he said, nodding to himself. "It's Rose's, or at least it belonged to her Dad, your old Uncle David. He wrote nature notes for the parish magazine. Honestly, Frankie, the only time I ever touched the thing was to carry it upstairs and put it at the back of the wardrobe. You see, after he died Rose couldn't bear to part with it."

"But how would the killer know it was in your wardrobe? And how could he have taken the thing away, written the notes and returned it to your bedroom?"

I expected him to come back with my line to Ned that the typewriter had never even been taken from the bedroom and had been used there and then to write the whole series of notes. But Joe just shook his head in bewilderment.

"I've no idea. But I'll tell you what I do know, Frankie. This guy's out to destroy me. And at the moment he's doing a pretty good job."

Just then the telephone rang and we both nearly flew out of our skins.

"Let me get it," I said, jumping up and moving towards the door. "I'll tell them you're in the bath."

But it wasn't the nick keeping tabs on its prime suspect. It was Conrad.

"Frankie, is that you?"

"Yeah hi, Conrad. Did they tell you I'd called the uni on the off-chance you'd be in on a Sunday?"

"Indeed they did. Sorry I haven't been in touch before. Bit busy. I'm guessing there's another clue."

When I read him the latest message, he solved it in no time at all and asked if I knew the exact date of Lord Haw-Haw's execution. I told him it was 1945 or 1946. Then I had a brainwave.

"Joe," I shouted, "when did they hang William Joyce, you know, Lord Haw-Haw?"

Hardly a second had gone past before the shout came back, "Third of January 1946. At Pentonville."

"Did you hear that?" I asked Conrad.

"Yes, very impressive. Give that man a coconut. Now let me have a second to work it out."

During the silence on the other end of the line I commended myself on my hunch that Joe, who had helped send most of the major Nazis to the gallows, would know exactly where and when they executed one of the few he hadn't dealt with.

Conrad's voice interrupted my self-congratulation. "It's going to be next Sunday, a week today. Fourteen minutes to eight in or around the Coliseum Theatre on the pier. The scene of all your triumphs."

There was silence for a few moments as we both digested this. Of course, if the venue was a theatre it would have to be Sunday, the only day when there were no shows.

"Thanks, Conrad."

"No problem, my friend. Now I really must go. We've got this damned inspection over the next few days."

"What, like the boy scouts?"

"If only! No this is the uni bigwigs poking their beaks in to see if we deserve the extra money we requested - or can even keep what we're getting at the moment."

"So now wouldn't be the best time to ask how you worked the date out?"

"No, but we should be clear by Friday. Why don't we meet up for a drink then and I explain how the binary thing works? I'd let Paddon enlighten you but he'll be at it as hard as me. Besides why would you want to talk to him when there are perfectly decent gateposts to share your thoughts with?"

I was smiling broadly when I strolled back into the lounge and told Joe what Conrad had said. I was about to add the joke about the gateposts, which I thought was rather good, when Joe spoke up.

"I want you to do something for me."

"Name it."

"Tell Ned that this rendezvous with the killer is in a fortnight's time."

"But it's next week. Weren't you listening?"

"I was listening very closely."

"Then what are you up to?"

Joe rose from his chair, limped towards the window and gazed out. Thirty seconds elapsed before he turned back to me with a tight and somewhat sad smile.

"This guy wants to make it personal so I'm going to let him. Face to face. And no-one else gets hurt except for him - or me."

At that point I realised he'd actually slipped his moorings.

"There's no way," I told Joe, "that I'm letting you tackle this madman on your own."

"Why, it's not you he's after? I'm at the centre of it all."

"True, but he killed my good pal Wilf and nearly did for me too, so I reckon I also have a dog in this fight. Well, two dogs if we're counting you."

He took a quick step forward and briefly I feared he was going land me one. Then, for the only time in his life, he embraced me. I had to confess it was not a comfortable moment.

"Frankie," he said, almost sobbing, "you really don't have to do this."

Well, no I suppose I didn't; what with this maniac having got the better of around half a dozen victims, some of whom were better equipped to fight him than I was. But when duty calls and all that.

"Look, Joe," I said, detaching myself carefully from our awkward embrace, "I'd rather we got other coppers involved in this malarkey. However, if you don't want to go in mob-handed then I'm right behind you. But, whatever we're doing, we need a strategy."

"Now, you're talking, Frankie" he replied. "And as it happens, I have had one or two ideas."

For the next half-hour we kicked around various plans. At one point, Joe became particularly animated over the idea that by now I knew all the theatre's nooks and crannies - until I reminded him that the killer was also familiar with the building's layout having already committed one, and nearly two, murders there. Curiously this didn't dampen Joe's new-found enthusiasm for the enterprise at all and I began to develop a queasy suspicion that there could be more to this than met the eye. What if, under the cloak of catching a killer, he was actually setting me up as the next victim? It was an uncomfortable thought and one I tried to banish by changing the subject.

"Did you tell Ned that you'd kicked the sh ... had a fight with Olly not long before he was strung up?"

His smile vanished. "No. Did you?"

"Of course not. But he mentioned it to me, so someone's been talking."

"Huh, yet another stick to beat me with. This character's thought of everything hasn't he? But hold on, the only other person who knew that Olly was here ..."

For the second time in twenty-four hours the pair of us jumped out of our skins as the front door slammed.

Rose opened the lounge door and stared at us both.

"What are you up to this time?"

Snared once more like naughty schoolboys, neither of us had the guts to return the same question to her.

Joe merely replied, "They've suspended me."

Rose's face fell. She threw down her bag, rushed over to Joe's chair and flung her arms around him.

"How could they?" she complained bitterly. "You've just seen your best friend killed and they do something like that. Honestly, Joe, you're better off out of it. And I'll tell them I can't go. Those machines can go hang."

For a second, I thought this odd comment was part of some sort of code between them and wondered why Nancy and I did not have similarly esoteric interactions; until I saw that Joe was equally as puzzled.

"Sorry, darling," he said, "I'm not quite following ..."

"Oh, I am a fool," Rose replied tearfully, banging the palm of her hand against her forehead, "I thought I'd already mentioned it to you."

It turned out that in her short stint at Tatlocks Rose had already impressed the management enough for them to offer to pay for a four-day course so she could refine her skills on the very latest counting machines, and recommend whether they were worth investing in. However, the venue was a hotel south of Birmingham and there was no way Rose was leaving Joe on his own at the moment. Yet surprisingly, Joe was having none of it.

"For goodness sake, Rose, you must go," he urged. "I can look after myself and if I'm struggling, I'm sure Frankie here will give me a lift."

"Er, yes of course you've no worries on that score," I told them and added, god knows why, "but before you go, Rose, why don't you get a few tips from Conrad? He knows all about number machines."

The name was hardly out of my mouth before I remembered the cosy scene from a day or two before. Rose obviously recalled it too.

"The machines I'm working on," she said, "are not computers, they're just glorified abacuses. I think they're a bit beneath Conrad."

I was about to inquire if the word wasn't in fact 'abaci' but the look on Rose's face was enough to make me realise that this would not be wise. In any case I was interrupted by the telephone. It was Nancy ordering me to get back to the hotel pronto. Relieved, I called the cab firm and prepared to take my leave of the loving couple.

"Don't go yet," pleaded Rose. "Your taxi won't be here for at least ten minutes."

"Ah, no, cuz, my personal cabbie Ted's always on the ball. In fact, I can hear him right now."

Wishing them both luck, I quickly took my leave and hung around at the end of the street for twenty minutes before the now familiar jalopy came clanking and wheezing into view.

My journey back to the hotel was spent trying to ignore Ted giving his expert opinion on Marilyn Monroe's upper body and damning to hell the Arthur Miller who didn't kill Butterthwaite's rats for a living.

While he ranted on, I considered the triangle that appeared to be developing between Joe, Rose and Conrad. It was, I reasoned, unsurprising that my cousin should be drawn to the computer scientist. Conrad was happily blessed with large doses of romantic dash, charisma and joie de vivre while, even to his best friends, Joe could hardly be described as a gay cavalier. More a plodder or perhaps more accurately a limper. But Joe was a plodder/limper because he'd put his life on the line in some of the war's fiercest fighting while Conrad, for all his elan, had been a glorified puzzler. Vitally important war work I suppose but still…

Back at the hotel I found Nancy hard at work behind the large leather-topped desk in our suite. Not so hard, however, that she couldn't pause to extract the latest news from me. I'd already phoned to tell her the awful story of Ray's death and now she was demanding the gen on Joe.

After asking all the right questions about the gun and the typewriter she had the brass neck to solve the cryptic note almost immediately, and compounded the offence by quoting the correct date of William Joyce's execution. This was too much.

"How the heck do you know that?"

"Lord Haw-Haw was an answer not long ago in our weekly quiz."

"Quiz? What quiz?"

"Oh come on, Franco, I must have told you a hundred times about our team. The Golden Girls!"

I was saved from further perplexity over The Golden Girls - whoever they were - by a tentative knock on the door.

"Ah, here he is," Nancy said, with a satisfied smile.

"You're referring to the room service waiter with our delicious Sunday roast dinner?" I inquired hopefully.

"Let's wait and see."

I'd already begun to tuck a metaphorical bib into my imaginary dress shirt before I was rudely dragged back to earth. For when Nancy threw open the door, there on the threshold stood Barney in his Sunday best. That wasn't all. The pesky pipsqueak's hair was tidily combed and the trademark line of grime around his collar had disappeared. He even smelled of something that was only vaguely unpleasant.

"Sorry, I'm late, Mrs Thirkettle," he whispered respectfully.

"Nonsense, Barney, you're not late," Nancy fussed, ushering him in. "And how many times must I say, it's Nancy not Mrs Thirkettle. We'll have no airs and graces here. Now get your coat off and sit down."

He did as he was told while giving me a brief nod of acknowledgement.

"Now then," smiled Nancy when everyone was more or less comfortable - me squatting on the bed as there were only two chairs in the room - "let's get down to it."

And so we had a couple of hours of detailed discussion about every aspect of the act; its changing dynamics, the way forward and, most importantly, tomorrow evening's vital performance. Unsurprisingly, it was Nancy who made the early running.

"These Blackpool bookers," she told us, "are looking for something different, but not so different that it would frighten the punters."

"Makes sense," I agreed.

"And in you two, I believe we have the ideal mixture. Here's Frankie, for instance, a name well-known for more than twenty years, a proven funny man guaranteed to bring the crowds flocking in."

I sensed Barney was anxious to add his two pennorth to this but Nancy cut him short with a raised hand. Nobody was going to stop her flow.

"And over there we have Barney, a new, original and exciting talent who can take a double act in surprising directions."

She glanced over towards the bed as if daring me to put my oar in but I was canny enough to say nothing.

"Then we have the tools of your trade. The hook for instance. An inspired idea from Barney brought to life by Frankie's skill, would you not agree?" And she gazed expectantly at Barney.

"Well there was that time he nearly dragged off that woman's bra ..." he began before noticing the warning signs in Nancy's eyes. "But yeah, I'd say he's pretty skilled at handling the hook these days."

I tried not to grin too much. Nancy was demonstrating that it is indeed possible to wring blood out of a stone.

"Then there's the box," she continued, "which I think, with all due thanks to St Mungo the Magician, has added a new and exciting dimension to your act. I mean, I just adore the idea of the useless conjurer and his even more gormless assistant. It has, I feel, an almost endless capacity to impress the Blackpool people."

Later, I would wonder if they'd cooked up what happened the following night between them, but for now I listened to Barney as he had his moment in the spotlight. And unusually he seemed to strike the right note. Nodding thoughtfully at what Nancy had said, he proceeded for the first time to put me centre stage.

"I think Frankie is the key to the whole thing," he said with some fervour. "I mean look what happened at yesterday's matinee. OK, Frankie got it wrong by overbalancing the box and being unable to get out but he did open up the routine to all sorts of new possibilities. I think we should use the box tomorrow for all it's worth."

True to form, even while praising me, he'd made me look a proper Charlie but Nancy did not appear to notice. Indeed, in her eagerness, she went on to suggest a couple more box-related stunts we could pull. I know if I'd done the same, I would have been on the end of a tongue-lashing and branded a bubble-headed twerp. But Barney just nodded serenely and complimented Nancy on her inventiveness.

I felt the discussion was by now crying out for my input but before I could weigh in, the hotel's reception rang to announce that dinner was served. Nancy may not have organised a room service meal but she had made sure her boys would eat well in the hotel dining room.

For the next couple of hours the three of us worked our way through a roast beef dinner accompanied by fine red wines, all courtesy of Star-Protheroe, the company run by Nancy and my original agent Eddie Star, who set me on the road to serfdom, sorry stardom, with instructions not to object when I was pinballed around the London Palladium by those veteran (even then) pranksters, The Crazy Gang. It was therefore fitting we should raise a glass of the finest to Eddie, now approaching his dotage and content to leave spotting and cultivating the talent to Nancy while he remained in London counting his money and his blessings.

Recognising the personnel on our increasingly rowdy table, one or two of the other diners began to sidle over and request autographs. Even though we'd all been necking vino like it was Ribena, we each clicked into gear to do our showbiz duty - in different ways.

I was charm and bonhomie itself - twenty-odd years in the business had taught me never to take my public for granted; Barney was obviously more taciturn but even he managed to crack the odd smile; Nancy, meanwhile, organised the punters into a very orderly queue. And when finally they'd all drifted away the three of us ended the meal with a toast to tomorrow, whatever it might bring.

12

Take the Money

IF PUSHED I'D HAVE to admit that within those aforementioned twenty-odd years there were as many near calamities and outright disasters as triumphs. Frank Randle warming up a bolshy Bolton audience (is there any other kind?) for me by challenging each one of them to a fight springs to mind. As do The Crazy Gang's Palladium antics which left me in the orchestra pit wearing the lead violinist's toupee. Then there was the time that dear old Wally Simple, bless him, landed on my head as I took a bow. Everyone had forgotten that the Crazies had left him up there earlier in the week. However, I'm also forced to admit that for sheer gut-wrenching awfulness the evening show on that Monday could not be beaten. Never, ever, ever. Furthermore. they even called it a triumph!

It all began encouragingly enough with Nancy and I observing a wine-fumed truce as we awoke from a long lie-in. In truth neither of our very thick heads could have stood up to the usual to and fro. And when I got to the theatre Barney too was unusually respectful to me, a situation which continued until he went into his trademark trance before the matinee, when I could have been the Queen Mother and he still wouldn't have noticed me. Incidentally, I once got a proper dressing down from the Queen (as she was then) for standing idly by as her hubby King George VI nearly choked to death while I was persuading him not to boycott The Festival of Britain. This incident is detailed in my first volume but as I'm sure you've already noticed, if you wait long enough, I'm bound to tell the story again.

However, warning signs were already on the horizon. Near the conclusion of an otherwise uneventful matinee I couldn't get out of the magic box as the antique lock had seized up. Of course, the audience were in stitches at my predicament and laughed all the more at my ripe selection of curses and oaths. And when I finally managed to kick open the door, I came shooting out and ended up spread-eagled across the stage.

Luckily the audience thought it was all part of the act, but even their generous reception could not erase my sense of humiliation. Back in the dressing room I braced myself once more for another of Barney's ritual denunciations - which never came. On the contrary, he seemed rather pleased. I even managed to wring a tribute from him.

"You flying out of the box like that," he said, shaking his head in admiration. "Who on earth taught you how to aquaplane on your chest? Absolutely inspired stuff."

"It was flamin' embarrassing."

"But you got the biggest laugh of the show."

"It wasn't planned though. It only happened because that damn lock stuck."

At first, I thought Barney hadn't heard me because he stood stock still wearing a completely blank expression.

"Did you hear what I said?"

"Yeah," he said, snapping out of the trance, "I'm really sorry about all that, Frankie. I'll get Arthur Askey to put some oil on it."

Now what the heck was he talking about?

"Now what the heck are you talking about?"

"The caretaker."

"I don't know if you've noticed, but Pitt's so big Arthur Askey could fit in his top pocket."

"Yes but they're both Scousers, aren't they? I suppose I could equally have said Robb Wilton."

"Did I ever tell you about the time that Robb, myself and Ted Ray…?"

"Strangely enough you did, Frankie. And I was as unimpressed then as I would be if you told the story yet again. Which, of course, you wouldn't dream of."

It was actually some comfort that Barney had lapsed back into his usual unpleasant self. The globe was firmly back on its rightful axis.

"And having the merest passing acquaintance with Robb Wilton," he continued in the same snooty vein, "doesn't automatically turn you into a top comic. I once had dealings with Cary Grant but I don't stroll around calling myself a film star."

"Nor are you well-groomed, sophisticated or the least bit charming so I fully take your point, old fellow … hold on a minute, what could Cary Grant possibly want with you?"

"He came backstage after a show in Hammersmith to congratulate me … and in return I gave him a few tips on comedy technique."

I studied him carefully but he didn't seem to be joking. So I stroked an imaginary beard.

"Yes, I can really see that; Cary Grant, the foremost comic timer in the movies taking tips from a scruffy kid. Pull the other one."

"Have it your own way."

I certainly intended to; it was the most unlikely thing I'd ever heard. And yet, in the not too distant future, I would discover that Barney had been telling the truth all along, although exactly what benefit Cary Grant ever derived from his advice has alas gone unrecorded.

Characteristically Barney was unwilling to enlighten me any further and sloped off to give Pitt his instructions on mending the lock on the magic box. In light of what happened a few hours later I should have had him followed.

Instead I filled those few hours with a trip to the same café at which my comic partner and advice-giver to the stars had feverishly recorded on paper napkins the idiocies and foibles of holidaying Lancastrians, and where Ray had revealed he was about to be the father he sadly never became.

Not surprisingly the visit filled me with gloom, only partly lifted by an elderly couple of diners, Len and Mabel from Bacup, who told me I'd been their favourite comic for decades. So I arrived back at the theatre feeling marginally more contented but considerably older than when I'd left. It was fortunate that I didn't know how much worse the day was going to get.

As the evening show drew nearer and Barney, as usual, retreated into the familiar realm of Trancelvania, I began to feel uneasy. Don't get me wrong here. I never go on stage without harvesting my own personal swarm of butterflies and I can't think of a performer - apart maybe from Cary Grant - who doesn't. But this was a different feeling. A premonition of doom as if the whole world was about to crash down round my ears. However, I was lulled into a degree of comfort when the first part of our routine went to plan and I managed to successfully manipulate the hook without maiming anyone too badly, myself included. Then the stagehands wheeled on the magic box and my nightmare began. It was bad enough Barney referring to me as 'my lovely assistant', but as I entered the box and the door clicked shut behind me, I was hit by a feeling of dread, as though something had already gone badly wrong. Strangely, this was because we were getting too many laughs. Our usual routine built up, through question, answer and the almost inevitable misunderstandings, a steady sea swell of laughter which would rise to a crescendo before I came flying out. But tonight, the laughter started even before the door was properly closed and reached a climax in the following few seconds. What the heck was Barney up to? He hadn't even begun to ask me the usual questions like, "are you allowed visitors in there?" And he was doing something odd to the door - there was an ominous scratching sound followed by an unfamiliar click. By now the audience were wetting themselves - and all this before I had done a single thing.

Although it wasn't really part of my repertoire, I resorted to a stage whisper.

"Hey, cowpoke, you're not plannin' on saddlin' up and ridin' into the sunset without me?"

OK, not exactly Groucho Marx but it did get a bit of a laugh. Yet why did I have the uneasy feeling that the crowd were still responding to what Barney was doing rather than what I said?

"No sirree, pardner" came the confident reply, accompanied by an appreciative titter from the audience. The guy caught on quickly, I'll give him that. "I reckon the fine ladies and gentlemen would rather I stayed here than vamoose, ain't that right y'all?"

There was a resounding yell in the affirmative.

"So what's goin' on out there?"

"Well, Frankie, it might be better if you saw for yourself."

I didn't need a second invitation and decided to make my reappearance with a pratfall, as this had worked so well in the matinee. So I shoulder-charged the door … and shot backwards to the other side of the box.

"What in tarnation, Frankie!" Barney drawled. "You went the wrong way, pardner. The door's on this side." And he gave a sharp rat-a-tat-tat on the box.

"No, I went the right way." I shouted to gales of laughter. "The goddam door's jammed again."

"That's because I've goddam locked it."

Even though everything happening was completely off-script I tried desperately to play along with it.

"But the lock's never worked properly," I ad-libbed.

"You're right so I asked Mr Handy, our handy handyman to put a new one on. He's very good is Mr Handy. You have to watch his hands, mind."

The thought that William Pitt wouldn't be guffawing like the rest of the theatre as he planned revenge for Barney's slur, was scant consolation as I realised I had been royally set up. Could I possibly rescue anything from this fiasco?

"But why has Mr Handy put a new lock on it?"

"To protect the precious things in the box."

"But there's only me in here."

"I know, I did tell him that!"

I'll spare you the excruciating details of what happened in the next ten minutes, for my sake as much as yours. Suffice to say that, while I raged, the audience howled louder and louder with uninterrupted laughter as Barney turned every one of my insults and threats into a gag. He also apparently kept a straight face (but then how would I know?) as he tried to explain to them that I might be in the box and not be in the box at the same time like something called Schroedinger's Cat. If a comedian in a box fell over in the middle of a forest, he began to wonder, would anyone hear him bawling like a maniac? It was the unlikeliest comic material yet the crowd loved it. And, just to illustrate his total domination, Barney brought my torture to a climax with his own homage to Take Your Pick, possibly the most popular show on the TV.

Doing a passable imitation of 'quiz inquisitor' Michael Miles, he asked the audience a very familiar question. And it wasn't in the least bit gratifying for me to hear that, far from wanting him to open the box, most of the audience were urging Barney to take the money.

To put the seal on my humiliation he elected to open the box after all - at the very moment I'd decided to kick my way out. God knows how he'd guessed the exact timing, but as I launched myself at it feet first, the door swung open and I shot across the stage collecting splinters in my backside.

"Ah," observed Barney as I flew past him, "my driver's here ... but he appears to have forgotten the limousine."

By now, even though everyone in the audience was weeping with laughter, I was still fuming and determined to rip out my partner's throat. As he helped me to my feet, however, Barney whispered urgently that I'd been fantastic, the crowd loved me, and I should at least wait until we were back in the dressing room before killing him. All said through a huge grin while he waved to the crowd and held up my right arm in triumph. So, ever the trouper, I merely placed my hands round his neck in simulated strangulation and together we milked the huge waves of applause and goodwill. I even noticed Nancy a few rows back, clapping and whistling through her fingers - the things they teach at those Swiss finishing schools! I also saw that she kept turning to two elderly well-dressed fellows either side of her, the bookers presumably, who were clapping as enthusiastically as she was.

We did three curtain calls before I managed to break free and stomp off to the dressing room. Barney didn't follow me immediately but when a figure eventually came through the door, I grabbed him by the collar, eager to extract my revenge. It was therefore unfortunate that my intended victim wasn't Barney at all but one of the elderly bookers.

"Franco," barked Nancy, who was right behind him, "remove your paws from that man's windpipe at once."

Of course, I couldn't apologise enough and the fellow to his credit was extremely magnanimous about it.

"I see that you remain in character," he said, while straightening his tie. "Most impressive. David Noble by the way."

We shook hands.

"And this here is my partner in crime Charlie Westerman."

He indicated a stout, bald chap who'd just come in chatting avidly to Barney.

"If we can't rustle you up a Blackpool spot before long then I'm a Dutchman," David added.

Charlie looked up from his discussion with Barney and nodded in agreement.

"Well said, pardner," he boomed to polite laughter before turning to me. "How long have you been rehearsing that routine?" Charlie asked in wonderment. "I mean, the timing alone was first class."

Before I could reply Barney put his arm round my shoulder.

"Both my colleague and I take our comedy extremely seriously," he said reverently.

The bookers and Nancy signalled their approval with earnest nods. They obviously understood that good comedy was no laughing matter.

"What you saw on stage tonight," Barney continued, "was the culmination of weeks of rehearsals we undertook in order to move our act into new and exciting directions."

He then came up with an unexpected stinger.

"Frankie suggested we should do it, which I'm sure you'll agree is to his great credit."

Well, it was hardly the time to tell them that my partner was talking the most almighty bollocks so I nodded modestly as David and Charlie slapped me on the back, both echoing each other that I was the very best type of good egg.

Nancy too was most enthusiastic.

"The audience adored your mute impotence, darling," she said before planting a huge kiss on my cheek. "They thought it was a scream. Although I doubt Schroedinger's Cat ever made that sort of racket. Dead or alive!"

Everyone laughed apart from Barney, who was too busy scribbling something on an outsized beer mat which had magically appeared in his hand.

Having calmed down somewhat, I felt I couldn't exactly go full bananas at Barney. So when the bookers left shortly afterwards, trailing a promise of untold fame and riches, I contented myself with one or two grumbles to my wife.

By now, however, Nancy had stopped smiling and ordered me to play along as a prisoner in the box from now on.

"But I'm not a straight man," I wailed.

"I'm afraid that's exactly what you are, darling," Nancy told me. "Furthermore, you do it brilliantly. For a start you're so bad-tempered. Grrrr! And the most important thing is that you really, really impressed Chas and Dave."

I glanced at Barney, vaguely wondering about his take on things, but the big drip was still scribbling away on his big drip mat, studiously ignoring both of us.

I gave it one final shot, but a throwaway mention of the London Palladium saw Nancy leap in with a two-footed tackle.

"And if you so much as mention The Crazy Gang, *I'll* bloody well string you up naked from the dress circle by your ankles."

"That's hardly the way to treat a comedy legend, Nancy," said a voice behind us. We both turned to see Conrad craning his head round the door like an eager glove puppet.

"I can't stop," he said, "but I had to tell you that I'm so relieved I awarded myself an evening off. That was just astonishing stuff. You two really should have your own TV show - on the box so to speak! Ha, ha, ha. Sorry, that one needs a bit of work."

I'd have been more than willing for Conrad to stay and ramp up the praise to even higher levels but, pleading pressure of work, he quickly took his leave with a promise of meeting up in four days' time.

Those days scurried past in no time at all, due in no small part to the continuing tremendous success of the act. Word of mouth ensured that every day at both houses the theatre was bursting at the seams. And, even though I was still very much less than keen on being made to look a dick twice a day with only Sundays off for good behaviour, I had to admit that Barney had struck gold.

After each successful second show I would hurry back to Joe's where, over one or five whiskies, we would refine our plans for Sunday's showdown. With Rose still on her course and Nancy working hard at the hotel and content for me to lodge once again at Joe's to keep him company, we were free to put as much away as we could manage while discussing every angle. Our major resolution was that we would be armed. Both of us realised that the killer would have us in his sights at the theatre on Sunday and we didn't plan on making it easy for him. However, thoughts of what he might have in store for us did begin to weigh heavy as the week wore on. Late on Wednesday evening, just as I was planning to hit the sack, Joe put his hand on my arm as I got up out of the chair.

"You don't have to do this," he told me solemnly.

"Yes I do. I'm really knackered."

"You don't fool me, Frankie. You know what I mean and I repeat, if you want to back out then I won't think any less of you."

"The only way you'd persuade me not to do this," I told him with equal solemnity - we had put away the best part of half a bottle - "is if you told Hallows the truth and the whole station went in mob-handed."

He shook his head violently.

"No, whatever all this is about it's my fight now. And I'm not risking any more lives apart from mine and …"

Suddenly reddening, Joe clammed up and to save him from further embarrassment I interrupted his sentence with the message that I would be beside him to see this thing through to the end.

Yet, despite our burgeoning buddydom, we were both relieved when Friday arrived to rescue us from each other. Naturally Joe was looking forward to his reunion with Rose who was due home in the late afternoon, while I was anticipating a more intellectually stimulating exchange with Conrad, who had phoned to invite me to an early lunch at a country pub. I felt duty-bound to invite Joe along as well, although when he refused, the relief I felt was deliciously guilty. I experienced even more guilt when he offered to drive me to the Horse and Hounds.

"The buses there are few and far between," Joe explained, "and I think you've donated enough to Coastal Cabs to hold shares in the company."

I accepted his generous offer and a couple of hours later as we arrived at the pub and I was climbing out of his jalopy, Joe laid a hand on my arm.

"Don't tell Conrad anything about the plans we've made for Sunday evening."

"That might be difficult if we don't want him blabbing to Hallows about the real date."

"Good point but I'm sure you'll think of something."

As he drove off, I spotted Conrad's Triumph Roadster tucked away in the far corner of the pub's car park, followed immediately by a sight of the man himself lounging at a wooden table near the front entrance overlooking the village green. He was dressed so very casually that I could tell he'd taken a great deal of trouble about it. The cricket pullover draped artlessly over his shoulders for instance gave him the look of a film star; a young Cary Grant maybe. Perhaps Barney could help me with that. Despite my pleasure in seeing Conrad, I was secretly relieved that Rose had been out of his orbit for a week.

"Did you get everything done at work?" I asked as he placed a welcome first pint in front of me.

"I think so; the money men are happy at any rate," he replied, dropping a menu next to my drink. "Allow me to recommend the steak sandwiches."

His endorsement proved sound for when the food arrived, I had to admit I hadn't sampled such tasty meat since before the war. Conrad of course had the reason.

"They get it from a farm down the road, and furthermore it's …"

"You live near here then?"

"Not far."

For some reason I was mildly surprised he hadn't mentioned this.

"Anyway, you were saying about the meat."

"It's freshly slaughtered or so I'm told."

"Which brings us to …"

"Ah yes, the reason you're here. You want to know how to work out the dates. It's simple really."

And with a few deft strokes he sketched out on a paper napkin a basic outline of binary theory full of noughts and ones and how the numbers in each message fitted together. It appeared so simple that I cursed myself for not working it out before.

"As I might have mentioned," Conrad explained through a mouthful of steak sandwich, "although binary is a second language to mathematicians like myself and Paddon, virtually anyone could master the basics after a couple of hours in the branch library."

This, I gloomily reflected, allowed for a depressingly large number of suspects.

"So, what's the plan for Sunday?" he asked keenly. "The full team? Spotters in place hours before? Sniper Joe positioned in the dress circle?"

"Yeah, something like that. Now back to binary. Do you think someone with a public school education …?"

He waved away my comment impatiently. "Look, anyone can understand it given the right prep. But I'm more concerned about what you might actually be facing on Sunday. That's why I'm planning to drop in on Chief Inspector Hallows this afternoon. I have one or two ideas of my own about how to trap this fellow."

Oh great, Joe *would* be pleased. I had to tread carefully.

"Er, Conrad, I wouldn't do that if I were you. Hallows is not very receptive to interference from outsiders. I should know."

"Yes, Frankie, but he needs to hear exactly how this character may be setting you all up for some kind of theatrical finish. I know I'm no copper but I've been giving this a lot of thought and I'd hate to think of people I now count as good friends being hurt."

I took another bite of my sandwich and chewed it carefully, all the while considering my options. If Joe wanted to do it his way these really boiled down to a single choice.

"Listen, Conrad, I - that is Joe - may not have been entirely straight with you."

I then admitted how we'd fooled Hallows into thinking the operation was a week hence so no lives would be at risk apart from Joe's and my own. As I spoke, Conrad expressed incomprehension quickly followed by alarm.

"This is absolute madness," he whispered urgently, glancing around to check that drinkers at adjacent tables were not ear-wigging in on our conversation. "The two of you venturing alone into the lion's den. It's completely crazy."

He stared pleadingly at me.

"Look, Conrad," I told him. "Even if I wanted to, I couldn't shift Joe from his course. And I'm under strict orders not to let you give the game away."

"How do plan to do that? Shoot me?"

I glanced up to see if he was joking. He clearly wasn't.

"No, I'm not planning to shoot you. Obviously I can't stop you doing what you want to do. But I can ask. As a mate. A really good friend."

There was silence for thirty seconds while Conrad's gaze remained impassive, a perfect blank. Then he said, "Fine, put yourselves in the most deadly danger. I won't peach on you ..."

I gave an involuntary sigh of relief which quickly died at the back of my throat as I registered Conrad's follow-up.

"...but I'm coming as well."

This was all getting a bit too complicated and I actually found myself longing for a return to the relative simplicities of binary notation.

"Conrad, please," I implored, "Joe and I have been planning this all week and we're down to the fine details, the main one of which is ..."

Quite suddenly I found myself unable to speak as Conrad's right hand had appeared across my mouth.

"Not another bloody word," he hissed urgently. "Did they never teach you that walls have ears?"

He glanced furtively round the pub garden and slowly moved his hand away from my face. Strangely enough, it had smelled of wine gums, the green ones. For the next couple of minutes, he picked absently at the last of his steak sandwich.

"I don't want to interfere with your plans," he mumbled eventually. "I just want to tag along. Who knows I might even be of some use."

I shook my head. "You don't get it, Conrad. *I'm* only part of this mission on sufferance so if I tried to introduce someone else, I'd be out of the picture too. Then Joe would probably have to shoot us both."

He gave me an odd look which quickly changed to one of genuine alarm.

"I'm kidding of course but you can see why the idea hasn't got wings. Plus, you're not exactly ..."

"Exactly what?"

"Well, to be brutal, you're more of a brainbox than a man of action."

Conrad's face and shoulders drooped and I felt genuinely sorry for him. It wasn't his fault that he'd been playing with nutty numerals while the rest of us were getting shot at. To his credit he could accept the point - up to a point.

"Very well," he conceded, "I admit I'm not the world's most physically impressive specimen but I have done my bit for the Third XV. Taken the knocks."

"But, Conrad, even if your idea was feasible, we need someone who can hand out the knocks. And can shoot his way out of trouble. Ever handled a gun?"

"Oh yes indeed. My dear old Dad had a nine-millimetre Luger pistol he took from a German in east Africa during the Great War. He sometimes let my brother and I handle it. Sensational piece of kit."

"But did you ever fire the thing?"

"Well, as you ask, no."

"Have you ever fired a gun?"

"Not as such."

"Then I'm afraid you won't be much good to us on Sunday evening anyway. In fact, mate, I'll go so far to say that you could even be a liability. We might be looking out for you when we should concentrate on the killer. I'm afraid we just can't risk it. Sorry."

Conrad nodded sadly, finally appearing to accept what I was saying before slowly getting to his feet, pint glass in hand.

"One for the road?" he inquired hopefully.

I glanced at my watch and my regret intensified.

"Sorry again, Conrad, but I need to be getting back to the theatre. Apparently, some genius is plotting to lock me in a magic box during the matinee. I think the bus is due any minute."

Conrad put his pint pot firmly back on the table.

"I won't hear of it," he said. "Let me run you there. Atone for embarrassing you just then."

I hadn't been all that embarrassed but I was happy to let him think I had. I was just relieved that I'd managed to put him off telling Hallows about our plans and getting involved in them himself. So I graciously allowed Conrad to drive me back into town. After all, the buses *were* terrible.

As we arrived at the pier entrance Conrad leaned over and grabbed my arm.

"Don't do anything silly, old fellow," he said with a weak grin. "It would be nice if that splendid steak sandwich lunch wasn't our last."

I nodded in full agreement.

To my mind, if you've just been told not to do anything silly and then promptly allow yourself to be locked in a gaily coloured box while five hundred people mock you, then you deserve all you get.

This conclusion arrived as I sat glumly incarcerated in my gaudy prison. Even though I still had to give Barney routine angry responses so he could weave his menace and magic around them, there was plenty of time to philosophise. While the existence of Schroedinger's cat might have been a justifiable starting point, my musings took a more menacingly feline-related course. What if I was going into the lion's den - thanks for that one, Conrad - with the King of Beasts himself? Suppose Joe planned to shoot and then frame me for the murders because … well I don't know, because I was in a big daft box with nothing else to think about or do. I tell a lie, I did have one duty; fall out of the box at the wrong moment, ie the right one for maximum jollity. Given that my mind was elsewhere it was, sadly, a task I failed at on this occasion - an omission which produced a stream of volcanic rage from my partner back in the dressing room.

"It should be literally impossible to cock up the job of a straight man," he raved.

"I keep telling you I'm not a bloody straight …"

"But still you manage to fuck things up with ease. I was going to say enviable ease but quite frankly who'd envy you?"

By now a moustache of foam was forming on his upper lip.

"It's embarrassing and everyone could see it. Frankly you're really just a … oh bloody hell why did you do that?"

The guy was so up himself he really didn't comprehend why I'd punched him in the mouth and sent him spinning across the room. Though I'll give Barney this, he didn't lack courage. He was up in a flash and throwing himself at me in a mad revenge attack. And at one point, I was alarmed to find he was even getting the better of me. But after I'd flattened him again with one to the chin, he just lay there panting and confined himself to hitting back verbally.

"You're just a rotten bully, a talentless hooligan who can't even be unfunny convincingly. Good god, I'm I really looking forward to …"

"To what, Barney?" I said as he swallowed his words. "Thinking of going solo, are you? Well get on with it 'cos I can't bloody wait!"

That was only the first in a series of awkward encounters - depending what you take to mean by the word 'awkward'. In my opinion the definition could definitely stretch to the first three. But the final one? You'll have to make up your own mind.

After Barney came Hallows.

Between shows the following day, I went as arranged to visit the chief inspector in his lair and to say I was on edge would be something of an understatement. I'd been walking on eggshells in the two shows since my bust-up with Barney and the fact he'd been glacially calm and professional before, during and after each performance had unnerved me even more. Back at the other palace of varieties Joe had been his usual surly self and even Rose had snapped at me when I'd asked if she'd enjoyed her little holiday. Some people!

I therefore approached Hallows with a degree of care which proved to be unwarranted. After I'd delivered Conrad's supposed confirmation that the latest message predicted the next outrage would take place in eight days' time, Hallows merely nodded and gazed at me expectantly. At first, I thought it was the calm before another explosion but he surprised me by asking, "So, no requests?"

"Requests, sir? In what respect?"

"You're normally itching to get a gun in your hand and fight the good fight alongside us."

For a moment I worried that he suspected my unusual reticence meant I was hiding the truth from him. But when he clapped me firmly on the shoulder and said, "I'd really like to have you on the team," I realised that he had actually begun to value me. Which of course made me feel bad for conning him. But hey ho!

"Sir, I'm honoured you want me there when we finally trap this maniac and I'll join the mission in any capacity, however lowly."

Hallows looked as if he was about to blub.

"Frankie, we have not always seen eye to eye but during those awful times when Ray and Wilf were fatally injured you proved to be a cool head on a willing body."

That sounded a touch dodgy if you ask me but, again, time to play along.

"How could I do anything else, sir? They were both my friends. As this maniac will find out if, sorry, *when* I get my hands on him."

As he ushered me out with the advice to get plenty of sleep in the next few days, I managed to bite my tongue and stop myself asking after Jenny. That would definitely have spoiled a beautiful moment.

The third potentially awkward encounter came at the time I least wanted it, in the middle of Sunday morning - D-Day if you like, although Joe would hardly have welcomed that description. In direct defiance of the Chief Inspector I'd spent the night tossing and turning and was feeling fairly wretched, when another summons arrived from the mayor. Just when I felt I needed to be alone with my thoughts, I was handed the phone receiver by an unsmiling Rose.

"Your podgy pal wants to see you again," she muttered, and, following a short one-sided conversation, I was once more on the way to Boardman Towers.

Of course, I could have refused the mayor's invitation but something was nagging at me. It was perfectly possible, I reasoned, that in a few hours' time Joe and I could be lining up in a fight to the death against Boardman senior or junior. And, while my appearance would hardly be guaranteed to have the mayor or his son quaking in their size twelves, I was keen to see what they were up to and if either might let something slip.

So off I went, transported inevitably by Ted the chattering cabby who remained keen to give me his views on

Hollywood weddings when I really could have done without his prattling. It was actually a relief when I escaped from Ted's world of pain over Marilyn into Boardman's realm. That respite, however, was fleeting as the look on the mayor's face suggested that he was facing troubles of his own. It turned out that, like me, he had his worries about John.

"Why are you so concerned, Ken? You've not lined up more fights for him?"

Boardman managed to crack a smile for the first time since I'd arrived.

"Yeah," he said, "I thought he could box young Brian London, you know that big lad from up the road. The one they call The Blackpool Rock."

Now it was my turn to look concerned.

"Jesus wept, Ken. Hasn't John taken enough punishment?"

Boardman's smile grew wider.

"I got you there, Frankie. Besides Brian, who's a very nice lad incidentally, tells me he's turned pro. No, our John's says he's hung up the gloves. But I'm still concerned about him."

"How old is he for goodness sake?"

"It doesn't matter. He's still my son. We never stop worrying."

Worrying that he might embarrass your mayoralty, or even worse, land you with a huge bill for something or other, I thought.

Nevertheless, when Boardman told me what had been going on, I had to admit it was all a bit odd. I mean, even when John was supposedly on the rails, he'd spend his days terrorising bakery employees before evenings at the club drunkenly bullying anyone in his vicinity. But, through all that, at least his Dad knew where John was while he was misbehaving. Whereas nowadays, Ken reckoned, his son was prone to skip work altogether before going missing all night. What on earth was he up to?

"He's probably got a girl," I said, doing the minimum I could to lighten Boardman Senior's mood. "I did see him at the dance recently toe to toe with a little stunner."

The fact that he'd also gone toe to toe with Ray and ended up virtually dragging the poor girl off by the hair went unmentioned.

Boardman grimaced. "Tiny little thing? Red hair, really good looking?"

"That's the one. They looked like a match made in heaven."

"Yeah, until she set the cops on him a couple of days ago. Officially he's not allowed within half a mile of her now."

"Why not?"

"You don't want to know. You've got a son, haven't you?"

"Two actually but the oldest isn't …"

"… a twenty-two-carat prick without a civil word in his head?"

"I was about to say the oldest isn't seventeen yet. And the younger one is only eleven."

"Then you've got all this joy to come," he replied morosely.

On the contrary, I was looking forward to seeing both my sons when school broke up and they made the trip to Lancashire to visit their old Dad. But I kept quiet about it so as not to make my host feel any gloomier.

"Anyway, it's time I got my skates on," I said, moving towards the door.

Boardman looked startled. "No don't go," he pleaded.

At that point I realised that, while the mayor might set limited store by my lukewarm advice, what he desperately needed from me was companionship. To put it bluntly, the man was short of real pals. Most people in the town either feared or loathed him and nearly all kept their distance.

I was about to pledge that I'd keep my eyes open for anything his son and heir might get up to (I was determined to do this anyway after hearing of John's unexplained absences, which had put him near the top of my personal list of suspects) when the man himself hove into view. John had slouched halfway down the wide staircase before he noticed me loafing in the doorway to the drawing room, trying unsuccessfully to take my leave.

"Ah, the entertainment's arrived," he drawled. "My cue to exit stage left, I think. Don't want to die laughing or suchlike."

Behind me, I could sense his Dad beginning to bristle with rage so I quickly hit back verbally before Ken could unpack his fists.

"John, allow me to commend you on your performance against Brian Pike. It was a masterclass in the noble art - from Pike at any rate."

"I suppose I should be grateful he didn't kill me," was John's fairly honest assessment of his fighting prowess. Of course, being John Boardman, there was a sting.

"But I never really fancied dying on the public stage. Talking of which, how's the act going?"

I could see that Ken was reaching boiling point but fortunately John had noticed it too.

"I'm only kidding, Dad. And I'm sure he's dealt with keener critics than me in his time. Speaking of which, Frankie, how's your extremely talented partner. Barry is it?"

"Yeah that's right. Be sure you tell everyone about Barry."

Ignoring my sarcasm, he opted instead for a spot of sage advice.

"Do you know what you should do?"

"Look, John, I don't give you advice on how to fall over in the boxing ring without hurting yourself so …"

John shrugged. "I was only going to say that you should forget about aping those clowns on Variety Bandbox and try to take a leaf out of Tony Hancock's book."

This vaguely constructive criticism intrigued me so much I couldn't help asking John to elaborate.

"Well," he said rubbing his cheek, "it is true that Hancock's also straight out of the variety tradition."

"Very perceptive of you, John."

He grinned malevolently.

"Yeah, but now he's moved way past that tired old music hall crap."

"I wouldn't describe …"

"Have you listened to his show on the Light Programme?" It was the first time I'd seen John become animated about anything but now he was positively fizzing. "Bloomin' hilarious, it is. I nearly pissed myself last week when him and Sid got that three-legged greyhound."

And then he only went and did a passable impression of the lad himself. "'Dear, oh dear, oh dear, stone me, Sidney, what a bleedin' life!' And now he's on the television. You could pick up a fair few comedy tips from watching him."

"Pity I don't have a telly."

I wasn't sure if Ken had actually been listening to our to-and-fro but he must have been because the next moment he'd grabbed my arm and was steering me back into the parlour.

"Well, you can watch that," he said proudly pointing to the corner of the room and a slightly larger than usual television set in a gleaming mahogany cabinet.

"It's a Ferranti deluxe console with a seventeen-inch screen," he bragged, puffing out his chest as if this should mean anything to me. "And, listen to this. It's got 405 lines."

Given that I was a guest, I was prepared to be impressed but John remained in a less amenable mood. Raising his right eyebrow slightly, he asked, "Do you have the faintest idea what 405 lines means?"

Ken glared at his son. "Do you?" he snapped back.

"I certainly don't but then again I don't pretend to. That's why I'd like you to enlighten me, pater. You've always been such a fount of knowledge."

I watched in fascination as Ken oscillated between the urge to throttle his son and a genuine wish to share with us his understanding of the new medium. Which turned out to be basic to say the least.

"Well, you see 405 lines means that this TV has," he said, glancing at me in desperation as if I could be some help unravelling the science, "that is, it has … a touch more than 400 lines."

What a relief he'd cleared that one up. John, however, was still not entirely satisfied.

"I once got 400 lines at school," he revealed with a straight face, "when the head reckoned I was talking total bullshit about televisual communication."

"You cheeky little …"

"But my mitigating plea that talking bullshit ran in our family didn't seem to cut much ice with him."

Boardman senior clenched his huge fists.

"I wasted my bleedin' money there. I should have sent you to the council school."

"Console yourself with the thought that you have always been free, father dear, to spend your considerable fortune in any way you wish," John replied cheekily. "Just as I'm able to choose to drink myself into as much of a stupor as my meagre allowance will allow."

John turned and walked towards the door before his Dad had the chance to detonate. But after a couple of steps, he turned to me with a surprisingly solemn look.

"I was really sorry to hear about what happened to the big copper," he said. "I'm told he was a pal of yours. We didn't get on much as you're probably aware but, well, I'd never wish that on him."

You just might though, I mused as he slammed the front door and roared off to god knows where in his Jag.

Ken seemed to echo my thoughts.

"Goodness knows when he'll be back," he grunted. "You will have lunch?"

I didn't fancy any more argy-bargy so I agreed I would stay. And, from a gastronomic viewpoint, I was glad I did. Far from lobbing me one of his meat and potato specials in a barm cake, Ken once again pushed out the boat. Like last time, I was treated to an upmarket lunch which included roast saddle of beef and glazed parsnips accompanied by the offer of an impudent Bordeaux which I regretfully declined in view of my approaching adventure with Joe. Looking back, I'm still not sure whether I shouldn't have necked the whole bottle.

The food and excellent wine aside, my lunchtime with the mayor proved uninspiring fare. Chief item on our conversational menu was a one-sided grumble from Ken about how much time his missus Marjorie spent caring for her ailing friend Polly. Apparently, this selfish harridan had had the gall to be struck down with a bowel disorder just as Boardman was planning a classy night of fun on the sofa for him and Marjorie - most likely goggling at Double Your Money on the Ferranti while munching Spangles. Ken v Colitis, I mused, blocking out the rest of his rant before opting for an easy away win.

Increasingly conscious of what was approaching, I set about disentangling myself from my host's grasp. Despite my insistence, Ken said he wouldn't dream of me phoning Ted and for an awful moment I thought he was going to offer to drive me back himself, even though he had shifted seven-eighths of the lunchtime bottle of wine.

"Nay, I'm not that bloody daft, lad," he replied to my expression of concern. "My driver'll take you."

"I can't imagine the Mellish ratepayers will be happy to see a comedian being ferried around in the mayoral limousine," I told him, failing to add that this was exactly what they'd normally witness.

"Don't worry Terence'll be driving my Jag."

I couldn't argue with that. As I settled into the soft leather passenger seat and opened the window to bid farewell to my host, he leaned down and stuck his face so close to mine I could smell the vineyard on him. I thought I was about to get a warning - maybe 'buy our pies or I'll do you' - but Boardman's message was less threatening if no less heart-felt than that.

"Just keep an eye out for John," he pleaded with a damp stare. "You will, won't you, Frankie?"

I assured him that of course I would - and immediately put his plea out of my mind. Yet it turned out that the chance to have an influence on John's future would arrive far sooner than either of us could have imagined.

Outside Joe's, I thanked tiny Terence both for the lift and his commendable silence on the journey. I also slipped him a couple of quid. After all, it made a welcome change to travel in a vehicle not driven by the poor man's answer to Tommy Handley. And, as I'd suspected, the chauffeur *did* need to sit on a cushion.

Letting myself in, I expected to be greeted by the usual smells and sounds of Sunday afternoon; lamb, mint sauce and Take It From Here. But the place was aroma-free apart from a faint trace of Rose's most recent menthol cigarette. The silence also remained unbroken by radio funny men. Troublingly this dead atmosphere brought to mind the stillness of my own home a decade ago, immediately before I was attacked by that Russian thug intent on doing me terminal damage. To mask my screams, he'd turned on the wireless which blared out what else but Handley's ITMA programme complete with its brain-dead catchphrases. With the Ivan's huge hands tightening round my throat, I'd resigned myself to leaving this world accompanied by the ironic request, 'Can I do you now, sir?'

Given these happy thoughts and the fact that I believed the house was empty, it came as a jolt to find Joe at the dining room table brandishing a knife. In front of him was a medium-sized wooden box. He didn't see me for a moment and when he did, he merely placed the knife next to the box on the table. It was an evil-looking serrated-edged thing.

"You taking that on our big adventure?"

"No chance. I might hurt someone," he said without a smile.

"Then why are you messing about with it?"

"As a reminder."

On a day like this I really didn't need to hear what a deadly weapon reminded him of.

"Where's Rose?"

"Gone into work. Something about the course. Debriefing we used to call it."

"Bit of a liberty making her work on a Sunday."

"Probably for the best," Joe replied, opening the box and pulling out a .455 Webley Revolver. For a second, I flinched but Joe didn't appear to notice.

"As you see the safety catch is on," he said handing it to me. "That's because it's fully-loaded. Get used to it while I nip upstairs for a kip. If I'm not down wake me at five."

I was about to ask how the hell he'd managed to conceal this weapon and presumably another for himself from his colleagues' searches, but he was already out of the door.

13

End of the Pier Showdown

LIKE A FEW OTHER British seaside towns, Mellish once boasted not one, not two, but three piers to delight its visitors. Many theories exist about how the central pier came to be blasted into oblivion on the night of May 17th 1941. Some locals blame it on a Schnapps-befuddled Dornier bomb aimer who, peering cross-eyed into his crosshairs, understandably mistook Mellish's memorial boating pool for Liverpool Docks. Others maintain that a huge naval mine, released by a passing U-boat to damage incoming ships, bobbed gently into the pier's supports with predictable results. And one or two reckon an embittered RAF Halifax pilot who'd paid good money to see George Formby at the pier's Grand Palace Theatre in 1937 took appropriate revenge. Whatever the truth, the calamity left Mellish with just one pier (the southernmost version having been washed away during a violent storm in 1927). And yet, despite their turbulent ends, neither the south nor central piers witnessed any fatalities on the nights of their demise or indeed at any time before that. Which is more than can be said for their less fashionable cousin, the north pier, which had already been the scene of one violent murder and was about to record another.

If that uncelebrated pier, resting uncertainly at the point where the town ended and its outer wasteland began, had eyes which opened at a quarter to six that wet Sunday evening, it would have been intrigued to observe the approach of an unlikely brace of gunslingers. For a start, the peering pier might have struggled to identify the duo as quick-on-the-draw merchants, as our firearms were very much not on show. We might even have been mistaken for a pair of shoplifters on the run, as Joe had insisted that we took care to hide the weapons. Mine was in a concealed shoulder holster and sniper Joe had tucked his Lee Enfield rifle in the carefully-prepared lining of an old-fashioned grey gabardine mac. How he'd known it was going to rain was beyond me.

These arrangements had been finalised half an hour earlier, not long after I had struggled to wake him from his slumbers. Knowing Joe's intermittent sleeping patterns, I would have bet good money on him being wide awake at four o'clock and pacing irritably back and forth. Instead, when I poked my head around his bedroom door at a quarter to five, he was still sleeping contentedly. No wailing or thrashing around. And definitely no ranting about Freddy!

He was wide awake now though as we left the last street in town and crossed Marine Parade to the pier entrance. One or two people were milling around but not many. Even if the weather hadn't been blustery and wet there was precious little to do on the pier before you reached the theatre, apart from sit in one of the shelters, observe the sea and wish you were somewhere else. The usual fun stuff, slot machines, a little fairground with a twisty slide and a miniature train had all been features of the central pier which disappeared forever that fateful wartime night.

Despite the lack of crowds though, we were watchful as we made our way along the boards. After all, it was not beyond possibility that one of this bored-looking lot might turn out to be our murderer. Particularly that shifty cove picking his nose. But by the time we reached the theatre, there were even fewer people around and not one paid us the slightest attention.

Joe insisted we go in by the stage door but before we could set off round the side, he placed his hand on my arm.

"You can still sit this one out, Frankie."

"Thanks, Joe, I'll nip back and catch the last few minutes of Ray's A Laugh."

Joe grinned for the first time since he'd woken from his nap.

"I had to ask."

"No, you didn't but thanks anyway."

We were about to set off when Joe grabbed my arm again, a move which frankly had begun to annoy me.

"Look, I told you I'm as committed to this … good god, Joe, what's wrong?"

He was staring in horrified amazement past my left shoulder. I turned to look … and gasped. Wilf's two small garden boxes which had been smashed to pieces the night he was murdered were back there on the window sills, newly painted red, yellow and blue as if nothing had happened. Furthermore, they contained the same neat assortment of sea pinks, cornflowers and geraniums which had ended up scattered across the boards among lumps of soil and wood splinters. As on that dreadful night, the sight of these flowers, now fluttering harmlessly in the stiff breeze, terrified me.

"Perhaps your boss did it as a tribute to Wilf," Joe said, trying to convince himself that this wasn't one more thing to be deeply worried about.

I shook my head. "Mr Shelvey would have taken soundings from everyone at the theatre before doing something like that. No, Joe, this is the killer telling us he's in charge."

"Then you and me, Frankie, we'd better go and see what other pretty delights he's prepared for us."

We crept around the side of the building, trying unsuccessfully not to make the boards creak and think too much about what was waiting for us inside. Hopefully we'd be early enough to surprise The Mellish Maniac when he made his entrance for the 7:46 denouement.

I carefully unlocked the stage door and, sneaking past the poky dressing room I shared with Barney, wondered if I should grab my cricket bat as a lucky charm. Good god, it already looked as if we needed something extra. But Joe whispered that this would complicate matters as each of us was already carrying a gun. It came as a relief when our more detailed plans then kicked in. I began to make my way down to the wings in a particularly noisy and conspicuous manner while Joe quietly climbed the stairs to the circle to see if the shadowy character our roller-skater Dot had glimpsed from the stage was once more hiding up there.

Watching Joe disappear up the wide main staircase, I stole a glance at the double front doors out on to the pier and for a moment wondered if it might be more judicious to … but any thoughts I had of fleeing the ordeal to come disappeared as I became aware of an indistinct yet pervasive sound coming from the auditorium. Resisting making a frontal assault, I continued down the corridor to the wings.

Peeping out into the auditorium, I could clearly see Joe crouching up in the circle. He gave a signal that he was quite alone up there but I was aware that, like me, he had become transfixed by the curious tableau on stage. Barney's magic box stood there upright and lit by a single spotlight from above. Nothing too unusual about that. But here was the thing; the box appeared to be making the most god-awful racket as if someone was being tortured, and furthermore enjoying the experience. It took me a few moments to realise that the noise was a recording of that old music hall standard, The Laughing Policeman, complete with its manic cackling. For a brief moment, neither of us was sure what to do, then Joe signalled that I should tiptoe down into the auditorium.

Seconds later I was crouching at the end of row B, sweeping my pistol across the stalls and up towards the circle. Although there was no-one in sight, I remained in place for a couple of minutes scanning the scene, during which time the record mercifully stopped - and then started again. I noticed that the stout lock which Pitt the caretaker had sneakily fixed to the magic box's door had gone. In its place was a hook and eye.

I looked up at Joe again and pointed to the box, clearly indicating I was about to approach it.

"Not from the front," came the hoarse and urgent stage whisper from above. He was right of course; there was little sense in making myself too much of a target. It was at that point that I had my brainwave. I crept forward to the side of the stage and from it I pulled my trusty hook. If there was a bomb or any other grim greeting when I opened the box, this would give me a fighting chance. Carefully manoeuvring the hook along over the centre of row A and the orchestra pit, I played it out to its limit until the curved end was touching the box's door. From the corner of my eye I could see Joe signalling urgently for me to step aside a couple of paces. It was a good job he did too because, as I skilfully steered the end of my trusty hook under the makeshift lock and raised it slowly, the magic box's door swung open. And the theatre exploded.

The seats next to me disintegrated and the hook flew from my grasp as I was thrown to the floor. Peering up though a film of smoke, I could see that what remained of the seats in the centre of rows A and B were covered in pellet holes. Had the trap worked I would have been blown to bits. And still that fat and jolly policeman laughed until he cried.

Struggling to my knees, I saw that amid the smoke and debris sniper Joe had already rushed downstairs and was crouching behind a seat, aiming his rifle directly at the box, which to my surprise was still largely intact. The only thing that had changed was the door had been blown clean off its hinges. Oh, and there was a man sitting inside it, facing us with a shotgun resting between his legs and pointing our way. With his rifle still levelled steadily at the box, Joe barked an order at the seated figure.

"Put the gun down and come out with your hands up," adding melodramatically, "the whole building is surrounded."

But the man in the box with the shotgun did not move a muscle. I gulped and stared harder through the clearing smoke. There was something exceedingly familiar about our assailant but it took another few moments to understand what I was looking at.

"Jesus wept, Joe," I cried, "it's Barney!"

It looked very much as if my partner in comedy had turned to crime.

"Talk to the fellow then," whispered a perfectly focused and unemotional Joe. "Tell him to give himself up. Let him know that I never miss."

"Joe, I'm the very last person he'll take orders from."

"Why's he just sitting there?"

"Because he's an idle swine. He only really comes alive when he's tormenting me."

"Perhaps we'd better ask him what's going on then."

Both of us crept carefully to end of the rows of seats and ducked down by the orchestra pit. Slowly we rose until we were crouched staring right into the box. Then I saw it - an envelope pinned to Barney's coat collar. Immediately I jumped on to the stage.

"No, Frankie," Joe yelled in a desperate warning but I already understood that Barney offered no threat to me - nor would he ever again.

I walked slowly up to the box and stared at its occupant. Barney looked quite dead but as I was about to check for a pulse there was another shout from Joe.

"Watch it, he might be booby-trapped!"

I stepped quickly back and scanned the immediate area. There didn't seem to be any wires around but Barney did have a suspicious bulge under his coat. I also noticed a Dansette record player at the back of the stage, the source of the policeman's manic laughter.

"Switch off that rubbish," Joe shouted, "but, watch out, the record player might be wired as well."

I signalled to Joe who passed me what remained of my trusty hook; it was now minus the hooked end and about half of the shaft had been blown off. However, there was enough of it to enable me to carefully lift the stylus from the spinning black disc. The cracked voice of Charles Penrose was suddenly silenced - no more laughter from that quarter. Ah, how could I forget dear old Charlie and his missus Mabel, who was a fair bit younger than him. I remembered when we'd both been playing Bradford Alhambra in 1937, Mabel had confessed she carried a bit of a torch for me. In fact, that torch turned out to be a bloomin' great …

"Jesus flamin' Christ!"

With that oath, Joe had leapt back from the box and was gazing in horror at his chest, which was covered in blood. For one terrible moment I thought the box had been booby trapped after all and Joe was a goner. But then I saw that, as he'd carefully opened Barney's coat to assess the damage, a strategically positioned bag of blood had burst all over him.

It wasn't just Joe's chest that had been stained red either. Blood was smeared all over his face and hands, giving him the look of a mad butcher but I kept silent about this as he pawed at his shirt front in anger and fear. Perhaps I would have been more sympathetic if I hadn't been staring in horrified fascination at the inanimate shell of my former partner. It had taken a professional lifetime but poor old Barney had finally died on stage.

I carefully reached in to the magic box and checked my stage partner's pulse to make sure there was nothing there. Sadly there wasn't, although I did catch a lingering whiff of BO. Unpinning the blood-covered envelope from Barney's coat, I handed it to Joe. Both of us moved well away from the box before we read it. What proved to be the oddest message yet read, 'Domus et placens uxor.' And afterwards, in Roman numerals, one, four, three, one, eight, four.

"What the hell is all that about?" said Joe staring at me in bewilderment.

"Dunno but it does ring a bell."

In fact, I vaguely recalled Guy Burgess spouting something similar at me but I was buggered if I could remember what it meant.

The next quarter of an hour was spent with our weapons drawn, nervously searching the building but there was no one else to be found. Eventually Joe lowered his rifle.

"I need to phone this in," he said, hands still trembling.

The police telephone box was by the entrance to the pier, which was now completely deserted. This was fortunate as Joe looked like he'd been auditioning for the part of ship's surgeon on Nelson's Victory. He urged his colleagues to get to the pier immediately as there was one man dead, the comedian Barney

McAskill. We would soon face an incendiary Chief Inspector Hallows but that was not what concerned me at that moment. As Joe closed the police box door, I tugged at his blood-soaked sleeve and pointed across the road to a patch of waste ground.

The boot of a dark green car was sticking out from behind one of the large thorn bushes that dotted the area. The vehicle looked very much like a Jaguar.

"That's John Boardman's jalopy," Joe exclaimed excitedly. "I bloody well knew it. Come on let's nail the swine."

"Careful," I said with my hand on his arm, "there may be more surprises in store."

Raising our weapons, we zig-zagged towards the Jag, taking cover behind piles of earth and discarded bricks. And, sure enough there *was* another surprise. Even though we could see no figures in the car, it was clearly rocking not so gently up and down on its springs. I glanced at Joe but he appeared as baffled as I was. Creeping nearer to the bouncing Jag, we could now make out the figure of a man on the back seat.

"I'll get the door, you cover me," Joe whispered.

Taking a very deep breath, he rushed at the car and threw the door open while I stood behind him, trembling but ready to fire. However, our precautions proved unnecessary. Although the normally menacing John Boardman was indeed in the car, he had his trousers and pants round his ankles, while his naked white buttocks heaved up and down like a couple of very unappetising blancmanges. The man was only having sex with a woman on the back seat.

John spun round to face us, first in murderous fury and then puzzled fear as he registered the two lethal firearms that were pointing at his head. For a moment, I couldn't see the woman's face but as John roughly detached himself from her, she too gazed fearfully up at us - and screamed in terror when she saw her blood-soaked former fiancée, pointing a rifle directly at her.

"Please, Joe, don't kill us," Marjorie whimpered.

Joe, obviously in shock, didn't say a word but motioned John to get out of the car, which he did quickly enough while pulling up his trousers.

"It's not a crime, you know," he sneered in the moment before Joe smashed him across the face with the stock of his rifle.

"But murder is a crime," Joe replied, pointing the weapon at John who, despite being flat on his back, was ready as ever with an answer.

"I'm not the one covered in blood."

Joe looked as if he was about to hit John again but before he could, Marjorie swung her legs out of the car and grabbed her former lover's arm.

"Joe," she pleaded, "I don't know what you suspect him of but John has been … with me all afternoon."

I pulled Joe away from her, unable to divine from his expression what he was most put out about: a) the fact that yet again we had not cornered the killer; b) that he'd been watching some pillock shagging his old girlfriend; or c) that John Boardman was having sex with his own step-mother.

John staggered to his feet, looking mean enough to risk having another go. Which was probably not the cleverest idea when there's a sniper's rifle pointing at you.

"Don't even think about it," Joe spat. "I'd shoot you down in a heartbeat like the dirty dog you are."

A mixture of b) and c) then.

For an instant everything hung in suspense but thankfully John leaned back against the car and Joe lowered his rifle.

"So, what's this about another murder then?" John asked.

By way of reply, Joe reached into his pocket and handed John the blood-soaked note that had been pinned to Barney's corpse.

"Make yourself useful for once. You did Latin at that posh school of yours. What does that lot mean?"

John took the note, glanced at it cautiously and gazed equally warily back at Joe.

"It says, 'Domus et placens uxor.' You're right it's a Latin quote. From Virgil."

"But what does it mean?"

"Er ... 'domus et placens uxor.'" John was now concentrating as if his life depended on it. "Er 'a home and a pleasing wife'. That's it."

While John had relaxed, Joe looked even more horrified.

"Wife! You're sure?"

"Yeah 'uxor' means wife. Or as *you* might say 'trouble and strife.'"

By now John was beginning to look pleased with himself - as much as you could appear self-satisfied with your nose splattered across your face and your shirt flapping in the breeze.

"Oh, and I've just remembered," he added, "it's not by Virgil."

"I don't give a toss who it's by," growled Joe, who was glaring at Marjorie, as she desperately tried to get her clothes in some sort of order.

"Just for the record anyway," sneered John, "it's actually by Quintus Horatius Flaccus."

"Never heard of him."

"You might have; he's the Roman poet better known as Horace."

The final word hit Joe like a bullet. He staggered back and stared aghast at John.

"Horace? You sure."

"I didn't completely waste my time at school."

Eyes flashing wildly, Joe pointed at Marjorie who was now sitting in the back seat, pulling her shoes on.

"Get out," he yelled, dragging his ex from the car and throwing assorted items of clothing after her. I was then astonished to see him pull open the front door and jump into the driver's seat.

"Come on then," he shouted at me and I barely had time to clamber into the Jaguar before we roared off, bouncing across the waste ground.

And there, among the mayhem, with a bleeding John Boardman protesting loudly about the theft of his car, a half-dressed Marjorie staggering around screaming and our crazed policeman driver doing terminal damage to the Jag's gearbox … amid all that chaos, Joe decided to tell me a story.

14

Battered, Thence Ring KO (Free, Wine)*

* See end of chapter

MORE ACCURATELY he completed the story he had begun a couple of days before, although circumstances dictated it was heavily edited, as the journey would not be a long one. When we arrived home to find it empty, he took a brief glance at his notebook and then we were off again, with Joe still driving like Mr Toad's far more reckless brother. Over those few miles he outlined the bones of a tale that put everything that had happened in context, although I didn't immediately grasp that. Of course, much of the detail was omitted as we flew round corners and scraped kerbs. But in the months following that terrible day - not yet at an end for the purposes of this narrative - I managed from various conversations to piece together Joe's encounter with the German sniper on top of that tower during a baking hot day in Normandy twelve years before. And although he didn't actually say some of the following words, I'll put the story in Joe's voice as I promise it's totally faithful to the gist of what he blurted out to me during that drive. Plus, in this instance at any rate, his delivery was far better than any comedian's.

... either I got lucky or I was actually aiming properly, I just can't remember but anyway I must have hit him because I see him fly backwards. Dead or wounded? I dunno but I'm going

to find out. I vault over the wall and get to the side door of the church.

I'm expecting to have to kick it in but on a push the door swings open as if the church is inviting me in. If I hadn't been half-crazy with grief and anger, that might have worried me - heavy symbolism and all that - but at this point I'm not afraid of anything. Anyway, I figure the sniper won't have had time to get down the tower so I'm OK taking the spiral steps two at a time. I come round the last turn of the spiral and there's the door to the roof. It's open so naturally I ignore all my training and go barrelling through it - don't forget at this point I'm so pumped up I'm immortal - and go arse over tip when my feet come into contact with a wire strung across the doorway.

Worse than that, my rifle goes flying out of my hands. I smash down face first and wait for the inevitable shot, the coup de grace ... which doesn't come. Very slowly, I look up. About seven or eight feet away is my rifle. At the far end of the tower, about the same distance again from the rifle sits the sniper, who looks a lot younger than me. He's leaning on the parapet and like me, he's breathing heavily. Breathing heavily because he's bleeding from his side. So, wounded not dead.

Slowly pulling my feet clear of the trip wire, I make a quick calculation. I'd easily get to my rifle before he was out of the blocks. However, he's holding a weapon and, judging from his performance so far, he wouldn't have much trouble hitting a sitting duck from fifteen feet. He reinforces this impression by gently shaking his head. I notice his hair and face are grimy and the parts of his uniform not covered in blood are dusty and dirty. As I sit up slowly and raise my hands, he points the rifle at my side - at my water bottle.

"Wasser. Haben Sie Wasser?"

I nod and remove the water bottle from my belt. He signals for me to throw it to him and points the rifle at my head to warn about what might happen if there's any funny business. But there's no funny business as my boiling anger has dissipated a little, maybe because my faceless foe now has a human form. I gently underarm the bottle which skids to a halt just next to his left hand. With another deep breath he carefully lays the rifle across his knee, picks up the bottle, opens it and drinks like a sailor on leave, not taking his eyes off me for a second. He then pours the remaining drops on his face and rubs it before picking up the gun again and pointing it at my head.

"Even if you kill me," I say, "you're dead. They'll bring up the artillery and blast this tower to pieces."

"Warum ... er why do they not do that already?"

The guy's sharp, I'll give him that. It's as if he's read our useless lieutenant's mind. Best to be straight with him.

"Because we didn't want to destroy this precious old building."

He laughs hard at this and then grimaces as the effort obviously hurts him.

"If you had looked, you would see the church is from achtzehn-hundert sechs und achtzig, eighteen ... eighty-six."

"I was a bit too preoccupied to read the date stone."

He smiles grimly and lowers the rifle a fraction.

"I will not kill you. I will not kill you if you - ach wie sagts versprechen?"

Don't ask me how, but I know what he means.

"To promise. What do you want me to promise?"

"Ja, if you promise I am prisoner and not shot. Meine familie. My family, I must again see them. Mutti, Vati und Liselle ..."

Liselle? Who is she, I find myself wondering? Sweetheart, sister, faithful family dachshund? I don't pursue the point though as he's snapped out of the reverie and the gun is once more pointing straight at my face. I suppose I could toss him some rubbish about the Geneva Convention but I haven't the energy so I give it to him how it is.

"I can't guarantee you anything. I'm not the lieutenant. I'm just a foot soldier like yourself. Besides you have killed my friends."

"I have killed meine Feinde ... my enemies."

"A philosophical distinction that might just be lost on that mob down there."

Understandably that goes beyond him so I get back to basics.

"Besides how would you know whether to trust us?"

He considers this before replying.

"I would have your lieutenant's word ... as an officer and a gentleman."

Unlike the rest of his halting English, this rolls lightly and easily off the tongue and I guess he's practised saying it. Maybe it's part of his training like 'Nicht shiessen' and 'Haende hoch' is part of ours. *Our officer's word, eh? I wouldn't trust that bastard Iris as far as I could dropkick him.* I don't say that out loud though.

"What is your name? Wie heissen Sie?"

"Friedrich. Fredi."

He stares expectantly at me.

"Joseph. Joe."

"In another world, Joe."

Again, I can tell it's a practised phrase but said in a way that I feel is not insincere. I will try to help him.

"Fredi, listen, I'm going to put what you've said to our officer. As I mentioned, I can't promise anything but I'll give it a go, eh?"

Fredi takes a good long hard look at me and then nods. I stand up carefully, keeping my hands in the air, and move towards the low wall of the tower. I shout, trying to make what I say as loud and clear as I can.

"Sir. Lieutenant Rossetti. The sniper here - Fredi - says he won't shoot me if you, as an officer and a gentleman, agree that we will take him prisoner and not kill him. You should ensure that everyone else in the platoon honours that promise as well."

No harm in the sniper thinking there's a horde of well-armed Tommys down there instead of two useless idiots and a cripple.

There is an agonisingly long pause before the reply, in that familiar and very irritating drawl, drifts up to the top of the tower.

"Tell your new friend that I agree - as an officer and a gentleman - to his terms."

"And the rest of the lads?"

There is another pause before the lieutenant replies, "Yes, they all agree too."

I turn back to Fredi.

"Did you get that? Verstehen Sie?"

"Ja, I understand."

"Can they treat the wounded?"

"Ja. Yes."

I walk three paces back to the wall and lean over.

"Sir," I shout, "you can check on Private Maybury and Corporal Gibson."

For a few seconds nothing happens but then I see first Olly and then the lieutenant climb to their feet and proceed cautiously out of the copse and across the open ground where Maybury is stretched out staring at the sky and clutching his wounded shoulder. Gibbo lies still, his brains oozing out on to the grass. I note that both the lieutenant and Olly are carrying weapons.

I turn back to Fredi.

"You can get up now," I tell him.

He does not move.

"You heard my officer. He's agreed."

Fredi gives back a hard stare and signals for me to approach. I take a step towards him but then turn back and shout down across the open ground.

"I'm getting him up now. Don't shoot."

With my help the sniper struggles to his feet, still holding his rifle. I offer my arm as a support and matters appear to be going swimmingly. But, just as Fredi leans forward to take my arm, things go completely and murderously awry. There is a shot, and the German staggers backwards and away from me. He's been hit in the shoulder. I look down in horror and see Iris, Lieutenant Rossetti, aiming his rifle at us.

"No," I yell in panic, "for god's sake, you fucking promised!"

I turn back to the sniper who is struggling to aim his weapon at me. Just as he gets steady there's another shot which sends him flying across the roof, his weapon spinning from his grasp - but not before he's managed to fire off a round straight into my right knee. Absolute bloody agony it is too. So we're both out for the count. Except he isn't. Despite wounds to the side, shoulder and hip, he's crawling towards his weapon which is about equidistant between him and me. I quickly realise I'm too *far from the door to escape, even if I could move properly, and my own rifle is even further away than his. There's no alternative then. I too start to drag myself towards his rifle. It should be no contest really as, while I am hit in the knee and it's hurting like hell, he has three wounds to my one. But he's going as fast as me on his belly towards the gun; we're like snakes - a pair of arthritic serpents. He also has the look of a man on a mission and his face is contorted with hate. This is not the time to plead my case that I wanted no part in this outrage.*

Almost inevitably we grab the rifle at the same time. He has his hands on the barrel and I've got hold of the stock which should give me a big advantage as the trigger is just by my right hand. But this lad is good. Before I can wrap my index finger around the trigger, the stock is propelled hard into the bridge of my nose and I let go of the weapon with a scream of pain. I'm saved by the fact that again he decides to use it as a club rather than a firearm and swings the thing at my head. But his shoulder is (literally) shot and, because he can't put much power into the swing, I have little difficulty avoiding it and manage to lunge forward and smother the rifle. But the sniper throws himself across my back, puts his hands around my throat and starts to throttle me. I try to prise his grip away but it's no good. He's far too big and strong for me. So I take my right hand away and punch it into his groin. It doesn't connect fully with his balls but is hard enough for him to relax his grip a fraction of a second. I twist and bring my left elbow into his face, sending him flying backwards. I turn towards him, grabbing the rifle as I do but again he's quick and I end up on my back clutching the gun with the German trying to force it down into my windpipe. It's no contest, like one of those arm-wrestling bouts against a bigger stronger opponent. You can hold out with maximum gut-wrenching effort for a few seconds but it's only a matter of time before he forces your arm down. And now sure enough my arms begin to weaken and he starts to inch the rifle barrel towards my throat. He still looks crazed but the hate has gone out of his eyes. He's simply concentrating on the job in hand. An insect buzzes around his head and I pray that he pauses to swat it away. He doesn't, and the shiny steel tube is now pressing against my throat. Another few seconds and I'm gone.

I'm saved by one of my colleagues down there. Not the two useless articles - Rossetti and Olly - who should have been charging up those spiral stairs as soon as they saw the German flying back across the roof of the tower. No, I'm saved, yet again and for the very last time, by the man who lies dead on the open ground below. Summoning my final ounce of strength, I manage to push the rifle a fraction away from my throat and yell straight into the sniper's face.

"Frieeeeedrich!!!"

The sudden shock makes him relax his grip just a fraction but it's enough for me to lift myself up a couple of inches, reach round my back into my belt and take out the large commando knife sheathed there. The one that Gibbo drummed into us that we must all get before D-Day. Without a second thought, I drive it straight at the sniper's face and its blade disappears into his right eye. The German screams in pain and fear and falls backwards clawing at his face, trying to pull the weapon out. But its serrated edges have snagged against the bones of his eye socket on the way in to his brain and his motor functions are already rapidly diminishing. He manages to haul himself part way up, still flailing at the knife handle but his legs are beginning to buckle. Finally, with a look that seems to despair at my betrayal, he crashes back to the floor, twitching two or three times before becoming still. It is the most horrible thing I have ever seen.

I lie back down for a few seconds, panting desperately. The sniper's rifle is by my side and when I can finally catch my breath, I quickly check the magazine. It's good. I begin to drag myself towards the edge of the turret. Using the rifle as a kind of crutch and leaning on the low wall I manage to haul myself into a standing position ...

At this critical point, Joe's narrative was inconveniently interrupted by the Jag smacking into the kerb, bouncing back across the white line and throwing us both sideways. It seemed that Joe had taken his eyes off the road. Luckily there was nothing coming the other way and he managed to steady the vehicle. As he did so, I was able to register our surroundings for the first time in the twenty-minute journey. It had stopped raining and the early evening sun was casting long shadows down the high street of a rather well-heeled looking country village with a solid brick-built pub across the green. The place looked somehow familiar but I gave it no further thought as I forced my mind back to Joe's grim tale.

"So, what the hell what comes next?" I demanded.

"This," Joe replied, suddenly speeding up and doing a quick right turn into a cul-de-sac of fine detached houses. He screeched to a halt, inevitably mounting the kerb as he did so, grabbed his rifle, and was out of the Jag before I could pick myself up from the passenger well and demand to know what the blue blazes was going on. Throwing open the car door, I caught up with him as he was being assailed by an elderly fellow who'd paused in the task of mowing his vast front lawn.

"Those tyres won't last long if you carry on driving like that," the old man grumbled to Joe, who had half-turned away from him while he carefully checked his rifle.

"And if you're visiting that place," he pointed to the half-timbered 1920s home outside which we'd stopped, "you might tell them to keep the racket down while you're at it …"

The complaint tailed off as Joe turned towards the pensioner. His misty eyes had become horribly fearful when he registered that Joe, covered in poor old Barney's blood, was brandishing a weapon. He really did look like something out of Madame Tussauds. With not another word, the old man turned sharply away from the lawnmower and retreated quickly into his home.

He had a point about the noise though. Joe and I stared at the large lounge window from behind which Bill Haley's Rock Around the Clock, so popular at the rugby club dance, blared out across this otherwise quiet backwater. Beyond the net curtain we glimpsed the outlines of two people apparently throwing each other around in abandonment.

Joe nodded at the window.

"The dance of death," he said without emotion.

His wartime story had shocked and disconcerted me. Now, as I began to gather my wits and noticed that 7.46pm was fast approaching, I realised that it wasn't beyond possibility that he'd prepared the whole gruesome tableau in the theatre whilst I was at Boardman's place just to throw me off the scent. And had now brought me to this quiet spot to finish off the job. OK, I still couldn't quite believe he'd really done that, but I decided to go on the attack.

"You seem to be rather good at death don't you," I told him angrily. "It follows you around like a bad smell."

Joe appeared totally unbothered by my tirade and continued to gaze through the window at the sprightly scene. Then he turned to me and I couldn't help flinching in fear as he put his hands on my shoulders.

"You're so right about death and me, Frankie," he said with a shake of his head, "and it's not over yet. Stay outside."

"Not on your nelly. I'm coming in."

"Please, I must go on my own. Then you'll be in no danger …"

"What *is* the danger? What have you not told me?"

"All will become clear, I promise. Now give me your gun."

Without thinking I gave him the revolver and in return he handed me his rifle.

"You'll have a better chance with that," he said, nodding at the Enfield.

"How do you mean?"

"I mean, if you hear shots, you'll be able to kill the first person who comes out of that door. Even if it's me."

I stood there open-mouthed, as Joe smiled thinly, patted me on the shoulder and walked slowly up the drive. Without a pause, he pushed at the front door which swung open, went inside and closed the door quietly behind him. How he knew it would be unlocked was beyond me.

I stared at the rifle which I was holding as if it were one of Pitt's brooms. Kill the first person who came out? No chance, mate! Joe might be a trigger-happy lunatic - the Mellish Maniac himself perhaps - but I wasn't his sidekick. If I was going to shoot someone then I'd need to know a lot more about why. And I didn't have much time to find out.

Hurrying down the side of the building, I opened a small gate and stepped into a large lawned garden bordered with rhododendron bushes. In front of me was a half-brick, half-glass summer house attached to the back of the building, and through its windows I could see closed double doors to what looked like the dining room; there were chairs and a large table stacked right up against them. To my left was the back door which opened as easily as the front one had. Did nobody in this part of the world know what locks were for? Closing the door, I found myself in a large old-fashioned kitchen. Its ample work surfaces were well-scrubbed, and both the chrome rail on the Aga cooker and the Belfast sink taps gleamed in the sunlight. Whoever owned this place was extremely house-proud.

The music had stopped, but the incomplete silence held the sound of indistinct voices. About to creep out of the kitchen into the hall, I was diverted by the sight of a serving hatch in the far wall which looked like it opened up into the dining room. The hatch was hinged like a door and, as I pulled at it slightly, I saw that beyond was one large room which ran the length of the house. This had been largely cleared of furniture and in the middle of this empty space stood Rose, gazing fearfully at the door where I presumed Joe was standing just out of my line of sight. Beyond Rose was Conrad. He too was looking apprehensively towards the door.

"Joe, you've got to believe me," he pleaded, his fear not even below the surface, "I was only teaching Rose to do the jive. It's a dance. Just a silly dance."

"He's telling the truth, Joe," sobbed Rose. "Please put the gun down. Oh my god what on earth have you done?"

"Don't worry, darling," Joe replied without emotion. "It's not my blood."

Hardly the most comforting news you'd want from a gore-covered intruder brandishing a pistol.

"Please put the gun down," Rose implored Joe, "and we'll talk about whatever is bothering you."

There was a moment of silence ended by Conrad, his voice still tinged with terror.

"I think I know what's bothering Joe, Rose."

"What are you talking about?" Rose snapped back, as if it were unthinkable that he could know more than she about her husband.

"I didn't want to upset you with my suspicions."

"Which are what exactly?" Rose, probably without realising it, was nearly screaming.

"Which are that … oh god I can't believe I'm about to say this."

There came a sour chuckle from Joe.

"Go on, Conrad, say it anyway. You'll feel a whole lot better."

I could hear Conrad breathing very heavily. "That … that Joe killed Ray, Olly and those other poor souls."

Rose gasped. "What absolute and utter nonsense. Tell him, Joe."

But again there was silence. I edged the hatch open a touch further and saw that Joe had stepped towards Rose. He offered her his gun and she took it as if she hardly knew what she was doing. Joe then stepped backwards, away from his traumatised wife and out of my view.

"What … what's all this about, Joe?" Rose eventually managed to ask.

"Something that happened during the war. To Lieutenant Horace Rossetti."

"Your officer who got the posthumous medal? For killing that sniper?"

Rose had obviously heard a rather different version of the story recently relayed to me. But before Joe could reply, Conrad butted in, his voice back to its authoritative self.

"Joe, please tell Rose how Second Lieutenant Rossetti actually died," he said.

There was another short hiatus during which I could hear Joe breathing heavily. Finally he sighed deeply.

"I never wanted you to hear this, Rose," he said.

"Hear what for goodness sake? You're frightening me, Joe!"

"It was me not Rossetti who killed the sniper. Fredi was his name. I stabbed him through the eye at the top of the church tower. With my Gibbo knife."

"Oh my god, no!" Rose, still clutching Joe's pistol, sank to her knees, bent double and began to sob.

Joe forced himself to continue.

"The sniper had been shot by Rossetti straight after he'd promised him 'as an officer and a gentleman', that he would have safe passage."

"That," shouted Conrad, "is a barefaced lie!"

Joe ignored Conrad and, sounding almost in a trance, he took up the story he'd been telling me as if there had been no interruption.

So Rossetti caused me to have to brawl for my life with a wounded man and kill or be killed. So I killed. Then I hauled myself up and gazed over the parapet. Down there on the open ground it's as if time had stood still. Pete Maybury lies there, eyes open, still holding his injured shoulder. There's a big red stain on his tunic and Olly, a first aid kit open beside him, is frantically cutting at the bloody material with a pair of what appear to be nail scissors. The lieutenant stands looking down on them as if he isn't really part of their world at all. Which I suppose he isn't. Iris and Olly! Sounds like a comedy double act which I reckon in a grim way they are.

I take the rifle in both hands, give a loud whistle and shout as clearly as I can manage.

"Lieutenant Rossetti. Horace!"

Still holding his own rifle in his right hand, he looks up. Whereupon I shoot him twice. Once in the chest and then through his right eye. He falls dead where he stands, just next to Olly who gazes up at me, terror-stricken. Looks like he thinks he's next. But that is it for me. Justice done. I drop back onto the leaded floor of the tower roof and lie down on my side, facing the dead German sniper ten feet away. I idly wonder how he hadn't spotted my knife in its sheath while we fought. In the distance I'm sure I can hear the rumble of an M4 Sherman tank approaching.

Well, I hadn't seen that one coming and neither had Rose, who stared at her husband in disbelief and utter horror.

"I can't dress it up, Rose," he told her. "It happened exactly like that as god is my witness. Fredi was trying to kill me so it was him or me. And I don't regret killing Rossetti either. It all came about because of his pig-headed incompetence - and his foul and deliberate lie."

I watched uneasily as Conrad gave Joe a long cold look before shaking his head in disgust.

"Oh, and one other thing that needs to be mentioned, my darling," added Joe, almost as an afterthought, "is that Second Lieutenant Horace Rossetti was Conrad's elder brother."

Rose's sobbing stopped and she looked up towards her husband.

"But his surname's Ross …"

The obvious corollary to her statement went unsaid. I watched as my cousin slowly and unsteadily climbed back onto her feet.

"Rose," Conrad pleaded, "this is a complete pack of lies. My brother was an honourable man and this maniac murdered him in cold blood. And now he has even more blood on his hands. Look at him! He must be stopped before he kills again."

Rose gave Conrad a quizzical, almost impatient, glance before turning back to Joe.

"Fredi? He's the name in all your nightmares."

"Every last one, my love. Friedrich Kesselman from Nuremberg, home of the master singers and the rallies. And the trials. You remember I was posted there after the war."

"Helping the tribunal make a case against the Nazi High Command."

"Yes, one of the easiest jobs I've ever had. And when I wasn't assisting the lawyers in Neave's investigation unit, I was engaged in a much more difficult task; spending countless hours and hours trying to locate Fredi's family. Of course, there was no trace of them. The RAF had flattened the place."

"What ... what did you want to say to them, Joe?" Rose sounded genuinely bewildered.

"I would have tried to reassure them that ... that Fredi died a soldier's death."

"With your executioner's knife sticking out of his right eye."

Conrad's harsh tone contrasted with Joe's almost wistful reminiscences.

"My brother, Olly, Ray, Barney and those poor ex-servicemen. Who's next in your killing spree, Joe? Rose and I?"

Joe began to laugh. It was the grimmest sound I think I'd ever heard.

"Of course you're right, Conrad," he said.

My grip on the rifle tightened involuntarily and through the hatch I saw Rose staring in horror at her husband.

"You're right," he repeated, "Barney is dead. This is his blood all over me. But how did you know he'd been murdered?"

"Oh for god's sake," Conrad rapped back, immediately. "This isn't the films and you're not Simon Templar. Rose, you must have heard the telephone ring when you were upstairs before?"

"Er, yes, I think I did," Rose replied uncertainly.

"It was one of the local police officers calling, a friend of mine from the rugby club, Alan Brabourne. He told me that someone had killed the stage partner of your cousin Frankie."

Rose gasped. "So Barney *is* dead! But why would Al Brabourne tell you of all people?"

"Because he knows Frankie is a drinking buddy of mine and wanted me to warn him that he could be in danger."

That was it. The pub across the village green - with the delicious steak sandwiches. I knew I'd seen it before.

My thoughts were interrupted by Rose's voice which was growing noticeably shriller.

"Why didn't you mention this to me then? Why did you just let us keep on dancing?"

"Because I had no idea where Frankie would be if he wasn't at the theatre and I told Alan that. There was little else I could do."

The sound of slow applause came from the direction of the doorway. "It's a pretty tale, Conrad," said Joe. "And full marks for thinking on your feet. But if you're such good pals with Al Brabourne how come you don't know that his name is actually Alistair?"

Conrad stared towards the door, his eyes heavy with a mixture of anger and fear.

"For goodness sake," he spat, "unlike you, I don't spend my life checking the diminutives of everyone I come into contact with. Look, Rose, the fact is he killed my brother, the sniper and five others and he's come here to shoot both of us."

"You're in no danger from me, Rose."

Joe sounded almost matter-of-fact.

Conrad gazed at her pleadingly.

"Rose, give me the gun, I beg you! He's going to take it from you and use it on both of us."

Rose was completely silent. I guessed that she, like me, was weighing up what she had just heard. And, like me, she was struggling to come to any coherent conclusion. Finally, she turned to Conrad.

"Why did you come here?"

"My job brought me here of course."

"But you work miles away, in Altonford."

"Yes, Rose, and I'd grown heartily sick of the town so two years ago I bought this place. And I'd probably have lived here happily ever after but for a visit from Olly. Sorry Bernard Ollerton, Esquire, if we're using exact names. He told me everything that had happened, much as you've heard from me today."

"So what did you decide to do?"

Now Rose was sounding like the investigator.

Conrad breathed heavily.

"I didn't know what to do, Rose. I mean how could I accuse a so-called pillar of the community of committing two murders a dozen years ago? And then carrying on his killing spree ever since."

I so wanted Joe to snap back at him. To tell Conrad he was spouting nonsense on stilts. To take the nagging suspicions out of my - and Rose's - mind once and for all. But he didn't. And because of that omission, Conrad began to press home what he clearly saw as an advantage.

"It comes down to the life you want, Rose. You've got a choice. An empty nest here or a much brighter future."

Rose was now holding Joe's pistol by her side.

"What are you talking about?" she said flatly.

"Come with me, Rose. Leave him to face the consequences. We'll go to a place where the past doesn't matter. California! It's where all kinds of exciting things are happening."

Poor Rose, she was as perplexed as I was.

"Things? What are you talking about, Conrad?"

"The future. One day soon they'll build ... *I'll* build a computer that's ... that's ..."

"That's no bigger than a garden shed?" Joe had finally woken up. "And then you could do us all a favour by locking yourself inside it. For good."

If it wasn't up there with Barney's greatest zingers (I could afford to be magnanimous now the blighter was gone), it was definitely one of Joe's better ones. And evidently the barb had hit home. Conrad moved out of my vision yet his voice was still crystal clear.

"But first we must make things secure and get justice," he told Rose. "For both of us."

There was another cry from Rose and a click which told me Conrad was now holding a weapon of his own. I opened the hatch a little further and had to suppress a gasp as I saw Conrad's gun was a nine-millimetre Luger. His father's? The one he claimed he'd never used?

"It's to protect you, Rose," he said quickly, noticing her look of horror. "Look, I admit, *I'm* not the best shot in the business but I'm all that stands between you and oblivion. Can't you see? I mean look at him. The jealousy is oozing out of him."

"What's he jealous of?"

"Why us, of course. What we've got - and he can never possess. Take care or he'll have that pistol."

For ten seconds nobody spoke and then Joe's monotone cut through the stillness.

"I'm so sorry for all this, Rose," he said simply. "I shouldn't have lied to you all this time."

Now knowing what needed to be done, I looked down automatically to check the rifle but before I could raise it there was a single shot. I rushed out of the kitchen into the hall. And when I burst into the lounge, rifle cocked and ready to fire back, I saw the maniac who'd held a town in terror for weeks stretched out on the floor, killed by the woman he loved more than anything else in the whole world.

*The Reckoning

15

The Two Frankies

"WE HAD ALL long believed Joe Trueman to be a man to whom you could entrust your life."

A grim-faced Chief Superintendent Michael Hallows paused and gazed down funereally at his sober-suited audience.

"And so many of us did trust their lives to him, in no small part because we all recognised that Joe was an authentic hero of the war. But then … then came those terrible events of six months ago. And it was at that point we were forced to revise our views and admit that Joe …"

Hallows paused again, apparently overcome with emotion. But he bravely took a couple of deep breaths and somehow managed to carry on.

"It was only then we realised that Joe Trueman …"

By this time many of the sober-suits looked close to tears.

"…that Joe Trueman was also a true hero of the peace."

"Which clown writes this guy's scripts?" I whispered as I stared from the wings of the Collins Hall's temporary stage at the uniformed figure struggling to contain his emotions.

"You're looking at him," Joe whispered back while gazing at his boss. "Perhaps you should line him up as Barney's replacement."

"Don't need a replacement," I muttered, "but if I did it'd be a toss-up who'd prove more annoying."

Hallows, meanwhile, was back in full flow.

"And so I call upon our Mayor, Alderman Kenneth Boardman, to present the 1956 Ralph Duvall Memorial Medal for Outstanding Achievement in the County Borough of Mellish and its Environs to my valued colleague Detective *Inspector* Joe Trueman."

"Over the top," muttered Joe as he strode on to the stage, leaving me to wonder if he was talking about this public ordeal, Hallows' delivery, or the ornate name of the medal. Whatever it was, I had to admit Detective *Inspector* Trueman looked mightily pleased with himself as Boardman pinned the gong to his lapel and encouraged the emotional crowd's cheering affirmation. When the applause finally died down I, along with everyone else, expected Joe to say a few words but it was Boardman who grabbed the microphone from a startled Hallows.

"Can I just say," he boomed, "that without Joe here we wouldn't have had such a special - and extended - second half of the summer. There were a record number of visitors in July, August and September and that meant … more pies sold than ever before."

There was a smattering of lukewarm laughter, as if the crowd was weighing up who in Mellish might have benefited most from this mass pastry scoffing.

Regardless of this, Boardman's delivery continued on its upward trajectory.

"But none of it would have happened if this brave feller hadn't stopped the Mellish Maniac in his tracks. Ladies and gents, I give you Joe Trueman."

Again, there was thunderous applause as Boardman handed the mike to Joe, who cleared his throat theatrically before speaking.

"I sincerely thank the municipality of Mellish for this great honour which I feel I do not fully deserve."

Cries of 'nonsense' rippled around the hall.

"There were other people …" he gazed down at Rose looking radiant on the front row "… who also deserve recognition." He then glanced at me.

"Again, I thank everyone for the medal and look forward to serving our great community for many more years."

At that the whole place was on its feet and it took a full two minutes for the crowd's enthusiasm to abate. Finally, as the standing ovation began to die down, Boardman leaned into the microphone.

"Well, I reckon that just about wraps things up so …"

Joe urgently tapped the mayor on the elbow and signalled with his eyes towards me. For a moment Boardman looked puzzled but then he nodded.

"Oh aye, we've got a bit o' summat for t'comic an' all."

It was the first time I'd been in the building since the night Boardman junior had had his clock thoroughly cleaned nearly six months before. In the meantime, it had been confirmed that John had hung up his gloves. With regard to the matter of whether he had also given up restricting his love life to the immediate family, I neither knew nor particularly cared.

In the days after the dramatic events that ended the previous chapter, Ned Clarkson, in charge of the investigation, had kindly kept me informed of developments. And extremely troubling some of them were. For instance, it was entirely likely that it was me who should have been in that terrible box in which two people had died on stage; yours truly (many times) professionally and Barney (just once) but actually. Reliable evidence pointed to the probability that Conrad had planned that Joe would find me (actually) dead up there so further suspicion would fall on him. When he realised he'd killed Barney by mistake after our last show, he quickly organised the elaborate trap with the gun to catch me. After all, he knew Joe and I would be at the theatre because blabbermouth me had told him so. Even so, you had to admit the guy was an operator.

"But how could he be sure it would be me who copped it and not Joe?" I asked as we'd sat in Ned's office three days after the drama.

"Joe would naturally believe the greater danger lay up in the circle after Dot's tip-off," he replied. "So he'd be the one to go up there. And besides you were familiar with how the box worked," he added with the trace of a grin. "After all you'd spent enough time in it."

"Very funny but that's still only a theory."

Not quite, added Ned. There was sound forensic evidence that Barney had been attacked and strangled in the darkness by the stage door as he was about to leave the theatre the previous evening. He'd then been bundled into a cupboard where he lay until he was readied for his macabre encore. Apparently, they'd discovered a napkin in the cupboard with Barney's scribblings all over it. They guessed it was his because one of the things written on it said, "As usual FF fucking hopeless tonite. Prick really has to go." But it turned out that Barney was the one who'd had to go and not just because of his dodgy spelling. You see, we had both changed our usual habits after the show ended. For once Barney had hung around that night instead of doing what he normally did and clearing off at the first opportunity. Ironically, he'd probably been plotting how to get rid of me, professionally of course, although you could never be sure with that two-faced pipsqueak. Meanwhile, in a break from my normal routine, I'd left safely through the front doors, with Nancy on my arm, minutes after the final curtain. Ah well, a happy ending of sorts.

However, the legacy of Barney had nowhere near played itself out. In the days after my unfortunate partner's murder and all the rest of the stuff, Henry Shelvey had once again done the decent thing and mothballed the theatre for a week. About five days into the closure, I dropped in to pick up a few odds and ends including my notebook. The act had to go on after all but I was stumped if I knew in which direction. Yet before I started to miss Barney too much, it turned out that, of all people, William Pitt the Welder (ret) was about to unwittingly provide the solution to all my problems.

I was in the dressing room gloomily scanning my incoherent exercise book ramblings when the creepy caretaker crept in unannounced and loomed over me.

"Come in, please, why don't you," I muttered.

"I just have, haven't I?"

So much for Scousers instinctively understanding the power of irony.

"I've got this for you," he said, plonking a battered old cardboard suitcase on the table in front of me."

"How did you know it was my birthday?"

"Well, I didn't."

"Well, it isn't."

Pitt looked at me pityingly.

"All the rubbish in there," he said, nodding at the case. "It's your mate's stuff."

"What mate?"

"I've been tidying things up and I'll tell you this for nothing. That old lead-swinger left the place in a right state."

Big and tough as he was, I wasn't letting Pitt get away with this slur on my old pal Wilf.

"Hold on a minute, chum, he was my friend. Don't forget how all this lot started. And how you got your job."

With sadness I remembered how, despite being mortally wounded, Wilf had saved my life by signalling that the killer was lurking behind the door, poised to dispatch me.

My words made even Pitt pause for a couple of seconds. Then he ploughed on much as before.

"Anyway, I was doing what the old git never did and cleaning everything top to bottom when I came on this 'ere thing tucked away under the floorboards in the props store."

I stared at the suitcase. It didn't appear to be much of a final testament to a life well lived. But at least Pitt, thoughtless prick though he was, had found the thing and it could now be returned to its owner's family.

"Thanks, William. I'll make sure it's safely delivered to Wilf's sister."

Pitt gazed at me as if I was some kind of imbecile.

"No, it's not his. It's yon feller's."

"Who the heck are you talking about?"

"Your other dead mate. Benny was it?"

"This is Barney's?"

"Yeah, I had a quick gander at it. Dunno why he hid it. Pile of old rubbish if you ask me."

And on that note, he turned and left the room before I could come back with a witty riposte. Which, I have to say, was becoming par for the course.

At first glance, the suitcase's contents did seem pretty standard stuff. There were a couple of letters from Barney's mum urging him to stay safe and wash regularly - nuggets of advice he'd singularly failed to heed. I remembered his mother from the sparsely-attended funeral. She was a small, bird-like woman who gazed at me vacantly when I presented my condolences.

"I didn't realise Barnabas had a stage partner," was all she said in reply. It could have been the requiem to my career - but for that suitcase.

Other than the letters, it contained a pile of playbills, one or two press cuttings and a few daft props including Barney's magic wand. Maybe he was planning to make me disappear from his life for good. To my great surprise, I also discovered a signed photograph of Cary Grant, thanking Barney for his valuable advice. So the annoying swine had been telling the truth after all. Either that or he was a moderately decent forger.

And *then*, hidden away under the suitcase's lining and obviously unnoticed by Pitt, were items I hadn't known existed - Barney's bibles; four hardback account books loaded to the hilt with comedy gold. I'd never realised it but those scribblings I'd watched him compulsively make on beer mats, fag packets and napkins had all been neatly transcribed into these tomes. And, if he'd lived long enough, the misspelled message, 'As usual FF fucking hopeless tonite, etc' would doubtless have appeared between their covers as well. The blighter must have hidden the books so I wouldn't get my paws on them. Well, how ironic did that turn out to be?

Even a preliminary skim through Barney's scribblings revealed immediately that his books provided a masterclass in humour. There were surreal ideas for sketches (even one involving a dead budgie nailed to its perch), myriad ways to humiliate your partner without him even realising it (cheers, buddy) and acid monologues that took my breath away and had me chortling so much that at one point Pitt came bundling back in, worried I might be having a heart attack - and he'd have to sweep me up.

"What's so bleedin' funny anyway?" Pitt grumbled.

"Why, William, it's my new act," I said, brandishing my slim exercise book; Barney's bibles having been quickly tucked out of sight down the side of my chair. "I think even you would warm to it."

And a fortnight later, I did indeed discern the merest trace of a smile on his lips as I glanced into the wings while taking my bow after yet another smash-hit show. Of course, I hadn't been able to do much with the sketches without hiring a partner, and that wasn't going to happen; I'd decided I was well and truly done with double acts. But the monologues, with their gigantic leaps of logic and breathless risk-taking could be used almost unchanged. And when it came to the bits involving ritual humiliation, I used audience members, just like Barney had. I take great comfort from the thought that it's exactly what he would have wanted.

Ned Clarkson's investigation turned up one or two other surprises as well. Not just that a trawl through Conrad's place showed he'd been obsessively planning his murder spree for years, and the motive was the violent death of his useless and murderous brother. That seemed obvious enough. As did his plan to frame Joe, meticulously plotted down to the finest details. These included the brilliant blue contact lenses he'd worn during the attacks, the limp with which he'd fooled Wilf's pub pals and the single undetected burglary at Joe's when he'd stolen the revolver and typed out all the cryptic notes.

But the identity of a more distant relative of Conrad's was altogether more surprising - and troubling.

"Here," Ned had inquired as we'd snatched a quick pint after the evening show, "ever heard of a cove called Kim Philby?"

"Er, the name does ring the faintest of bells. What of it?"

"Well, it turns out this Philby's some kind of diplomat who was suspected of spying for the Russians until he was cleared by the Foreign Secretary ..."

"You don't say!"

"... and it turns out he's a distant cousin of Conrad Ross."

Well blow me down! So that solved the mystery of how Philby had suddenly disappeared that day. Conrad was obviously lurking nearby in his RAF blue sports car. But it didn't really get us any nearer as to why Philby had been stalking me over the sand dunes, other than that he wanted to find out what Burgess had been up to. Ned admitted he was in the dark about it as well.

"There were half a dozen letters from Philby to Conrad," he told me. "Innocent stuff on the surface; Great Aunt Mabel's bunions, that kind of business. But you never know, it could all have been an elaborate code."

It was payback time.

"I think you're right, Ned," I replied, wearing my most earnest expression. "In fact, it's my strong suspicion that Philby planned the whole murder spree and used his cousin as a pawn. I'd drag him in for questioning and ensure he gets a scrupulously fair trial. Then lock the swine up and throw away the key."

But even if Ned was game for all that - and to be fair, he didn't look too enthusiastic - the whole thing proved academic because by then Philby was out of everyone's reach in Beirut, working as a journalist, and getting up to his usual mischief.

"Got time for another?" said Ned.

"I shouldn't but go on."

When he came back from the bar with the beers Ned sat in silence for a few minutes. Just as I was thinking this last drink had been a waste of time he came out of his trance, shaking his head vehemently.

"Everything goes back to the bloody war doesn't it," he spat.

I found that hard to argue with.

"Look at all those poor veterans on their uppers who were slaughtered," he continued, "plus Wilf, Olly, Barney and yeah, even that murderous bastard Conrad. They all died because of the bloody Second World War."

Again, I couldn't disagree but wasn't entirely sure where Ned was going with this.

"I mean," he went on, "there are guys in the station, young coppers who were in short pants when the war ended but go on about it as though they were in it. I'm not kidding they really, really want to have been there. So I tell them to take a lead from Joe, a true war hero if ever there was one, who never mentions the bloody thing. But do they listen? No they do not! I blame the comics."

"Nothing to do with us, Ned, although the quality of some ENSA acts might well have encouraged folk to take up arms against us."

Ned grimaced. "No Frankie, I meant the kids' comics like Hotspur and Wizard. It's all Union Jack Jackson this and Blazing Ace of Spades that. And don't get me started on the war films."

"But it's just kids pointing sticks at each other and going 'bam-bam.' Been going on since Adam was a lad."

Ned sighed and shook his head. "It's been nearly a dozen years. Are we never gonna move on?"

Amid this philosophising about warfare and violence, the one thing Ned and I did not get around to discussing was who fired the fatal shot in Conrad's palatial lounge six months before.

I'm fairly certain that Rose had been holding the pistol when I burst in, but after checking Conrad really was dead, I looked up to see the gun in Joe's hands. Before I could get properly worried, he'd put the weapon on the table and ordered me not to touch it.

"We don't want the fingerprint boys confused."

When I pressed him later, the most he would say was, "I didn't take the blame for his brother so I'm not going to miss my chance to accept it for him."

There had been one more significant incident which came a few weeks after I'd taken my final (extremely successful) bow at the end of Mellish Pier. One evening in early November I found myself alone in our London home. Nancy had travelled to Nottingham to run the rule over a couple of promising comics and the kids were in various parts of the country having all kinds of interesting notions stuffed into their bonces.

I had just grabbed the opportunity to gulp down a particular favourite of cheese and black pudding on toast, all lashed with Worcestershire Sauce (Nancy had banned the dish) and was about to snuggle down in front of our new television (a Ferranti 405 lines no less) with a coquettish Beaujolais when the doorbell rang.

Silently cursing, I flung open our front door to be confronted by someone I'd never met, a well-dressed cove with the look of a nightclub bouncer, who wanted to know in a Geordie accent if I was Francis Thirkettle.

"Depends who's asking."

He smiled. "I was in Joe Trueman's unit during the war. Peter Maybury."

He held out his left hand to shake mine and before I could go on wondering if he had Masonic or Boy Scout connections, I remembered he'd been shot in the right shoulder. Like Joe's knee it obviously still gave him trouble.

Of course, I immediately invited him in, sat him down and poured a generous dollop of plonk into his glass. Like Olly, Maybury wore an extremely smart overcoat; unlike his former comrade in arms the rest of his outfit also had a prosperous feel to it. And I'd have bet anything that, unlike Olly, he'd paid for his own coat.

Maybury didn't waste much time with chit-chat and went straight into his story. He told me that around two years ago he'd had a visitor to his home just outside Newcastle. It was Conrad, keen to establish the truth about the death of his brother.

"He didn't believe the finding of the military tribunal that said Iris had been killed by the sniper."

"Unsurprising really as Joe had shot him," I observed.

"And equally unsurprising as Olly had already told him his version of what happened."

He paused for a drink.

"Canny vintage is that," he muttered appreciatively, his vowels slipping back into the vernacular. "Anyhow, he was eager to get my version of events and I was equally keen to give him the bare minimum. I didn't want Joe in any more trouble, see. So we danced around things for a bit, Conrad got himself a bit wound up and then he ... left."

"And you're here to apologise for not spotting he was a potential murderer. Well don't. None of us did."

"I read about what had happened - and your part in it - and I wanted to get things off my chest like."

I thanked him and refilled his glass. He then recounted with pride the success he'd made of the firm he founded in 1947 which manufactured electrical components. But he seemed proudest of the fact that he was an enlightened employer who encouraged worker participation in the running of the company.

"I mean god knows I'm no Socialist but I reckoned most of those lads deserved better than what my Dad got after the first lot; finding someone else sat at his desk in the town hall when he got home from France."

"And that's to your great credit, Pete. I wish all employers thought like that."

My mind had already drifted back to the questionable industrial practices of my cotton-mill owning father-in-law. That man couldn't walk past a chimney without wanting to stuff an infant up it.

Maybury took another appreciative swig and stroked his chin. "Ever read a book called Brideshead Revisited?"

It was an odd question but I answered it truthfully. Yes, I had read the thing, mainly because it was written by someone I'd briefly come across during the war - or Waugh as you might say if you were a proper clever clogs!

"Good one that," Maybury said with more kindness than the comment deserved before continuing. "Don't get me wrong, it's a good book, perhaps a great one. I'm not the right fella to judge. But do you remember how it ends?"

I didn't, although I guessed that everyone wasn't exactly happy ever afterwards.

"There's this chap called Hooper, a junior officer who's billeted at this stately pile, Brideshead. We're supposed to mock or despise him because he represents the common man who's about to beat down the gates to the Garden of Eden."

"I bet you've never used that one before."

He smiled back at me.

"Only a couple of hundred times. But it *is* my own phrase."

"Then I commend you for your way with words."

"Thanks. Perhaps it's a Geordie thing. But seriously do you know what? It was Hooper and millions like him who won the war for us - ordinary fellows like Corporal Gibbo and poor old Mack Mckenzie - and I always thought they deserved much more than that sort of patronising rubbish. And that's why I … I'll get off me soapbox now and leave you in peace."

As I opened the front door for him something struck me.

"Did you mention the word 'execution' to Conrad?"

He stared back at me with an odd expression.

"No, why should I?"

"Well, you saw everything."

"Aye, I was flat on my back - not out of choice, mind - and I had a perfect view.

Maybury leaned against the front door and it closed quietly but he hardly noticed. His face wore a faraway expression.

"I remember that after Iris had fired at the sniper, I yelled at him and Olly to get up the tower pronto. But he just stood there like the wazzock he was. 'Let's see how things go,' was all he had to say. I was screaming at him to do his duty and save one of his men but to no avail. A couple of minutes, a couple of lifetimes later, Joe finally appeared at the top of the tower. And that's when it happened."

"He shot and killed the lieutenant."

Maybury gave me another extremely odd look.

"Yes, I suppose he did. But not before Iris shot at him."

For a moment I thought I'd misheard.

"Shot at Joe! Why on earth would his commanding officer do that?"

"Don't think I haven't asked myself that over and over and I still can't give an answer. But there it was. Despite me yelling at him to stop he kept on firing. Maybe he'd just lost his wits. In the end Joe snapped back and … I don't blame him. I'll tell you another thing, I've never lost a moment's sleep over protecting Joe by telling the tribunal the sniper killed our lieutenant."

Well this was a shock and no mistake. Joe wasn't an executioner; just someone battling to stay alive. Another thought hit me.

"Did you tell Conrad about his brother going potty with the rifle?"

"Of course. I mean, I thought it's what Olly would have said to him. But well … the little sneak hadn't. So Conrad went completely berserk like, accusing me of making the whole thing up and I had to kick the bugger out. He obviously didn't believe a word of it but it's the truth. Again, I'm right sorry I never spoke up about him. I should have guessed he was … well, potty."

I could see why Olly would lie for advantage but what possessed Joe to go along with the fiction that he was an executioner? Perhaps after Iris had caused the death of his best buddy in the whole world that's how he wanted to see himself.

Maybury reopened the door but before he left, I had to ask him one final question.

"Joe and Gibbo, I'm not prying but were they …?"

Maybury put his massive hand across my forearm and smiled.

"Have a good life, Frankie. And if you're ever playing in my neck of the woods, I'll try to catch one of your shows."

"You're in luck, I'm doing Sunderland Empire next …"

But he'd already gone.

Back in the Collins Hall I watched as Joe, still clutching the Ralph Duvall Memorial Award, tried his utmost to be sociable but as usual failed abysmally. Even as people warmly congratulated him and queued up to shake his hand, I could see his eyes wandering over their shoulders towards the exit and blessed solitude. I hadn't mentioned the Maybury visit to him and I strongly suspected I never would.

"Penny for them."

Someone had lightly grabbed my elbow and I turned to see Joe's altogether more sociable better half.

"So, what did they give you?" asked Rose, pointing to the framed certificate under my arm.

"Oh, it's er … well here have a look yourself."

Rose took the frame from me and examined it.

"'Certificate of Thanks from a Grateful Municipality.' Not exactly the Freedom of Mellish is it."

"Maybe not, cuz, but I reckon it means they won't get too upset when I drive my flock of sheep up and down the pier."

"Your sheep might not be so pleased though."

I chuckled, relieved to see Rose in such good spirits. But then again, her sunny mood was hardly surprising.

"So how long to go?" I said indicating the football-sized bump beneath her dress.

"Ten weeks. I can't wait."

"I can believe that," I replied with a smile. After all she had been waiting years.

Then Rose took hold of my arm and pulled me towards her.

"There's no doubt about it," she whispered seriously. "It is Joe's."

This had me desperately wondering how to fashion a suitably diplomatic reply, when I was saved by an unlikely source. Miles Paddon, Conrad's old computer buddy, appeared by our side and introduced himself to Rose. He seemed a much more amenable soul than the arrogant character I'd met at the university. And, although he didn't exactly apologise on Conrad's behalf, he appeared keen to transfer some of the blame on to his own shoulders.

"Conrad would go missing for hours, sometimes days on end," he told Rose. "And I said nothing. I even covered for him with the university authorities."

"You weren't to know, Mr Paddon," replied Rose awkwardly, her face reddening. "Conrad fooled everyone. Myself, Francis here and even my husband Joe. Excuse me."

As she moved off for a word with Ned Clarkson, I mused that in fact Joe had been the only one who hadn't succumbed to Conrad's charms, unsurprisingly in view of what appeared to have been going on. But I kept that to myself. Something else was bothering me.

"Would you say Conrad was a patriot?" I asked Paddon.

He looked puzzled. "What makes you say that?"

"It's a simple question but I'll put it another way. Would he have considered betraying his country?"

Paddon weighed the matter up for a few seconds and then held out his hands in bemusement.

"He was undoubtedly proud of what we'd achieved at the university but as for what else he believed, I've no idea."

I wasn't letting this one go yet.

"But if he'd, say, wanted to sell secrets to a foreign power would they have welcomed him?"

"Oh my goodness!" Paddon's eyes widened with a fervour I'd not seen in him before, "they'd have greeted him with open arms and the town band. What we're doing already has the potential to influence societies now and in the future. Anyone with access to someone like Conrad would immediately possess huge social, military and economic advantages …"

"I sense a 'but'."

"Well, you don't just waltz into the Russian embassy and offer your services, do you? There has to be contact of some kind and I never saw evidence of anything like that."

"I guess you wouldn't though. Did Conrad ever mention his family?"

"Only his Dad. He was a diplomat but he's long dead."

"Nobody else?"

"Were you thinking of anyone in particular?"

"Probably not," I lied, thinking only too vividly of the mysterious car that had undoubtedly picked up Philby from the dunes. "It's not important now anyway is it?"

I was about to move on but then I remembered something else.

"Was it you I saw at the boxing tournament?"

Paddon's face reddened, which came as a shock. It was the first time I had seen him embarrassed.

"Oh, you did notice after all. I was really sort of hoping I hadn't been seen."

"Why?"

"Well," Paddon said awkwardly, "Conrad told me he had a ticket but couldn't go so I could use it. I'm not that keen on boxing to be honest but when he said the ticket included a meal, well, you know."

"Fair enough, a man has to eat. But why were you hoping I hadn't seen you?"

"He told me to make sure you got a glimpse of me but no more."

"Why?"

Paddon looked even more uncomfortable.

"Just for the hell of it, he said. Tell you the truth I'd had second thoughts about the idea because he could have some very odd notions. So I'm sorry you actually did see me."

He paused before continuing.

"It's funny but everyone thought it was only me who'd been badly damaged by the war. Up here I mean." And he tapped the side of his head. "That bugger wasn't even in the fighting and look what it did to him."

"Yeah and then pressure of work didn't help, I'd imagine."

Paddon looked sharply at me.

"What do you mean?"

"Well, that last week he never stopped did he. For the inspection."

"What bleedin' inspection?" Paddon was sounding a lot more like the curmudgeon we'd all grown to love just a very little.

"The one to determine how much funding you got. Conrad said he was working …"

I stopped speaking. The look of irritation and bafflement on Paddon's face told me all I needed to know. I'd bet a large portion of my father-in-law's fortune that Paddon hadn't even seen Conrad in that final week. And if he wasn't slaving over a hot keyboard then where …?

I glanced across at Rose who was now being talked at by Boardman senior. In that precise moment she swung round through ninety degrees and looked straight at me. Again, she reddened before turning away.

"He must have had more important things to do," sneered Paddon. "I mean when you're a busy murderer every second must count."

"I suppose so," I replied automatically, as he walked away. I watched as Rose patted Ken Boardman's arm and began a slow walk towards me.

"Francis!"

"Yes, Rose."

"I'd like a chat with you if possible. In private."

"No, Rose, not possible I'm afraid. I need to talk to my wife. Why don't you chat to Mr Paddon? After all, you should both have no trouble in making things add up."

I turned away towards Nancy who'd just shaken off Hallows' attentions.

"So, what secrets did Minnie Mouse impart to you?"

Good god in heaven! Nothing got past Nancy. But this needed burying once and for all.

"Well, darling, Rose was just telling me how much she's looking forward to having a baby with Joe's sunny demeanour and smiling face."

"Let's hope so. I'd hate to think she was carrying the spawn of Satan. Who's the coffin-faced chap with her?"

"Satan's sidekick. Fancy an introduction?"

"No. Let's go over there where it's quieter. I've got some news for you."

As Nancy dragged me into a far corner of the hall, I fervently hoped she wasn't going to tell me she too was expecting (a fourth) happy event. Or even, god forbid, our daughter Julia was - despite that box full of johnnies. Luckily it turned out to be neither of the above.

"I've been talking to Bill Cotton," she told me with some excitement.

"I didn't know you were pals with old Wakey Wakey."

"Not Billy Cotton the band leader, you oaf. His son Bill. He's just joined the BBC as a light ent producer and he phoned me at the office a couple of days ago."

It turned out that young master Cotton had been in the audience on Mellish Pier days before my fabulously successful solo run ended in September, and he liked what he'd seen.

"Bill said he was particularly taken with the dead budgie malarkey," Nancy told me. "How the heck you suddenly dreamed that one up I'll never know. My theory is that you've always been a bit sick in the head."

"Thanks, darling. Did you reach that conclusion before or after our first sweet kiss?"

"It's not important. What does matter is that Bill Cotton is putting together a new telly programme.

"A TV show? Now you're talking!"

"Yes. It'll be a mixture of old and new comedians."

"Which category does he think I'm in?"

Nancy stroked her chin.

"That's the thing. If he hadn't seen the show on the pier, he'd have lumped you in with Arthur Askey, George Formby and that maniac Randle."

I shook my head vehemently.

"Sorry but I'm not working with Frank Randle again. I did my time on that particular coalface twenty years ago at Bolton Grand. Remember?"

The memory of Frank whipping out his teeth and throwing them at the audience still made me shudder.

Nancy smiled.

"You don't have to worry about Randle - or his false chompers - because with all that jazzy material, Bill reckons you belong in there with the new boys. People like Tony Hancock and Spike Milligan."

Hardly new boys as both had had fabulously successful shows running on the radio for years. But, that said, this was sounding very promising.

"Anyhow, Bill reckons he wants to pair you up with one of them."

"A double act, Nance," I said doubtfully. "After Barney, I vowed I'd never team up with anyone again." I paused for effect. "However, I suppose if push came to shove, I could work with Hancock. Strictly joint top billing of course."

"Oh no, no, no." Nancy shook her head vehemently.

"Oh, yes, yes, yes," I shot back. "I've had enough of hanging on to some latecomer's coat-tails."

"You ass. I'm just saying it can't be Hancock or Milligan. They're both teamed up with others anyway. No, Bill wants to put you on the telly with another comic who's been around a bit but whose stuff appeals to the modern audience.

"Who?"

"None other than Frankie Driscoll. You'd be The Two Fabulous Frankies."

God bless us and save us!

"Er, actually Nancy you've done really well but I'm not sure it's a good idea."

"Why ever not?"

"Well, for a start, Frankie Driscoll's miles older than me."

"He's three months younger than you actually. And he's let it be known that he very much admires your back catalogue."

Only five past one and already I was deep into double-entendre hell.

"Anyhow," Nancy continued, "he's on in Manchester so I've arranged for you to go and see him tomorrow morning."

"Tomorrow? Actually, Nance, I've got something on."

"*What* have you got on?"

"I'm, er, polishing my speech for Barney's memorial service. It's at Westminster Abbey don't you know. There's a full house booked as well. He'd have appreciated that and it's rumoured there's even a guest turn from the Archbishop of Cant …"

"Stop blathering. Now!"

I decided to stop blathering.

"I'll run you over," she added.

"Bit much, Nance. Blather never hurt anyone."

"I'll *take you in the car* to Manchester and then you and Frankie can get down to it. Apparently, he's got a nice cosy suite at The Midland so you won't be disturbed."

As ever, and even from the grave, it turned out that Barney McAskill had had the last laugh.

Milton Keynes UK
Ingram Content Group UK Ltd.
UKHW020720030424
440506UK00002B/335